RICHARD HUMMEL

RADIOACTIVE REVOLUTION

D1599940

Author: Richard Hummel
Cover Artist: Dusan Markovic
Typography: Bonnie L. Price
Formatting & Interior Design: Caitlin Greer

Copyright © 2018 Richard Hummel
ISBN-13: 978-1-7323374-3-5 (Paperback)
ISBN-13: 978-1-7323374-4-2 (Hardback)
ISBN-13: 978-1-7323374-5-9 (Digital)

Hummel Books Newsletter

If you'd like to keep in touch and follow progress on my next book, join my Newsletter!

Check out my website - https://hummelbooks.com

You can also keep in touch on my Facebook Group, Facebook Page, Discord server, or Twitter.

To our new baby boy.

THE STORY SO FAR

Nuclear war devastated the planet and the nuclear fallout rendered much of the planet inhospitable. Pockets of survivors carve out a living while society's elite flourish in floating utopias.

Professor Igor, sympathetic to those dwelling below, synthesized bio-nanites and dispersed them over the earth's population. The tiny machines gave humanity the ability to survive radiation poisoning. This miraculous technology had unwarranted side-effects resulting in the need to reset them every few years or risk falling prey to the radioactive waste blanketing the world. The nanites also included a hidden mechanism that could change everyone's fate. Unfortunately, the professor failed to send out instructions for this hidden technology and it wasn't until Jared Cartwright accidentally stumbles upon the secret that mankind realizes they can be so much more than human. They can be super human.

Jared makes the discovery, while also uncovering the fact that dragons are real. Experimenting with what he thought was a rock

1

that gave off an electrical charge, Jared unknowingly triggers the nanites fusing a bond between himself and Sildrainen Maildrel (aka Scarlet), the only heir to the queen of fire dragons.

Jared and Scarlet set out to discover who they are, tangling with mercenaries, killer bunnies, and a giant Godzilla worm. With each creature they kill, the pair becomes stronger and gain abilities that propel them to heights previously thought impossible. During their exploration, Jared nearly dies at the hands of a deranged water dragon called Razael. He recovers after spending weeks trapped in his own mind. Jared creates a plan to destroy the manic being that nearly ended him.

Secrets abound as Jared uncovers a hidden military complex, Razael imprisoned beneath a lake, and an entire colony of people warped into mutants by the once great water dragon. The malevolent dragon eliminated, Jared takes these people, aptly named water folk, under his wing to help them survive and grow in strength.

Beset at every turn by the cruel overlords in the floating cities, Jared and Scarlet realize they need to bring in the cavalry and set out to find Scarlet's family hibernating deep beneath the earth's surface. A harrowing journey into the depths of the earth finally see the bonded duo emerge victorious, ushering in a new era where dragons once again walk among men.

01 HOMECOMING

"**G**o!"

In one quick leap, Kitty cleared the lip of the nest and disappeared inside. A moment later a piercing cry ripped through everyone's mind. If Jared hadn't fortified himself and had the mental enhancements he did, the sound would likely have crippled him. He watched Vanessa and Elle farther down the cliff drop to their knees, hands over their ears. A pained sob from inside snapped his attention back to the nest.

Leaping onto the edge of the nest, Jared watched Carla on the creature's back expecting her to stab it with the injector, but her hands were empty.

"Carla! Where's the injector?"

"I dropped it!"

By this point, the large, bird-like creature had risen to its feet and stood a towering twenty feet high. Carla clung to its back with everything she had. Fear shone bright in her eyes, and Jared surged into motion. He dove at the creature's feet, desperately searching for the injector. In his haste, he missed a claw descending for him, and a searing line of heat ignited up his back. Jared shrugged off the pain, wrapped his hand around the injector, and somersaulted away from the creature. His dive carried him to the other side of the nest, Carla's back now in front of him.

Jared leaped, activating *Maximum Muscle,* and vaulted up to meet Carla's outstretched hand. She nearly lost her grip on the bird's back as it crouched to leap into the air. As quickly as she could, Carla slammed the injector home and jammed down on the plunger.

Another piercing shriek tore through the air and penetrated deep into the minds of those less protected. It nearly dislodged Carla from the back of the creature. Somehow, she maintained her grip, but appeared paralyzed in fear.

The griffon launched itself into the air and rapidly climbed altitude.

"Scarlet, come!"

Scarlet swooped lower, and Jared vaulted twenty feet into the air to land on her back. They ascended and chased the fleeing griffon. His primary concern was making sure Carla survived this bonding.

As if the creature had heard his thoughts, it jerked through the sky to throw Carla off its back. Horrified, Jared watched the frail woman press herself to its body, burying her hands and arms in its feathers or fur. Jared wasn't certain what this creature was, nor did he know anything about a griffon.

Since Scarlet didn't know much about them either, it was merely a guess, but he had nothing else to enlighten him about the massive creature. Scarlet positioned them behind it while it continued evasive maneuvers to knock the pest from its back. Carla might have been a tick for all the jostling did to dislodge her.

The fierce determination of this tiny woman impressed him beyond words. They'd known this wouldn't be an easy task, but this might've been more than Carla had bargained for. Yet she handled it like a trooper, refusing to give even the slightest inch to failure. Her courage and strength of resolve spoke well to the remaining colonists. If everyone behaved in such a manner, their efforts to get everyone bonded might go faster than originally thought.

Their only hindrance was a lack of creatures worth bonding. Sure, Scarlet's brothers were on the way, but already several of them didn't want to bond. They had forty-four people needing companions. Only Carla had found something worthy of bonding. In a best-case scenario, only nine of Scarlet's brothers would accept a human companion. That left thirty-four more creatures to find.

"Dive under them, quick!" Jared's heart leaped into his chest as the griffon flipped upside down, and Carla's tiny form detached from its back. Only her vise-like grip on the creature's fur kept her from falling to a painful death. He saw the strain on her face and the white-knuckled grip.

Hold on, Carla, you can do it.

Several tense moments passed while Scarlet maneuvered herself beneath the griffon so they could catch Carla if she fell. Finally, the giant airborne creature righted itself.

Carla wrapped her legs around its back as best she could and reaffirmed her grip.

Why did I agree to this?

This griffon was way out of Carla's league. When Jared had finally caught a good look at the creature, he'd balked. Even with his enhancements, he hadn't wanted to get too close. Its beak could easily bite him in half, and the razor-sharp talons looked vicious. Its strong, muscular body barely resembled a bird, but rather the powerful body of a lion. When Scarlet called it a griffon, he'd questioned her at first, firmly believing they were simply a legend, but bit his tongue. Dragons had been only a legend to him mere months ago, so it shouldn't surprise him more creatures of legend existed.

He'd nearly called off the mission when he'd seen the creature sleeping in its nest. They were in way over their heads, especially Carla. She was no more than five and a half feet tall and barely weighed a hundred pounds. The griffon's head was as large as her entire body.

When he'd voiced his doubts, Carla had vehemently opposed him. Her heart and mind made up, she had to have this creature as her own.

Jared realized it was partly his own fault for inciting a sense of urgency in everyone about the bonding. When he'd gotten home the previous day, he'd told everyone about their journey and what had happened with the cities.

Home.

There was a novel concept. He'd told everyone it was just a staging area, a temporary shelter, but it felt like home. It could've been the people, the place, or a sense of belonging. He didn't know for certain, but it was wonderful having a place to return to. Though, after this little adventure, he wasn't so sure they'd welcome him back with open arms.

As Carla clung to the griffon for dear life, a sense of dread pervaded Jared's thoughts. He wondered if he'd been premature in his wishes. If Carla didn't survive this encounter, he had only himself to blame. He'd agreed to this too quickly even when Vanessa had expressed her doubts. He'd told her Scarlet could handle the creature and keep Carla safe, but they hadn't anticipated the speed and agility. It was incredibly fast. Faster than Scarlet could fly. It was all she could do just to stay close enough to catch Carla if she fell. Jared didn't know why the nanites hadn't taken effect yet. Or, if they had, then it was a completely different process to the one he'd experienced.

If Carla dies, will Vanessa ever forgive me?

Jared's thoughts spiraled into despair. Yesterday, when he and Scarlet had approached home, he'd wanted nothing more than to see Vanessa again, wrap her in a fierce embrace, and return the kiss she'd sneaked in before they left to find Scarlet's family. The anticipation had built to a crescendo, and when they'd finally touched down, he'd found her running toward him with a wide grin splitting her face. She'd thrown herself into his arms, and Jared's heart had soared. His lips tingled, remembering the kiss she'd planted there weeks earlier.

That tiny jolt of electricity turned into cold fear the longer the chaotic flight through the sky transpired. If Vanessa did forgive him, he'd need to find a way to forgive himself for letting them all down.

Jared snapped out of his reverie when he heard Carla cry out. He focused on her tiny form clinging on with everything she had. He wished there was something more he could do, but every scenario he considered put her in even further danger. In hindsight, he should've had Scarlet restrain the griffon from the onset. He'd stupidly thought the creature would just freeze up when injected with the nanites. Clearly, that hadn't been the case.

Thankfully, it couldn't twist its head around far enough to get at Carla on its back. If that'd been the case, Jared would've had Scarlet bring it down even if it'd be more dangerous for Carla. She needed to survive the encounter, or everything was for naught.

"Scarlet, is there anything else we can do? Can you talk to it with telepathy?"

"I tried. The creature does not understand. In its current state, I do not believe it would heed anything I said if it could. It is scared, angry, and in pain."

Jared grunted in frustration. He hated this waiting game with Carla's life hanging in the balance. If something happened to her, he'd have a hard time looking Vanessa in the eye as the guilt ate away at him.

"Scarlet, can you fly above them?"

"Jared…"

"I've got to do something."

"This is too dangerous."

"It is, but I'd never forgive myself if anything happened to her. Vanessa wouldn't forgive me. You can be absolutely certain George would use this to his advantage to sow more discord with the group. No, I've got to do more to help."

Reluctantly, Scarlet climbed above the griffon, and Jared prepared to jump. The creature flipped, and again Carla dangled from her mount. Jared growled in frustration as Scarlet dove beneath them again.

"As soon as it rights itself again, we move."

One of Carla's hands came loose.

Hang on, hang on…

He couldn't take this emotional roller-coaster. Just when he thought she'd fall, the griffon flipped back over.

"She won't survive another one of those. Let's move!"

Scarlet flew above them, and Jared jumped. He landed on the griffon's back and straddled Carla, wrapping his arms around her. He grabbed fistfuls of the creature's fur, wrapped his legs around tight, and secured Carla to its back. His enhanced strength would help hold them in place if it flipped over again.

"Carla, are you okay?"

She didn't respond, but Jared felt her squirming beneath him and knew she was still conscious.

"Carla?"

Jared craned his neck around to see her eyes closed and moving in a silent prayer.

"Carla, can you hear me? Nod if you can."

Still nothing. Jared grew concerned after several more attempts to speak with her.

"Scarlet, she won't respond to me. I can see her lips moving, but it's like she's in a trance."

"Perhaps it is the bond finally taking effect."

"How is she clinging to its back if she's not aware of her surroundings?"

"Instinct?"

"I don't know…maybe? Just be ready to catch us if we need to abandon it. I'll jump straight off its back so follow below and behind us."

"I will be ready."

Jared knew he'd need to tell everyone about this experience when they got back. He hated to do it, but everyone needed to know the dangers involved. He knew this was yet another reason George would speak out against him. The man had largely shut up when they got to their new home, but small things made Jared realize he still worked against him. It wasn't as brazen and open as before, but George had managed to sow seeds of doubt in people's minds. They'd started questioning Jared's choices.

Vanessa assured him she'd take care of things and make sure there was no doubt in people's minds. They only needed to remember he'd saved them from the lake.

Jared had his doubts since George could turn the tables and suggest he'd only rescued them because he knew they were there and hoped to use them as pawns in a larger game. Jared really hoped no one believed that. He'd done nothing to show any malicious will toward these people, but after everything the water folk went through, it was tough to take the word of a stranger when compared to someone who'd spent a decade imprisoned with them.

"Scarlet, can you still reach Vanessa and Elle from here?"

"Yes."

"Good, can you send them back home please? I…don't think we should

leave everyone else alone for long. There's nothing they can do here anyway."

"I relayed your message."

Both had come on the trip to capture the griffon. Elle had come because she knew the way, as she and Kitty had explored the path a few days prior. Vanessa had come because she didn't want to leave Elle's side, but Jared hoped another part was she didn't want to leave Jared again so soon after his return. He needed to have a long conversation with her after this. They owed it to themselves to figure out their feelings for one another.

A part of him longed for a relationship with another human and he really wanted it to be with her. The feeling actually surprised him. He hadn't realized he had anything left to give. For years he'd wandered aimlessly, avoiding human interaction. Now, he hoped for a relationship and realized he did have room in his heart to love another.

"Scarlet—" Jared's next words died on his lips as a familiar high-pitched whirring noise reached his ears, " —get down!"

Jared flipped backward off the griffon, putting his trust in Scarlet to catch his fall. He wrapped his arms around Scarlet's neck and they rocketed toward the creek running between the cliffs. Thankfully, the griffon leveled off and there didn't seem to be any threat of Carla falling off, but there was still a risk of discovery from the drop ship.

"Carla! If you can hear me, you and the griffon need to get down and out of sight!"

Jared lost visual on them when Scarlet entered the gorge and abruptly flared her wings to halt their rapid descent. A shared worry emanated between them. Jared dared not fly out of the ravine to see if Carla had gotten the message or been able to control the griffon enough to send it down. A jolt startled him, but it was only Scarlet landing on an outcropping. The moment they landed, she tucked her tail and wings close to her body and made herself as small as possible.

Fortunately, the forging she'd undergone in the earth's belly made her scales dark enough to blend with the dirt and rocks around them. Her wings and the fire pulsing through her veins stood out like a beacon for anyone paying attention, so he hoped the ship didn't see them. If Carla hadn't heard his cry of warning, perhaps she was small enough that the approaching drop ship wouldn't see her clinging to the griffon's back. Based on what they'd seen when observing the explorers encounter with the machines from the city, he suspected they'd shoot the bird down if they found out a human could ride on it.

The ship was liable to shoot first and investigate after—if they even investigated. The machines hadn't bothered to figure out how the two explorers that managed to reach their city as stowaways got there several weeks earlier. They simply executed them on the spot. Thinking through the scenario left a hollow pit of fear eating away at his stomach. Carla still hadn't responded, and the ship had to be overhead already. Sure enough, the next instant the ship screamed by, headed on a direct path for the waterside town they'd bombed weeks earlier.

Jared wished he was closer to their new home so he could warn everyone about the ship. They all knew the sound, and knew to be on the lookout, but it'd help his peace of mind if he could get them a warning. He should've brought along the talkie things Pete had scavenged for them.

"Next time we head out, remind me to bring those devices from Pete that let us talk over a longer distance. I know we've told everyone to keep an eye out, but I'd feel much better warning them."

"Very well. Do you want me to get a warning to them?"

"No, at this point the ship's already past them. At least, I hope."

"I think we would have heard something."

"Good point, let's hope for the best. Give it another minute, and let's head up to find out where Carla went."

A minute later, Scarlet launched herself into the air, using a thermal current rising from the valley to push them over the cliff's edge. Looking around, he saw no sign of Carla in the immediate vicinity.

"Carla?" Getting no response, he projected his thoughts harder *"CARLA!"*

A screech shattered the silence, followed by a loud *boo* in his mind. Jared nearly fell off Scarlet's back in fright as the griffon banked just above them, gliding forward in near silence. They'd not even heard its wings beating, so quiet was its flight. In contrast to the griffon's stealthy approach, Carla sat atop the creature's back laughing hysterically. She turned around to look at them as she passed, a brilliant smile adorning her face. The smile was infectious, and Jared smiled right back.

She did it!

"Jared, we are almost there."

Scarlet interrupted his thoughts, and he craned his neck to look at the forest below. Sure enough, he could see the faint outline of the cliff peaks above their home. From the direction they flew, it was impossible to see into the valley and pick out the people inside, which is part of the reason they'd chosen the dwelling. Concealed from any casual passersby, it made the perfect place for them to recover, grow, and prepare for war.

"Can you let everyone know we're coming? I don't want stray bullets coming our way."

A few moments later, Scarlet unleashed a wave of mental energy as she informed them of their return. The pressure on his mind had faded since his over-exertion in the tunnels beneath the earth, and her psionic announcement was no more painful than her normal telepathy. Jared hoped the pain of those experiences increased his abilities and fortitude to endure more, but he wouldn't know until he pushed himself to the limit once again.

Their presence announced, Scarlet headed for the clearing a short distance from the cliff. While they descended, Jared could see almost everyone running toward them. He smiled as Vanessa, Elle, and Kitty led the way, no doubt having just gotten back. Though it'd only been a few hours since he'd seen Vanessa, his stomach fluttered, and he felt a flush creep up his neck. He hopped off Scarlet's back and walked in Vanessa's direction.

Before he'd gone a few paces, he turned back to Scarlet. "I'll gather everyone for the evening meal and let them know what happened. Please keep tabs on your brothers' progress, and let me know when they get closer. I want to be there to greet them."

"It should take them several more days to reach us. I talked with Malsour as we left, and he said they would take their time getting here. They want to remain hidden and use the time to gain strength along the way."

"Thanks, Scarlet. Oh, since we didn't share any images yesterday, let's keep them to ourselves for now." Jared smirked. "I want to see the look on everyone's face when they see them for the first time. No doubt they'll look stupefied like I did."

Scarlet snorted her agreement.

He turned to head for the group advancing on them but barely made it through the turn when a fragile body leaped at him, making him stumble a few paces back as he scrambled to grab his assailant. Vanessa clung to his neck tightly. Jared's smirk morphed into a huge smile, and he returned the hug before he grabbed her slender waist and gently set her down.

"What was that for?"

"That creature was so scary, I thought—"

"Hey, it's okay. It was a little scary, and we definitely underestimated it, but with Scarlet there, we succeeded."

Her concern touched him deeply. Impulsively, he tilted her head up and planted a tender kiss on her lips, returning the favor she'd granted him weeks earlier. Her cheeks flushed a light pink, creating a contrast against her pale skin that Jared found endearing. He tucked a lock of her raven-colored hair behind an ear, exposing the gills on the side of her neck. He hardly noticed the mutations anymore. She was beautiful, inside and out, and it didn't matter what Razael had done to her.

Once Vanessa gained control over her nanites, she planned to revert her body back to human form. She was already beautiful to him, and he couldn't wait to see the result.

The rest of the group caught up to them, everyone clamoring to speak and ask questions.

Jared held up his hand. "All right, all right, I'll answer all your questions, but not here. Let's gather everyone for dinner tonight, and I'll tell you what happened with Carla."

"Did it work?" someone from the back asked.

"It did, but, again, wait until dinner and I'll explain."

Eventually, they agreed to hold any further questions until dinner. While Jared and the majority of the people walked back to their homes in the cliff wall, a few remained behind to get a better look at Scarlet and her recent changes. Jared suspected they also wanted to catch a glimpse of Carla's companion. However, he'd asked Carla to keep flying with the griffon and land after he'd calmed everyone and explained the situation.

A few minutes later, Vanessa on his arm, they walked into the third level room provisioned for Jared, Vanessa, Elle, and Kitty. The room looked much the same from the day before, but there were now furs hanging in all the windows and covering the beds. There were even a few folded next to the furniture. It looked like the hunters had stayed busy. These hadn't been there the day before when he got home. Jared suspected it was simply they didn't know when he'd get back with Scarlet and had only just brought them up.

Walking to his room, Vanessa still attached to his side, Jared pulled out the only spare change of clothes he had and laid it on the bed. Elle and Kitty had left for the dining hall, leaving Jared feeling slightly uncomfortable and unsure how to put action to his feelings. He wasn't quite ready for anything beyond what he'd already shared with Vanessa, but here they were...alone in his bedroom.

"Ahem." Jared cleared his throat. "I need to get undressed and cleaned up."

Vanessa let go of his arm and smiled coyly.

"Do I have to go?" A mischievous smile graced her features.

Jared's cheeks turned red, and he stammered incoherently.

Vanessa held up a hand and said, "Don't worry, I'm teasing."

The way she said it sent shivers down his spine. Even though she hinted at something more, Vanessa turned and walked from the room.

As soon as she'd left, Jared collapsed in a heap on the bed. He'd never felt so conflicted in all his life. His body screamed at him to rush over to Vanessa and embrace her, giving in to his desire. That portion of him nearly won out as he lay there panting from the rush of emotions he'd just experienced. Though, with each breath he took, the emotions receded, and his willpower became his own again. He cared for Vanessa deeply, but he didn't know if it was the same way his father had cared for his mother.

Is she the one?

The question echoed in his mind, but with a torrent of emotions swirling through him, it was a question he couldn't rightfully answer at the moment. He felt his physical desires for Vanessa, but his heart felt at odds with it as he worked through his feelings. He didn't want to give in to the physical urges until he was certain his heart and mind agreed. If he chose a partner, lover, and wife, he wanted to choose one for life. She'd be the only woman in his life he shared physical intimacy with, and he wanted to be one hundred percent certain she was the one he'd spend the rest of his life with. These feelings needed careful consideration, but at the moment there was a village full of people waiting on him.

He took a full fifteen minutes of meditation to calm himself. If Vanessa had returned to the room, he wasn't sure he'd have been able to resist. He cobbled together enough control to push the tumultuous thoughts and feelings to the back of his mind for another day.

Calmed, Jared dressed himself in his last pair of clothes and joined everyone in the dining hall. A quick headcount revealed that everyone was present and the food ready.

Eating his fill and waiting for everyone else to finish, he reached out to Scarlet.

"Is Carla okay flying around, still?"

"She is more than fine. I can hear her thoughts from miles away. She had a similar reaction to you when you first flew."

"Okay. Please keep an ear out for her and any ships that might pass. We're eating and then I'll share the details of our adventure. Once I'm done, I'll come down to the clearing, and we can take care of Carla and the griffon."

Jared gathered his thoughts before telling everyone about the bonding.

"It was a success, but it could've gone better. Scarlet can show you exactly what happened if you want. Honestly, I think it was a bit more than we should've taken on."

Someone in the room snorted, and Jared glanced up to find the person responsible. He had an idea who it was, and one look at George confirmed his guess. The man stood against the doorframe with his arms crossed and a sneer plastered on his face.

Jared sighed inwardly. He'd known this was a possibility, yet he needed to be truthful with these people. He'd deal with the fallout when the time came.

"I'll be brutally honest with you. When I thought of what to share, I almost withheld some of what we witnessed. However, I realized that was wrong, and all of you deserve to know the truth." Jared looked around the room to see people nodding their head in agreement and looking at him with respect.

"I've also decided that you have a right to see everything that transpired under the earth when we went to find Scarlet's family. Though, I've asked Scarlet to withhold images of her brothers because I want to see your faces when they get here." Jared smiled mischievously, which earned him another scowl from George and a playful punch from Vanessa.

"I also have something more to confess." Jared furrowed his brow, plotting the best way to reveal the information. The looks of respect he'd received just a moment ago disappeared, replaced by ones of alarm. "I wasn't entirely truthful about everything. For a good reason. However, I plan to remedy that now. When Scarlet helped you recover from Razael's influence, she wasn't just curing you. She also examined your loyalty and motivations."

Jared held up a hand to forestall the outbursts he saw on several people's lips.

George looked ready to strangle him right there on the spot. Several others looked like they might join him if he tried. Even Vanessa looked affronted by the admission. Granted, she didn't look appalled by the idea. Surely, she had an inkling of an idea Scarlet had done this as part of evaluating them for the vow they eventually made. All except George, at least.

Jared grew uneasy as he looked around the room. He'd second-guessed himself about this decision, but the truth was out there now, and all he could do was continue and hope they understood.

"Dragons do this instinctively. At the time, we decided it was in everyone's best interest to exclude that little bit of information. I asked Scarlet to ensure everyone's motives, but also to gauge your mental stability to see if you could handle the truths we shared. Should I have asked your permission first? Perhaps, but after Razael, the state you were in made me realize most of you would've denied my request. Because of the experiences we had at the hands of the Daggers, I couldn't risk it. We almost died once at the hand of humans. We also didn't know if Razael held sway in your minds. I understand it'll take time for me to garner some of your trust again after violating your privacy, but I felt it necessary and I would do it again if presented the same scenario."

Vanessa laid a hand over his. "I understand." She looked over the rest of the table and met everyone's eyes. "We understand."

She turned back to Jared with a smile and bade him continue.

Even as she said it, Jared saw the doubt in her eyes as she gazed at George and a few others. The moment she finished speaking, George stormed from the room.

Holding her proffered hand, Jared squeezed it for reassurance and recapped some of their story from the other day, promising that Scarlet should show them if they desired.

"Scarlet? Can you come up here for a few minutes?"

"One moment."

"Will Carla's companion be okay?"

"Yes, he will be fine for a time."

"Good, I'd like you to show everyone the events of the last couple weeks, culminating with Carla's experience. Just leave out images of your brothers. I still want to surprise everyone."

Jared didn't know if that was the wisest decision given their experiences, but he believed he knew many of them well enough by now to know they'd be just as awed as he was. Plus, everyone knew they were part of Scarlet's family, so they shouldn't be frightened.

He motioned to the entrance. "Scarlet is coming up here, if you would like to see what happened."

As one, everyone stood up to file out of the room. Jared left first and stifled a chuckle at the scene before him. Scarlet was perched on the ledge, George plastered against the wall a few feet away. Scarlet had her head close to him with a sinister grin on her face.

"All right, Scarlet, you've had your fun."

Amusement flitted along their bond, and Jared turned away from the terrified man to cover the smile creeping over his face. Thankfully, no one else saw, and he managed to compose himself before everyone filed out.

"Place your hand on Scarlet, and she'll take you through the events leading up to today."

Everyone but George placed their hands on her, and she recounted all of the events. She started with the encounter of the ship in New York City, the subsequent butchering of all the people on the ground and on the floating city. She took them through their trip down into the earth, lingering on Jared's fight with the first batch of lizards. She showed her mad descent into the tunnel and all the fantastical creatures she encountered. She paused the images on a gigantic stone creature seemingly composed of rock and molten lava. It was slow, and Scarlet managed to tackle it to the ground before she continued her flight. She ended the recounting when she reached out to her brothers for help.

The next scene was somewhat confusing as she shifted to Jared's point of view and showed his fight with the lizard horde in amazing detail. It was like watching a movie play out in front of his eyes. He hardly believed it was himself dancing through the air, leaving large swathes of dead lizards in his wake. The fight scene with the large praying mantis scared him just watching it. He felt twinges of pain in his ribs and arm as he recalled the impacts from the creature's limbs.

Scarlet wrapped up their quest to find her brothers by showing her arrival and the destruction she caused to the reptilian horde. Somehow, she managed to leave out anything that showed her brothers, though they did get a glimpse of the different flame bursts. Finally, she showed them arriving back home, skipped over the day of recuperation they'd had, and went straight to the moment Carla leaped into the griffon's nest. The crowd gasped every time the creature flew upside down and Carla barely managed to hang on. Cheers sprang up when they saw the bond was successful.

"My brothers will arrive in two days' time." Scarlet's voice echoed in their minds. **"I spoke with them, and they are making steady but careful progress. They have already hidden from at least one drop ship, and a couple of explorers. They are doing their best to avoid detection."**

Vanessa reacted strongly to the scene of Jared broken and bleeding after his battle. She ran to him and threw her arms around him, forcing him to grab hold or they'd fall over.

"You could've died," Vanessa sobbed into his shoulder. "I—" Jared almost said he was fine but thought better. "I came close to dying, yes. Ever since I told all of you the truth, you've known there will be times when our lives will be on the line. Some of us may not survive the coming war. Those of us who do will have scars that may never fade. We all chose this path, we forced no one into it, and we all have obligations to see it through to the end. That includes putting ourselves in harm's way, facing near impossible odds, and emerging from these tribulations triumphant. I believe in our cause. More importantly, I believe in everyone here. Together we are strong enough to achieve victory."

Vanessa dried her eyes on his shirt and composed herself. She put on a strong facade for her people, but Jared saw through to her fragile state. The years she'd spent holding their group together had taxed her greatly. Jared knew those years were catching up to her, and at any moment she could fold under the strain. Somehow, Jared needed to help her heal, and make sure she could be the leader these people needed. Over the next few days, Jared planned to spend time with her to talk through her issues.

Everyone needed to recover from their ordeal and operate on all cylinders for the next phase of their plans. In contrast to the sober mood of the crowd as they dispersed, Jared felt only excitement.

It's time to build our army!

02 CLEAR MIND

mmediately after everyone dispersed, Jared joined Scarlet in the clearing to wait for Carla's return.

"Where are—"

"There."

Jared looked up to find the griffon not more than fifty feet away coming in for a landing.

"Scarlet, this griffon is amazing. I can barely hear it. If not for the shift of the air, there's no way I'd hear it coming."

"Wherever this creature came from—or whoever created it— designed it in such a way that the wings do not make a sound as it flies."

"We need a few more of them to build out a scouting force. You know, now I'm thinking of it, we didn't check that thing's nest for eggs. Hey, Carla, do you know if there were any eggs in the griffon's nest?" Jared had to shout before she heard his question.

Laughing, Carla said, "*He* doesn't have a mate."

"Too bad. Can you understand him? Are there more griffons?"

"I—he doesn't quite understand anything I ask, but if I'm

interpreting him correctly, he believes he's the only one around. But, it's more like he is the only alpha, maybe? I'm sorry, it's hard to understand."

"It's okay. Maybe Scarlet can have a chat later and understand what he's saying." Jared patted Scarlet's side. "Sorry girl, I hope that's okay with you?"

"I am intrigued by this creature."

Some of the water folk saw Carla return and started for the clearing, but she jumped off of her new companion and rushed out to greet those approaching. She held up her hands to forestall the rush of people from surrounding the bird.

"Wait! Please. He's scared and doesn't understand what's happening. He has a sharp mind, but is not intelligent like Scarlet. If you give me some time, I'll work to make him more comfortable. In the meantime, please give him some space."

Jared walked over to Carla and agreed with her request, asking for everyone to vacate the area.

"Don't worry, everyone will get the chance to meet Carla's new companion in time. We expected that many of these creatures wouldn't be as intelligent as Scarlet. That will change as their intelligence increases. In the event you bond with a dragon, that won't be an issue, but any other creature will probably require you to dump their nanites into *Mind* right away. We'll discuss plans to get everyone else bonded later."

The crowd dispersed and Carla and Jared walked over to her griffon. Cautiously, Jared approached the beast with his hand held in front of him. Sniffing, the creature extended its beak to prod his open palm. If not for his hardened skin, the sharp beak might've drawn blood. Even with *Natural Armor* and his *Skin Hardening*, he felt the razor edges.

As gently and quietly as possible, Jared spoke to him.

"Hello, I am Jared."

The griffon recoiled at the words but didn't attack or fly away. It was a start.

"Scarlet?"

Jared beckoned for her to come closer and speak to the griffon. "Carla, let's give the two of them some time to speak. Right now, your griffon's mind is primitive, and it would be good if Scarlet could get through to him on an instinctual level."

Carla hesitated, looking at the griffon in concern.

"It's okay, I promise. Scarlet won't let anything bad happen to him."

Appeased, she followed Jared. He heard a small snippet of telepathy from Scarlet, introducing herself to the griffon. This was all unexplored territory, but he had faith Scarlet could get through to the griffon and it would all work out to their advantage.

"Will he be okay?" asked Carla, the worry obvious in her voice.

"He'll be okay. We won't go far. Let's head up to my quarters there." Jared pointed up to the open balcony leading to his bedroom. "You'll be able to see him from there."

Before they made it to the stairs, Vanessa, Elle, and Kitty joined them. Vanessa ran up to Carla and gave her a hug.

"Are you okay? Did it work? What happened?" Vanessa's questions tumbled out in a rush.

Laughing good-naturedly, Carla said, "Yes! It worked! My companion is working with Scarlet to understand the changes. He's...Vanessa, I flew! It was amazing!"

Laughing along with her, Vanessa hugged her again and threw Jared a quick smile.

Jared winked back and motioned up the cliff wall. "We're headed up to my deck so I can teach Carla how to assign nanites and she can keep an eye on her new friend." Jared gestured behind him toward the clearing. Together, the four of them ascended the steps to his room. Kitty paused on the steps and nudged Jared.

"May I see?"

"The griffon?"

"Yes."

"Carla, Kitty would like to go see Scarlet and the griffon. Do you mind?"

"I...will that be okay?"

Jared nodded his head. "I think so. Scarlet has it under control, and Kitty knows enough not to startle him." Carla nodded her head in agreement and Jared motioned for Kitty to head over to the clearing.

"Scarlet, Kitty is on her way over to you. She wants to join you while you work with the griffon."

"Very well."

"All right. Scarlet is okay with it and will make sure everyone stays safe."

They headed to the balcony and sat across from each other. Vanessa and Elle remained just inside his room on the bed, watching curiously.

"You ready?"

"Yes!" Carla said, giddy with excitement.

"Okay, the first thing you need to do is will your status screen into focus. If you've never done it before, you need to relax your gaze and mentally command it to expand in your view."

The only indication she'd listened to him was a slight widening of her eyes when the status came into focus.

"You'll notice that there are quite a few new options besides the countdown timer. There are two primary categories, *Mind* and *Body*.

When I first enhanced myself, I focused on physical enhancements and augments since it was just Scarlet and I facing down beasts. In hindsight, I wish I'd focused on some mental attributes, but I'm fairly certain the physical changes saved my life many times. As you can see, it's a tough choice and one you must make on your own. However, I'd recommend you focus on *Mind* first."

The lesson went on for some time as Jared outlined the various ways to enhance mental attributes. Unfortunately for Carla, she didn't have a wicked smart companion like Scarlet, so she didn't get the breakdown of categories and different ways to assign the nanites. They needed to experiment to see if she could force certain categories like specific senses or intelligence. As it stood, she had *Mind* and *Body*, and that was it.

It didn't really surprise him, since he'd had Scarlet to understand the additional categories. Clearly, this griffon wasn't smart in the same sense. Jared had no doubt he was a keen predator and sharp enough to stay on top of the food chain, but that didn't equate to intelligence and rational thought. Since Carla had none of that to work with, Jared went through all the categories available to him, and described each of them. If, and when, she understood the nanites enough she'd understand all the ways to use them.

"Honestly, Carla, I think this will be a lot of trial and error. I've no idea the dispersion of nanites when assigning all to *Mind*. Nor do I know how long it'll take until you gain sufficient awareness of them to isolate different parts of your mind and body for enhancements. Like I said earlier, I don't think you should worry about physical changes just yet. I understand you'd want to reverse modifications made by Razael, but without an understanding, there's no way you'd be able to assign the nanites into *Remodeling* and direct them to counter the changes.

"Let's push everything into *Mind* for now since you're unable to put anything into *Body Manipulation* and *Regeneration*. I'd recommend doing the same for your griffon. At least until you both understand everything and can make more informed decisions."

"Now? Didn't you and Scarlet wait until you slept?" Carla voice held a note of fear.

"We did, but you can assign them now. They're programmed not to begin until the host is unconscious. I don't think you'll experience any pain. I had unique circumstances with Scarlet and her mother, such that the pain I felt was likely much worse than anything you'd go through. It might not be painful for you at all. Though, we heard you scream during the bonding with your griffon. Was that pain? Fear?"

"Definitely pain. At first nothing happened. I could feel a slight tingling over my body for several minutes, and then the message from Professor Igor showed up. As soon as I finished reading it, an intense burning covered my whole body. It felt like I was on fire. My body tensed, and for a moment I thought I'd fall off, but then you showed up to help. Even now, it feels like I have a terrible sunburn over my whole body, but from the inside out." Carla shivered at the memory.

Jared assumed it was like his experiences when he bonded, again, when Alestrialia had "assessed" him, and finally with the Godzilla worm and lake. Pain seemed a constant companion for him ever since finding Scarlet, but the pain brought with it some major advantages Jared wouldn't trade for anything.

"Okay, go ahead and make your selections."

Carla squinted in concentration. A slight widening of her eyes was the only outward indication she'd pulled up her status screen.

Carla – Nanites Available: 100%

Mind – 100%

Body – 0%

"Done."

"Excellent. Once the two of you undergo the enhancements tonight, we'll see what changes for you and if you're able to unlock or understand more categories. Since you don't have Scarlet's help, it will be up to you to create the categories when you understand them sufficiently. We'll see what this current batch does and if you're ready, I'll make a trek down to the lake with you. There's a lot of nanites there, and you'll be able to absorb as many as your body can handle in one sitting, but never, ever go down there by yourself. If you can't break the connection, it'll burn out your body."

Jared painted a grim picture, but he needed her to understand the risks, stomping out any notion she might have of rapidly enhancing herself. "Scarlet and I experienced the start of that burnout multiple times and found out the hard way that only a forced removal from the source will stop the flow of nanites."

Wide-eyed, Carla nodded her head vigorously. "I promise I won't go down to the lake without you."

"Last thing. I'd like for you to sleep up here. I want to keep an eye on you throughout the night and make sure you're safe. Scarlet will do the same with your griffon. I recommend you eat a big meal and send your griffon to do the same before nightfall. Normally, the meal is more important when enhancing *Body*, but it'd be a good idea to prepare for any eventuality."

Carla made to leave and do Jared's bidding, but he stopped her. "You should be able to communicate from here."

"Really, how?"

"You already know how to use telepathy with touch. It's the

same way with your companion. Focus on the bond you share and push your words in the same way you do through touch. This will only work with your companion because of the bond. We're close enough you should be able to reach him. When you've upgraded telepathy more, then you'll be able to project thoughts to anyone, like myself and Scarlet, without touching them."

Carla wrinkled her brow in concentration, creases appearing on her forehead and the corners of her mouth. The intense concentration on the little woman made him smile. Carla appeared to give everything her all. She held nothing back when putting her mind to a task. The moment Carla's eyes lit up in joy, Jared knew she'd heard her companion.

"Okay, now, tell him to remain with Scarlet. She'll accompany him to find food. Then, have him come right back here and stay with her overnight. Guessing by the size of your creature, he no doubt has a lot of unassigned nanites and the changes he'll undergo tonight will significantly improve his mental prowess. Let's hope it's sufficient for him to understand at a more cognitive level."

Wrapping up, they walked back into his bedroom to join Vanessa and Elle, who had eavesdropped on their conversation. They'd sat in rapt attention, drinking in his words. Elle seemed especially thoughtful as she fiddled with something none of them could see.

"Elle?"

"I work on *Mind*. We got more nanite hunting done while you went with Scarlet. I make changes like you say too." Jared grinned at Elle and Vanessa. Ever since she'd moved into his living space, it felt like having a little sister. Their biggest challenge was education. She'd also picked up a lot of bad habits during the years spent with Kitty, and it would take quite some time before her knowledge caught up to her age.

"We will go hunt now."

"Thanks for letting me know. Please stay safe out there, and make sure Carla's griffon—" He wanted to say *make sure he doesn't escape*, but Scarlet beat him to the punch.

"I will not let him or Kitty out of my sight."

"Thanks."

Jared returned his attention to Carla and Elle. "Scarlet is taking our companions out on a hunt. They'll be out for a few hours."

Carla protested, but he anticipated her argument with a raised hand.

"I know you're concerned, but I promise you that Scarlet will take care of him. She's promised not to let him out of her sight."

Although the words calmed her some, Carla still looked worried. Any time he and Scarlet were apart for any length of time, that same worry set in. It wasn't strong now, especially as she was just out on a hunt, but he understood Carla's fear. The worst experience of separation had been when Razael nearly overtook his mind. Though Scarlet had remained by his side for the weeks under his influence, they couldn't talk or share anything across their bond. It had been a miserable experience and not one he ever wanted to repeat.

"Jared?" Vanessa beckoned at him from their doorway. "It looks like everyone's out here waiting for you."

"Why?"

"They want to know the plans for bonding. You did tell everyone you'd brief us."

"Right, sorry. I didn't think that meant tonight. All right, let's do this, then." Jared left his room with Elle and Carla in tow.

"Thank you for coming, everyone. I know all of you are excited about Carla's new companion and want to get a closer look at him. Again, thank you for heeding our wishes to give him some space. The griffon's mind is predatory. Although intelligent in its own way, it does not have an intellect like Scarlet, or even the mind that Kitty developed over the years. It will take time before it can achieve that level of cognizance. Please consult with me or Carla before you attempt to approach..." Jared paused. He tired of calling it "the griffon."

He glanced behind him at Carla. "Do you have a name yet?"

Blushing, Carla looked down and whispered his name. "Attis."

Jared had never heard of the name before and wondered at its meaning. Curious, he reached out to Scarlet and informed her of Carla's choice.

"Scarlet, Carla has chosen the name Attis for her companion."

"A fitting name."

"You know what it means?"

"It means handsome. My mother was a fan of Greek mythology and became fascinated with their time period. The term dragon is of Greek origin—"

"Sorry," Jared interrupted. *"I would love the history lesson, but I'm in the middle of speaking with everyone. Let's chat later tonight?"*

"As you wish."

Picking up where he left off, Jared continued. "Please ask Carla before you approach Attis. It is a fitting name that means handsome. You'll see that she chose well when you're able to get a close-up view of him. He really is incredible. He's also very fast and stealthy. On our way back, Carla flew circles around Scarlet and me.

"Now, the main reason you're all here." Jared's voice had an edge of seriousness to it. Everyone stopped their side conversations, and the room went silent. "The bonding for Carla differed significantly from my experience, and it could've ended badly. The nanites did not affect Attis right away, and he leaped into the air with Carla on his back. It was everything she could do just to hang on while he flew in erratic patterns through the air.

"Not only that, but while she was on Attis, a drop ship flew overhead. I don't think Scarlet showed that to you earlier, but no doubt you all heard the ship and hid like we practiced." Many heads nodded around the room in agreement. "Thankfully, it didn't appear as though they saw Carla clinging to the griffon's back. If they had..."

Jared's voice trailed off. He didn't need to finish his thought, as everyone knew what would happen should the cities find out what they could do.

"Not only was the process dangerous, it was also incredibly painful. I'd hoped that it wouldn't be the same for everyone as it was for me, but it looks like that won't be the case. Carla can tell you personally that it was probably the most pain she's ever experienced."

Carla nodded her head vigorously, shivering as she relived the pain.

"As you can see, this was not an easy task. Unless you bond with one of Scarlet's brothers, I imagine this will be the same for most of you. It will probably be best if a dragon is always present to help restrain whatever creature you've chosen. They can physically restrain something, or perhaps use their telepathy to daze whatever it is you've chosen to bond with. What I don't want is a repeat of what Carla had to endure. It was just too dangerous. We need everyone for the coming war, and we can't afford you to become mortally wounded, or worse, die a meaningless death."

"Why did you let Carla go?"

Jared looked for the speaker, but couldn't see who it was.

"I—"

"Yeah, she could've died."

Again, Jared couldn't identify the speaker, but it was definitely a different person. "I know that now, we—"

"You shouldn't make decisions for us."

This time Jared knew who'd spoken and his blood boiled.

George.

"Listen here—"

Vanessa laid a hand on Jared's arm and stepped forward. "Look, I know what you're feeling. If something happened to Carla—I understand. But nothing happened to her, and now she has a wonderful creature as a companion. Jared risked his life to keep her safe. You all saw what he did."

"She shouldn't have been up there at all!"

"What's the reason for having a dragon if she doesn't help us?"

Jared knew this would happen if he left George unchecked. Now the man started sowing discord among the group. Who knew how many he'd infected with his insidious nature.

It was Jared's turn to step in front of Vanessa. He didn't want her labeled as the bad guy in all this. He needed her to remain strong and true to her people. If anyone wanted to point the blame at someone it should be him. He could at least try and alleviate their fears though.

"Look, I apologize for not seeking everyone's counsel. It hadn't even crossed my mind. I'm not…"

Jared frowned, trying to think of the best way to phrase his next words. "I'm not a leader. There's a reason I've asked Vanessa to lead this little colony. In matters of how best to live and survive, I defer to her. However, when it comes to bonding, battle, and the war with the cities, I will make the hard calls. Everything I've done up to this point has been in your best interest. I'm fighting for all humanity here on the earth. Yes, even the Daggers. I want the world to go back to the way it used to be before the nuclear bombs destroyed everything.

"That means I'll need to make unpopular choices. You may not agree with me, I get that, but I promise I'm not doing any of this for myself."

It probably wasn't the best way to end his monologue, but he wanted the seriousness of the situation to sit in the forefront of everyone's minds. They needed to know how dangerous it was, but also that everything he did was for them.

After everyone returned to their rooms, he made his way over to a fire pit, asking to be left alone. The pit overlooked the small valley they'd claimed for themselves. Many of those here called it Haven. It was a simple name, but for many, it represented safety. A second chance in the world.

"Jared?"

Glancing to his side, Jared smiled. "Hey, Pete, what can I do for you?"

Hesitating, Pete glanced down before he spoke. "I...c-can we make a t-t-trip to our old home t-tomorrow? I want to g-get appliances for the kitchen and we c-could use more wiring. Also, if s-some of those electric vehicles survived the explosions..."

Smiling at Pete's enthusiasm, Jared held up a hand. "You had me convinced at kitchen appliances. We don't have too much going on right now and, so far, no one's requested a specific companion. I think it'd be good to get out and do some salvaging. Let others know we'll be making a journey there. If we do this, I want to be back in two days. That's when Scarlet's brothers should be here, and I don't want to miss their arrival."

Pete left to get things ready, snippets of his excited chatter floating in his wake. Turning back to the fire, Jared stared into the flames, lost in thought. The ambience was peaceful, and he'd had little time to just sit and enjoy himself recently. Fire danced hypnotically, jumping from log to log. The crackle and pop lulled him into a meditative state. Conversations around him became a buzz in the background.

Jared quickly found himself in his mental room of doors, the highway of his mind where all thoughts flowed back and forth. There was no intent or purpose to Jared's meandering. His consciousness drifted among the byways where snatches of thoughts and actions briefly passed through. The more his mind wandered, the easier it became to understand the numerous thoughts rampaging through his mind.

Many thoughts demanded attention, emotions warred within him, and inner conflict of his recent actions fought for control.

There were fragments of pain and loss from those that had passed on, and if Jared let even one of these fleeting events fixate in his mind, the doors around him slammed shut as his entire focus latched on to that one ephemeral object.

Frowning to himself, Jared focused on the room he stood in, a massive, infinite space with no real boundaries. The doors at first glance appeared finite, but if he focused on enumerating them, it quickly became impossible. The room itself was a construct of his own making. His mind didn't have boundaries, and there was no way for him to prevent a thought from occurring. All he'd done so far was cast strands of thought away, or refuse to acknowledge them because his fickle mind couldn't handle it, or so he thought.

In the calm center of his mind, Jared understood he couldn't bottle his thoughts up anymore. He needed to exist within them, let them flow through him.

Staring into the fire, Jared blocked any external stimuli from his mind. Breathing deeply to prepare for what came next, Jared closed his eyes.

His entire focus inward, he obliterated his room of doors. Hundreds, thousands, perhaps millions of thoughts and fragments of memory flooded through his mind. The moment his boundaries disintegrated, a message flooded into view, and Scarlet's words echoed in his head.

"Well done, Jared!"

Clear Mind Unlocked!

Mental boundaries and limitations no longer exist. This is an active and passive ability. Every enhancement to the Mind will also improve this ability. The state you reached to achieve this level of understanding will often elude you until it grows in strength. The stronger your mind, the more this ability moves into a passive state. Enhancing your mind sufficiently will allow you to maintain a Clear Mind indefinitely.

Jared's mouth dropped open in surprise. In the next moment, the barriers of his mind slammed shut, and he snapped his eyes open. Not really seeing anything around him, his eyes darted around seeking the enlightenment he'd achieved, but his thoughts were in too much turmoil to revert so soon. Shaking his head, Jared willed himself to focus. The level of awareness he'd achieved felt the same as sharing a thought space with Scarlet. Limitations and shackles in his mind dissolved, and limitless possibilities emerged.

No matter what it takes, I will make this ability permanent, Jared vowed to himself.

03 IT TAKES WORK

Jared's mind reeled from the ability he'd just unlocked. The possibilities seemed endless. It was no wonder dragons were so smart. They always had a *Clear Mind* and could process thought so much faster than humans. Mastering the ability would take a long time, but it would be invaluable in their fight.

"Scarlet, this ability—it's incredible!" A sliver of mania tinged his thoughts. *"Is this what...how...did you learn how to do this the same way?"*

Scarlet sounded amused as she replied. **"Yes, in a way. I did not have to unlock the ability. It was always there for me. From the moment I was born, I could see and hear every thought. The harder part for me was figuring out how to process everything at once, but that came in time as my mind evolved."**

"I can't imagine living every moment like that. It's overwhelming right now." The sheer number of thoughts that bombarded him when he'd achieved *Clear Mind* staggered him.

"Now that you've learned how, you must learn to quiet your mind lest you become sluggish. If you dwell on every possibility for everything you do, it will slow your reaction time down."

Scarlet reverted to teacher mode, no doubt multi-tasking while she was out hunting with Attis and Kitty. "**You could counteract it with** *Hyper-Cognition***, but it would be better if you learned how to quiet your mind using active meditation."**

"What is—"

"**Active meditation differs from what you use to enter your mental storage. Active meditation is something you can do physically. Find a rhythm to everything you do such as the way you walk, how you perceive your environment, or how you blink. These are all physical actions you can use to help focus your mind."**

Jared thought about all the individual actions and realized he'd never considered them before. They were subconscious thoughts, and his body did them in the background. However, in a *Clear Mind* state, he realized his body unconsciously processed them with little effort. Perhaps focusing on them to harness the jumble of thoughts would work for him.

"**You will also want to find a tempo or cadence to the thoughts running through your head. When we shared a thought space, your mind opened to the possibilities, but what you likely did not notice is the order to my thoughts. It is not chaotic because I learned to harness the thoughts and direct them. Do you remember experiencing my thoughts as I fly?"**

He cast his mind back to that first time they'd shared a thought space in the air and remembered thinking it was amazing she could consciously force her body to fly amid the hundreds of other thoughts running in her mind.

"I remember thinking how incredible it was that you could multi-task while flying."

"**Exactly. That is one way in which I practice active meditation. It is almost subconscious for me because I practiced with my mother for hundreds of years while incubating. When the time** came for my hatching, I'd already mastered the ability through my mother's experience. You have no such experience and must start from the beginning. I will help you along the way, but I recommend you activate the ability and practice as often as you can."

"Do you have any idea how it'll work when I assign nanites to this ability? The description you wrote for me suggests that eventually it'll become a passive skill without the need to activate it. How does that work?"

"Think about it this way: the more nanites you allocate to the ability, the more it builds additional neural pathways through your mind, increasing its ability to see and understand the information passing through it. *Hyper-Cognition* works the same, only at much greater speeds and only temporarily. My mind can do this natively."

"I've been thinking about this, and what you described makes it more relevant. Let's say I do this and become dependent on this neural framework built in my mind. What happens if we come across a technology that can make the nanotech stop working?" Jared had thought about this before and dismissed it because the nanites coursing through them were a biological hybrid, but they still kept some electrical properties.

"I do not know. I am not familiar with any technology that can do this."

"I remember reading about electromagnetic pulses, or EMPs, that can destroy any electrical circuit. When you get back, we can share a thought space and you can go through the lessons I had on it. It isn't much, and definitely won't help us answer the question now, but it's something we should think about."

"Yes, we need to think this through."

"Is there a way for me to make these changes more permanent? Could I use Remodeling to build these neural pathways?"

"Possibly."

"I wonder if it's possible for me to hold the Clear Mind ability active, while also directing nanites in Remodeling to build the pathways the ability creates. For that matter, I could do that with all my abilities. I wouldn't need to depend on the nanites anymore!"

Scarlet didn't answer for a time and Jared became increasingly agitated as he waited for her to think through the possibilities. If he could make them permanent, it almost made him regret enhancing any of his current abilities and physical attributes. He should've pushed everything into *Remodeling*. Then again, he'd needed to increase his mind sufficiently to even get to a place where he could understand the nanites and how to do any of this. One thing was certain. If he could do this, he'd need to change up his instructions to Carla and Elle.

Finally, Scarlet responded. **"I think you might be onto something here. If you can hold your *Clear Mind* state and force your mind to sleep while maintaining a single thread of awareness, I think you'll be able to trick the nanites into thinking your body is asleep. I'm able to do it because I partition my mind. For you, it will be a much harder task and I think you should experiment with tiny portions at first. As for constructing the neural pathways yourself, I also think you can do this. You already understand nanites at their base level because of your enhanced Intelligence. If you are merely following a framework established by the technology itself, it should be trivial to replicate it using *Remodeling*. It could take a long time, and a lot of nanites, but I think it is possible."**

"If I can do it with my mind, I should be able to do it with the rest of my body too!"

"Yes, but there are things you cannot do permanently, like your *Natural Armor*. That is a shield made up of nanites."

"Yeah, that makes sense, but most things I can and should be able to

replicate. Like my enhanced vision. We know that the nanites contract the lens so I can see farther, right? If I use Remodeling to add muscles to that effect, I won't have to rely on the nanites. Same thing with Heat Vision. Right now, the nanites detect the heat wavelength and relay to the cones added to my physical eye. You told me it used something called the trigeminal nerve, right? If I can replicate it, then it would work. Night vision is even easier because I only need to change the optic nerves to increase my pupils to absorb more ambient light."

Scarlet laughed. **"Yes. I can see that it intrigues you. Let us discuss more at length when I return. It will go much easier and faster when we share a thought space. In the meantime, keep practicing your new ability."**

"All right, all right. I'll wait until you're back, but Scarlet —"

"I understand. This could change a lot."

Jared spent the next two hours staring into the fire, periodically activating his new ability. Each time he activated *Clear Mind*, he examined the nanite coding and their areas of assignment. It was easy for him to see what each of them did and where they resided in his body. Scarlet had a point; some skills he couldn't replicate. *Natural Armor* and *Telepathy* were two he couldn't figure out how to replicate. Perhaps studying Scarlet's mind would help him understand how she used telepathy without nanites. With the little understanding he had, it looked like magic.

Feeling something bump into his shoulder, Jared opened his eyes and found Vanessa sitting next to him. He hadn't heard her approach and didn't know how long she'd watched him.

"Hey, Vanessa." Jared put his arm around her, and she rested her head on his shoulder. "How long have you been sitting here?"

"I think a few hours. I watched you staring at the fire, and you got this really surprised look on your face, but you didn't seem to realize I was here. Then your face took on that faraway look it does when you're conversing with Scarlet for long periods of time."

"Sorry, I was preoccupied. I gained a new ability. Well, I guess it might not be new, but I managed to unlock my mind? It opened new possibilities and gave me clarity I never had before. Scarlet called it *Clear Mind*. It basically allows me to break down any mental barriers and process all of my thoughts, conscious and subconscious, at the same time. It's the same way her mind works. It's just another skill I need to activate at the moment. However, as I add more nanites to it, it'll become a passive skill. Meaning, I'll always have a *Clear Mind*."

"That sounds difficult. How do you think about many things at once?" Vanessa wrinkled her brow in concentration. "If I think about multiple things or try to multi-task, it isn't at the same time. It's more like quickly switching back and forth."

"Exactly! The same thing happened when I used *Hyper-Cognition*. When I went into the hyper-speed mode in my mind it didn't let me think through every scenario at once, just rapidly speed through a lot of different pathways in succession. After the last round of enhancements to my mind that changed. I could reach a meditative state to see and control the thoughts in my mind. It was like standing in a room with a lot of doorways. All I had to do was open one and the stream of consciousness continued. I'd reached the point I could open half a dozen of these doors simultaneously, but mostly when I was in a stationary, meditative state. I think the most I managed while active is three, and that's likely because my life was in peril when we went looking for Scarlet's family."

"What changed now?"

"I'm not entirely sure why it was different now, other than I've practiced a lot. This time I let my mind wander and destroyed the room I'd constructed on a whim. The moment I obliterated the room, everything rushed in. Even more incredible, I understood and could process all of these threads at an instinctual level. That's when I got the skill. I suppose it's like the skills we get passively when the nanites adapt to our surroundings. If we use an ability enough or get exposed to something a sufficient amount of times, the nanites adapt. I unlocked neural pathways I didn't know I had and now everything is clear, a *Clear Mind*."

"It sounds incredible! I can't wait until I have a companion and can do the things you do. I feel weak and helpless as I am right now."

"Vanessa." Jared lifted her face to look at him. "You are one of the strongest people I've ever met. Through sheer will you helped every person in this colony survive. If our roles were reversed, I don't know if I could've done it. The person you see in me today is not how I used to be. I left my home colony because I couldn't bear the loss of my parents. I ran from my issues. You..." Jared was at a loss to find the words to convey what he felt. "You faced those trials head on. You became separated from your sister." Jared pointed a few yards away where Elle sat beside another fire pit chatting amiably with other colonists. "You lost both your parents to Razael. For nearly a decade you survived and willed others to survive beneath a dark, foreboding lake with no hope of ever seeing the light of day again. I hope that someday, I have even half the strength of will I see in you. You are an incredible person, and I'm so glad we can work together to free others from the slavery forced on them."

While he spoke, tears trickled down Vanessa's cheeks. They were tears of sadness at the loss she'd endured, but tinged with happiness when she gazed over at her sister.

"Thank you for saving us, Jared. You—" Vanessa's voice cracked, and she stopped to compose herself before continuing. "You can't imagine the years we spent under the water. Sometimes when I close my eyes, I panic. Many times, we were so deep in the lake no light made it through, and it was endless floating in nothingness. We couldn't see and never developed any kind of night vision like you."

Jared drew her closer and squeezed her shoulder. "You're safe now, Vanessa. I'll do everything I can to protect you and the others."

Jared held her close while quiet sobs wracked her body. She barely made a sound, and it didn't attract anyone's notice. Jared saw the scars left behind by Razael, the veil of strength and willpower she put on for everyone else, gone.

He admired her strength and willingness to put others before her own needs, but it was clear to him she needed emotional support and someone to confide in.

The two of them sat for some time, enjoying each other's company. Slowly, the rest of the colonists filed into their rooms until only the two of them remained. They didn't need to share words. The mutual feelings of contentment and belonging were close to euphoria. Something both used to think was far beyond their reach.

Every day, his feelings for Vanessa grew. At first, he'd felt like a guardian and had a strong desire to protect and nurture all of these people, Vanessa included. Over time, those feelings had morphed into a friendship, and looking forward to their next meeting. He enjoyed being near her, talking with her. In this moment, with them side by side, and his arm around her, Jared knew their friendship had turned a corner and a seed of love started to blossom in his heart. He gazed at her form snuggled up to his side and knew he never wanted her to leave it.

"Vanessa, I—" Jared began, but Scarlet's thoughts intruded into his mind.

"Jared, we are back."

"Sorry, Scarlet just told me they're back from the hunt. We're going to head back to the old colony tomorrow, and I'd love it if you came with. I...want to spend more time with you, and maybe we can talk more about, well. Us."

"Thank you, Jared." Vanessa sounded out of breath, and her

cheeks flushed slightly. Standing on her tiptoes, she wrapped her arms around him and embraced him tightly.

Jared returned the hug before he turned and headed down to meet up with Scarlet and the other companions.

He didn't expect Attis would suddenly understand him, but perhaps Scarlet could share a thought space with him and show what they spoke about. Once he finished here, he needed to find Carla and make sure they assigned any new nanites before sleeping. Although he could make the trip down to the valley floor in two swift jumps, Jared took his time, activating *Clear Mind* while walking. If he used it enough, it might be easier to convert it into a passive skill.

The walk down was insightful. Scarlet had explained active meditation, but he hadn't tried it until now. It was surreal for him to be processing the act of walking, breathing, blinking, watching, and listening all at the same time. Things he'd taken for granted when managed by his subconscious now found their way into this purview. It wasn't as though he needed to manage them, or force them to happen, but focusing on them helped to quiet the cascade of other thoughts running rampant through his skull.

The descent passed rapidly, and the clearing came into view. Scarlet sat in the center with Attis just in front, facing her. Kitty paced off to the side weaving in and out of the desiccated trees. The moonlight cast the area into shadows and the white of the trees stood in stark contrast to the pitch black of night. Jared paused to admire the amazing creatures. The moon reflected off Attis' feathers like a polished surface. Scarlet appeared a black hole, drinking in the surrounding light with only her molten eyes and burning veins standing out like burning sentinels and tiny rivulets of lava. Kitty's pacing amongst the trees made her look like a shadow flitting through night.

Magnificent. What will this place be like when everyone finds a companion?

Approaching the trio of otherworldly beings, Jared called out so as not to startle the griffon.

"Scarlet, Kitty, Attis!" As one, they turned toward Jared, and Kitty stopped pacing through the trees. "Kitty, you can go find Elle if you'd like. Scarlet and I can take care of things here. Also, have a chat with Elle about nanite assignment if you gained any tonight. She's got some new plans for increasing her mental."

Kitty growled in agreement and silently slinked off into the night. Turning his attention to Attis, the creature stared at him. Its expression neutral, it didn't shy away from his approach.

"Scarlet? Is it okay for me to speak with him? I don't want to freak him out if I talk into his mind."

"It is okay. I spoke with him at length, and he accepts it, albeit grudgingly. His mind is primal, and he does not understand human speech. You may have better luck projecting images and thoughts through physical contact, similar to how we used to do it."

"Can I even do that? I don't..." Jared's brow furrowed in thought. "I've never done that with anyone but you. I assumed our bond allowed me to do that?"

"It does, but I believe you reached a point you can project the same to others. It will not be as effortless but should be possible."

"All right, I'll give it a try. Attis?" The griffon's head twisted to the side in recognition of the name given to him by Carla. "Yes, that's good." Jared pointed to him and said, "Attis." He then placed a hand on his chest and said, "Jared."

Slowly, Jared approached him with his arm extended in front of him. Although eyeing him suspiciously, Attis made no move to prevent Jared from placing his hand on the griffon's side. As gently as possible, Jared spoke into his mind.

"Attis, my name is Jared. Scarlet is my companion."

Awkwardly, Jared imagined an image of Scarlet and himself with a glowing bond pulsating back and forth between them. Then he showed an image of Attis and Carla with a similar bond pulsing between them. Although he used no words, the griffon understood him to a degree.

Next, Jared showed Attis the conversation with Carla. At least, he tried to show it, but it was more like a bunch of still images in his head bombarding Attis. The creature shook his head at the influx of images, not understanding.

"Sorry, Attis. Let's try this slower."

It was a test of his patience for certain. After learning how to eliminate the boundaries in his own mind, this process was almost painful as he severely limited the flow of information. Besides taking it slow, he had to play a game of charades in his mind, acting everything out.

Eventually the creature understood Jared's crude mental performance. Rather than prolong what would prove to be a futile conversation, Jared left the griffon alone. He'd try again after his mental faculties improved.

Scarlet sent him a mental shrug, no doubt understanding his frustration trying to communicate with something that had only ever known instinct and survival.

"It will take time. With as many nanites as he has, it will be sooner than we think, but it is difficult to say exactly how long."

"Did you get through to him at all during the hunt? He understood pictures, but literally nothing else I showed him."

"Let me show you." Scarlet lowered her head to the ground.

Sitting next to her, Jared rested his back against her side.

"Activate your ability before we join thoughts. Compare your mind with mine."

Following Scarlet's instruction, he activated *Clear Mind*. No matter how many times he'd done this in the past few hours, it still felt like a revelation, or a higher plane of existence. It was like his mind was a prison, and in this state of clarity, he was free. He calmed his mind as much as possible before letting Scarlet know he was ready.

In the next instant, his awareness multiplied exponentially. Sharing a thought space had become a common exercise between them over the past month, but with nothing else to compare it to, he'd thought it was just two sides to one coin. Now, however, he compared the vast difference between his ability and Scarlet's mind. The comparison to his *Clear Mind* and Scarlet's own made him realize there was still a world of endless possibilities before him. Before nanites his mind was a mere spark, then a tiny flame with *Clear Mind*, but Scarlet's mind was akin to a raging bonfire. It was so infinitely complex it made his mind spin.

"Scarlet, I—"Jared didn't really know what to say.

He'd felt proud of his accomplishment, but next to Scarlet he was small and insignificant. She'd simultaneously wowed and humbled him in one go. He purposed in his heart to strengthen his mind any chance he got. One day he'd reach the pinnacle of human development and transcend beyond.

"See how my thoughts follow an ordered path? Without seeing the whole picture, it looks chaotic, but immerse yourself with my mind and see all. Trust me when I say it took hundreds of years for me to reach this level of mastery and control. I also needed to grow and mature and that is part of the reason it takes so long for a dragon to hatch. A human mind, yours in particular, is already very mature and developed. The problem stems from humans not using their mind in its entirety."

"Before I met you and enhanced myself, I'd disagree, but I know you're correct now."

"It happens at a young age for humans when they ignore portions of their mind. They learn how to perform tasks, and it becomes a subconscious activity. The mind no longer actively dwells on it, and over time you lose the capacity to use those portions of the mind. You unlocked that access again, and now you must learn how to use it all over again. Only now, you have a much greater capacity to understand, and you have absolute control over your own mind."

"I have a lot of work to do for certain. Let's get back to the reason for this exercise. Can you please help me sort through these thoughts and find where you hunted with Attis?"

Scarlet's thoughts shifted slightly. Not that they diminished or there were less of them, they simply re-focused. Like shifting a focal point from something near to a distant object. It became clear as if it was always there. The implications of always knowing everything in his mind excited and exhausted him. Shaking off the melancholy thoughts, he focused on how Scarlet communicated with the griffon.

She used no words, only impressions and feelings. Urges, desires, instinct, primal desires to kill, and hunger raged through Attis. He didn't understand speech or any complex thoughts. Images sometimes worked when Scarlet showed them, but it startled the griffon so much Scarlet stopped showing them and focused on her own dragon instincts to guide Attis. It worked better than any kind of rational thought or reason. Eventually, Scarlet found a pack of wild dogs and pushed urgency and the scent of blood to Attis. He eagerly followed in her wake until spotting the dogs on his own. Then, like a rocket, he dive-bombed the creatures again and again until not a single one of them remained. By the time Scarlet and Kitty caught up, all six of the dogs lay dead and Attis ate one. The faint glow of nanites swirled into the griffon, but he didn't seem to notice, nor did he care as he consumed the meal.

Scarlet broke the connection and Jared returned to his own thoughts.

"He doesn't really understand much of anything." Jared's shoulders slumped in disappointment.

"He understands only survival and instinct. Any of his intelligence comes from learning to survive other predators. The bond made him manageable, but even now he eyes you like prey. However, he knows you are with me, and he fears me more."

"Scarlet." Jared looked at her forlornly.

"I know. We have much to do and the task seems insurmountable. Let me remind you that there are twelve of my brothers on their way here. We can all help the others as they bond, just as I did with Attis. Even if my brothers choose not to bond, they will help us domesticate the creatures we find and bond."

Relief washed through Jared at Scarlet's words. Without Scarlet and the other dragons, he didn't think they'd ever be ready to take the fight against the cities.

"They are still two days out?" asked Jared.

"A day and a half. Though, they are taking their time so it may be close to two days for them to arrive."

"Thanks for helping out with Attis. I'll let Carla know your thoughts. I've asked her to push everything she has into *Mind* for the time being. At least until she understands the nanites better, and Attis can think about more than his next meal. They'll also come with us to the old colony tomorrow, and we'll let them replenish their nanite stock in the lake."

"They must rest if they are to be ready in time. They will need

time to get used to the changes when they wake."

"I'll head back up and tell Carla now. I'm having her stay in our room to keep an eye on her throughout the night. Please do the same with Attis."

Jared turned and headed back to his home. He had an equal amount of excitement and trepidation. If every creature proved as primitive as Attis, they had their work cut out for them.

Maybe I should put more priority into reaching out to the other dragons?

If they had the other thirty or forty air, water, and earth dragons added to their number, then everyone would have a battle-ready companion, and they could spend their preparation hunting and growing stronger rather than finding more creatures. He had no idea how many of the dragons would join them. Scarlet was the queen of her kind and still several of her brethren outright refused to bond.

Sighing, Jared trudged up the rock wall. *Yes, we've a lot of work to do.*

The short walk did nothing to diminish Jared's concern over their current progress. They had several tasks ahead of them, and all he could do was take it one day at a time. By the time he returned to his home, the girls were all in Vanessa and Elle's bed chatting.

He walked into the room and sat on the edge of the bed.

"I can see you all are ready to turn in for the night." He smiled, attempting to put them at ease, but it never reached his eyes.

Vanessa, attentive to his mood, frowned. "Is everything okay?"

He really had tried to put on a facade for them, but saw it wouldn't work with Vanessa. They'd spent enough time together over the weeks that she picked up on subtle cues others missed.

"Nothing's wrong exactly, it's just...disappointing." Jared explained to them everything Scarlet had said and also tried to show them exactly how Attis thought by sending them impressions through physical touch. He wasn't nearly as effective as Scarlet, but it was sufficient to get the point across.

Carla looked downhearted, but Jared quickly re-assure her. "Carla, please don't worry about it for now. I probably expected way too much. My experience with Scarlet didn't exactly prepare me for anything like this. Truth be told, George and some of the others are probably right."

"Jared, he's just trying to get under your skin."

"Maybe, but why? I mean, what purpose does it serve? He's right in that we went about this the wrong way and put Carla in unnecessary danger. If we'd waited until Scarlet's brothers got here, it could've gone much better."

"I don't know why either. He didn't do anything like this before…you know."

"How long did you lead everyone after your parents went away?"

Vanessa shrugged and tilted her head in thought. "I can't say exactly, but maybe half the time we were down there."

"Maybe he didn't try anything because no one would've listened to him or cared what he had to say. Now that everyone has their freedom back, he's decided he wants to be in charge."

"To what end? None of my people would follow—"

"Damien?" interrupted Jared.

"But Damien came around after a while."

"He did, but you heard him in there. He was quick to back George up. Worse, there's others agreeing with him now."

"I'll talk with them. I'm sure it's nothing."

"I hope so. George is still the one person who hasn't said the vow to protect and uphold human and dragon life. I don't particularly trust anyone who can't say a simple vow to protect humankind."

Vanessa looked torn between a duty to her people and her

growing feelings for Jared. She was between a rock and a hard place, and Jared didn't want to make her choose between the two.

"It's okay, Vanessa. I understand. I'll try my best to get along with him. Maybe we just need to sit down and hash it out. Sorry, I didn't actually come here to talk about George and my problems. I wanted to update you on Attis. I mistakenly assumed it might go faster based on the level of intelligence Kitty has, but I was wrong to have set such high expectations. Kitty bonded with Elle nearly a decade ago. They've had time to learn from each other, and their need for survival drove them into such a close relationship that they've understood each other in ways that few of us will ever achieve."

Hope returned to Carla's eyes. "I'll work with him every chance I get."

Squeezing her hand, Jared reassured her they'd work through it as a family. "I know. We'll get there. Scarlet can communicate with Attis at an instinctual level, and once you've upgraded his Intelligence enough, she'll be able to have more conversations with him and teach him. When Scarlet first told me, I got discouraged, but she reminded me that her brothers can help with the process when we find more companions for others to bond. It will take time, but we can do it."

Jared stood and stretched. "Please try to rest. I'll stay up throughout the night to keep an eye on you. Scarlet will do the same for Attis. The moment you both awake, we want to get you together and work through the changes. Then, we'll set out for the old colony. You can load up on nanites in the lake. It's hard to say how many nanites you and Attis have with no baseline to work with. Tomorrow will be telling for you and those waiting to bond."

Tomorrow would indeed be telling. Jared suspected that everyone had a ton of dormant nanites swirling around inside their bodies, but they wouldn't know for sure until after they went through the evolution process. Only a few hours remained before they found out.

Jared spent the next few hours cleaning and organizing his weapons and equipment. It gave him a chance to finally examine the phase rifle in detail.

He picked up the gray and white weapon, turning it over in his hand. It was smaller and weighed significantly less than the rifle he'd taken off the mercenaries corpse months earlier. The top part of the weapon was round with a hole bored through the top lengthwise which functioned as a sight. Inside, there was a digital targeting reticle that glowed a faint green. The finger guard curved down into a sweeping point that ended just before the handgrip. The grip itself was made of the same material as his phase pistols.

The safety was quite different compared to traditional weapons and both points on either side of the grip needed constant pressure to activate the weapon.

Picking up the battery, Jared found a couple different buttons. Depressing one, a bright, neon green glow lit its side to show the remaining charge. Another button to the left of it showed a heat gauge in bright red. The last of three buttons read *vent*. He didn't know what the button did, but he suspected it was a way to purge the heat when used too much and the gun stalled from the heat. Baffled by the technology, Jared finished cleaning the phase weapons and put them back into his pack. In hindsight, he probably should've tried to understand the technology before cleaning it, but there really weren't many moving parts and the main source of confusion came from the battery itself rather than the weapon.

Unceremoniously, he field-stripped his 9mm taken from the Daggers and performed a quick cleaning. He hadn't used it much, and it was still in good shape. The mercenaries weren't the best of people, but it appeared they knew how to take care of their weapons.

A fleeting thought popped into his head about Loch and Iliana. He wondered where they were and if they'd safely made it back to their base. They'd kidnapped him and tried to steal from him and Scarlet at least twice, but Jared wasn't a cold-hearted monster to kill them outright. He genuinely felt sympathy for their plight. They'd fallen in with the wrong crowd, but similar to him, they wanted to bring justice to those deserving. The biggest distinction between them was they didn't care who they stepped on to make it happen. Definitely a big difference between their agendas. Where Jared planned to go very far out of his way to make sure nothing happened to innocent people, the Daggers couldn't care less, the end justifying the means, as the saying goes.

Finished with his cleaning task, Jared picked up his now dry pack and was about to put everything back into it, when he heard a light clink. Frowning, Jared shook the pack and heard it again. Turning it over he shook it out, but nothing tumbled free. He opened every pocket but found nothing to make the rattling noise. Confused, he set the pack down in thought.

What—

"—Aha! There you are!" Jared flicked his eyes to Vanessa's room to make sure no one heard him. He hadn't meant to speak aloud but had gotten carried away. Underneath the flap was a layer of material that peeled away from the rest of the bag. If someone didn't know where to look, it was easy to miss. The seam followed the same contour as the flap itself and a tiny concealed zipper under the buckle held it shut.

Realizing what he'd put in the flap months ago made him excited. The handful of credits he'd retrieved from the dead explorer's pack beneath the streets of New York remained secured in the pouch. The credits could net their budding colony some much-needed items. Probably the one thing he wanted most was a press so they could pack their own bullets. The credits could buy a lot of them, but the ability to pack their own, with the large barrels of gunpowder he already had, would be a better investment. Jared kept the credits concealed in the flap for now but catalogued them in his mind so he wouldn't forget.

An idea struck him as he finished gearing up. They had a leatherworker now; perhaps they could make him something that would fit the oddly-shaped phase pistol. On their way out, he'd stop and ask.

Jared stood in the room looking around for something else to keep him occupied. He could sit and meditate for a while, but he felt like he'd done enough of that over the past couple of days, and he was antsy. In his room, his meager possessions looked pitiful in the large space. A single change of well-used clothes lay folded on a shelf. After Vanessa found out he only had a couple spare shirts, she'd scrounged up some spares along with a couple pairs of pants.

A few small tools and knives lay scattered about on the stone dresser. The only item of any significance in the room was the box of explosives and manuals in the closet. They had no way to secure the stuff in a locked room so it remained in his closet where he hoped it was out of sight enough that people wouldn't get harebrained ideas and try to take any of it.

He walked over to the box with the manuals and selected a few at random, in addition to the book on explosives. When he went back into the room, he saw Carla tossing around in her sleep. A few more minutes of restlessness and she returned to her calm state. There was no evidence she was in trouble. It was likely just some pain seeping through to her conscious state.

Before cracking open the book, Jared activated *Clear Mind*. He wanted complete cognitive function so that everything he read he understood in absolute clarity and could recall in a moment's notice.

It'd been a few hours since he'd last used the ability, and it took a few moments to center himself and calm the raging highway of thought speeding through his mind. After he'd found a center, Jared used active meditation to order his mind.

The first several chapters proved an introduction to all things explosive. They included details about high temperature burning substances to short, forceful detonations. Liquid chemicals, solid object reactions, and heat regulated materials made up most of the different explosives. The list of different compounds used was immense, many of which should be easy to find. The section on ammunition reloading piqued his interest. Skimming the segment, everything made sense to him and brought back memories of helping his dad hand-load their bullets.

When he got to the section about blasting caps and primers, he paused.

"I forgot all about primers. How could I forget about that?" Closing his eyes, Jared did a mental inspection of everything in the weapons and explosives cases he'd rescued from beneath the tunnels. There was no press, nor were there any primers. They had gunpowder for the bullets, but no way to prime them for use.

He should've remembered the primers. If he'd spent a few minutes recalling the experience when he was younger, he would've remembered. During the many times working with his father, he recalled handing him primers while packing the bullets.

Is there a way around that requirement? Can we make them ourselves?

He kept reading through the book and flipped to the index, where he found a section dedicated to primers. He could make primers himself but needed to find mercury, nitric acid, ethanol, and something to use for the metal caps. He could make nitric acid from mercury using electricity, and they could make ethanol from yeast, which they shouldn't have trouble finding. It would be quite the production, but at least they had the option to make it themselves.

Why must everything be so difficult?

Every facet of life was difficult in this world. Those in the floating cities had every form of convenience at their fingertips, like automated robots to perform all their menial labor. No concerns of dying by radiation or mutated creatures. Extravagant cities with lush vegetation, and likely any food they wanted.

Someday that will change. Someday, they'll experience our life, or we'll bring their life to the rest of the world.

04 COMMUNICATION PROBLEMS

J ared continued reading through the night, pausing occasionally to check in on Carla and make sure she was okay. From time to time he reached out to Scarlet to check on Attis. He needn't have worried since all appeared in order.

As with his own changes, they took quite a while for Carla, and it wasn't until late morning when she woke. By that point Vanessa and Elle had already left the room, leaving Jared alone. When Carla woke and looked at Jared, he immediately noticed a change in her demeanor.

Jared rushed over and helped her sit up. "How do you feel?"

"I…different?" Carla shook her head to clear the remnants of sleep from her mind. "I can't place my finger on it, but I feel different."

"It will take you a while to get used to all the changes. I'll walk you through some instructions that Scarlet gave me after upgrading my mind for the first time. First, can you try to speak using telepathy? I want to see how far you progressed with these enhancements."

"Can you hear me?"

"Yes, I can! We'll have to test your range when we get outside, but the fact you can already speak like this is great. Though, you could already use telepathy in a limited fashion, so perhaps it's not all that surprising, but I'm still happy to see the change. Next, explore the nanites in your body. There are several ways to do this, but I'll repeat what Scarlet told me. Follow the nanites."

"Follow them?" Carla cocked her head to the side, confusion etched onto her face.

"Cryptic, right? Yeah, Scarlet has an odd way of answering questions, but it really is an accurate way to describe this. Examine yourself and *feel* the nanites. Once you feel their presence, you can delve into them with your mind. It's a little disconcerting at first, but you'll get the hang of it with practice. I want you to do this for the rest of the day, even while we fly back to the old colony if you can manage it. If you think it will split your concentration too much while atop Attis, then wait until we get back."

"I'll give it my best shot." Carla looked determined to learn and progress as fast as possible.

"Awesome, that's all I ask. The sooner you understand and can work through all of this, the faster you can upgrade to the next level. Not that you couldn't keep enhancing everything now, but you need to get used to the current changes before adding anything else. If you can learn how to add categories, your options for enhancement paths will broaden a lot. I've been doing the same for any changes I go through. It helps if you break it into chunks." Jared rubbed the top of his head, thinking back to the first set of enhancements he'd gone through, the increased strength, and the subsequent idiocy when moving large pieces of concrete around.

"Let's say I've experienced too many changes, too fast. I recommend taking things slow. Take the time to get used to the changes, and then you can do more enhancements and upgrades. We have an entire lake of nanites to burn through. While we don't know how many are there, we'll keep using it until they run out, and then move on to hunting creatures in the wild."

"I'll practice every chance I get and let you know when I'm ready for the next lessons."

"Thanks, Carla. Now, let's round everyone else up and go see Attis. I'm curious to see what changes happened to him."

Vanessa and Elle joined them as they headed over to Attis. Jared wasn't sure what to expect. He hoped for the best, but it was difficult to say how much the griffon's intelligence would increase overnight.

When they reached the clearing where Scarlet and Attis resided, it was clear something had changed. The giant bird of prey was no longer cowering off to the side, eyeing everything like his next meal. He stared at the trio with cold, calculating eyes.

Staring into the solid black eyes of the creature, Jared imagined the bird was trying to understand what he saw. Before today, everything was another meal. Every encounter with any other being, be they human or animal, was just another battle in his struggle for survival.

Now, however, it appeared the griffon looked at them in a new light. Not necessarily as prey, but as an entity he didn't quite understand.

Carla rushed over to Attis, but Jared cautioned her enthusiasm, voicing his concerns.

"Be careful. I don't think he'd harm you, but this is all very new to him. If you notice his behavior, he isn't treating us like enemies anymore, but his mind is sharper, and we don't know what he's thinking."

"I can hear him. He's confused."

"All the more reason to be cautious. Just approach slowly and take this one step at a time. Scarlet is right here if you need any help.

We'll take as long as you need before heading out. Since we are all flying, this trip won't take long at all. While you get re-acquainted with him, I will go have a chat with Casey, Pete, and Marie to see if they need anything from the old colony."

"Scarlet, please keep a close eye on them and be ready to intervene should you need."

"I will keep an eye on them and try to listen to their communications if I can. Though, I do not think we have anything to worry about with the two. I do not trust Attis not to hurt anyone else, but for myself and Carla, he will not harm us."

"Thanks. I'll be back shortly."

Jared left with Vanessa, Elle, and Kitty. The giant cat refused to let Elle out of her sight. It was probably a precaution with Attis around since no one knew the bird's motivations and if he would attack. Jared didn't blame the big cat at all, and that was part of the reason he wanted Scarlet to remain vigilant.

"Vanessa, Elle, can you two go around and see if there are any small items anyone needs? Let them know we'll be out for a short time and can look for some things in town. We won't spend hours scouring the area, so if it's not something we'll easily find, it'll need to wait. I want to be back by the time the dragons get here. This trip is mainly about getting Carla more nanites from the lake and a couple items for Pete."

Jared grabbed Vanessa's hand, beckoning her to stay for a moment. He led her over to the side of the clearing. "I think it might be better for you to stay here today. As much as I want to spend the day with you and continue our conversation, Attis concerns me. Scarlet and I can handle anything he might do, but if something happens—"

"It's okay. I understand." She looked a little disappointed, but Jared knew she saw the wisdom in the decision. "I'll use the time to talk with my people and see if I can get to the bottom of the resentment and unrest caused by George.

"Vanessa, please be careful. If George is willing to go against me when I have a dragon to back me up, there's no telling what he's capable of."

"He won't hurt me. He'd have to contend with the entire group if he tried."

"You're probably right, but promise me you'll only confront him in a public place? I mean, I know you probably don't want everyone overhearing your conversation, but at least do it someplace where others can see you."

"All right, I promise."

"Thanks. I just want you to be safe."

Vanessa looked up at him and smiled.

Jared gazed into her eyes, drinking in the sight of her beautiful face. He loved how her smile crinkled her nose and created tiny lines at the corners of her eyes. He almost bent down and kissed her, but she broke the connection and followed after Elle. Before Vanessa left the clearing, she glanced back at him, her eyes smoldering and cheeks flushed.

It took Jared more than a few minutes to recover from the encounter. It left him weak in the knees, her presence intoxicating to him. Once he'd recovered, he followed the pair to ask Pete what he needed from the colony.

As usual, Jared found Pete in his room, which doubled as his workshop. Every time Jared walked into the room, it seemed more cluttered and packed than the time before.

"Pete? You in here somewhere?"

A crash in another room—followed by muttered curses—reached his ears, and he smiled.

Maybe that'll teach him to clean things up, Jared thought, the corner of his mouth ticking up in a smirk.

"I-I'm back here."

Jared picked his way through the maze of gadgets and gizmos on the floor and every flat surface within the room. Pete was in the bedroom, using one of the flat counters as a desk. He had a small desk lamp pointed at an array of parts on the counter.

"What are you working on?"

"Nothing in p-particular. I'm just taking stuff apart to figure out how it works. This happens to b-be one of those wind-up walkie-talkies. I'm trying to f-figure out how it recharges the device. If I c-can f-figure out how to replicate this and store the energy, we m-might find another source of power. If you hadn't n-noticed, the smog in the air p-prevents a lot of direct sunlight, and we always have to ration our electricity."

"I noticed, but to be fair, it's not like we have a lot of things that use electric—" Jared paused, looking around the room. "Well, most of us don't have a lot of electronics. I'm not even sure we have a single one up in our room. Though the girls might have something I've not seen. We don't need a huge abundance of electricity—unless you are cooking up something I don't know about?"

"No, n-not really. I mean I've always g-got projects going, and we c-can never have enough electronics, b-but there's nothing special. It's mostly for m-my work and making sure I have enough to test and keep building."

"Good idea. As far as I know, you're the only one of us technically inclined to understand all this stuff. I was thinking the other day about how we have so much talent with our small group. When we take the fight to the cities, we'll need someone who knows the technology and can help us make sense of everything up there. I think you are just the man for the job."

"B-but," stammered Pete. "I know n-nothing about their tech!"

"Right now you don't, but I think we'll remedy that in time. If these phase pistols weren't so valuable, I'd let you disassemble one. For now, though, I think I've got something to tide you over." Jared slipped his pack off his shoulders and extracted one of the spent battery packs. "This one no longer has any charge, so it probably won't help you figure out how to replenish the energy, but at least you can work with it safely and not worry about blowing the whole area up."

Pete's eyes grew to twice their size as he stared greedily at the object in Jared's hand. Wanting to have fun, Jared moved the battery around in a circle and Pete followed it like an eager puppy, not caring Jared teased him. He was so eager to get his hands on the technology.

"All right, this is yours, Pete, but please reassemble it when you're done. Once we get some kind of trade relationship going with other colonies, I'd like to exchange some of these depleted ones to see if they can get them recharged by the cities."

"Yes! I will!" Pete snatched the battery pack from Jared's outstretched hand.

The small man already had a stammer occasionally, but excited as he was, it escalated to a whole other level and it became hard to understand him. Jared turned around to walk out but stopped himself. He'd come here to ask Pete what he needed.

"Oh, the reason I came in here was to see what you needed from the old colony."

The only reply was an incoherent muttering from Pete, as he'd already turned back to his makeshift workbench. He slid all the walkie-talkie components out of the way. Though Jared noticed that even in his excitement, Pete was careful not to disturb the order in which the parts lay. Jared shook his head, amused. Pete had seemed eager to get his hands on some appliances yesterday, but now he had a new object to occupy his attention, he forgot all about his original request. Jared left Pete to his project and walked to Casey's medical station.

Touring the room, it turned out Casey was not present. Before leaving, Jared quickly checked the storage closet to check in on their supply of boosters. Surprised, he found he wasn't able to check on them, since Casey had fashioned a door with a combination lock attached. He didn't know where the parts came from or how whomever did it affixed it to the rock, but it made him happy to see someone had locked away the precious items for safe-keeping.

His last stop was to see Marie, their cook, to find out if there was anything she needed. Jared hiked back up to the top platform and found her tending to the stock of meat. One of the back rooms they used as a meat locker also had a door on it, and they'd fashioned rubber strips around the outside of the door that functioned as a seal. Praising their ingenuity, Jared approached Marie.

"Hey, Marie, is there anything you need from the old colony? Carla and I are heading over there. We'll be flying, so I can't bring too much, but I thought I'd ask, anyway."

Marie's response was immediate. "Salt."

Jared chuckled. "Salt it is. Anything else?"

"We could use more seaweed if you don't mind swimming."

"I don't think that's a possibility, unfortunately. We're bonded, and the moment we step foot in the water, we'll absorb the nanites. If we spend too long in there it can really hurt us. I don't entirely know what would happen if we let it continue past our pain threshold, but it could kill us."

Marie blanched and took a step back. "I didn't know."

Jared held up his hand. "Don't worry about it. Now you know. It's not a big deal. We'll send out a foraging group tomorrow or the day after. Right now, I want to go with Carla so we can get back quickly. The dragons should arrive tomorrow!"

From the look on Marie's face, she didn't share his enthusiasm. Frowning, he wondered if more people felt that way. It could be they didn't know what to expect. After Razael and then Scarlet, they might be scared of a group of massive dragons looming over them.

They were no longer scared of Scarlet, but then she'd earned that trust and was Jared's companion; not to mention she was only a third the size of her brothers. These other dragons were an unknown entity, and they had no loyalty to humans. What Marie and the other water folk didn't realize was that Scarlet's word was infallible. Her brothers could no sooner go against her wishes than stop being a dragon. He'd need to reassure everyone before they arrived to make sure there were no incidents and that everyone knew what to expect.

Again, Jared found his thoughts wandering back to George. This man was such a pain in the neck, Jared almost wished he'd just disappear. He realized the thought didn't make him feel guilty either. Perhaps his encounter with the Daggers jaded him against George's type. Jared quickly dismissed the thought and cast George from his mind. He had other things to dwell on, and fretting over something he could do nothing about right now wouldn't help anyone.

Jared ignored Marie's obvious fear for now. "Where's the best place to find salt? I don't want to go ransacking every home looking for tiny amounts."

"Check the school house cafeteria. They kept large containers of it there."

"I don't recall going through any schools. Where is it?"

"Do you remember where the solar panels were? And that large building you said was on top of the garage you found in the underground facility?"

"Yes, I remember."

"It's not huge—the school, that is—but it's just across the street from it. We didn't have very many children in the colony, so we used an old office building and turned a couple rooms downstairs into the cafeteria."

Jared pulled up an image of the area and quickly found the two-story building described. It was roughly three times the size of most houses in the area, but he hadn't had time to explore it before. Right around the time he'd wanted to head that way was when the drop ship came to destroy everything. After that, he didn't have the will to scavenge further.

"Okay, I'll check the cafeteria. If that fails, I'll look in some old diners."

"You probably won't find too much in them old diners since we didn't use them all that much, but you never know, it might be worth a shot."

Thanking Marie, Jared headed back to the medical facility to see if Casey was back.

"Casey? Are you here?"

"Just a minute!" Casey appeared carrying a handful of clean pelts. He set them on a chair and turned to Jared. "What's up?"

"I wanted to see if you need anything from the old colony. Carla and I are making a run today and we can pick up small essentials."

Casey looked around the room, taking stock of his equipment and items. "No, I think we're all set here. We've had no serious injuries, and that crate of supplies you pulled from the military complex is more than sufficient to handle anything we need. I also recycle wraps and bandages whenever I can."

"Excellent work. Oh, before I go, how did you get this door installed?"

"Two of the guys loaded up a smaller cart in one of their forays to that ruined city at the tip of the lake. They brought a few doors, and they also found some…what did they call them? Self-tapping nails?"

"Ah, that explains it. Okay thanks for the info. Do you know if Johan got one of these installed in the temporary armory too?"

"I'm not sure." Casey twisted his face in thought. "I know Marie got one installed on the meat locker."

"Yep, just came from there. No worries, I'll ask next time I see him. It would be a good idea to make sure we get all of our valuables locked away. Eventually, it'll be nice if everyone had a door installed to their room. It would be a good protection against any creatures that might roam around. Maybe then we wouldn't have to set a night watch. Anyway, I'm rambling. I'll let you get back to whatever you were doing."

Leaving the medic, Jared rejoined Scarlet in the clearing to wait for Elle and Vanessa. Sitting next to her, they watched Attis and Carla from a few yards away. The small woman stood in front of the giant griffon, her hand resting on his beak.

"Any update on them?" Jared thought to Scarlet.

"Not yet. They are making progress. The few thoughts I heard proved the creature understands much more than before. He still seems primitive; he does not understand everything Carla says, but she is patient and using images and impressions to get her points across."

"They have a long way to go. It might be faster if Carla just learns to communicate at an instinctual level than to teach the thing to understand the spoken word."

"I believe you are correct. Eventually, he will come to understand words, but right now he needs an image for association. This form of speech is much slower and difficult for both."

"What about a shared thought space?"

"I do not know if that is the answer either. What would Carla's mind have to endure, sharing the thought space of a non-intelligent

creature that only thinks in predator and prey mentality?"

Jared didn't reply immediately as he thought about the consequences. It may cause issues for Carla, but the benefit would be faster reaction times, accurately assessing danger, and predatory instincts. All of those were valuable assets, especially if they wanted to use her as a scout. She could easily go unnoticed atop the griffon and maybe the cities wouldn't care about it flying around.

"Scarlet, I think you're onto something there. If Carla takes on the characteristics of the griffon while in a shared thought space, that might be beneficial for us. That bird is fast, silent, and knows how to avoid danger. If Carla becomes our scout, she might get close to the cities and gather intelligence for us."

"That is a good point. I agree, but we also do not know how long it will take for them to share a thought space. You had to upgrade your mind a lot before we could, and even then, it was I who initiated it."

"That's fair, but I don't think it'll take them as long. Carla can already project her thoughts to me without touch. If you tried a shared space with her, would that work?"

"It might, but I am not sure having her know everything running through my head is a good idea, either. While I trust them, I do not know if I trust her that much."

"Why don't you trust them?" Jared looked at Scarlet in alarm. "Didn't you root through their minds yourself?"

"Yes."

"Then what's the issue?"

"Jared, we have not exactly had the best experience with humans now and in the past."

"I...you're right, but I thought if you could trust anyone it would be these people."

"I trust them more than I thought I would any human, but that

does not mean I want them privy to all my thoughts."

"Understood. Just to sate my curiosity, do you think it's possible?"

"I do."

"Let's keep it as a last resort if we need to go there. If Carla becomes our primary scout, then she'll need all the advantage she can get. I totally understand not wanting her rooting around your thoughts, but maybe you can erect a mental barrier of your own and prevent her from accessing things you want hidden."

"I...can do that. Normally, we only shield our thoughts from external influences, and I have not tried to lock anything down internally. I will think on it in the event we need it."

"Thanks! Hopefully it doesn't come to that, but it's nice to have options."

Jared slowly walked over to Carla and Attis, careful not to do anything Attis would interpret as hostile.

"Carla, are you ready to go? I overheard a little bit of your conversation and understand the frustration in communicating with Attis. Scarlet and I were just discussing it and think you should try to understand his thoughts better on an instinctual level rather than force his mind to your own. It'll get easier the more you upgrade *Mind*, especially when you can share a thought space as we do, but for now this might be the best option. I won't pretend that it'll be easy, but you will get there, and I don't want you to get discouraged."

"Thanks, Jared. I'm ready to go. It's something I must get used to, but I think we can understand each other enough for now."

"Good. Let's get this trip done, and you can spend more time with him. Keep trying to *follow the nanites* as often as possible too until you understand them. I think it'll speed things up and you'll adapt faster."

Vanessa, Elle, and Kitty sat off to the side of the clearing waiting for them while they conversed with their companions.

Jared called them over. "Did anyone need anything?"

"Nope," Elle answered in a cheery tone. "There were a couple odd requests for furniture, but we told them you be flying, and they change mind."

"Thanks, Elle. Your speech sounds much better!"

"Vanessa work with me every day." Elle looked at her sister with love.

It encouraged him to see the sisters together. When he watched them interact, the world's ugliness faded into the background. There was good left in the world worth fighting for and these two reunited siblings were the constant reminder he needed.

Since leaving his colony a couple years ago, there hadn't been much to put hope in. Everywhere he went there was death, destruction, and chaos. He'd only visited one other colony in that time, and it was much the same as his own. They were a small group of people completely isolated from the outside world. Occasionally travelers would stop by, but that had only been in the last decade since the technology existed. Other than that, only drop ships visited, and that was often an automated transaction. All the colonies he knew about were normal societies that worked for the common good of everyone and they rarely ventured outside the boundaries of the safe zones.

Jared imagined it was much the same as pre-apocalypse government. In the case with his colony, the elders voted on someone to lead, and they had security forces to help keep them safe. Though it wasn't like the old law enforcement, they made sure no one did anything against the tenets of the colony. Because it was such a small group of people, they rarely had any issues, and everyone realized that working toward the good of their colony was of utmost importance.

That sheltered upbringing hadn't prepared him for the hostile world in which he found himself. When he looked back at the experiences of the past few months, it was obvious he'd been unprepared for reality. He hadn't known there were so many violent people in the world. Even the cities hadn't seemed bad at the time. It wasn't how he'd grown up, and with no outside influences on his small bubble of reality, there had been nothing to prepare him, save for the rude awakening he'd experienced.

The world was harsh, but hope existed, and he planned to cling to that lifeline for all he was worth. Otherwise, his mission and vows were pointless. He needed to be a protector of humankind.

"I'm so happy for the two of you. Truly. The relationship you share gives me confidence of a future absent hardships and fear like we suffer today. Never change."

Vanessa laid a hand on Jared's arm and drew him into a hug. "Thanks to you. None of this would be possible otherwise. I have the same request of you. Never change. Your compassion allowed you to do these things. It drove you to protect us and help Elle. Even now you tirelessly work to increase the strength of others before yourself. You've selflessly offered to settle your differences with George for the others. It is something I… we admire about you."

Jared watched her cheeks flush a slight shade of pink, and he smiled. In the months they'd been out of the water, some of their natural color had returned. Just a month ago, he wouldn't have seen her blush, since her skin had still had a slight bluish tint to it.

"Thank you, Vanessa. Though, it's not all selfless. I have ulterior motives to all of this. Eventually we'll take the fight to those above. At some point I'll ask everyone to put the good of the world above themselves, and there will be risks. When that time comes, it'll be challenging, and people may get hurt or die."

"I understand that, and we all agreed to take that risk. If not for you, we'd still be at the bottom of a lake, clinging to an absurd lifeline that one day we'd see the light of day. Already, every one of us has experienced more life than we ever thought we would. We all said the vow and will follow you wherever that may lead."

Jared tightened his grip around Vanessa. This woman was amazing, and he wanted nothing more than to protect her from the harshness of the world. It pained him to think he would need to ask her to follow him into a battle one day. They needed to get stronger. Everyone needed to get stronger.

"All right, we must go. Please stay safe and we'll be back in just a few hours."

"We will. Be careful out there."

Jared turned from Vanessa. A momentary pang of sadness pulsed through him as he mounted Scarlet. Glancing back at Vanessa, Jared winked and patted Scarlet on the side.

She bunched her legs and launched them into the air.

"*Carla, can you hear me?*"

"*Yes, and you, me?*"

"*I can. Stay close. If you want to have Attis stretch his wings, that's fine, but try to stay within sight. We can test your telepathy distance too. I imagine it isn't very far just yet, but I could be wrong. We'll head directly to the old colony first, and then to the lake. We're going to the old school so I can find salt for Marie.*"

"*Okay, I'll stay within sight.*" Immediately after Carla spoke, Attis banked sharply.

"**He is beautiful and graceful.**"

"*He's also extremely fast and silent, making him a deadly adversary. A great addition to our fighting force.*"

His thoughts ever-turning toward their coming confrontation with the cities, Jared knew the fight was much closer than he wanted. Starting with the destruction in New York City and the destroyed underground facility, the cities knew something was afoot.

05 SO IT BEGINS

I t only took less than twenty minutes to reach the old colony, and that was at a leisurely pace. Both Scarlet and Attis could fly extremely fast if they wanted, and it was only a twenty mile stretch in a straight line, something that took them two days to walk the first time.

Jared instructed Scarlet to head for the old school building and shared with her a picture of where it was. Scarlet banked with Attis close on her heels. They touched down in front of the building. Jared hopped off and double-checked all of his gear.

"Ready, Carla?"

He received a nod in response, and they entered the building.

"Stay behind me." Jared pulled out his phase pistol in case there was anything lurking in the building. "Do you remember the layout?"

"No. I didn't go to school here. I was old enough to work in the colony, and my dad taught me whatever else I needed to know. My mom helped with my education since my dad was always out taking care of our colony. My mom passed when I was little. She got sick, and—"

Jared turned to face Carla and lay a hand on her shoulder. He saw the unshed tears in her eyes. "I know what it's like. I lost my mother to the radiation."

"It's so unfair, you know? We have this technology that could've saved her, but it was a few years too late." She looked at Jared and the same questions he had shone in her watery eyes.

Jared dropped his hands and turned back down the hall. "It might've saved her," he said over his shoulder. "But you can't know for sure. My mother still died from it and she had nanites in her body."

Carla lifted a shoulder and nudged a stack of books laying in the hallway. "I guess. Still, she didn't have to die."

"On that point, I'll agree. If they really do have full nanites as Igor suggested, then they wouldn't need to worry about radiation at all."

"They need to pay for everything they've done to us."

Jared glanced behind him and saw the fire in Carla's eyes.

"We'll have our vengeance, Carla. You and all the others must get stronger first. A single phase round would be enough to take all of you out. That's to say nothing of the rifles and cannons they also have. Let's focus on what we came to do here, which puts you one step closer to that goal."

Carla nodded her head tersely, and they continued searching the building. Jared hadn't seen or heard anything to indicate danger, but he'd rather exercise caution and check the whole building to be sure.

It wasn't until they reached the opposite end of the building that he found the small cafeteria. Rummaging through the cabinets, he found a couple containers of salt and put them in a satchel he'd brought for the occasion. It wasn't a lot, but it'd be enough to tide

Marie over for a while.

"Okay, we got what we came for. Let's head over to the lake. I want to see if there's anything of interest along the way. I didn't see any creatures when we flew over here. It seems strange given the large volume that used to live in the lake. I don't know if they're still scared of Razael, or if they wanted to leave the area altogether, but it seems unnatural that so many predators fled rather than try to assert dominance over the area."

Walking through the small town was uneventful. Just as he'd seen from the air, there was nothing living down here. The only items of interest in the streets were a variety of furniture pieces some of the water folk had hoped to bring back to their new home. Looking at the furniture, Jared smiled. While it would be nice to have some modern amenities and more comfortable items, the water folk hadn't thought through how to transport the stuff.

"There's the lake, Carla. When we get there, just hold up for a minute while I make sure there's nothing lurking under the surface. I've got an ability called *Heat Sight* that will let me see if there's anything close by."

"That's neat! I can't wait to get abilities of my own."

"To be fair, *Telepathy* is an ability. It's just not as cool for you since you've had it for years. Some of these abilities become so innate that I don't even realize they're an ability anymore. They become a natural extension of myself. My *Night Vision* and *Temperature Regulating* are like that. Before I ever met Scarlet, or had the ability to enhance myself, I could use them."

Jared stopped a few paces from the shoreline and held up a hand for Carla to wait. He walked up to the water gently lapping against the beach and flipped over to *Heat Sight*. It took a slight moment to adjust, but when it cleared, he found no threats in the immediate vicinity. He saw a faint glowing outline far out into the water, but nothing close.

"Okay, it looks safe."

Carla immediately started forward, an eager glint in her eyes.

"Whoa, whoa." Jared stepped in front to bar her way. "You know this will hurt, right?"

Carla paused and looked at him, eyebrows raised. "It will?"

Her question came out as a squeak, and Jared had to stifle a chuckle. He admired her eagerness, but she needed to know what was in store for her.

"The amount it hurts largely depends on you. If you absorb only a little, it won't hurt, but if you want to push yourself to the limit, then yes, it will hurt a lot. Even Scarlet experienced pain because she couldn't handle the torrent of nanites flooding into her."

Carla looked from Jared back to the lake, and back again. Slowly, her expression transformed from fear to determination. Her body tensed as she stepped forward.

"I can do this!"

"I'll be here every step of the way. When you can't take it anymore, yell out for me and I'll break your connection. If you want the best results, you need to hang on until you think you'll pass out from the pain. Though, if you do pass out, I'll pull you out myself. I don't really know how much our bodies can handle so I'd prefer if you were conscious when you finish."

Jared heard an audible gulp and Carla's breathing quickened. He laid a reassuring hand on her shoulder. "I'm here. Before you go in, please let Attis know this will cause you some pain. I don't want him to think I'm hurting you and attack. Scarlet will take care of Attis when it's his turn to absorb."

Attis and Scarlet had landed a few paces away while Jared explained. Carla walked over and laid a hand on the griffon. She spent several moments explaining what would happen, trying to make him understand.

"I'm ready." Carla walked to the edge of the water, but didn't step in.

"Whenever you want to start. At first, nothing will happen, but then you'll see a glow emanate from the lake, that will gradually grow until there is a stream entering your body. Don't pull back. When you've had enough, yell out and I will pull you back. At that point, you may not be able to break the connection yourself."

As soon as Jared finished speaking, Carla slipped off her shoes and strode into the water up to her ankles.

It took a few minutes, but the faint glow rose to the surface of the lake and grew in brightness. Slowly, a funnel of multi-colored light streamed toward Carla.

Her eyes widened to saucers as she scrutinized the beautiful colors swirling through the stream. The tide grew, thickened, and wrapped around Carla's feet. Her face showed elation as she watched the tiny machines, but the smile quickly faded as the excitement turned to pain. Droplets of sweat broke out on her forehead and her brow wrinkled in concentration.

An involuntary grunt escaped her lips and her shoulders hunched against the intense pain wracking her body. Jared knew exactly what she felt in that moment, since he'd experienced it several times now. At first, it felt cool, a stream of cold water wrapping around the body, but it quickly turned into a boiling inferno and every nerve ending screamed out in agony.

"It. H-Hu-Hurts," Carla stammered, teeth clinched tight.

"As soon as you say the word, Carla." Jared reached up his arms to wrap around her body.

"I…" Her voiced faded, and Jared saw her knees buckle.

He scooped her up, and the flow of nanites stopped, leaving a pulsating shimmer in the water. When he looked up, Attis was just a few feet away in a crouch. Even warned, it didn't quite sink in for him, and he was ready to rip someone apart for hurting what was now a part of him. Jared didn't blame him. He hated to see the pain wrought on someone else, knowing full well how much it really hurt.

"Scarlet, can you please calm Attis down and try to explain this to him? He's got to go next, but I don't think we'll be getting him anywhere near the water if we can't calm him down."

"I will try."

Scarlet snorted to get Attis's attention. When the griffon didn't immediately turn around, she issued a low guttural growl. Immediately, Attis folded his wings and lowered himself to the ground. He knew who was at the top of the hierarchy with Scarlet, but Jared was just prey that hurt his charge.

Scarlet and Attis stared at each other for long moments, Scarlet no doubt delving into the creature's mind, explaining the situation. Several moments later, the large creature turned back to Jared and Carla, nudging her with his beak.

"I told him she is fine and will revive soon. Well, revive is not quite the right way to describe it. I showed him Carla waking up and…flying."

"Whatever you have to do to get through that thick skull of his. We'll do whatever it takes to get him on board. Should we wait until Carla wakes up to have Attis step in?"

"I think that is best. He barely restrained himself from attacking you once you picked Carla up. I think only my presence kept him at bay."

"Sounds good. Let's wait. I know you're fast. I'm fast, and I've got a thick skin, but I wouldn't want to put it to the test against him and his wicked sharp claws and beak."

It took fifteen minutes for Carla to wake up. She groaned and hissed in pain as her eyelids fluttered open.

"Wh-what happened?"

"You blacked out from the pain. I warned you this would happen. You should've told me to stop it a few moments sooner, and you'd have been fine. Hurting, but fine."

"I tried to hold out...a long time."

"And you did great, but next time please be more careful. I can't see into your body to know if you were doing more harm than good. Also, if we needed to leave right away, or were attacked, you being unconscious could jeopardize your safety."

"Sorry," Carla said, lowering her head.

"It's okay. Everything worked out. Just remember for next time and make sure others you tell about your experience here know the consequences."

"I'll be more careful next time."

"That's all I can ask. Now, let's get Attis leveled up! First, you need to calm him and let him know you're all right. He almost bit my head off when I picked you up."

Carla looked at him in alarm, and he tried to maintain a straight face, but a crooked smile twisted his lips.

"Don't tease like that," Carla complained, playfully punching his arm.

"I was never in any real danger with Scarlet around, but he was ready to attack me if he thought I did anything to harm you."

It was Carla's turn to smile as she patted her companion on the side. Giving them space, Jared wondered if he should absorb any nanites while they were here, but realized he still had plenty to learn about his most recent ability before enhancing himself more. He needed to bring Elle and Kitty over soon to help them out, but he and Scarlet were strong enough for the time being. As soon as the other water folk bonded with Scarlet's brothers, they'd be back to get everyone else leveled up.

"He's ready." Carla motioned Attis toward the water.

He stopped just short and sniffed the surface. Tentatively, he put one claw into the lake, slowly followed by the other. Attis looked back at Carla and cocked his head.

"Good boy. Stay." Carla held up her hand to show the griffon what to do.

"Let's stand back, Carla." Jared waved his hand behind him. "If he gets startled, we don't want to get in the way. Scarlet will take care of him and make sure he doesn't absorb too many."

They walked back a few yards, and Scarlet took their place. It was difficult to see the water with their large bodies blocking the view, so Jared suggested they walk onto the dock to watch. Once there, they observed the familiar glow congregating around Attis before the stream thickened and rushed into his body.

Jared saw a shiver pass through Carla's body as she watched Attis. Jared knew her body screamed in protest with every movement. It'd taken him hours to fully recover and a couple times only sleep had quelled the burning sensation. Leaning back against one of the small outbuildings on the dock, Jared enjoyed the day. It was peaceful and the constant flow of nanites calming.

It took almost fifteen minutes before Attis showed signs of a struggle, and another two before Scarlet wrapped her tail around his body and yanked him back. Attis lay there panting, his wings feebly trying to push himself up.

Carla moved to go after him, but Jared held her back. "Give him a moment to recover. Scarlet recovers much faster than me, and Attis might be the same."

Carla was antsy and wanted to rush over to him, but she listened to Jared until he could hold her back no longer. Once she affirmed

Attis was okay, she returned to Jared's perch and thanked him for making the journey with them.

"You're wel—" A high-pitched whine cut off his words, and Jared's face turned white as a sheet.

"Scarlet!"

"I hear it too. Jared, there is nowhere to hide!"

"I know, I know." Jared searched frantically, looking for a way to avoid this confrontation. It was much too early to reveal everything they had up their sleeves.

"Scarlet, in the water! Can you hold your breath for a few minutes?"

"For a time, yes. But the nanites?"

"As soon as you feel it becoming too much, surface and take to the skies. If they are still here, we'll deal with it then."

Needing no further encouragement, Scarlet dove into the water.

"Send Attis into the sky and have him stay away from the ship. Quick, get inside this shack. We'll wait them out."

Jared and Carla ducked into the cramped building while Attis vaulted into the sky. A few seconds later, the whine of the drop ship's' engines passed overhead. Rather than continue on, it halted in place a short distance away. Holes in the small building allowed Jared to peer outside and see the ship hovering some three hundred yards away.

It slowly lowered itself to the ground out of sight behind the buildings.

"Scarlet, go now! Stay low to the water and fly away from here."

The waterline wasn't visible from his hiding place, but he heard a splash as Scarlet burst from the water and flew away. Her wings slapped the water in rhythmic patterns as she stayed as close to the surface as possible.

It didn't appear as though the ship could see her from their location, but Jared kept a watchful eye in the direction it landed just in case. Several minutes passed before he released a long sigh of relief. They were in the clear.

"Carla, can you speak with Attis from here?" Jared whispered in case there was some way the ship, and those aboard, heard him.

"I've tried, but I think he's too far away or he isn't responding."

"Okay, let me ask Scarlet to search for him and keep an eye out. If he's close to the ship, Scarlet won't be able to do anything, though. The risk is too great for her to be near that thing."

"Scarlet, can you see Attis?"

"Yes, he is with me. We are flying back home to lie low until the ship leaves."

"Thanks! If there's any way you can hide before you get there, do it. I'd rather have you near if things go south."

"I will look."

"Attis is with Scarlet. They'll find a safe place to lie low. I asked Scarlet to stay as close as possible just in case."

Carla exhaled a shaky breath, relieved Attis was in good hands.

"Don't worry, Carla, we'll be safe. No matter what happens, we can take care of this lone ship, even if it means destroying it."

They waited in tense silence for a long time. The minutes ticked by agonizingly slow and still the ship stayed grounded.

"Scarlet, I don't know what this thing is doing, but staying this long in town is not comforting."

"Should I come back?"

"Not yet, but get ready. I don't know what they're doing for this long."

Another thirty minutes rolled by, and Jared almost left the building to investigate. Before he made that decision, they heard a faint creaking, followed by a low droning sound that grew louder and paused. Jared withdrew from the peephole he was using and silently prayed there was nothing that could sense them through the walls.

A faint whirring and beep were the only warnings Jared received before a high-pitched alarm blared through the wooden barrier they stood behind. With no choice, Jared threw open the door to find a small spherical device with blinking red lights sitting on the dock in front of him.

The sphere had a lens on the front and a shimmer of red light washed over Jared and Carla as it scanned them. The shrill noise emanated from the tiny device. His path decided for him, Jared whipped out his phase pistol and burned a hole through the tiny device.

"We've got to move!"

"Scarlet, they have found us! Don't come yet, we'll see if we can find—"

Jared paused in mid-stride as he watched half a dozen of the balls roll out from the closest street. He also heard the faint metallic clang of something else approaching from just beyond his sight.

"Never mind, come now!"

"On my way! I need five minutes to get there."

Five minutes. Jared wracked his brain for a way to avoid a confrontation, but nothing surfaced. *I need to hold out for five minutes.*

"Carla, stay close and follow me."

Jared sprinted up the dock, carefully aligning his shots as he picked off the small spherical machines. One by one, they fizzled out as his phase rounds burned clean through them. Right before they rounded a corner, Jared glimpsed a metal leg entering the street in the same direction the scanner probes came from.

The color drained from his face as he recalled what had happened to the explorers who'd reached the floating city. If these machines were anything like those and had phase rifles, he and Carla were in serious trouble.

"Hurry, Scarlet! Those robots we saw kill the other explorers are here and coming for us."

"I am coming. Hold on!"

They silently sprinted down a side street. After running several blocks, Jared darted into an open home and shut the door.

"Carla, I don't think this will work. When Scarlet and I went back to New York to find her family, we saw some of these scanners. Somehow, they followed the path we took months after we'd traveled it. I think they're going to find us."

Jared peered out one window, looking for any signs it had followed them. Jared grabbed his second phase pistol and handed it over to Carla.

"Take this." He shoved the pistol at her.

She backed up a step and held her hands in front of her. "I don't shoot weapons. I-I was one of those who didn't want to."

"Carla, I understand where you're coming from. I know several people from my colony who felt the same way, but if we don't take out these machines, they will take us out. Us or them. Those are the options. I can't guarantee I'll be able to take them out solo. It depends on how many there are. They all carry phase rifles and the only way we make it out of this is if we work together. You, me, Scarlet, and Attis. Scarlet is several minutes away still, so we are on our own."

No sooner had he finished speaking when the robots rounded a house up the street.

"Here they come."

Carla accepted the pistol from Jared, and he gave her a quick demo on its use and the handgrip safety mechanism. Satisfied she knew how to fire it, he extracted his Colt and checked to make sure all the chambers held a round. Rotating the cylinder back into the revolver, he cocked the hammer and waited for the robots to draw closer. There were five of the robots, and a dozen of the spherical probes roving down the street.

"If they pass us by, we're going to sit here and do nothing, but if they find us, we take out the walking machines first and then the rolling balls. As far as I can tell, the balls are harmless."

"O-okay."

Jared gripped her shoulder firmly. "We will make it out of this. I promise."

He truly meant that promise. He'd do anything he could to make it happen. The steady metallic thudding of the robot's footfalls kept a steady beat in tune with his pulse. They were almost directly outside the building now and the spheres continued whirring through the street making beeping noises and flashing their scanners. The robots reached the house they hid inside, and it seemed like they would pass on when suddenly they paused and swiveled to face it.

"Come. Out."

The metallic tone brooked no argument. They expected immediate obedience, but Jared did nothing to alert them they were inside. So far, the robots hadn't raised their weapons, but they faced the building, waiting for his response. Jared looked to Carla to see the fear he felt mirrored in her eyes. Pursing his lips, Jared said nothing, nor did he move.

The robot amplified its voice and issued the mechanical-sounding command again. "Come. Out. Immediately."

Jared cringed; the sound was ear-piercingly loud. From his vantage, he could see the street in front, but he doubted the robots could see him unless they also had scanning abilities like the small spheres rolling around. That thought gave Jared pause.

They are robots, so it's possible.

When neither Jared nor Carla made a move to leave the building, the robot on the far right raised its metal fingers, and they all raised their rifles, pointed directly at him.

Yep, they can see me.

"Carla, get ready to move. It looks like they're focused on me right now. See if you can find a back exit and leave the building. I can outmaneuver these things, but I doubt you're fast enough."

Without a word, Carla crawled into an adjacent room to look for a back exit. One robot left the formation in front of him to circle behind the door.

"Carla, you're about to have company! Keep that pistol ready."

"Firing. In. Five. Four. Three—"

Jared froze as he realized they were about to open fire on him. His hesitation almost doomed him, but he got his body in motion and launched himself out the window directly at the line of machines. He tackled the middle robot, pressing the phase pistol to its head and ending its life, just like he'd done to the one he'd encountered inside one of their drop ships weeks earlier.

The lights in its body winked out of existence, and he rolled off the lifeless hunk of metal. He activated *Maximum Muscle* and vaulted on top of the adjacent building. They focused on him completely, leaving the building and Carla behind. The three remaining robots swiveled in place and chased after him. Unprepared for their next move, Jared's jaw dropped as all three of the robots crouched and jumped to follow him, the pistons on their legs easily providing enough force to propel them to the top of the building.

He dropped to the other side, sprinted down two houses and spun. As soon as the head of a robot crested the lip of the roof, Jared squeezed off two shots and watched in satisfaction as the head exploded in a shower of sparks.

"Yes!" Fist pumping, Jared prepared to fire at the remaining two robots, but they didn't appear over the edge.

Where are you?

A loud crash to his left answered his unspoken question. Diving forward, an energy blast sizzled past. The heat from the round seared the back of his neck, making him realize just how close it had come to killing him. They were smart and able to strategize. He needed to take the offensive before they managed to corner him. Jared advanced in the direction the shot had come from. He launched himself from behind the building at a sideways lunge, immensely grateful for his foresight as a round sizzled in the air right where his head would have been.

What is it with these things and headshots?

Taking advantage of the machine's missed opportunity, Jared sent a volley of rounds into its body, ripping the chest and neck apart. The metal body crumpled to the floor. Not wasting time, Jared turned in the opposite direction and ran. He wanted to put distance between himself and the last machine. Once in a defensible position, he'd turn to confront it.

He briefly thought about running back toward Carla's location, but he didn't want to lead another of the robots in her direction in case she ended up in the crossfire.

"Scarlet, I destroyed three robots already. There's one chasing me, and another one went after Carla. Please find and help Carla first. I can handle this last one."

"We are almost there."

Jared finished his mad dash across the street, leaping into the broken window of a two-story building. As soon as he cleared the windowsill, he reached behind him to grab the threshold and halted his movement. Taking up position to the left of the window, he sighted down the street, waiting for the machine to show itself. Several minutes ticked by. Nothing happened.

Jared worried it had gone after Carla, but a moment later, he realized what had happened. The high-pitched whine of the drop ship picked up tempo, and he watched the ship hover off the ground.

"Take out that ship! It probably sent a warning to the cities already, but we can't let it get back with any of the recordings and scans it took."

"Got it."

The next thing he heard was a great rending noise. Looking in the ship's direction, Jared watched Scarlet drop straight down on top of the ship, forcing it back to the ground. The pitch of the engines escalated as the pilot attempted to force it off the ground. The shriek of Scarlet's claws on the ship's hull grated against his nerves. Deep furrows appeared on the wings and body as she tried to gain purchase on the bucking ship. Jared watched all this happen as he jumped from the building and raced down the street toward them.

She used her wickedly sharp claws to sever the thrusters from the rear of the ship. The engines ripped free of their mounts and spun erratically through the air as the last of the power propelled them forward. One of the engines detonated high overhead, and another smashed into a house, obliterating it entirely.

Scarlet didn't even notice or flinch as the waves of fire and concussive force from the engine explosions rolled over her body. The heat was nothing compared to the extreme temperatures she'd experienced in the depths of the earth.

The ship banked hard to the right, no longer able to sustain flight after Scarlet had eliminated the engines on one side. Still, the whine of the remaining engines increased in volume as the pilot pushed them to the max, trying desperately to get away from whatever held the ship fast. It was no use, Scarlet was too strong, and missing half their thrusters, they couldn't stay airborne any longer. Another swipe of her claws and Scarlet removed the thrusters on the other side. Abruptly, the ship dropped like a rock.

The landing struts crumpled under the weight of the ship and

Scarlet. They weren't made to withstand a forced landing like that, and Jared only hoped it hadn't crushed the cargo hold too badly. He wanted to get into the ship and retrieve any valuables before they left.

"I'm almost there. Please make sure the robots don't leave the ship. Oh, and take out the phase cannon up front so it doesn't shoot me when I get in range."

"Done. I hear movement, but the ship is useless, and they are trapped within."

"Okay, thanks. I want to try and salvage some stuff. Hopefully, it's not destroyed too badly."

When Jared reached the scene of the ship's demise, he chuckled at Scarlet's handiwork. She wasn't kidding. The ship was a complete wreck. Not just from her wanton destruction, but the explosions from the engines had really done a number on it. The robot that had run from him, and the pilot of the ship were likely already slags of metal, and Scarlet had simply heard their death throes. With the immediate threat over, Jared turned around and ran through the streets looking for Carla.

He found her a short distance away from the house they'd originally hid in. She leaned against a building, the fifth robot slumped against the concrete steps a few paces away. Carla cradled her arm in one hand while she brandished the phase pistol awkwardly between them.

"Carla!" Jared dropped to his knees to check her injury. She had a wicked burn across her left arm exposing the muscle and tendons beneath. Tears streamed down her face, and every slight movement pulled the skin around the wound taught, inciting a hiss from Carla.

"Hold your arm steady. I'll wrap it up. Are you injured anywhere else? What happened here?"

"I got him."

She cried, sobs wracking her body which only caused more pain and tears.

"It's okay, Carla. We're here, and the robots are gone."

Jared followed her gaze to the downed robot. The entire side of the building bore evidence of her fight. Pockmarks and burns from phase rounds peppered the side of the house. Only a single hole went clean through the robot's head. Jared wondered how many shots it had taken to do that, unless she'd kept pulling the trigger after it was already dead. The important thing was she'd lived to tell the tale. If this fight showed him anything, it was that everyone in the colony needed to learn to handle and shoot weapons whether they wanted to or not.

As gently as he could, he pried the phase pistol from her grip, stuffed it into his pack, and pulled out a bandage to wrap her arm.

"This is going to hurt, but we've got to move as soon as possible. I'm sure these ships have a way to send warnings back to their city, which they probably did the moment the ship took off. We destroyed five of their robots, dozens of their scanners, and a drop ship. I'm positive there will be more incoming. Where's Attis?"

A loud squawk drew his attention above to where Attis was perched on the roof directly above Carla. He was too big to fit into the narrow street that ran behind the house.

"Can you walk?"

She answered by staggering to her feet and into the street. Attis alighted next to her, and Jared helped her clamber onto Attis' back. She gripped his fur with her free hand, and Jared asked Attis to be as careful as possible. Whether the griffon understood him or not, he didn't know. He instructed Attis to take Carla back to their home by sending pictures to him.

"Carla, Attis will take you home. Please don't alarm everyone about this. You can tell Vanessa and Elle what happened, but please let them know we're safe. Scarlet and I will be along shortly, and we'll brief everyone when we get there."

Carla agreed, and they launched into the air. Jared turned back to the dead robot and unceremoniously picked it and the phase rifle from the ground. He jogged back to the downed drop ship and deposited the lifeless hunk of metal. Jared spent a few minutes collecting the rest of the robots and their weapons. He put them in two piles, intending to have Scarlet pick them up. He found some duffle bags in a nearby house and stuffed as much of the weapons and robot parts in them as possible.

While he made the piles, he'd heard the metallic clanking from the ship, confirming Scarlet's words that one of the machines had survived.

"Scarlet, can you open up a hole for me to get inside?"

She walked over to the cargo doors and quickly sliced the hinges holding it in place. The door held fast, but a sharp kick from Scarlet dislodged it. Jared jumped back as the door toppled forward and thumped into the ground. He ducked inside the hold and found the source of the noise. One of the robots weakly tried to pick up a rifle lying a few paces away, but the bottom half of the robot had fused to a melted section of the wall where one of the engine explosions had torn through the ship. Jared didn't hesitate, and put a round into its head, ending the struggle.

Quickly, Jared ripped open all of the compartments left intact. Just like the previous drop ship he'd been inside, there were several weapons, battery packs, and medical supplies. None of the uniforms survived, but he still had a couple he'd taken last time. His job completed, he left the hold to discuss next steps with Scarlet.

"All right, here's what I think we should do. We'll take these two piles of bodies and the duffle with the spheres and deposit them many miles from here in some secluded place. Then, you and I will take our loot back home and wait this out. The cities will probably send a response force, and we don't want to be anywhere near when that happens."

"Why are we putting these bodies somewhere else? Would it not be better to take them to have Pete study them?"

"Yes, that's exactly what I want to do, but we need to make sure there's no way the cities can trace them back to us. If they have a way to track them, I'd rather they lead away from our new home. We'll head in the opposite direction, and then we'll circle around, well out of range for their ships."

"There is much about your technology I have yet to learn."

"You and me both. If they don't find the bodies, Pete will have his hands full for quite some time as he figures out how they work. Maybe he can even reprogram them to work for us."

"That would help us significantly."

"Exactly. That's best-case scenario. Even if he can't reprogram them, maybe he can salvage parts from them and figure out how some of this more advanced tech works. I'd love to take parts of this ship, but we've no idea what everything does or what would be valuable. For now, let's follow this plan and see where it leads."

Jared vaulted onto Scarlet's back, holding his bags of loot. She picked up the piles of bodies and jumped into the air.

06 EVERYONE MUST FIGHT

S carlet flew to the opposite end of the lake from their home, and they found an empty building to stash all the parts. It only took a moment, and they were back in the air. They headed west for at least half an hour before she banked and turned south. The drop ships always came from the east, so it made sense to fly around.

"Make sure you stay low as well, Scarlet. I don't know what kind of technology they have for long-distance scanning, but I remember radar and sonar from my studies growing up. It could see large objects in the air above a certain altitude. They probably have something more advanced these days, but we can at least do everything we know to evade detection."

Scarlet dropped as low as she dared, her wing tips evading the treetops. It took almost two hours to get back home. They'd probably gone much farther out of the way than needed, but Jared didn't want to risk any possibility the ships would find them. Everything rode on their ability to maintain secrecy and build up their fighting force. They were in no position to start their campaign against the cities.

Carla had barely taken out one robot, and Jared suspected many of the water folk would fare similarly. He needed to make sure that everyone was ready for the eventual encounter, including those who didn't want to wield a weapon.

"We need to impress upon everyone how important it is they learn to shoot a weapon. I just don't know what else we can do to convince them if they aren't already. You showed them what happened to those people who stowed away on the drop ship, and those on the ground the ship massacred. What will it take for everyone to realize they need to protect themselves?"

"What happened?"

"Huh? Oh—" Jared snapped out of his introspection and realized Scarlet hadn't seen Carla and the scene with the robot and he quickly filled her in.

"Perhaps it is time to train everyone with these new phase weapons?"

"I think so. We have enough of them; it makes sense to use them for training and hunting. They are much quieter and more effective than traditional guns. I just hope it's enough to get everyone involved. I understand some people don't like weapons or are scared of them, but maybe after they see Carla's injury, they'll change their mind. Besides, it's much less scary to fire a phase weapon with no retort and recoil than traditional weapons."

Jared glanced at his Colt. No matter how many of the new phase weapons he gathered, it would always have a place on his side. It was the one weapon he could always rely on in a pinch, and he'd never had a malfunction with it.

Jared mentally inventoried all the weapons he'd collected so far and realized they had over a dozen phase weapons, including the more powerful rifles. He'd save one for himself, but the rest they'd dole out to those who had more experience with weapons. They also had quite a few batteries after the haul from the previous drop ship and this one. It was enough ammunition to last them a long time if they only used it for small practices and hunting.

Once more of the water folk bonded with creatures or dragons, they wouldn't need to use weapons as much. With Scarlet's brothers, they'd become a dominating force. He didn't know how they'd compare to the cities and the forces they could deploy, but at least they wouldn't need to worry about other creatures. The biggest issue they faced would be the dragons getting all the kills and nanites.

As little as her brothers had in the way of nanites, they didn't need them nearly as bad as the water folk. They needed to alter their minds if they ever hoped to operate on a level in harmony with the dragons. Jared was only now realizing how much he had yet to go, and he already had significant upgrades.

As soon as the cities cleared out of the old colony, Jared wanted to take a group of people out to find companions, those who hadn't yet bonded with a dragon.

He didn't know how far afield they would need to go, but it could take them a while. That was fine since having the other dragons around meant he didn't need to fret every second over everyone's safety while he was gone.

They were his people now, and their safety was paramount to him. As little time as he'd spent with them, not once in the past weeks had he felt like, or considered himself, an outsider. Maybe he wasn't a water folk, but he was a protector, and every person under his and Vanessa's charge were family. Well, most of them, anyway.

He still had issues with George, but thankfully Damien had come around and was a useful addition to their budding settlement. Though the recent developments suggested George was at it again, sinking his claws of malice into anyone who deigned to listen. Jared didn't know what it would take to bring George around, if there was even a possibility of doing so. A small part of him wanted to banish the man, but he knew that would get backlash from many others, possibly Vanessa as well. On the other hand, George knew too much, and Jared didn't like the idea of sending him off with that knowledge.

Jared shook off the negative thoughts as their home came into view. Scarlet circled once and landed in the clearing next to Attis and Carla. It looked like Vanessa and Elle were sitting nearby as well. The moment they landed, Vanessa and Elle ran over to greet him.

"What happen—"

"Are you okay?" Vanessa's question cut off Elle as she ran up to him.

Jared smiled grimly, hoping to put them at ease, but it only made Vanessa's frown deepen. "I'm okay. I'll explain in a moment. Where is everyone else? I'd like to make sure everyone is inside. We can meet up in the dining room, but no one should wander off right now. Scarlet? Will you be okay here?"

"Yes, the trees and surrounding cliffs provide enough coverage."

"Let's round everyone up and head to the dining hall."

Thirty minutes later, everyone had assembled in the dining room, and Jared addressed the crowd.

"As most of you know, I took Carla back to the old colony and the lake to absorb nanites for her and Attis. That mission went well, but before we could fly away a drop ship appeared from the cities. Dozens of probes and a few robots disembarked and searched the city."

"How many?" The icy voice startled Jared. He didn't have to search the crowd to find out who spoke. He only needed to look toward the door to find George in his usual spot leaning against the door frame.

Jared was about to respond, but Vanessa laid a hand on his and gave an almost imperceptible shake of her head. He bit his tongue and continued the recounting.

"We encountered five outside the ship."

Though it answered George's question, Jared said as much for the benefit of everyone else. Out of the corner of his eye, he saw George's eyes widen at the number. Jared swore he saw the corner of his mouth tick up, but when he flicked his eyes over, George wore his usual scowl. Jared closed his eyes for a brief moment to compose himself and keep from lashing out at the man. He wasn't violent, but something about the man set him on edge.

"They found our hiding place, forcing me to react. I took out three. Carla brought down another one, and the other fled back to the ship to take off, but Scarlet intervened and brought the ship down."

Eyes widened when he'd said Carla destroyed one, since most knew she hated weapons. Jared didn't know why she was so averse to them, and it hadn't come up in their short adventure earlier. The fact that she'd bonded should have been enough to drive her to change her mind so she could protect her companion. Perhaps Jared could use that as leverage later if she ever balked at using a weapon again. The surprise on everyone's face increased when he said Scarlet had brought down the ship.

"You took down a ship? What will the cities do now?" Vanessa sounded scared and angry.

Jared turned his head to glance at her and caught sight of George smirking at her response. That was enough to set Jared off.

"What is your problem, George?" Jared jerked to his feet and started toward him.

Vanessa stepped in front of him and shot him a look of annoyance.

Vanessa's intervention did nothing to cool his anger, but he didn't move any farther toward the smirking idiot. "Do you not understand that Carla almost died out there? If we hadn't taken the ship down, they'd know about Attis and Scarlet. You realize that they'd probably experiment on you, or kill you outright if they knew about you, right?"

George didn't answer him, but rather stormed out of the room, completely blowing off his questions.

Jared clenched his fists and closed his eyes. He spent several long moments composing himself before he turned to look at Vanessa. The look she gave him promised a discussion later, and he wasn't particularly looking forward to it.

"D-d-did you b-bring any of the-the parts b-back?" Pete looked ready to race back to the scene and confiscate the parts himself.

"Yes and no." Jared smirked when he saw Pete's face light up and then cloud over. "I've got these—"

Jared dumped the duffle onto the table. Six phase rifles, three pistols, and a dozen battery packs fell out. A collective gasp filled the room.

Johan rushed over to Jared's side and picked up one of the rifles.

"This is amazing." Johan held the rifle reverently, inspecting it from every angle.

"Careful, everyone. Yes, I agree this is quite the haul, and no, Pete, it doesn't answer your unasked question. Scarlet and I took all the destroyed robots and the sensor probes, but we didn't bring them here. Instead, we flew north and left them near the opposite end of the lake. I don't know if there's a way for the cities to track them and didn't want to risk bringing them back. Does that answer your question?"

"Y-y-yes! When can we g-go s-s-study them?"

Jared held up a hand to slow things down. "I'm not sure how the city will respond to our actions. They could swarm over the place and we might not get back there for a while. In a few days, we'll go scout the colony from a distance to see what's happening. If there's no activity, then we'll go check on the parts to see if they're still there. My guess is that they'd want to confiscate and bring them back to the city, so we don't get our hands on them and learn how they work."

Pete nodded his head vigorously and ducked back to his seat.

"Now, for these weapons. Here's what I'd like to do, and I know some of you won't like it. Johan, I'm remanding these over to your custody, but I want every single person to learn how to fire them."

A cacophony of voices rose in protest, but Jared silenced them all before he continued. "Carla?"

"Yes?"

"After the events of today, do you still wish you'd stayed away from weapons? Or do you wish you'd learned how to use them?"

She glanced at the bandage on her arm and a determined look crossed her features. "I will learn how to shoot better."

Jared took a moment to look around the room. Several of those who had previously refused to take weapons sat with their mouths open in shock. Carla was spritely, but she wasn't violent and had been one of those more vocal against using a weapon. Seeing her reverse her position set them back on their heels.

"I know some of you don't like this idea, and I haven't talked to Vanessa about this yet, but we must prepare for the inevitable. That means everyone here needs to learn how to use these. For those who feared using traditional pistols and rifles, these will be much easier to use and learn. There's no recoil, it's not loud, and you don't have to reload anything except a battery pack."

Jared watched the naysayers consider his words and slowly nod their heads, accepting his ultimatum.

"Each of these battery packs can shoot around three hundred rounds. Well, at least that's how many I fired with the phase pistols before it ran out. That means with the batteries up in my room, and these, we have enough for over five thousand rounds. That's not a ton of ammunition, but it should be enough to get everyone here familiar with their use. We've also got the weapons I raided on the last ship. Everything considered, we're doing pretty well. These weapons on the table here are worth more than a dozen colonies combined. I think we'll run into more ships and robots before we can get everyone bonded. These might save your life."

After his speech, no one was on the fence, and without George in the room, there was no one to inject criticism and doubt into his plan. The small group that Carla had formed initially to take a stand against using weapons now rallied around her and voiced their agreement to learn.

Carla explained to a few around her and met Jared's eyes briefly. "We'll do what we must."

Jared nodded once and gathered the weapons together before bagging them and handing them over to Johan for safe-keeping. He turned and left to put them in the armory right away.

"Hold up, Johan. Just a couple more things. I'd like everyone to remain inside for the next few days. It's okay if you need to move from room to room, but please don't hang out on the platforms or the riverbed. I'm almost certain there will be more drop ships coming, if they haven't already, and we don't want to give them a reason to visit us. Scarlet and I will go investigate in a couple days."

Receiving nods from everyone present, Jared called a close to the impromptu meeting and everyone filed out of the dining hall to their own rooms. Pete, Vanessa, Elle, and Carla remained behind.

"What's up, Pete?"

"The p-parts, probes, and ship? You have p-parts for them all? They d-didn't g-get destroyed too b-b-bad?"

"I didn't get any ship parts since I didn't know what would be worth salvaging and we didn't want to stick around longer than we had to. If there's any of it left when we visit, then I'll see about bringing it back. The rest of the parts are all yours if the cities don't find them. We need to figure out how they work and how they're programmed. If we can somehow control them, we'll have a major advantage when we attack a city."

Pete bowed his head and left the room without another word. Everyone else moved next door to Jared's home.

"Jared, do you mind if I move in here?" Carla gestured at the empty bedroom next to Vanessa's. "I want to be close to Attis, and he doesn't fit on the lower ledges well, plus there are more people down there, and he's wary of them."

"As long as Vanessa has no objections." Jared looked at her.

Vanessa shook her head. "None here. She already asked me."

"Then absolutely! Sorry, I should've suggested it myself. In fact, I'll go grab your things from your other room in a bit. While we're all here, we should talk about assigning your nanites. I know we talked about pushing all into *Mind* but add some to *Body* this time around to make sure you can recover from injuries like this faster. Any nanites assigned to *Body Manipulation* will help you to heal faster. You can also use them with *Remodeling* to revert your appearance back to how it was before…" Jared's voice trailed off. He hated bringing up their experience with Razael.

"Thank you for all the help. I'll put half into *Mind* again and the rest into *Body Manipulation* to help me heal."

"Wait, you have the category for it already?"

"I do! I did what you told me and studied them. I can see their purpose, even if I don't understand them all. The categories are already there, they just didn't show up on my status screen, but once I thought about it, they were there. I don't know if I understand them at the level needed for *Regeneration,* though. I'll talk with Scarlet soon and see if she can help me."

"Good! I'm hoping everyone has a similar experience and their first enhancements unlock more pathways for them. Once you understand *Regeneration*, you can use *Remodeling* to change your body. Obviously, you've been working on understanding the nanites, but definitely spend the next couple days in confinement to study more?"

"I will."

"There isn't a lot I or Scarlet can do to help you, aside from providing guidance. This is a journey of self-discovery you must make on your own."

Jared suggested Elle and Kitty do the same thing. They had two whole days to work together and they could learn a lot in that time. He didn't know if Kitty really understood, but Elle understood the concepts well enough to start working with Kitty on it.

"I feel them!" Elle squealed and ran off to her room, Kitty on her heels.

Shaking his head, Jared went and grabbed Carla's extra clothes from her old room, depositing them in her new one.

With nothing more to do, Jared went to his own room and stripped off all his gear. He needed to downsize soon. All the extra stuff he carried with him was getting cumbersome. If he couldn't move quickly enough, or if something impeded his movement, it could mean his death.

There wasn't much he wanted to part with, but he forced himself to leave all the extra weapons and only take the two phase pistols, his Colt, and the phase rifle with one spare battery each. He also carried only one box of ammo for his Colt. Medical supplies weren't super crucial anymore, given his many enhancements, so he only kept a few bandages. After he'd cleaned everything out, he placed the extra items onto a shelf and sat down on his bed.

Taking a page out of his own book, Jared started his meditation process. The moment he closed his eyes, he heard Vanessa enter the room and clear her throat.

Sighing, Jared opened his eyes. He knew why she was here, and he really didn't want to have this conversation.

"Do we need to do this right now?"

Vanessa planted herself firmly in front of the door, hands on her hips. "We do."

"Vanessa, look—"

"No, you listen first."

She didn't say it in a rude way, but it made his mouth snap shut all the same.

It was her turn to sigh before she continued. "I understand your frustration with George, Jared. I do. But I also have to put on a strong front for everyone else. If I didn't stand up for one of my people in there, how would that look to everyone else? I told you I was going to handle him, and you promised you'd try to work with him."

"What else do you want me to do? You see how he treats me. I'm supposed to just set our differences aside and let him undermine all my decisions?" Jared involuntarily clenched and unclenched his fist when talking about George.

"To be fair, you put me in charge of the people here," countered Vanessa.

"Yes, but these choices are about protecting everyone and fighting a battle *everyone else* agreed to." Jared emphasized the fact that George was the only one who hadn't vowed with the rest.

"Part of being a leader means you need to work with even those who don't like you. Do you think everyone always agreed with my parents, or me?"

"But that was different, you—"

Vanessa rounded on him. "How was it different? Because we were under the water and couldn't go anywhere?"

Jared shrugged. "Well. Yeah."

"We still had disagreements, and not everyone agreed with the way I handled everything. George didn't give me any grief, but there were others who…well, let's just say they didn't survive. I did what I had to do to keep Razael happy and my people safe. That meant working with the literal devil himself to ensure we made it."

"All right, all right. I get it. It's just hard. I grew up with a bully much like him, and now that I can defend myself, I hate taking a beating, verbal or otherwise, for no reason."

"I know it's difficult to stomach, but that's part of being a leader. Unless George does something to hurt someone or put anyone in danger, I have to stand between the two of you in public. George has spent a few weeks trying to get others to see things the way he does. I don't think he'll succeed, but if I show complete trust to you at the expense of him…" Vanessa lifted a shoulder in sympathy, a sly smile painted on her face.

"It will further erode trust in you and give him a platform to stand on. I get it, but that doesn't mean I have to like it." Jared sighed. Being a leader wasn't easy and he had a long way to go before he'd call himself one.

"Nor should you. I've dealt with him for a decade and know how obstinate he can be. If we work together and you don't let him rile you up, we can present a unified front to everyone, and it will cut his legs out from under him, giving him no ammunition to make people doubt us."

"You're much better at this sort of thing than me."

"Jared, I've been doing it for years. Up until a couple months ago, you had only yourself and previous to that your parents. Becoming a leader requires you to change the way you think about people. You have to get to know and understand them."

"Thanks, Vanessa. I thought this talk was going to be much worse, but I needed to hear it. Even as a part of me rails against ignoring George, I get your positioning."

"You're welcome. I'll let you get back to what you were doing. I'm going to go check on Elle." She stopped halfway out the door. "And Jared?"

"Yes?"

"If there's ever something like this you need to talk through, you can come to me about it. I know you usually talk with Scarlet, but I'm here to listen if you want."

Jared gave her a warm smile and promised he would let her know. Feeling much better and relieved the conversation hadn't spiraled out of control, Jared had no trouble entering a meditative state.

He activated *Clear Mind*, and his awareness blossomed into infinite possibilities. It was such a different way of looking at the world and understanding his surroundings; it continually amazed him. A random thought floated by, about the fight hours earlier and his failure to use *Clear Mind* during the scuffle. He needed to make this second nature so that it was his default action whenever a difficult situation presented itself.

Though the ability hadn't activated, the events of the day had turned out well enough. He'd had the foresight to take weapons and battery packs while depositing all the robot parts far away from them. If they managed to learn the secrets of the robot technology, then perhaps they didn't need to defeat them at all. Jared's people could just take control.

Wait. If we can take control of them…

The thoughts spilled forth like a gushing river, and his excitement grew. If they took over the robots, they could, in theory, take over all the drop ships, and the cities wouldn't know. They'd load onto the drop ships and make it onto a floating city without being detected.

There was much to think on, but for starters, they could get to the cities quickly, quietly, and without fear of automated defenses triggering. Their flying companions could meet them after they'd taken control of the city, or at least anything that might shoot them down. They'd want to bring some of their companions in the drop ships, but how many was the question. The only person who had a companion confined to the ground at the moment was Elle.

"Hey, Scarlet, I had an idea."

"Yes?"

"If the cities don't find the stash of robots and we can get Pete to study it, we might gain a major advantage. It may take a while, but if he can figure out how to control the robots, then we have a free ticket to the cities aboard the drop ships."

"That could work?"

"It all depends on Pete. If he can figure out how to reprogram them, it should be possible. Obviously, we don't want to fully rely on it for our plans, but it would be awesome and could save lives."

"We can check on the robots we hid after we are certain the cities have abandoned the area."

"That's what I was thinking. Maybe we can scout the area tomorrow to see what it looks like. Did you let your brothers know there could be a lot of drop ships incoming?"

"I will try to reach them, but they may be out of range. They understand the danger, and I gave them clear instructions not to engage."

"That's the problem. It might not be possible to avoid them. It really depends on what they send to find out what happened to their ship. I don't know how they alert their home base about threats either. Do they send a video? Is it verbal communication?"

Jared sighed. She could probably pick up on his emotional state, but there wasn't much he could do to mask the worry from her. There was just so much they didn't know about the cities. He wished there was a way to infiltrate one and gather more intelligence.

What defenses do they have? How big are their armies? How many ships do they have? Why haven't we seen any humans?

Questions upon questions only led to more questions. As far as it concerned him, the information about the cities was a black hole, and they had no credible intel aside from watching two poor saps turn into a pink mist. No trial, no explanation, just a swift end and turned into a cloud of blood. If they figured out the technology, then maybe he could make a solo scouting mission and figure out what they faced.

If Pete managed to figure out the tech, they could lure a bunch of ships to one location and capture them. Once captured, they'd learn to fly them, how the communications system worked, and then use them to infiltrate the cities.

While Jared knew how some of the controls on the ship worked, there's no way he'd get to a city in one piece, let alone land the thing. He would need to practice flying the ship, or Pete needed to figure out how to instruct the ship to fly back on its own, like it had with the other explorers aboard.

What if the ships are from different cities and we split our fighting force?

Exasperated, Jared cut off his ability and stood. There were so many variables; it was impossible for him to settle on one path. In time, that path might become clearer, but for now he'd continue the one he'd set weeks earlier: Get everyone bonded.

Not all the dragons wanted to bond right away, but at least many of them had said yes. Maybe the others would come around after they saw how important it was to grow stronger. None of Scarlet's brothers needed a size increase, but they could increase their defenses, perform some *Remodeling*, and upgrade their fire-breathing.

Malsour was so close to his final evolution of flames that the nanites would give him the push he needed.

Stretching, Jared walked into the common area and set all his weapons on the table. With nothing better to do, he started field stripping and cleaning them again. His Colt only needed a light wipe down since he hadn't fired it in the earlier confrontation. The phase pistols similarly only needed a light dust-off. In reality they probably didn't need any cleaning, but he found the actions surprisingly therapeutic.

Vanessa also came over to watch him strip and clean everything. After he'd finished with his Colt, she picked it up and copied his every move.

He'd made an involuntary move to snatch the weapon from her hands but he'd checked himself. If he couldn't trust Vanessa to handle the weapon, then he had no right trusting her with other people's lives and the management of their small colony.

Jared set the phase rifle in front of him and examined every inch of the weapon. It had a scope on it, but it wasn't a normal optical scope. Instead, it was a digital one, that had a glowing red reticle inside. Interestingly, it automatically turned on and off, so there must've been a sensor on it. A touch pad on the side of the scope allowed him to zoom in and out, alter the reticle, and change its color.

It was shorter than the automatic weapons he'd seen as a child, but not by much. That's where the similarity stopped. Instead of all the moving parts, chambers, magazine holder, and thumb safety, the rifle had a single sleek body. The only moving part was the battery back that slotted into the center of the rifle, directly under the scope. The handgrip sported the same rubber-like material as the pistols.

Jared really wished he knew what it was, because it never accumulated dirt and grime, and no matter if it was wet or dry, his grip was always sure. Thinking back to his battle in the tunnels, waiting for Scarlet, he wished he'd had similar grips on his knives. Losing one of his daggers inside the eye of the massive praying mantis creature could've been the end of him. If he'd had grips like the ones he now held, he'd have held on to his weapon.

Again, more questions and no answers. There was no end to them lately and nothing he could do to resolve them. Only time would reveal them. Time and getting to a city to explore the technologies the robots had created. For all Jared knew, they had the technology to fix the earth, but didn't want to give up their thrones.

Sick to his stomach at the idea, Jared retired to his room for the night. Tomorrow, he'd try to get more training in and make sure Carla and Elle were on the right track for development.

07 FIRST ENCOUNTER

Jared woke the next morning feeling refreshed. He'd slept for almost twelve hours, yet he had assigned no nanites to keep him in that slumber. It spoke to the events of the previous day and how much they'd taxed him physically and mentally. Jared found Carla already working on her meditation, and his entrance did nothing to disturb her.

Not wanting to intrude, he went to look for Vanessa and Elle. He found them in the dining room next door with a dozen other members of their small colony. It looked like they'd brought things up from their rooms to hang out all day. Jared didn't blame them. If he didn't have his meditation exercises, he'd get bored too.

"Hey, Elle." Jared beckoned her over to a quieter part of the room. "I'd like to go over some of your training while we have the time, if that's okay, Vanessa?"

"Of course, please help my sister. Can I listen in? Eventually I'll be in the same position, and it might help to hear it."

Jared agreed and in fact announced it to the room. Everyone crowded around them. Elle didn't like all the attention, but she relented when Kitty lay against her back, creating a buffer between them.

"If you want to listen, please be quiet. If you must talk, use your touch telepathy. What I've got to say is too important for distractions."

Jared explained things in the same manner he had with Carla, only he went further with Elle and dissected everything as best as he could. It was a tricky balance to maintain. While Elle had had nanites for almost a decade and had actively used them, she didn't really understand them. The lesson lasted for hours. The session was just as valuable to him as he better learned how to teach everyone about the technology. He briefly wondered if this is what it was like for Scarlet to break things down for him. It was probably even worse for her because there was a bigger gap between Jared's mind and Scarlet's than there was between his and Elle's.

It turned out Elle was a very quick study after she grasped the fundamentals, and in no time at all she dove into her body, exploring the nanites. Jared remained by her side, practicing his own meditations with *Clear Mind* and answering any questions Elle had while exploring. Before he'd unlocked his mind, there was no way he'd have been able to maintain his meditative trance and answer Elle. Now it was easy, and he had no difficulty responding to her bombardment of questions.

Her understanding was of a more instinctual nature than a real understanding from a biological and scientific standpoint, but she got the gist of it, and that was all that mattered in the end.

"Vanessa, do you know where we can get our hands on school books? I don't remember seeing any at the school house unless they're locked away somewhere. The ones I saw in the hall didn't look like textbooks."

"They should be at the school, but many parents taught their kids at home."

"I think we should try to find some for Elle. While she understands all of this to a degree, it's more of a feeling for her than anything else. To do more advanced things, like directing the nanites to enhance only certain portions of her body or heal specific areas, she'll need to understand things from an educated point of view."

"I'll teach her what I know."

"Yes, we can all teach her as much as we are able, but I'm not a teacher and, no offense, you were only a teenager when you went into the water. I think we need to have real educational material, or a teacher. I suppose no one here has experience?"

"No teachers. They all died years ago."

Mentally adding it to a running list of needs, Jared stood and stretched while Elle worked.

"Let's give her some space for now. She'll be at this for a while. If she has any more questions and I'm not here, please try to remember them, and I'll do my best to answer when I come back. I'd like to make rounds to check on everyone else. It's been half a day, and everyone being cooped up is liable to cause restlessness."

Thoughts of George ran through his mind, and Jared shook his head. Even after his conversation with Vanessa, he couldn't shake the feeling that the guy was bad news. A part of Jared he didn't like secretly wished George had been one of those who'd died in the blast that killed Razael. At least then Jared wouldn't need to contend with the man.

Everything seemed calm as he wandered, finding people arranged in casual groups, talking.

Approaching the medical area, he heard Casey before he saw him. The man sounded like he was having a conflict with himself, but Jared couldn't hear what he said. Jared paused at the threshold of the room, a bewildered expression on his face.

"Uh, Casey?"

More grumbling ensued.

"Ahem, Casey?" Jared tried again, but louder.

"Huh? Oh hey, I'll be right there."

A loud clatter—followed by cursing—announced Casey's arrival with an armload of items.

"What are you doing?" The corners of Jared's lips quirked upward as he looked at the flustered Casey.

"Organizing."

Apparently, it should've been obvious to Jared, but it looked like an explosion had detonated in the room, scattering medical supplies everywhere.

"I see."

Jared's eyes roved the piles of bandages and the random piles of junk heaped haphazardly across the floor. "Don't you usually make things neater when you organize? What exactly are you organizing, anyway?"

"Well, it will get better." Casey sounded annoyed. "I'm putting everything into more convenient places. I've been at this for a month now, and I have a good idea what everyone needs to treat common injuries so I'm making sure everything I need is easily accessible without taking out half the supplies from the closet." Casey pointed to the makeshift closet door sitting slightly ajar. It was mostly empty, with only their more valuable medical supplies sitting inside. The boosters occupied one of the highest shelves, keeping them safe and out of reach for some. He stared at the boosters for a time, marveling at how lucky he'd been to find them before the cities blew up the facility.

"Do you want me to help with anything?" Jared turned away from the liquid elixirs and raised an eyebrow.

"No. Nope, I got it. You'll just get in the way, and then I won't know where everything is. The whole point of this reorganization is to speed things up, and if I've got to search for items, then it was pointless."

"All right. Well, if you need anything, just let me know."

"Yeah, okay." Casey waved him away. "Oh, wait. I actually could use some stuff next time you go back to the colony. I wish I'd thought of it sooner, but we had a hospital there. I doubt any of the medical supplies survived the years, but the old doctor kept a shelf of textbooks in his office. At least, that's what I assumed they were." Casey scratched his head as he tried to remember. "I only saw it one time in passing. I—" Casey's cheeks flushed, and Casey looked away. "Let's just say I was in the hospital for a dumb reason, and my brother insisted he give me a tour after. He hadn't finished his medical training under the doctor yet, but he knew so much more than me. If he'd survived, we'd have all the medical expertise we could want."

"Hey, man, don't be so hard on yourself. We do the best with what we have, and you're doing a great job here. Your brother would be proud of you."

Casey looked away and cleared his throat. It seemed like a universal response from men who didn't want to be caught crying in front of anyone. Jared respectfully excused himself and promised to look for some of the textbooks next time they went into town.

Jared then made his way over to Johan's room and their armory. He entered, announcing his presence as he did. "Johan?"

Jared walked farther into the room and nearly tripped, stumbling on something. Looking down, he drew back startled. "Johan?" Jared crouched next to the man, shaking him. He lay on the floor, a half-disassembled rifle on the table beside him. He moved over to Johan's head and nudged him again. His hands came away slick with blood.

Alarm coursed through Jared and he drew back, searching the room for any obvious threats. He ran through the two rooms and down the hall to make sure nothing lurked in the shadows before darting away to grab Casey.

"Casey, drop what you're doing, Johan needs you. Head wound, not sure what the source is."

When he got back, Jared found Johan stirring and mumbling to himself.

"Johan? Johan!"

The man glanced up at him, wincing in pain as he grabbed the back of his head.

"Hey, careful now. Just lie back. Casey's on his way to treat your head. You have a nasty bump that's bleeding. What happened?"

"George." Johan spit his name out, anger evident in his tone.

That cold, hollow pit that had become all too familiar opened in Jared's stomach.

No, not now.

The timing for George to go rogue couldn't be worse. Scarlet's brothers were almost there, and the cities likely had a response force on the way after their little escapades earlier.

Jared waited a few more moments until Casey arrived and then bolted from the room.

"Jared? What's wrong?"

"George attacked Johan."

Jared heard Scarlet's growl as he sprinted up the stairs to George's room, but he wasn't there.

This is bad.

Jared's skin crawled with the realization that George might have chosen this time specifically because the cities were in the area.

Exiting George's room, he sprinted to his own, grabbed all his gear, and strapped on his pack.

"Vanessa?" Jared projected his thoughts to her instead of shouting. He didn't want to upset those around her with the information just yet.

She looked at him from across the room and left Elle's side to join him. Seeing the concern etched on his face, she mirrored the look with one of her own.

Vanessa grabbed his arm, following his example and using telepathy. *"What's wrong?"*

"It's George."

A brief flash of annoyance crossed her face, but the seriousness of his demeanor must've made her realize it was more serious than a brief spat between the two of them.

"What did he do?"

The other people in the room were staring at them, probably wondering what they were talking about. Motioning outside, Jared led Vanessa a few paces away and switched over to a whisper.

"He attacked Johan, and I don't know where he is right now."

"He what?! Did you check his room?"

"That's the first place I looked before I sprinted up here. I've got to go after him. I'll do a room by room search before I go, but I think he's headed back to the old colony. He probably thinks he'll get special treatment if he rats us out to the city."

Vanessa gasped. "You don't think he would?"

"I do. I told you before, he doesn't like me, and Scarlet could never get a read on him. I think there's more to him than we know. Do you remember when he joined the colony before everything happened with Razael?"

"No, I—"

"He might've been someone who knew about Razael. It's possible he was from the city and wanted to keep an eye on everything. There's a lot we don't know, but if I find George, I'll be having a very long discussion with him." Jared grabbed Vanessa by her shoulders and looked deep into her eyes. "I will do whatever it takes to pry the truth from George. If he doesn't come peacefully, he may not come back at all. I want you to know I'll go to the ends of the earth to protect you, the people here, and the dragons. If George is trying to expose us—"

Vanessa placed a finger on Jared's lips. The gesture sent shivers racing down his back. She leaned in and planted a timid kiss on his lips. She lingered there, allowing Jared to overcome his shock.

Hesitant at first, Jared returned the kiss, his lips parting slightly as his senses exploded in euphoria. A moment later Vanessa stepped back, and the world dimmed slightly as the sensation vanished.

Jared knew he looked like an idiot with a cheesy grin plastered on his face, but he didn't care.

"Go. Find George and bring him back. Do whatever you must."

Snapping out of his stupor, Jared's spirit plummeted. To go from such a euphoric experience straight into a desperate hunt for a malevolent person that may end in someone's death was not the way he'd imagined their first shared kiss to go. Sure, they'd shared a couple quick pecks before, but this was so much more, and he longed to ignore the man hunt and find a quiet place to be alone with Vanessa. It made him resent George all the more.

"I'll be back as soon as I can. Please keep everyone inside. If we attract the city's attention in our hunt, things could get ugly fast. Scarlet's brothers should be close if we need help. She asked them to be more cautious in case the cities retaliate."

"All right, enough talking. Go." Vanessa gently shoved him toward the stairs.

One by one, Jared searched each of the rooms for George, startling many of the water folk. He didn't have time to explain the situation to every person.

"Sorry, is George in here?" The response was always no.

Every room searched thoroughly, Jared knew George wasn't in their little settlement anymore. Thankfully, he hadn't broken into the medical room to steal any boosters, but then maybe he'd already grabbed some before they'd installed the door. Jared also didn't know how many weapons the guy had taken.

They'd faced a lot of dangerous creatures, but nothing scared him more than another human hell-bent on their destruction. It was the Daggers all over again. He knew he had to find George and bring him back before it was too late. Though he'd never trusted him, there'd been no reason to kill or exile the guy. Vanessa was right. If he'd tried to exile George, he'd have lost the trust of other people.

If George succeeded in contacting the cities, they were all doomed. If Scarlet's brothers hadn't reacquired their ability to fly, they'd be sitting ducks for the drop ships.

"Scarlet? Kitty? Elle? Meet me in the clearing now!"

It took only a few moments longer for Kitty to arrive with Elle seated on her back.

"We need to search this area for George. I think he's headed for the old colony, but we can't risk it if he's hiding nearby and leave this place defenseless. Kitty and Elle, please help us search on the ground. Scarlet, fly overhead and use your *Heat Sight*. I'll search further east and follow the river back to the ruined town and lake. I'm sure he's headed east and then north, but I want to be certain."

Kitty turned to leave, but Jared stopped her. "Please be careful and use your camouflage. He knocked Johan out and stole weapons. I don't know how many, or which kind, but we need to treat him with extreme caution. If you find him, shout out mentally for help and Scarlet and I will come."

With that, Kitty bounded toward the west to search the surrounding trees and river. Scarlet leaped into the air, and Jared took off at a sprint to the east. Following his own instructions, Jared flipped back and forth between *Heat Sight* and his regular vision to make sure he didn't miss George hiding nearby. There was no way to track George across this terrain. The ground was hard and there was no greenery to announce the other man's passage. Jared had to hope there was no place George could hide.

Jared grew worried as he reached the ruined city. He still hadn't seen George in the six and a half miles between their settlement and the tip of the lake. He seconded-guess himself on which way the man had gone, and he was too far from Kitty and Elle to find out if they'd seen him.

"Scarlet, when's the last time Elle checked in?"

"They are fine and have not found him. Should I tell them to head back home?"

"Yes, if they didn't find him yet, he is far enough away there won't be an immediate threat to everyone else. We'll keep hunting him."

"They will head back and patrol around our home in the event he doubles back."

"Thanks, you see anything up there?"

"Not yet. I will head toward the old colony."

"Please be very careful. If you see or hear anything to suggest a drop ship, get out of there as fast as possible."

"I will be careful."

Jared set out in the same direction. He could've had Scarlet pick him up, but there were many places for George to hide along the way, and they needed eyes above and below.

A feeling like an icy splash of cold washed over his body as Jared had a bad premonition. Fearful of what might happen, Jared checked in on Scarlet's family. *"How far away are your brothers?"*

"They are close, but as we warned them, they are exercising caution in their approach. They planned on finding a place close

by to make their home. While many, if not all of us, could fit near our little clearing, there is little room to do anything other than lie down."

"That's a good idea. Hopefully, it's not too far away."

"If they cannot find a natural place, then they will clear the forest, or attempt to burrow into the ground."

"I think we should do that too."

"Clear the forest?"

"Burrow into the ground. Well, it might not matter if George reaches out to the cities. If we're able to stay in our homes there, we should have a back door to escape, should anyone, or anything, ever come for us."

"It is a wise decision. Though I do not know where you would begin."

"We'd have to start somewhere you can fit. We don't have a lot in the way of digging implements. A few shovels, but it would take us much too long to create anything worthwhile. I was thinking you could use your fire to burrow into the earth like your mother."

"I can, but it will take some time. I will ask my brothers to stop searching for a place and head over to the clearing now."

Jared thought about it for a few moments before responding.

"It's liable to raise a lot of smoke and ash, and it would be a beacon for anyone nearby. If George is trying to rat us out, that's probably not a good idea."

"Excellent point."

"Maybe just have them stick around in case we need them?"

"Very well."

The entire conversation with Scarlet only lasted a moment, and he'd already run a mile toward the old colony.

"You see anything yet?"

"I think—I see something, though I do not know if it is a human yet."

"Can you get any closer?"

"I—"

Scarlet's words cut off, and a spike of alarm pulsed across their bond.

"What is it?"

"Ships. Lots of ships. I can hear at least five."

"Hide, quick!"

Jared sprinted for all he was worth toward the old colony. If it was George who Scarlet saw, he needed to get there as soon as possible to take him out. He didn't even want to question the man any longer. It was clear where he wanted to go, and his motivations plain. The man wanted to rat them out, but what he didn't realize was that they would likely kill him on sight.

"How much farther was the heat signature you saw?"

"You were nearly ten miles away."

George must've run the whole way to get so far ahead of him, if it was George anyway. Pushing himself to his limits, Jared flew across the ground. He only hoped none of the ships passed overhead. If they saw him running this fast, they'd realize he wasn't a normal person.

"Please stay close, Scarlet. If any of these ships see me, I'll need your help. Are your brothers well enough to fly yet? We might need them."

"Ashazad, Kanundran, and Malsour regained their ability to fly. The rest need more time."

Jared prayed that was sufficient if they got into a heated battle with these ships. Hopefully, it didn't come to that, but Jared's luck had been off lately, and he didn't want to rule out the possibility.

The miles passed much too slow. Even running as fast as he was without tiring, it seemed a snail's pace compared to what he was used to. When he'd travelled ten miles from their home, Jared heard the ships. Scarlet said she heard five, but from his position he only heard two. The sound rose and fell as if the ships were flying in circles.

Jared kept a wary eye on his surroundings, always cognizant of places to hide in the event a ship flew overhead. Another mile ticked by, and Jared worried. He might already be too late. If one of these ships found George, there's nothing he'd be able to do but try to take the ship out to keep their base a secret. He hoped that the cities would shoot the man down where he stood, but there's no way he'd rely on good fortune.

"Scarlet, I don't know about this. I still haven't caught up to him yet, and from the sounds, these ships are getting close."

"I can alert my brothers?"

"Not yet, but there's a good chance we'll need them."

Another two miles and finally he caught sight of someone stumbling down the road. Jared used his *Magnified Vision* to zoom in and identify George. He carried one of their phase rifles, and based on the bulges in his backpack, he'd stolen a decent amount of their gear.

You conniving little…

Jared's thoughts trailed off as anger clouded his mind. This guy was selfishness incarnate. He'd gone through the same trials as the rest of the water folk, yet he'd turned his nose up at all of them and decided his life was worth more than anyone else's. It grated against Jared's nature, and he wanted nothing more than to teach him a lesson he wouldn't forget.

Jared crouched low, prepared to activate *Maximum Muscle* and sprint the remaining distance, but he faltered when the familiar scream of a drop ship roared into the area. Jared's fears came to fruition as the drop ship zoomed into focus. Jared dropped to his belly and made himself small, hoping he'd avoid detection.

George dropped to his knees, holding his hands above his head. Jared watched the ships phase cannon pivot to point at George. It hovered in place for an agonizing amount of time before lowering itself to the ground.

"Jared? What happened?"

"There's a drop ship headed right for George. I think we have to take it out."

He searched the sky for signs of other drop ships, but it was impossible to say. They moved so fast at full speed it didn't really matter if he saw one now or not.

"Get ready. The ship is touching down."

The ramp of the ship lowered, and the ever-present spherical probes rolled out. Fully expecting more robots to come pouring from the hold, Jared's jaw dropped open when a human being flowed regally down the ramp.

"Scarlet! It's a human from the cities. They're walking down the ramp toward George. I can't tell if they're male or female from this distance, but they look…normal. They're wearing a uniform similar to the ones I stole."

George waved frantically at the person walking down the ramp and collapsed at their feet. He piled the weapons and bag in front of the mysterious person and waved back the way he'd come.

Resigned to what was about to happen Jared made up his mind. *"It's time. We've got to take them out."*

"On my way."

"Please have your brothers ready. If this person can use nanotech like us, they might be able to alert their allies the moment they see us."

Jared drew in a deep breath, feeling as though the universe was out to get him. Ever since he'd come to this area, he'd experienced setback after setback and nearly died. He'd found the water folk, which was a break in his bad luck streak, but now one of those same people threatened to upend everything he'd fought for. If more drop ships came to support this one, things would get dicey fast. Rather than delay the inevitable, Jared activated his abilities and launched himself forward. When he got within half a mile, the city-dweller looked up and zeroed in on him.

The man pushed George violently to the side. It seemed a casual gesture, but George went flying several feet away.

"This guy looks very dangerous. He batted George aside like a rag doll. He—" Jared dove out of the way as his opponent detached a long rifle from his shoulder and in one swift motion sent a ray of death streaming for him. The move was so smooth and practiced it amazed him. There was no hesitation, and his accuracy was superb. If Jared had not reacted immediately, there would be a smoking hole in his body.

"Take him out!"

"Almost there."

Almost as if the guy had heard him, his head snapped up to the sky, and Jared, his vision still magnified, watched him squint. Glancing in the same direction, Jared saw Scarlet approaching.

"How did—"

The man reattached the rifle to the back of his uniform, threw the weapons and ammunition George brought up the ramp, scooped George up, and threw him headlong into the hold. The ramp hissed shut behind them, and the ship rose off the ground.

"Hurry, Scarlet!"

He needn't have worried, because a moment later Scarlet crashed into the drop ship from above, ripping and slashing with her claws. Like the previous ship, she sliced off the engines on the back, so it had no thrust. It smashed back to the earth on the half-retracted landing struts and the ramp hissed open once more.

The human he'd seen before literally flew from the hold in a headfirst dive that carried him a dozen yards from the downed ship. He spun in the air with two massive pistols in his hands and fired on Scarlet.

The rounds sizzled into her side, leaving black scorch marks on her scales. Scarlet roared in pain and anguish as the rounds impacted. The barrage was steady and had amazing precision as the rounds hit the same location over and over.

Jared cried out in pain, every round sending a lance of fire through their bond. Scarlet said nothing, but Jared knew how much it hurt.

"Scarlet, get out of there!"

08 AERIAL BATTLE

Steely resolve settled into Jared, and he whipped out his own phase pistols. They were laughable compared to the ones this other person held. It looked like the cities had reserved the latest in technological upgrades for themselves. Yet another example of those above treating the rest of humanity with disdain.

Jared roared in fury and rocketed forward at the enemy. He brought his pistols up and squeezed the triggers. His foe somersaulted backward, and the rounds sizzled harmlessly into the dirt. It was as though the guy had eyes in the back of his head.

His adversary brought his pistols up to fire, and Jared leaped, soaring twenty feet into the air to drop down dozens of yards to the side. The guy's eyes widened in surprise, but the moment passed so fast Jared doubted he'd seen it. Midway through his leap, the man blurred into action, pivoting to face him. Before Jared touched down, there were already phase rounds headed directly at his landing spot.

Jared performed an aerial roll, throwing his body into a different trajectory and barely avoiding the bolts of energy seeking his flesh.

He landed hard, the wind knocked out of him. On instinct he

continued the roll, avoiding another barrage of super-heated energy boiling the air next to him.

"Scarlet, this guy is good. I'm not sure I can take him out on my own. He's fast, and his reaction time is on a whole new level."

"I will help. He cannot hope to take us both."

"Be careful. I saw what he did to you already. Is the wound deep?"

"It burned through my protections, but I will survive."

"Please be careful. If he gets a few more shots…"

Jared left the rest unspoken. Scarlet wasn't invincible, and this guy's weapons were much stronger than Jared's phase pistols.

No matter where he went or how fast he was, his opponent anticipated and reacted to his every move, refusing to let up for even an instant. Jared's diving maneuvers brought him close to some wrecked cars on the side of the road, and he dove behind one, hoping for some respite. However, the phase rounds burned right through the rusted bucket of metal, one energy beam leaving an angry red line burned down his arm.

Jared cried out in pain and sprinted in a zig zag in the opposite direction, hoping distance would help. The fire was relentless, and he couldn't get any breathing room to go on the offensive.

"Scarlet, I think this guy is biding time for reinforcements. We've got to take him out now before it's too late."

"Almost there—"

Jared whipped his head around the moment he heard Scarlet breathe fire. The barrage of phase rounds stopped, and the city-dweller's face flipped from impassive to shocked as the flames spewed from Scarlet's mouth. He escaped the majority of the flames, but the violet fire hungrily burned through his legs, the skin charring off of them.

Screaming in pain and unable to walk, he clutched his weapons and returned fire on Scarlet, but she'd already rocketed past him, and his lack of mobility prevented him from getting off a clean shot.

Jared reversed direction and ran flat out for the downed enemy. Bringing his pistols up, he loosed a volley of rounds that created a wall of deadly energy. The downed assailant saw the rounds at the last second and tried to get away, but he couldn't move fast enough. Several of the rounds missed as he moved his body in impossible ways, bending and twisting like a contortionist. Jared didn't let up, and a few of the rounds finally burned into the guy's body.

One round caught him full in the face and left a smoking ruin in its place. Exhausted, Jared flopped to the ground to catch his breath, but a movement drew his attention back to the downed ship.

George descended from the ramp holding a phase rifle with a white-knuckled grip.

"Come on, already." Jared groaned and rolled to his feet, once again finding himself on the defensive. Only this time, the shots were easy to dodge. Most of them went wide, and George fumbled with the rifle awkwardly. Using the man's inexperience against him, Jared quickly moved closer to him while evading the shots. Once he was certain he could take a shot without getting hit, Jared leveled his pistol at George's head and squeezed the trigger.

One shot was all it took, and a clean, cauterized hole appeared in George's forehead. The body, not realizing it was already dead, stood for a moment longer before collapsing to the ground, lifeless.

Jared sprinted for the corpses of both enemies. Unceremoniously, he collected the weapons and battery packs. Then, he sprinted up the ramp on the ship, grabbed the duffle George had stolen, and ransacked the interior of the ship.

This ship differed from the others he'd seen. There was no robot driving it, but a seat where a human fit comfortably. The interior also had more character, like someone had taken the time to add personal touches, paint, and decorations.

"Scarlet—"

"Jared, get out!"

It was too late; He heard the ships at the same time as Scarlet's shout in his head.

Reinforcements.

Jared didn't know what to do. There was no way they could take out more of the superhuman enemies. They'd only just taken out the other one, and he was by himself. If several of these guys showed up at once, he and Scarlet were in serious trouble.

"It's time to call your brothers in."

"Malsour, Kanundran, Ashazad! Come!"

The mental blast smashed into Jared's mind, sending a sharp stab of pain into his temples. He didn't hear Malsour respond, but he knew she'd reached him. Now they needed to hold out while they waited for the cavalry to arrive.

Though the ship he was in couldn't fly, Jared looked for a way to use the phase cannons.

"I hate to ask this, but can you keep them occupied while I search in here? I want to figure out how the cannons work and turn them against the other ships. If any of them land, let me know. Or, if any of them try firing on this ship, let me know so I can get out."

"I will keep them busy. When my brothers get here, we will take them down."

"How many ships are there?"

"I count six."

Six. Jared's mind threatened to spiral out of control as his heart tried to hammer its way from his chest. How did they hope to take out so many?

Six drop ships and only four dragons. The only saving grace for Scarlet was her speed and agility to fly circles around the ships. He hadn't seen any drop ship ever practice much in the way of aerial evasion, aside from the erratic jerking movements when there'd been stowaways aboard.

Scarlet's brothers were easily bigger in mass, but the ships were likely more nimble with four engines in the back and several on the bottom, allowing them to pivot and hover with precision. Jared almost communicated his thoughts to Scarlet, but she knew the stakes and what the ships were capable of, and his thoughts only wasted precious seconds.

Jared ran to the console, reading furiously. Before, he'd looked for ways to move the ship and hadn't paid a lot of attention to the other buttons. Now, he needed to find and activate the weapons system to shoot down its fellow ships, if that were even possible.

He hoped they didn't have some kind of friend or foe mechanism that would prevent him from firing on another ship. Regardless, he needed to even up the odds a little. Even if he didn't take any of the ships out, he would at least provide a distraction so the dragons could do their work.

He smacked his palm down in frustration. He'd forgotten to use his abilities, again. Activating *Hyper-Cognition* his world slowed to a crawl. He also activated *Clear Mind*. Everything in front of him came into crystal clear focus, and his mind fractured into a dozen thoughts, devouring the information in front of him.

There was a button for every conceivable thing the ship could do. Yawning, pitch, elevation readouts, flaps, wing tips, thrusters, communication displays, forward viewport, ground cameras, landing gear, upper hatch, ramp. The list went on and on. Nearly a hundred buttons, switches, and levers decorated the panel and Jared marveled at the complexity and convenience of having so much at the tip of his fingers.

In only a moment, his mind snapped into focus on a single section of the control panel that read *Weapons System*. The readout was simple, had several buttons, including one that read *Automatic Targeting*.

Bingo, Jared thought, deactivating *Hyper-Cognition* so his movements sped up. Sometimes he wished he could will his body to move as fast as his mind. He kept *Clear Mind* going so he had a complete awareness of the situation and could multi-task. Really, he should've activated the ability the moment he engaged the enemy. That might've been how his opponent had anticipated his every movement.

Pressing the automatic targeting, Jared hoped to hear the weapon engage and fire, but what happened next confused him for a moment. The forward display changed to show the surrounding landscape, but instead of an unobstructed view, the display had a digital targeting reticle, very similar to the ones in the phase rifles.

Text scrolled across the screen, and a synthetic feminine voice carried over the ship's speakers.

ACQUIRE TARGET.

Acquire target? How?

In his clear mental state, he ran through all the possibilities and realized that he needed to manually acquire a target before he could turn automatic targeting on. With nothing to lose, Jared grabbed the lever next to the buttons and twisted it. The targeting reticle moved in a circle, and he heard a mechanical whirring as the phase cannon mounted on top of the ship rotated. Taking a moment to familiarize himself with the directional movements, Jared tried to find the ships. It didn't take him long to see half of them hovering a short distance away while the other half pursued Scarlet through the sky.

Sitting ducks.

Carefully aligning the closest ship in the display, the targeting reticle blinked a furious red, and the same feminine voice sounded throughout the cabin.

TARGET ACQUIRED.

Jamming the big red button labeled *Automatic Targeting*, followed by the button that read *Fire*, the cannon chugged to life, drilling the other ship with a massive flood of phase energy. The thumping of the cannon vibrated up Jared's legs, making him smile in satisfaction. In seconds, the ship exploded into a massive fireball, rocking the two ships near it. Secondary explosions detonated as the engines blew up, further shaking the others. His momentary surprise over, the two remaining ships pivoted to face his own. The ships moved swiftly, but his mind processed the movement so fast it was almost like *Hyper-Cognition was still active*. The phase cannons swiveled into place and small pinpricks of light illuminated the tips of the weapons.

Uh-oh.

Quickly selecting the next target and depressing both buttons again, Jared launched himself from the cabin, scooping up the duffle bag on his way out. The two remaining ships' phase cannons kicked to life at the same time. The explosion and concussive force blasted Jared hard in the back, propelling him a dozen yards away. Thankfully, his *Natural Armor* held and protected him from the bulk of the blast. It still hurt, the pressure wave punching into his side at full force, but it caused no lasting damage.

Sparing a glance over his shoulder, Jared watched with extreme satisfaction as the second ship he'd fired on plummeted to the ground. The three smoldering heaps of wreckage sent great clouds of black smoke into the sky, acting as a beacon for anything—or anyone—nearby.

The final ship that'd been hovering in place was no longer content to wait things out, and joined in the fight against Scarlet.

Scarlet was fast. Faster than he'd ever seen her move, and a lot quicker than when he rode atop her back. She used the ships against each other, constantly putting them in their own lines of fire so that none of them managed to acquire her as a target. Based on Jared's experience, and watching the ships he'd just taken out, it only took a split second for the phase cannon to prime and fire. That hesitation in the weapons gave Scarlet all the time she needed to easily pivot away.

Jared tried to imagine the fight in her mind, the way she fractured her thoughts at all times and how she controlled her body. For someone like him, this would be an impossibility, but for her a slight challenge.

The display mesmerized him. He'd never had the chance to watch her in action like this. She pulled out all the stops, using momentary lapses in the ships' maneuvering to loose torrents of flame at them. She tried to target the ships' weapons with every blast, but they weren't helpless and often managed to dip out of the way to avoid the brunt of the fire.

The ships twisted and turned, trying to get a better line of sight on her while also trying to avoid each other. If they weren't in such mortal danger, Jared would've laughed at the sight as the huge ships tried to outmaneuver her. But if she stopped for even a moment, it would be game over. If the rounds from the city dweller he'd killed could punch a hole through all her layers of defense and scales, he didn't want to know what a phase cannon could do.

When the fourth ship joined the fray, it became much harder for Scarlet to avoid their cross-fire. Just when he thought he'd witnessed the extent of Scarlet's agility, she flipped upside down and dove backward through a gap in the ships and latched on to the underside of one.

"**Jared, watch.**" Scarlet's voice echoed in his ears, and a hint of pride preceded her brothers' arrival.

Jared blinked in surprise as they seemed to materialize from nowhere, descending from directly above the ships. Their speed was so great that each impact tore the wings right off the vessels. In swift, choreographed moves, the three giant behemoths made short work of the engines, and the ships crashed to the ground as all three dragons regained their flight. The final ship Scarlet clung to punched its underside thrusters and launched straight into the air. Scarlet's claws left huge gouges in the ship, but its upward thrust was too much for her, and she lost her grip. A split-second later, all four rear engines whined to life, and the ship shot away as if from a slingshot. Gone in a blink, there was no way the dragons could follow at that speed.

"That will be a problem."

"**There was nothing more we could do.**"

"I know, but... they saw the four of you. No doubt they'll be back with even more forces. We may end up leaving this area before long."

"**We will do what we must. Though, there are ways we can remain hidden.**"

"The den idea, right? Can you have your other brothers work on that? There's no reason to delay that anymore. If there were more ships in the area they'd already be over here and a little smoke won't change that."

"**I instructed them to begin the moment we engaged in this fight.**"

"Hopefully they don't burn down the forest. That would kind of defeat the purpose."

Scarlet looked at him sideways. "**My brothers are smart. They understand the situation.**"

Jared had meant it to be humorous, but he guessed his current mood didn't allow that sentiment to show.

"Sorry, I didn't mean to imply they weren't. Just my overly cautious nature. We've done so much to carve out the new home it would be a shame to leave it already."

"**We have not reached that point yet.**"

Jared ran to each of the downed ships, working his way through them and piling up the weapons and equipment he salvaged. In three of the six ships he found the remains of more human beings, but also several robots pinned into place by various pieces of the ship. Two of the robots were still functional and he ended them with a round to the head.

Each of the ships had markings on the exterior next to the hatch that read *Star – 1* and had nicknames such as "Avid", "Seeker", and "SMD". Jared had no idea what they meant, but suspected they were all part of the same fleet. It didn't matter, but he logged the information for later.

While Jared searched, he remembered Pete asking about the ship they'd destroyed earlier and whether Jared had parts for him to study. Jared studied the destroyed ships during his mad dashes between them and realized that not a single one of them remained intact. They wouldn't be able to keep one of the ships, but maybe they could salvage key parts and hide them where the cities couldn't find them.

"Scarlet, can you and your brothers carry one of these ships? Maybe pick the most intact one and carry it off?"

"**We will try.**"

"Thanks."

Jared resumed his task. Not only did he find more weapons,

battery packs, and medical supplies, he also found more uniforms. They matched the outfit the city-dweller he'd killed wore. The uniforms he'd stolen way back in New York City were much different, less…regal, and seemed plain compared to these. He found five uniforms. Two of the ships were still engulfed in flame, so he left them alone.

Once he'd gathered all the equipment, there was a pile of loot sitting on the ground, and he had no way to get all of that back home. Retracing his steps, he pulled open more of the hatches, searching for something to use as a transport container. Finding nothing to use, Jared searched parts of the ship they could rip off and use as a bucket.

Again, there was nothing. The ship was all flat angles, and the fuselage didn't have a top window or display. Jared had an idea, but it was morbid, and he really didn't want to go that route. However, after exhausting other possible ways to get all the gear transported, he buckled down to see it through.

He went to the corpses of the humans he'd killed and stripped off their clothes. He used these as makeshift bags and piled the weapons inside. The battery packs went into the duffle, since they'd be more likely to fall out. He used the sleeves of the shirts to tie around the middle of the bundles to secure everything inside.

His old phase pistols also went into the bundles, and he attached the new ones to his weapons belt. They were heavier, but the difference wasn't enough to be uncomfortable.

He didn't bother studying anything he'd gained. There would be time enough for that later. For now, they needed to get out of the area with the goods. They'd see what happened later. At least this time they didn't have George to muck things up.

This fight was both a blessing and a curse. They had gotten a whole arsenal of super powerful weapons and batteries. They now had uniforms to masquerade as the city dwellers, and they had tons of wreckage to study.

Jared hoped the city didn't find the wreckage, and that his people would be able to learn how the technology worked.

The short time he'd spent in the ships here should increase his understanding greatly, since he had *Memory Recall*. He could spend time later going over the controls in greater detail. It wasn't a substitute for practicing with them, but at least the next time he was inside one he would know what to do. His job finished, he watched as the dragons tried to carry the larger of the pieces of wreckage, but it was no use.

"It is too heavy."

Jared walked over to them and looked over the wreckage. "What if you slice it into chunks? We can take the most critical parts and leave the rest behind. The main thing I want here are the controls, communications system, and weapons array."

"We can do that."

Jared backed away, and they used their razor-sharp claws to dissect the ship into pieces.

"It would be a good to carry at least one engine away. Also, I want to bring some of these phase cannons with us. Actually, can you strip them off all of these ships? At least, the ones that are still whole? If we can figure out how they work, we will have some super powerful weapons on our side."

"After we take care of this ship."

"Okay, if it takes too much longer, we can just leave it be. I don't want to be here if or when the cities send more reinforcements."

"I think the cities will be much more cautious with the next round of ships and people they send here. We killed four of their own. No doubt they rarely see death. Not with the use of full nanotechnology to sustain their bodies."

"Good point. Though they could just send a huge army of robots here to take everything out."

"If they have an army, that would be my guess after our actions. The resources to create these ships are significant, and now that we have destroyed seven, it is enough to raise the enemies' ire."

"Well, let's not be around if that happens."

While the dragons finished their task, Jared went back into one of the drop ships and looked around for anything that would help him understand the phase cannon better. He wanted to figure out where its power source was, if it used a battery, or if the ship itself produced the energy. If Jared and the dragons took all the cannons, but then had no way to power them, they would just be useless hunks of metal. Well, they'd be useless to him, but no doubt Pete would have a field day.

"We are ready."

Jared jogged back outside, where four huge chunks of the ship sat next to the dragons. The smaller chunk was the entire cockpit. It looked as though Scarlet intended to carry the piece. There was a large portion of a wing with two thrusters underneath, and one rear engine hanging on by a single support. The other two chunks were part of the cargo hold. The phase cannons also lay in a heap next to the rigged bundles Jared made.

"Please take these pieces in different directions and stow them someplace we can find later. I'll wait here and keep looking through these ships for anything else we can take."

"Jared, what if—"

"I'll be fine." Jared waved her concern away. "We know how fast the ships can fly, and based on the distance to the city over the ocean, it will take them at least twenty to thirty minutes to return home and then another thirty minutes or so to come back."

"What if they sent news ahead of them and there are already ships on the way back?"

"Then, let's shoot for you to be back in twenty minutes to pick me and this equipment up."

Scarlet turned to her brothers and bobbed her head. "**Return swiftly. We need not take them far, just far enough they will not discover them without a tracking device built in. We must leave here before any more of these ships arrive.**"

Jared returned to the drop ship while the dragons grabbed their payloads and took off. He could tell it was heavy, as it took a while for them to gain altitude. Of them all, Scarlet looked to have the easiest time, but her brothers had only recently regained their ability to fly, so it stood to reason that so much extra weight was difficult at the moment.

Back in the half-destroyed cargo hold of a ship, Jared worked his way from one end of the ship to the other. At some point he'd activated *Clear Mind*, though he didn't remember when. It was becoming a natural thing for him to do, but would still be a while before it became integrated into his everyday life, as was evident in his failure to activate during his fight with the stranger from the city. It excited him to think he'd come so far, and he couldn't wait to see what the next breakthrough would be.

One by one, he opened all the compartments. There were no surprises and everything he'd seen before was also clear here. Since he had time, he raided the medical supplies and rummaged for anything else useful.

Once again, he focused on the weapons system. There had to be an ammunition source for the phase cannon, and he needed to figure it out before they left the area. Jared pulled an image to mind of the drop ship from above. He found the phase cannon and transposed himself into the image from inside the ship. He stood just behind the controls. The phase cannon was five feet in front of him, mounted on the nose of the cockpit. It rested on a swivel for a full field of view.

Pausing on the image, Jared magnified the view and saw something he hadn't noticed before. The cannon sat on the nose, but there was a track that ran vertically around the tip. He focused on the controls in front of him for the weapons system and saw *Top, Bottom,* and *Middle.* It looked like the cannon could sit on top of the ship, swivel to the bottom, or remain on the nose like he'd seen. That made these things even deadlier. They had full 360-degree rotation along with being able to fire on enemies above and below. The only blind spot was behind the ship.

It was a good thing they'd surprised these guys, because looking at everything they had at their disposal, it could've been a lot worse. Jared suspected none of the people and robots flying the ships had experience fighting against anything. No one dared attack the cities. They'd probably grown complacent, which was how he had escaped unscathed.

Almost unscathed. Jared looked down at the angry red burn on his arm.

Jared didn't think it would take long at all for the cities to mobilize and ramp up their offensive operations. Once they realized there were a group of dragons and a human with capabilities and skill equal to their own, things were liable to get hairy quick.

Turning his thoughts back to the present, Jared traced several paths from the cannon to parts of the ship's interior. There were a few compartments and panels around the control console he hadn't pried open because they didn't look like storage areas. He unsheathed one of his daggers and popped them open.

After the third panel, Jared heard several thumps outside announcing the return of the dragons.

"How's it going?"

"We are waiting on Malsour to return. Two more minutes."

"All right, I should be ready by then. I'm trying to find a source of power for the phase cannons."

Two panels later, Jared found what he sought. There was no label on it, but under a panel just to the side and back of the console, a huge battery pack sat inside. The indicator lights on the side glowed a healthy green to show it still had a lot of charge. Reaching to grab it, Jared paused. He didn't know what would happen if he unplugged it. Perhaps there was a shutdown sequence he needed to do. Time running out, Jared squeezed his eyes shut and yanked the battery out.

Nothing happened, and he opened one eye to look down. The battery was whole, and the only changes were the indicator lights winking out. Depressing one button on the side that read *Charge*, the lights blinked back on to show almost a full battery again.

"I found it! I need to get the batteries from the rest of the ships while we are here. It will only take a few minutes."

"You must hurry, Jared. Even by your conservative estimations, we are running out of time."

"I'll be quick. I promise."

He dumped the battery with the others in the duffle outside and ran from ship to ship, popping the panels open. He only gained three in total. The explosions had destroyed the other ships to the point he couldn't get to the panels, or the batteries had fried with the ships.

"Okay, here are the bundles we need to take." Jared pointed them out to Scarlet. He'd positioned them all farther apart so the dragons could pick them up.

He ended up with two bundles of weapons, one bundle for medical supplies, and a small bundle of clothes he planned to carry. Jared picked up the duffle of clothes and slung it over his shoulder before climbing on Scarlet's back.

Everything ready, the dragons launched themselves into the air and headed back to their tiny home.

It'd been a harrowing experience, but Jared smiled as he looked around at the four dragons and their bundles. They had their fighting force now, and this little foray had allowed them to gather a ton of weapons and gear for everyone. It had been a successful day—even if the cities now knew about the dragons.

09 LET THE BONDING BEGIN

It didn't take long for them to get home, and Jared saw the plume of smoke from the burning earth well before they made it back. Jared was glad the dragons had waited until after he and the others had engaged with the city's ships before working on the den. The smoke was an eyesore in an otherwise clear sky, and anyone from miles away would see it.

"Scarlet, I think we need to stop with the tunneling soon. If we saw the smoke from miles away, anyone can. If the city sends a response force, we don't want them zooming in on us like a homing pigeon."

"I think we should give them a few moments longer. They found natural caves beneath the cliffs here. The smoke is mostly from their initial descent and the trees that surrounded the hole."

A few of the trees in the immediate vicinity were gone, and in their place lay smoldering piles of ash. It was a good thing there were no leaves, because the whole forest would've gone up in a blaze. As it was, the fire still could've spread to the neighboring trees, and he was glad that hadn't happened.

"I see. Okay, we need to put some of these embers out to stop the smoke from rising into the air. Let me go get more people and shovels, and we'll throw dirt on the trees and ash."

He vaulted off Scarlet's back and ran over to the cliff.

"I need volunteers to help shovel dirt onto the burning trees out here."

Volunteers poured from the rooms as everyone was eager to get out and see the new dragons.

"Whoa, whoa…I don't need everyone. I promise everyone will have time to meet Scarlet's brothers, but right now we are in a rush to put out the fires so the smoke stops floating into the sky."

Jared chose five people at random, shoved the digging tools into their hands, and beckoned them to follow. All five immediately set to work. He started on the opposite side of the clearing and they met in the middle.

"Scarlet, can you take a tour from above to make sure we got everything?"

"**One moment.**" Scarlet launched into the air. "**There is a trickle of smoke just to the south, though it is not very noticeable unless you are directly over the area.**"

Jared looked in the direction and saw nothing from his vantage. They'd covered all the ash from the trees there already. He walked in the direction for a couple dozen yards before he saw what Scarlet saw. There, rising from the ground, a thin tendril of smoke escaped into the air. It looked like it seeped from between the rocks. Just to be safe, Jared threw dirt over them to cover any gaps in the rocks.

He walked back to Scarlet as she thumped to the ground. "It was probably the smoke from below where they are still clearing."

"**Let us go find out.**"

"Is there enough room for all of your brothers?"

"**Not yet, but soon they will hollow enough out for all of us.**

Enough questions. You will have answers in a moment."

Jared chuckled. She'd probably grown tired of his constant stream of questions and had been waiting to say something like that for a while. It was true, though. She only knew what her brothers told her, and it made more sense to see it with his own eyes before asking more questions.

"Everyone, listen up," Jared called to the five who had helped him out. "I'll go with Scarlet into the tunnel and check it out. I'd like everyone to go back up to the rooms. Once I've determined all is clear, we can work out a rotation of people to come down here to explore and meet Scarlet's brothers."

A collective groan escaped from their lips, but they reluctantly trudged back to their rooms, depositing their shovels into a pile.

"Everyone is eager to meet your brothers. That is a great sign after what they've been through."

"I only hope my brothers feel the same."

"At least some of them do, and that is better than nothing. Besides, even if they don't bond with anyone, having them around is awesome. What would've happened today if they weren't here? Scarlet, we took out six drop ships like they were nothing. If it were just you and me out there, we'd have died."

"That is not—"

"I know. It's a sobering thought, but it's reality. We need to get your brothers bonded as soon as possible to work on their defenses. If they increase the hardness of their scales and skin like you, then we will be much stronger and fights like these won't be quite as nerve-wracking. Do you know how many rounds that city dweller put into your side before it—"

Jared stopped, his heart clenching in his chest. He hadn't bothered to check up on her after their ordeal. He felt like such a bad person, and he couldn't believe he hadn't thought to make sure she was okay.

"Scarlet, I'm so sorry. I—"

"It is okay, Jared. The rounds did not seriously hurt me. Though if he'd landed a few more…"

Jared darted around to her side, examining the hole bored clean through her scales. The skin beneath was a charcoal color. Running his fingers around the edges of the wound, he carefully inspected it to make sure there was no lasting harm. If that guy had managed even just one more volley, it would have punched a hole right into her body.

"That was way too close."

"I agree. Now we know they have more powerful weapons. On the bright side, we no longer need to test the efficacy of the phase rounds against me."

A smile split Jared's face as he thought about their previous conversation, but then the embarrassment came back, remembering their conversation after.

"It is unfortunate you were unable to test your *Natural Armor* in the same manner."

Heat rushed to his cheeks. He knew she wouldn't let him live down his attempt to test a ballistic round against his newfound defenses. Well, it hadn't been a bullet, but rather him trying to shove his knife down against his hand. The moral of the story was they didn't need to test their own defenses. Nature and these battles they fought were more than sufficient.

Their conversation carried them into the tunnel and the caves below. When they stopped inside, Jared paused, his mouth dropping open.

Not only was there a massive underground cave system, an underground stream flowed beneath.

Why are all the trees dead if there's water? Looking up, he saw exposed roots, dried and shriveled. Not only did the roots not reach the water, they had to contend with the acidic rains. Until Mother Nature re-asserted her dominance and cleaned the atmosphere, he doubted they'd see widespread vegetation again.

"Do you know what this means?" He didn't expect Scarlet to answer, and continued speaking. "We don't have to go down to the lake anymore. At least, not for cleaning, bathing, and water for cooking. The only reason for us to go back to the lake now is for nanites. Is there any dirt down here, or is it all rock?"

"I do not know. My brothers only opened the larger chamber here. If you follow the water up or down the stream, you may find some."

"If we can find dirt, maybe we can grow mushrooms or some other plants that don't need light down here. Maybe Pete can route the electricity down here and we can—"

"Jared. Think about the others and their past experiences."

"What are you...oh, yeah. I wasn't thinking about that."

"Many recovered well from the ordeal, but they may be averse to living underground again."

"But there's so much potential here."

"There is, but you may lose people if you pursue it."

"What if we have no choice?"

"I cannot speak for them, but I know them well, and I doubt all of them will be receptive to it."

His joy dimmed, but not gone altogether, Jared's mind spun with the revelations of an underground bunker like this. It wasn't massive, but it would give their colony the edge it needed to thrive. They wouldn't need to risk going down to the lake all the time.

"We have yet to explore the tunnels on either side."

Scarlet's proclamation didn't dissuade him in the least.

Regardless of what they found, this was an epic discovery. He'd take a group with him to explore the tunnels later. With the dragons living in the main cavern, they didn't really need to worry about encroaching enemies, anyway.

"All right, Scarlet. It's been long enough. We should introduce the water folk to your brothers. Can all of you fit in here now? It looks like it'd be big enough for at least a short while."

"I think we can manage for a time, though we will want to enlarge it or move elsewhere soon. My brothers do not cherish the idea of remaining cooped up in a den after gaining their freedom once again."

"For now, let's get all of them in here, and I'll go round everyone up. I thought about doing this in two groups, but I'll bring everyone down. I'd like them to meet your family, but we also need to let them know what just happened with the cities."

"As you wish."

Leaving Scarlet's side, Jared walked back up the smooth tunnel created from dragon fire. It was awesome to have an entire contingent of dragons around. Already Scarlet proved her worth, and they rarely worried about their safety with her around. Jared should've felt even more secure, but after what they'd just encountered with the drop ships, even a full contingent of dragons wasn't enough to quell his fears entirely. It was a start, certainly, but they had a long way to go before he would truly feel safe.

Jared started at the top of the platforms with his room, then the dining hall. One by one, he called into each of the rooms until everyone was ready to go. They crowded the stairs, an excited murmur of voices accompanying them to the clearing and the tunnel leading down.

Since they couldn't all fly, Scarlet's brothers trudged through the dense forest of desiccated trees, careful not to disturb too many of them and ruin the cover they afforded. Every now and again, pieces of trees snapped off and made Jared cringe. They'd need to go and erase the evidence of their passage.

"Everyone, grab hold of someone to help you descend this tunnel. It's slick. I'll go first in case you fall."

Vanessa grabbed Jared's arm and walked with him. Slowly, the rest of the water folk edged themselves down the tunnel while Jared, Elle, and Kitty waited at the bottom. Elle and Kitty hadn't needed the warning. Elle had jumped on Kitty's back, and the large graceful feline walked down the sloping tunnel as if on a flat surface, her claws easily slicing through the super-heated dirt to gain purchase.

Finally, after what seemed an eternity, the group made it to the bottom safely and clustered together. It reminded Jared of the first time he'd seen them emerging from the lake. Every sound and movement had terrified them. They'd been little more than husks of the people he now saw before him. The pale blue of their skin had been transformed to a healthy skin tone. They were still pale compared to him, but they no longer looked sickly. It was more like a lack of sunlight. The gaunt nature of their bodies had disappeared, replaced by athletic builds as everyone worked tirelessly to better their small community.

They'd come a long way, and now here they stood in a large underground cavern created by a dozen dragons. Jared suspected they couldn't see all the dragons yet, nor the water trickling through the middle of the room. Their eyesight, while much better than it had been, didn't really let them see in the dark like him with his enhanced abilities. The only light penetrating the underground chamber was the shaft they'd walked down. It illuminated some of the room, but not enough.

"Hey, Pete," Jared called out. "Do we have portable lights in that workshop of yours?"

"Y-y-yes. There are some charging on my workbench. They should be ready to g-go by now. We've had clear skies, and the solar p-p-panels are working well."

"Okay, everyone hold here. I'll be right back."

Jared sprinted up to Pete's room. He found half a dozen of the portable lanterns. Unplugging them, he jogged back to the group. He passed three out to Elle and took the remaining three.

"Spread them around the room so everyone can get a good idea of the size of this place and see what's inside."

They placed the lanterns around the area, flicking them on to their highest settings. It wasn't sufficient by any stretch of the imagination, but it at least gave everyone a reference point to anchor themselves in the massive room.

"Okay, everyone stay close and follow me."

He walked a few dozen yards forward. Several people gasped as they saw the dragons for the first time. Excitedly, they jostled for better views and pointed in all directions.

"Listen up, everyone. There's a lot we need to discuss. I know this is exciting, but I promise everyone will have plenty of time to greet our newest allies and to explore this cave. I'll give you a brief introduction now, but there are also more serious matters we need to discuss."

He turned to the dragons. "When you introduce yourself, can you please dial back your telepathy as much as possible? If you feel you're unable to do so, just nod your head. These people, aside from maybe two, cannot handle the mental pressure, and it will hurt them greatly." Just talking about it made his temples hurt as he remembered Alestrialia's voice booming inside his mind.

One by one, Jared introduced the fire dragons. Thankfully, they were all able to dial back the psionic pressure on everyone's minds. He saw a few of the water folk squint and furrow their brows while the dragons spoke, but nothing to show it was overly painful. Introductions done, Jared moved on to other business.

"This chamber is large enough for the dragons to sleep and remain out of sight for anyone flying over the area. Initially, we'd thought they would need to find some shelter far away from here. It's awesome this cave was here for us to use. A stroke of luck, but unfortunately that luck didn't hold earlier today."

A few people cast confused looks his way, but he decided to save the bad news until after he'd finished explaining this new cave system. Jared made sure everyone was paying attention to him before continuing.

"Scarlet and her brothers will be enough to keep any creatures at bay, but we must explore the tunnel systems on either side of this cavern to make sure it's safe. Once things settle down, I'll take a small party with me and explore them to make sure we aren't sharing this area with any other creatures. So please keep your explorations to this main room until that happens. Also, please stay close to the rest of the group. If any of these dragons move, they won't notice a small human and could accidentally hurt one of you."

His message received, Jared paused to collect his thoughts. He furrowed his brow, thinking through the best way to broach the earlier battle.

"The next topic is not so pleasant." Jared hesitated as a ripple of fear passed through the group. "I…"

Jared didn't know how to continue. He'd killed George. Sure, the man had never pulled his weight and had gone against Jared most of the way, but he had been a member of their group. He'd survived nearly a decade enslaved like the rest. While Jared himself felt no remorse, some of these folks might. Especially Damien, since they'd been close. Though, ever since the story about Razael unfolded,

Damien hadn't given Jared much trouble, had pulled his weight, and fit in with everyone else.

With no better way to say it, Jared dropped the news.

"George is dead." He observed their faces but found he was the only one with a look of surprise. He'd expected some reaction, if not from Damien, then surely Vanessa would've had something to say about it. Only, no one spoke, and no one made an outward sign of caring.

"Um...I killed him?" Jared added a hint of a question in his words.

A few stray thoughts brushed his mind as several people sent telepathic words to their friends.

"Good riddance."

"It's about time."

"That's a relief."

He wondered where all the people were who'd agreed with George the other night. Specifically, when Jared outlined their plans. Not even Damien looked particularly crestfallen about his death.

"I see there was no love lost on him. I'm curious, why did none of you stand up against him when he fought us every step of the way? If I'd known you felt like this then, I'd have cast him out long ago, before he learned the secrets of bonding. He made quite a mess for us today, and we could've avoided it. He planned to turn us all in so they'd have had us for their new phase weapons. It's okay, Vanessa. I understand why you did, and I don't blame you. I didn't kick him out before because I knew you'd all been through so much in your time under Razael's influence, but I realize now, that wasn't the right move to make."

"Jared, we—" Vanessa collected her thoughts before finishing, "—we'd only just had our will returned to us. The experience was raw, and every person in our group survived. We saw anyone not us as an outsider. Even looking back at it, I don't think we would make any different choices. The conversation we had the other day—it was necessary, and I think you know why."

She didn't elaborate any further, and she didn't need to. Jared understood that she needed to stay a neutral party. If his actions went against the will of her people, she needed to side with them and reach an acceptable compromise later. Laying a hand on her shoulder, Jared nodded.

"I get it, I do. It's just unfortunate things turned out the way they did. George almost made it back to the old colony before we intercepted him. We'd almost caught him when one of the drop ships showed up. We got our first good look at the humans that live above. Let me start by saying they are much stronger and more powerful than us. The only reason Scarlet and I defeated him was through teamwork. If you look at Scarlet's side, you'll see that the guy we faced almost gravely injured her. His weapons punched right through her defenses and scales. If even one more volley hit her side…" Jared shuddered.

It was Vanessa's turn to reassure him as she reached up and squeezed his hand on her shoulder.

"After Scarlet left, it was everything I could do to avoid the phase rounds from this guy. His reflexes were fast and accurate. So fast, I couldn't even see him move sometimes. He predicted most of my maneuvers. Thankfully, I distracted him long enough for Scarlet to spew fire at him. After the fight, George tried to take me out with a phase rifle, and that's when I killed him."

Everyone listening to his words gasped. They directed words of outrage at the now deceased member of their group. They couldn't believe the guy would turn a weapon on Jared after he'd saved them from Razael.

Jared shook his head. Some people were fundamentally ungrateful, and nothing anyone did could change that. He finished his retelling of the battle and everyone started chatting about their encounter. Jared had to raise his voice over the noise to get their attention.

"Hold up a minute; I'm not finished. The credit for saving us goes to Malsour, Ashazad, and Kanundran. Without them coming to our rescue, I'm fairly certain Scarlet and I wouldn't have made it back. We are fortunate they regained their ability to fly on their way here."

Vanessa drew close and wrapped her arms around him in a hug. "I'm so sorry, Jared. You were right, and I should have listened to you when you expressed your suspicions about George. I never thought he'd do something like this. He never came across as outright malicious."

"Don't worry about it. I probably would've made the same choices in your shoes. You can see I'm protective of those I love. If someone came out of nowhere saying I shouldn't trust someone and to banish them immediately after meeting them, I'd be suspicious too." Turning back to the rest of the group Jared changed the topic. "It wasn't all a loss! We got a huge number of weapons, equipment, and medical supplies from the ships. If it weren't for the cities finding out dragons are real, I'd almost say George did us a favor."

"They know?"

"How?"

"I thought—"

"Whoa, okay, yeah. I kind of left that part out. I lost my train of thought when you all didn't react the way I thought you would. Yes, one ship got away and headed back to their city. I took out one, the second downed ship was from friendly fire after I used it to fire on them. Scarlet and her brothers took out three more ships, but as soon as the final one realized it had no chance, it bolted, and there's no way they'd have caught up to it. So, yes. The cities know there are at least four dragons in the area and that we can easily take out a few drop ships. It doesn't bode well for a surprise attack, but I got other stuff that might help us out. I'll show everything when we head up for dinner. For now, everyone should take time to introduce yourselves to Scarlet's family. Elle, Kitty? Can you two help me search down these tunnels? I want to make sure there's nothing immediately beyond this area. Everyone else, please stay down here and away from the tunnel to the surface. The cities will likely send an even greater response to our attack, and we must stay out of sight as much as possible. Once I've finished searching these connecting tunnels, I'll verify the coast is clear above and we can head up for dinner."

Jared turned toward the first tunnel, Elle and Kitty on his heels. "Kitty, do you mind taking point? Elle, you take center, and I'll guard the rear in case anything sneaks around us."

Kitty surged forward, her camouflage ability triggering. Jared flipped over to *Heat Sight* to make sure he saw anything lurking along the walls. Even with *Heat Sight*, he couldn't see where Kitty was. Her ability was impressive, and one day he hoped to learn how to do it. It was near invisibility and would provide a huge advantage if they ever infiltrated the cities.

They didn't have far before discovering the tunnel dead-ended and the water continued running under a rock wall. Jared suspected that if they cleared out the area, they'd find yet more tunnels, but for now they didn't need to worry about any intruders from this direction.

"All right, let's double back and check the other side."

When they got back to the main room, Jared watched all the water folk mingling with the dragons, several even had their hands on a dragon's side as they communicated using telepathy. It surprised Jared that the dragons were open to a more intimate form of communication. Jared found himself grinning as he entered the tunnel with the water folk. Everything had gone smoothly introducing the two groups together, and he hoped it would continue until every dragon found a companion worthy of the bond.

Kitty took the lead again, disappearing from sight. This tunnel didn't end abruptly as the other had, and they walked for nearly fifteen minutes before a scuffle ahead alerted him that Kitty had found something. He whipped out his new phase pistols. They functioned exactly like his previous ones, but were twice as heavy. They had the same safeties on the handgrip. The grip itself was of the same material. Overall, the main difference was the weight of the thing, a larger battery pack, and a grayish black color versus the white of the other.

A moment later, Kitty materialized in front of him, blood dripping down her snout.

"What happened?"

"Rats."

"How many?"

"None. They are no more." Kitty's lips pulled back into a mischievous smile, revealing bits of flesh and fur stuck between her teeth.

"Why must you and Scarlet—" Jared cut off his next words and shook his head. "Never mind. Did you take them all out?"

"They are all dead."

"Good. Where there's one rat, there's usually a lot more. Scarlet and I learned that the hard way and had to destroy an entire horde."

"Only three nearby, but more further up the tunnel, maybe."

"Let's keep going, but please be careful. If there is a den, I want to be first in line. I should be able to take them out easily enough with these new phase pistols."

Kitty turned around and headed back up the tunnel. A moment later, Jared and Elle passed the scene of destruction and found three mutilated rat corpses, large chunks missing where Kitty had indulged herself. Shuddering, he turned away from the shredded corpses and followed Kitty.

They encountered nothing else for another fifteen minutes and Jared called the search. If there was anything else, or another horde of rats, they were far enough up the tunnel it wouldn't be an immediate threat for anyone. Even if there was a horde of rats, the dragons could easily eliminate them.

Jared's biggest concern was the sanitation of the river that flowed through the cave system. The rats were upstream, and if they lived even remotely like those he'd encountered in the New York City subway, he didn't want to think what kind of nastiness pervaded the water. He'd make sure no one drank from the stream until it was verified safe.

They made it back to the large chamber quickly, no longer concerned with stealth. Several people standing by the tunnel had turned to leave, yet the majority of the water folk walked among the dragons conversing.

"Scarlet, how goes everything here?"

"Well! My brothers are very much enjoying themselves. I did not expect such a warm welcome."

"That's good news. Perhaps all of them will bond in time."

"It is possible."

"We didn't find anything threatening in the tunnels. Downstream is a dead end, so we don't have to guard that tunnel. Upstream, Kitty found a few rats and dispatched them in a most horrifying manner." Jared did his best to sound indignant, eliciting a chuckle from Scarlet.

"We are predators. We do not use forks and knives, as you humans." Scarlet radiated smugness and reveled in his discomfort.

"I don't think I'll ever get used to it. I still have nightmares when I think of the lizards you fried. I can still hear the sizzling and bubbling of their flesh."

"It was rather gruesome even for me, but the meat beneath tasted delicious."

Jared knew he wouldn't win this argument. He preferred to have his food prepared and cooked, but to Scarlet and Kitty any prey was good enough.

After double-checking everyone had what they needed, he let everyone know to steer clear of drinking the water for now. Then he led the group waiting by the exit up to their rooms. Just to be safe, Jared had Kitty and Elle scout the area first. Certain no city-dwellers or drop ships lurked nearby, they left the safety of the tunnel. Everyone piled into the dining hall since it was nearly time to eat. Marie directed several people to help prepare dinner while Jared, Elle, and Kitty returned to the cavern.

Before Jared made it a few steps into the room, Pete ran up to him, frothing at the mouth.

"I n-n-need a b-booster, now! Kirgor was talking about c-components and the nanotech, and we might have a way to—if we p-put together—and send to—"

"Pete?" He didn't respond, rambling on about parts and signals until Jared only heard gibberish.

"Pete!"

Blinking, the man looked up at Jared in confusion. "I need a booster!"

"You said that already."

"Kirgor and I were t-talking, and we want to b-b-bond. Did you know he's an inventor? He worked with humans in the past, teaching them about n-new inventions and ways to do things. His m-mind is fascinating and the short time we spoke, he already grasped the concepts of m-modern p-programming."

Smiling, Jared laid a reassuring hand on the man's shoulder. "Let's go speak with him and Scarlet. We don't want to make any brash decisions. If you two are a good fit, we'll get it done. I have a handful of boosters in my pack."

"Okay," mumbled Pete, his jubilation quelled temporarily.

"Scarlet, have you spoken with Kirgor yet?"

"Not yet, but from the snippets of conversation I overheard, it sounds like Pete could barely contain his excitement after speaking with him."

"Yes, Pete says they'd like to bond."

The news surprised Scarlet, and she had a similar reaction to Jared's own.

"Let us go speak with him."

Though Scarlet could easily speak with him across the room, they trudged over to where Kirgor lay. Once there, Scarlet bent her head to Kirgor's, and they conversed for a time. Whatever they talked about remained a secret, since Jared couldn't overhear a single word. For a moment he thought about asking if they could shield their conversations from eavesdropping but dismissed the idea. It was clear they could from this short exchange, and they didn't want him prying.

"Kirgor agreed to bond with Pete. They have kindred minds and believe they are an excellent match. I am sure Kirgor would be happy to discuss his accomplishments with you in great detail, but he is an inventor and revels in discovery of new technology, human and dragon alike."

"Wait, dragons have technology?"

"We do." Kirgor looked at Jared.

"That's what I w-want to learn m-more about," Pete stammered. "Kirgor will show me."

"Sorry." Jared looked back toward Kirgor. "I don't know a lot about—well, I don't really know much about you at all. The only history I've seen is that of your persecution and when you went into hiding. That, and some vague memories from Alestrialia. Even with *Memory Recall* I'm unable to remember the images and memories I witnessed during her departure."

"That does not surprise me. The memories are for her heir, not the mind of a human. Though you understood them at their imparting, it surprises me you remember anything at all. What you experienced was a mind meld that usually only occurs with dragons. In our natural language, we communicate with much more than words and pictures. We use a speech that transcends languages and visual cues. It also accounts for auditory and emotional cues that underline everything we say. If you saw an image communicated by our mother, but did not feel the emotional aspect, or hear the undertones of her voice, then you likely did not see or understand what you think you did."

Jared's head spun. "So, all of what I saw, including the dragons leaving the earth? All that might be wrong?"

"It depends, but if Scarlet's accounting of our mother showing this to you is accurate, then no. When she showed you the history, you no doubt saw it for what it is, but an entire lifetime of dragon memories cascading through the feeble mind of a human? No, most of those memories are likely false to you."

"Wow, all this time I didn't understand."

"That is my fault." Scarlet sounded chagrined.

"It's no one's fault. I didn't think to ask, and it isn't your job to educate me all the time. I should've asked more questions to learn more about you and your family. We need to remedy that soon.

Maybe we can spend a few days in shared thought space and go over some of your early history and this technology you speak of." Jared placed a hand on Scarlet's side.

Kirgor inclined his head. **"That is an excellent idea. If ever you reach the point to mind meld sufficiently outside your bond with our sister, I, too, can show you some of my history. Though Scarlet might show you our history, her view, or rather our mother's view, would differ significantly from my own. It will be useful to experience the same thoughts from all of our perspectives since we each have our own interpretation of history."**

"Thanks, Kirgor! I'm not sure how much longer it will be before I can do it, but it's increasingly easier to maintain a *Clear Mind* most of the time. Melding with Scarlet and entering my shared thought space is near instantaneous now. I don't think it'll take much more before I reach that level. When I do, I'll spend time with each of you, learning your history."

"It will be our pleasure after what you have done for our mother and sister."

"Thanks. Now, about this bonding—"

"Yes, let us begin with the process. If I understand it correctly, we need to fuse our nanites together using a shared booster. The process will force the nanites in my body to fuse with Pete's DNA."

"That's correct as far as I understand it. Pete, I'll warn you now, this process is very painful. I don't know how much pain Carla endured bonding with Attis, but she is a firecracker and probably would try to shrug off how much it actually hurt. Speaking from my experience, you need to prepare yourself for this to hurt immensely."

"I'm r-ready." Pete clenched his fists and approached Kirgor.

"It's best if you sit next to him for this. When I bonded with Scarlet, I was unconscious for a time. I think that was because Scarlet dug through my head. I'll also say Kirgor is much stronger than

Scarlet was at the time, so it might go faster and be less painful. But Scarlet had hundreds of years to study the technology. So, basically, I have no idea what will happen."

Extracting an injector from his pack, Jared passed it over to Pete. The man was a nervous wreck, his hands shaking. The jubilation he'd shown only moments earlier was gone as he second-guessed himself. He eyed the injector warily until a look of determination passed his features. With no further delay, Pete jabbed the plunger into his arm, depleted half the nanites, and then gently but firmly pressed the needle into the soft skin on Kirgor's underside and emptied the remaining nanites into the dragon.

Pete screamed, his body turning rigid. The injector clattered to the floor as Pete's hands spasmed uncontrollably. He lasted only a few seconds before his eyes rolled up into his head and he slumped against Kirgor.

Kirgor grunted as the nanites went to work, fusing their DNA together. Other than the short guttural noise from Kirgor, there was no outward sign it affected him the same. Neither Pete nor Kirgor moved a muscle after a few minutes.

"Let's leave them be. I'll keep an eye on Pete, but they could use the space." Jared walked away from the pair and made sure everyone left them alone.

Looking around the room, Jared grinned.

One down, eleven to go.

10 MATCHMAKING

Pete and Kirgor were the only ones bonded that day. Several other promising discussions took place, but only Pete worked up the gumption to get it done. No doubt it was the like-mindedness of the two that drew them together. Kirgor had already promised to bond with a human, so when one of them also happened to be an intellectual like himself, Kirgor had jumped at the chance.

Jared hoped this new bond would propel Pete's research to the next level. If he figured out a way to charge the phase batteries, or how the equipment and robots worked, they'd have a massive advantage against the cities that no one else in the world likely had. The thought excited him, and he idly wondered if there were any cities that didn't get along with another.

If there was in-fighting amongst the cities, perhaps they could capitalize on it. Or, maybe there was a city somewhere sympathetic to the plight of those who lived below and would aid them in bringing the other cities to heel. It was a frivolous thought, since if there was a city out there willing to help, why hadn't they done so in the hundreds of years they'd floated above the destruction below?

No, Jared needed to rely on only himself and those he'd surrounded himself with. Seeing things well in hand with Pete, Jared walked back to the dining hall for dinner. He had no specific plans for anyone, but he'd remind them to make sure of their choices to bond. The process was irreversible, and getting stuck with a lifelong companion they didn't get along with would be a bad deal for everyone involved.

Before heading back up, Jared turned to Malsour across the room. *"Can you please keep an eye on them? If anything happens, I'll come running."*

"I shall watch them."

"Thank you."

Several hours later, Jared found himself with nothing to do. Vanessa, Elle, and Carla were in the adjacent room talking about the dragons. He didn't want to intrude on their conversation, so he retreated to his room. Settling onto his bed, Jared practiced his meditation and abilities long into the night. At some point he'd fallen asleep. Interestingly, he woke with *Clear Mind* activated. Apparently, his subconscious could maintain the ability even while asleep. His arduous practicing had paid off already, and he didn't think it would be long before he could maintain it indefinitely.

Once that happened, he'd build the neural pathways into his mind to maintain it without nanites. Then, he'd focus on his other abilities. The one area he couldn't do anything about was *Body Manipulation*, which included his ability to regenerate, remodel parts of his body, and his nanite armor. If the nanites failed, those abilities also disappeared. It was not a pleasant thought when he remembered just how many times *Regeneration* had saved his life.

Rolling out of bed, Jared found he was the first one to rise for the day in their increasingly crowded home. Though he'd had Carla join him after she bonded, he didn't think Pete needed the same level of attention. He had a dragon to help him through the process. Carla needed the additional guidance since Attis wasn't much help. If it wasn't prey, it didn't fly, and wasn't bigger than him, Attis didn't know how that fit into his world. Hopefully that would change, but for now Jared planned to help Carla as much as he could.

After washing his face and donning a fresh shirt, Jared left his room. Thankfully, everyone had heeded his warnings and remained indoors. He saw no other people walking around as was common for the morning hours. As he walked past rooms, he heard conversations. He let the people know he'd be going down to the tunnel soon and if anyone wanted to go, to meet at the base of the stairs in a few minutes.

Jared quickly peeked in on Pete's room, but found him absent.

"Scarlet? Is Pete still down there?"

"He is asleep next to Kirgor."

"Any issues? Is the bond complete?"

"It is complete, though only just, and it took a lot out of Pete. My brother recovered quickly enough."

"And Kirgor? What does he have to say?"

"You should ask him yourself." Scarlet sounded amused. **"He has not stopped talking since the bond completed. His ideas and insight are—well, listen to him yourself. He has ideas about the technovirus and how to stabilize it already."**

"I'll be down in a few moments. I'm waiting for everyone who wants to go right now. One of us should be around to watch over everyone at all times. Especially with the cities' heightened awareness. There's no telling how many ships they send this time. And they might try to search the surrounding areas. I'm almost glad George got most of the way to the old colony. It will keep their search grid farther from us."

Jared finished his rounds of the rooms and went to wait at the bottom of the stairs. It didn't take long for everyone to assemble.

Performing a quick count, it looked like everyone wanted to go.

"Good morning!" Jared greeted his roommates at the head of the crowd. "I heard you chatting about the dragons last night. What did you think? Did you find someone to bond with?" Jared said it mostly for Vanessa, since Carla and Elle already had companions.

Vanessa slid her arm into the crook of his elbow and leaned in close. "Do you think any of them would want to? Bond with me?"

Jared smiled down at her. "If it were me, I'd definitely want to. Just take your time to get to know them. You probably know them better than me by now, since I've had little time to talk to any of them one on one. I had a couple short conversations with Malsour, Kanundran, and Ashazad, but thats about it. If I had to take a guess, you and Malsour might be a good fit. He is a strong, dominating presence and is also the de facto leader of his brothers. I think you two would have much in common based on personality. Though, he doesn't strike me as the compassionate type like you."

Vanessa said nothing in reply but leaned into him for support. Her presence always did wonders to lighten his mood and almost made him forget that they'd just poked a hornet's nest and were waiting for the response. She had a way of making him feel at ease in any situation, and he wondered if that's what her presence had been like when they'd remained captives of Razael. She was the stabilizing force that allowed her people to survive as long as they had. Sure, her parents had also played a role, but after they'd left, it was all on her.

"All right, everyone ready?"

A chorus of voices acknowledged they were, and Jared led them to the tunnel, always keeping a wary eye out for potential danger. He also strained his ears for any sounds of drop ships nearby.

The trip down the tunnel was much easier than the first time, as people got familiar with traversing the steep slope. Jared found Pete sitting in almost the same place as last night. He was awake and staring vacantly in front of him. The man didn't even look up as Jared approached. Waiting patiently in case he was in the middle of something, Jared stood a respectful distance away.

"Kirgor?"

"Yes?"

"How is he handling all of this?"

"Very well. In fact, he grasped the depth of the nanites quickly. I believe his *Intelligence* is high, since he can already do much of the things Scarlet told me took you some time to master."

Jared's eyes widened as he glanced between Kirgor and Pete. That was great news. If Pete could immediately explore the nanites and the technology behind them, it would help him understand the technology from the cities quickly. In turn, that would accelerate plans for exacting vengeance.

Deciding it wasn't the best time to interrupt Pete, Jared backed away to join Vanessa.

She stood hesitantly, casting furtive glances toward Malsour and Ashazad.

Grabbing her hand, Jared led her over to them and introduced Vanessa.

"Malsour, Ashazad, I'd like you to meet Vanessa. No doubt you had brief introductions yesterday, but I wanted to elaborate more. She is the leader of this small colony. I defer to her when it comes to the daily life of everyone here. She's kept her people alive for years, and it's a testament to her strength and will."

"Greetings."

Vanessa winced and shook her head.

"Apologies," Malsour was quick to add. **"We have not dealt with human minds for quite some time and forget we must tread carefully with our projections."**

"It's okay. I was just unprepared for it."

There was an awkward pause as human and dragons stared at each other. Instead of letting the silence continue, Jared elaborated on Vanessa's past actions.

"You recall my accounting of Razael's imprisonment, right?" He needn't have asked, but he did anyway to be polite with the subject. "Vanessa and her parents were in charge of the other humans during their captivity. Mostly, they kept the people together and encouraged them. If it wasn't for her and her parents, then many, if not all, of these people would've gone mad and died."

Malsour looked at Vanessa in a new light as she dipped her head, a faint blush rising to her cheeks.

"It—we—I didn't do much. I only tried to make sure everyone didn't lose hope after we were…changed. We learned to rely on each other and stay together so we didn't end up getting killed by other creatures."

"**Your… changes?**"

"Razael changed all of us. It helped us survive, but now we no longer need them, many of us wish to go back to how we were before."

"**I am sorry you had to endure such treatment at the hands of a dragon. It is not in our nature to behave so, though human history and lore says otherwise. We are peaceful, but we will defend our own fiercely. It is possible that is where the myths originated.**"

"We all thought dragons were a made-up story," Jared joined in the conversation. "I mean, we knew dinosaurs were real, and many firmly believed in the lake monster stories, but…"

"**Yes, it would seem true history has lost its way over the years.**"

"We're kind of getting off track here. I wanted to introduce the two of you because I think you might make good companions, and I'd like you both to think on it for a time if you don't mind."

"I will think on it and decide if I want to bond. It would mean giving up my newfound freedom."

"What freedom is this though?" Raising his arms, Jared spun in a circle to emphasize his point. "We burrowed into the earth to avoid the ire of those above, just as you did when you left humanity the first time. Is this freedom? Is this the closest we'll get to peace and acceptance of humans and dragons coexisting? I really hope that is not the case. I have much more grandiose plans to see all humans thrive in society and I want to see dragons soaring the skies once again, unafraid of persecution."

"We wish these things too."

"I know that this is a big decision, but to get there, I firmly believe this bond between human and dragon is our best hope. Look at Scarlet. Have you spent more time with her to understand the changes done to her body? Even with those changes, that lone human could have killed her if he'd gotten a few more shots off with these phase pistols." Jared held the new weapons up for Malsour to see.

"We will consider it." Turning to Scarlet, Malsour called his little sister over. "I think it is time we join our minds together."

"Let me get everyone out of your way first. My request still stands when you've had time to think on it. I'd ask that you spend time with Vanessa. I will not force any human or dragon to bond, but if the two of you agree, it would be a strong companionship."

It took Jared a few minutes to round everyone up and usher them to the mouth of the cavern. The only person who resisted was Pete. He wanted to spend more time with Kirgor, but Jared promised him he'd have plenty of time to discuss science with him later.

"If any of you wish to remain down here, you are welcome. I doubt there will be more to do for you while they converse. You won't hear anything, and chances are they will remain motionless for the duration. I don't know how long this will take either."

Everyone went back to their rooms. Jared used the time to instruct Pete, but it was obvious he'd already figured almost everything out about the interface, the description, and even understood the nanite structures. He was a very quick study, and the conversation they had about his enhancement path differed significantly from the one Jared had had with Carla. Pete didn't need to enhance his mind to understand himself to a greater degree, but his body could use help.

"I won't dictate how you assign them, but I will say it's probably good not to rely on technology one hundred percent of the time. We don't have a reliable energy source and you still don't know how to charge the battery pack—"

"Actually…" Pete's voice trailed off as he headed toward his room, motioning Jared to follow. They went into his workshop where Jared saw the remnants of the batteries he'd given the man to study.

Not understanding the technology even a little, Jared was at a loss as Pete looked at him with wide eyes.

"Help me out here, Pete. I know nothing about this tech. I mean, I know it needs charging, but that's it."

"L-L-Look at the light."

Jared peered closer at the parts on the table and the indicator field, showing how many charges it had left. There was one green bar as opposed to being depleted.

"Wait, you figured out how to charge them already?"

"Yes, but only p-partially."

"What do you mean, partially? Aren't these just energy weapons?"

"They are, but they require another force to create the energy b-beam. This chamber here—" Pete pointed to a small, square object, sitting to the side, "—is a sealed g-gas chamber of some kind." Pete picked up another part next to the object and brought it up closer to

Jared's face. "This is a plunger. It opens the gas chamber and lets out t-t-tiny amounts of the substance. P-presumably into a chamber on the pistol. The battery p-pack then uses the charges to ignite the substance, c-creating the energy beam."

Jared's face fell. They wouldn't be able to charge the weapons. They'd have to make do with whatever they found or stole from the cities. There was no way they could synthesize any kind of gaseous substance that would cause the reaction Pete explained, nor did they have a way to reload that gas.

"You're telling me there's no way we can charge them fully?"

"Correct." Pete sounded upset and a little angry with himself at the revelation.

"Hey, it's not your fault. No need to stress over it. I assumed this was an easy fix, but I should know better by now. If we could create highly volatile energy beams with only electricity, humanity would've figured this out way back before the nuclear war."

"I want to t-talk with Kirgor about it. He has an incredible mind. We talked about some things after our bonding, but we have much m-more to discuss."

"Thanks for working on this, Pete. It's disappointing, but at least we know and can plan accordingly. We do have a lot of ammunition from that last raid. Hopefully, we'll also have all the robots, phase cannons, and drop ship parts to bring back and study soon. If they are still there when we go check, we'll bring all the bigger parts into the cavern below so you can work on them with Kirgor. Hopefully, it won't take you long to share a thought space with him and communicate at a much faster and more intellectual level than telepathy or normal speech."

"I can't wait!"

Jared left the room feeling equal parts sad and happy. Sad about the weapons, but happy to see Pete so excited. The man was truly a genius, and he'd found a kindred spirit with Kirgor. Between the two, they'd find solutions to give them an edge over the cities.

Jared went back to his room and found only Vanessa waiting for him.

"Where are Elle and Carla?"

"They're in the dining hall with some others. Many people have questions for them about their bonds. I think several are close to asking some of Scarlet's brothers to bond. I haven't had that feeling yet, but I also haven't spoken with Malsour or Ashazad in great detail. Do you really think Malsour would make a good match for me?"

"Honestly, I don't know. You are both very strong, you've both led your families for years. He is thousands of years old, though, so I don't know. It was a suggestion, and part of me is being over-protective in wanting it to work out. He is stronger than any of his brothers and will protect you better."

Jared grabbed Vanessa by the shoulders and looked into her eyes. "I can't lose you. I won't lose you. If I can help you and Malsour bond so you have him as your protector, then I'll do everything in my power to make that happen. I know a couple months isn't all that long to get to know each other, but I've never felt the way I do about you with any other woman."

Vanessa's face softened, and a blush crept up her neck and into her cheeks. "Jared, I…" she began.

He pressed his fingers to her lips. "It's okay if you don't feel the same way, but I needed you to know how I feel. I can't handle losing any more of the people I love. If Malsour agrees to bond with you, it will give me peace of mind."

Vanessa reached up and cupped the side of Jared's face, sending arcs of electricity through his body. Slowly she leaned in and planted a gentle but firm kiss on his lips and then wrapped him in a fierce embrace. Her body shuddered as she clung to him.

Jared craned his head around to see tears leaking down her face.

What did I say? Jared thought, concerned he'd upset her.

"Vanessa? Are you okay? I didn't—"

She shook her head to stop his next words and looked up with her tear-stained eyes and a bright smile on her face. "I'm fine. More than fine." She collected herself, thinking through her response. "I never imagined I'd find someone like you to love me and to love back. The years we spent below—" Vanessa's voice caught in her throat. "I'm so grateful for everything you've done, and you've been so gentle these past months."

The tears flowed down her cheeks, a stark contrast to the brilliant smile splitting her face.

"I feel the same way about you, Jared. When you went away with Scarlet, I feared you'd never return. Yes, it's only been a short while, but, like you, I can't argue with the feelings I have. If there's one thing I learned from my enslavement, it's that life is unpredictable, short, and we must make the most of every waking moment."

Jared smiled at her, joy shining in his eyes as he bent and returned the kiss. Their feelings laid bare, he reveled in knowing she felt the same. He'd known deep down, but hearing the words of affirmation made it real. There was still a lot he didn't know about all of this, but they'd figure it out together.

He'd never been in a relationship with someone before and he wasn't sure what came next. His parents had married when they were young, but in a world as fractured as theirs, did marriage still exist, or was a mutually-agreed monogamous relationship sufficient for the day? Someone had married his parents, but they'd had a priest in their colony, and they'd tried to follow tradition as much as possible. Jared and Vanessa could visit a colony that had a priest, but given her mutations, they wouldn't be able to do that until she changed them back. *If* she changed them back.

No matter what they decided, he didn't want to rush things between them. For now, he was content to hold her hand and share the occasional kiss. He wanted more, but he also wanted to respect her. His upbringing had taught him to respect and cherish women. His parents had been a great example and whatever he did, he wanted to emulate their relationship as much as possible. They'd loved each other with every fiber of their beings, and Jared didn't remember hearing them fight even once as a child. Sure, they'd had their disagreements, but it was always civil and usually something trivial they worked out quickly.

For several long moments, neither he nor Vanessa spoke. They looked at each other, cheesy grins on their faces. After another short pause, they both exploded into laughter. They laughed at each other, letting all the pent-up emotions explode forth. Jared hadn't realized how nervous he'd been for this revelation, and judging by Vanessa's reaction, she'd felt the same. Now that it was all in the open, they'd figure out how to move forward together.

He smiled at her. "You know, a part of me thinks Carla and Elle did this on purpose. They're usually in the room, and being suspiciously absent is telling. I'm guessing we were the only ones in denial about our feelings. How much do you want to bet that this won't come as a surprise to anyone? Scarlet knows how I feel already. We've talked at length about it."

"You have? Why did it take you so long to tell me?"

"Well, it's only been a couple months. I didn't want to take advantage of you, following the ordeal in the lake. I didn't want you to feel obligated to like me for rescuing you."

"Thank you for being so sensitive to our experiences. Though I am indebted to you for saving us, my feelings for you go beyond an obligation. When I first saw you, I knew there was something different about you. The way you carried yourself and how you immediately leaped to protect us from those creatures even though you yourself had an injury. I'll forever be in your debt for rescuing us, but this…love I feel for you extends beyond gratefulness. I love you for who you are. For being someone worth loving and always putting everyone else's needs before your own. Even with your vows and plans, you've helped everyone else grow stronger first."

"Well, that is selfish of me. I can't defeat the cities on my own."

"Yes, and we're willing to give that help, but you helped us even when it inconvenienced you and set back your plans. You could've joined the Daggers and accepted the civilian losses that might follow, but you didn't. It's not who you are. You can't stand by and watch as innocent people get hurt. Your compassion is the characteristic I love most about you. Based on your past experiences, you have every right to be cold, hard, and no one would blame you, but you're not."

"You can thank my parents for that. They taught me to always value life and respect other people. It was rare for my parents to raise me that way. It wasn't something many other parents taught their kids."

Jared's mind immediately went to Tiny and his lackeys. They'd done a number on him more times than he cared to count.

"Your parents would be proud of you."

Jared felt tears glistening in his eyes and blinked furiously to hold them at bay. It didn't matter how much time passed since their death, anytime he really thought about them and reminisced on their life, the pain came back in full and it was all he could do to hold up the emotional dam he'd erected.

"They might be proud, but I realize the way they raised me doesn't work out here. In my colony, cut off from the rest of the world, sure. But out here? It's gotten us into trouble more times than I'd like. I understand that now and have come to terms with it. I didn't hesitate to kill the guy from the cities, or George when he showed his willingness to see us killed. I'll do whatever it takes to protect you and the others. No matter the personal cost."

"Still, you value life, and won't take innocent lives at the expense of seeing the cities pay."

"That is still true and will always be true. People will get hurt and there's nothing I can do to change that. I don't like it, nor will I shrug it off as meaningless. I'll need to live with the consequences, and that weighs heavily on me."

Vanessa snuggled in closer to Jared, spreading warmth through his body.

Jared kissed the top of her head, inhaling the scent of her hair, a mixture of nature and some kind of flowery odor. Jared breathed in the intoxicating smell, savoring every moment with this incredible woman.

They sat for hours, losing track of time while they chatted about their childhood. Jared was eager to discuss his feelings with Scarlet, but he'd have plenty of time to do so later. He wanted to share a thought space with Scarlet to truly show what he felt for Vanessa. Words alone were woefully insufficient.

Several hours later, Elle and Kitty wandered back into the room, followed by Carla. A quick glance confirmed Jared's suspicions about their absence. Both girls looked at each other conspiratorially and had massive grins on their faces. It was infectious, and Jared smiled back.

Vanessa saw him smile and twisted around to look at her sister.

Jared's smile widened when he saw another blush color Vanessa's cheeks. Jared gave her a quick peck on the cheek and stood.

This side of Vanessa wasn't something she showed often. When around others, she put on a stoic front and acted the part she played in their group. Behind closed doors, she let her guard down and wore her emotions on her sleeve.

Jared nudged Elle and Carla mentally. *"Thank you."*

They nodded. Elle ran up to her sister and gave her a big hug followed by Carla, making Jared smile. Elle and Carla immediately launched into a discussion about the dragons and the conversations they'd had as if they weren't in cahoots to give him and Vanessa alone time.

Before they completely immersed themselves in the intriguing discussion, Jared interrupted. "Hey Carla, where's Attis?"

"Down in the clearing. He's afraid to go underground."

"Okay, thanks. He's lived in this area for quite a while, so I don't think he'll set off any alarms if the cities see him. Just try to keep him grounded as much as possible these next couple days."

"I will," Carla said and jumped back into the other conversation without missing a beat.

Sometimes Jared didn't know how women multi-tasked. Sure, he could do it now, but he'd needed to make some serious enhancements to his mind. It seemed to come naturally for most women and he envied them for it.

Speaking of mental abilities…

"Vanessa, I'm heading down to see Scarlet," Jared called over his shoulder as he walked from the room.

The only response he got was a coy smile and a small wave.

Jared chuckled, his world bright and full of hope. He only wished this feeling would stay with him through the difficult times ahead. Normally, thinking about the future would dim his outlook, but today he didn't think anything could take that away from him.

He didn't tell anyone else he was going down to the den. He

planned to immerse himself with Scarlet for a time and didn't need to worry about others. He and Scarlet had many things to think about, including his new relationship with Vanessa. They also needed to figure out what to do about the cities and if they should even stay in the area. It might be time for them to head further inland and get as far from the coast as much as possible. Then, the cities would be no concern.

I wonder why the cities only float above the oceans?

Shrugging, he made his way down to the cavern. It was a thought for another day. For now, he needed to sort out his feelings and figure out their future. Not just his future with Vanessa, but the future of everyone in their small colony.

11 RETALIATION

Nearly to the bottom of the tunnel, a low rumbling echoed off the cavern walls and brought Jared to a stop. Cocking his head to the side, he listened intently to identify the source of the noise. It sounded like the low rumble of a thunderstorm, but he had seen no clouds in the sky, and it was persistent rather than booming and short like thunder.

"Scarlet, there's something going on up above. Are there any people down there?"

"Pete and a few others joined us a short time ago."

"Please have everyone stay down here until I can figure it out."

"We will be fine here. I will make sure none of the water folk leave."

"Thanks! I'll be back in a few. Can you also send a warning to those up in their rooms to stay put? I'm not sure my telepathy will reach everyone from here."

"Everyone, please stay in your rooms. Jared is investigating the rumbling sounds you hear."

Jared crept back to the top of the tunnel to see if he could identify the source of the noise, but he saw nothing. The sound steadily grew louder. It wasn't unbearably loud, or close by, but it wasn't something he'd heard before and had no way to pinpoint the source.

A couple quick leaps brought Jared up to their platform and the entrance to his room. He ran inside to make sure Vanessa was safe. The three girls were still talking in their room, apparently unconcerned with the sound. Or perhaps Scarlet's warning hadn't reached them.

"Vanessa, there's something making a lot of noise outside, and I don't know what it is. Please hang tight in here until I figure it out. If there's anything to worry about, I'll let you know."

"Be careful, please!" Vanessa ran over to give him a quick hug and a peck on the cheek.

Jared smiled as he disengaged from her. "I'll be careful, I promise."

He ran to his room, grabbed his gear, secured his pack and weapons, and went back to the entrance of their home. He poked his head out to see if anything had changed, but there was no evidence of something approaching even though the sound kept up a steady, rhythmic cadence.

Standing on the platform, Jared tried to think which way he should go. It was hard to say which direction the sound came from, and he could only see in a straight east and west direction from his current vantage. The top of the cliff was only a twenty or thirty-foot climb from his current position. That would put him above most of the desiccated forest and might give him a better view.

Jared found ready handholds to ascend the cliff and worked his way to the top. He could have just jumped, but he didn't want to risk injuring anything using *Maximum Muscle*. The recently-healed muscle in his leg gave a slight twinge as he thought about it. It hadn't taken much to push his body beyond its capability, and he had no desire to do so again, especially if whatever was making the noise proved an enemy.

Reaching the top, Jared tried to perch with just his head over the edge, but his grip was too precarious, so he eased his body over and lay on the ground. A quick look at his surroundings revealed no immediate threats, and he slid his pack off. Having confirmed he was alone, Jared looked around for a source of the noise. The west and south were clear, but the moment he turned his head to look north, he froze. Tendrils of paralysis turned his blood to ice. His breathing halted, and panic flared through his body.

"What's wrong?"

Unable to respond coherently, Jared managed the approximation of a grunt, using telepathy. It didn't do much to assuage Scarlet's fears as Jared felt her tension rising, but he couldn't bring himself to respond to her after seeing the source of the noise.

With a monumental effort of will, Jared activated *Clear Mind* and *Hyper-Cognition*. He needed the mental clarity and time-lapse to think through what he saw in the sky.

It was an entire floating city. The towering archways and spires peeked over the edge of the platform, resembling a giant porcupine. The underside of the floating monstrosity pulsed a light blue, while huge rockets propelled the island through the sky. A dozen drop ships escorted the ship through the air.

Wha—

Why—

How?

Even with *Clear Mind*, Jared found it difficult to process the thoughts. He'd never seen, nor had he ever heard of a city moving so far, so fast. From his understanding, they didn't really move at all. Some of them might move with the tides and various ocean currents, but he'd never heard of one moving like this over land.

Jared and the dragons had destroyed a few drop ships, but he never thought it would be enough to warrant this much attention.

However, the more he thought about it, the more it made sense. Someone—or something—that could take out half a dozen drop ships would concern the cities. If the water folk could take down drop ships, then they could reach the cities. It might be the first time the cities had ever encountered something that threatened their way of life, so it made sense they'd be afraid of whatever it was and come to investigate.

But a whole city?

"What is going on up there?"

"Scarlet, there's a city up here."

"Up where?"

"In the sky, headed toward the old colony."

"The city we saw over the ocean?"

"I can't say for sure, but it's coming from the same direction. I don't know how fast these things can move, but it's been a little over a day since we took down those other drop ships. If it started out as soon as the one that escaped got back, then the distance seems about right."

"How far out is it?" An edge of panic entered Scarlet's voice.

She was no doubt thinking through the same things as him. If the city got too close to their home, would they be able to get everyone out, especially the dragons? They were too large to go unnoticed and the cities were likely on high alert. If the cities got too close, there was a chance the dragons wouldn't be able to escape unnoticed.

"It's already too close."

"Jared—"

"I know, I know. They're likely scanning everything around them, looking for any signs of what took down their ships. Now is not a time to be moving around or think about abandoning the area. Even if you and your

brothers could carry all of us on your backs, which I don't think will work, we can't outrun drop ships. There's no way everyone would survive if we needed to take evasive measures in the air. We're going to have to wait it out."

"Please keep me updated on their progress and send Attis out to investigate."

"Good idea. Though, I'd need to risk bringing Carla up here to help interpret. Attis refuses to go underground, so you won't be able to help all that much. I can't understand the griffon enough to make sense of what he sees, but Carla should be able to translate enough to understand."

Jared lay with his back to the ground, not daring to move a single inch as the city drew ever closer. The size of the city was deceptive. He'd thought their people would be well away from the thing, but as it drew closer, he realized that wasn't the case. They were only twenty miles from the old colony, and this thing had to be at least twenty miles in diameter. Depending on where it stopped, they could literally be right above the water folk. Jared hoped the city centered over the lake to at least give them a little breathing room. Even then it would be a mere five to ten miles from them. Way too close for comfort.

It took another hour for the ship to reach the area. Its size easily eclipsed anything Jared had ever seen before. Even though he'd already seen it from a distance atop Scarlet, it was something else to witness it so close. Watching the angry hornets' nest that was the city, Jared realized he'd been stupid following the drop ship back last time. They didn't have backup then, nor were they as strong, and it would've taken very little effort for the cities to wipe them out. He and Scarlet had stayed far away, and they'd flown as high as they could, but in hindsight it was a stupid move.

When the city stopped moving, it rested near the location they'd downed the six drop ships. That made sense, but it also put the city much too close. There was no way the dragons could escape over land undetected. Either they'd need to wait it out or find another way.

The roar of the city's engines abruptly cut off, replaced by a thrumming noise so deep it rattled his bones. The blue light beneath the city intensified, pulsing in time with the beat.

A pressure in his chest forced him back to the ground. He could fight through it easily enough, but with every pulse from the city, it pressed down on him. It had to be the technology that allowed the city to float indefinitely. He idly wondered if Pete would understand how it worked.

"Hey, Scarlet, how far from the old colony did you and your brothers hide the ship and robot parts?"

"Maybe ten to fifteen miles?"

Jared sighed in resignation. *"I don't think we'll be retrieving anything. The city covers at least twenty square miles centered on the scene of our last battle."*

"We still have the original robots we took down in the old colony. Remember, we brought those to the other end of the lake."

"Yeah, I remember, but I was really hoping for some of these ship parts for Pete to study. At least we'll be able to retrieve something from this whole mess. I definitely think we need to find a way out of this area. I don't know when or how, but this thing is much too close for us to go on as we did before. We don't know what it's capable of, how far they can see, or if they have any scanning technology that can see us here."

Jared lifted his head up and rolled over the edge of the cliff when another wave of pressure flattened him back to the ground. The moment it subsided, he picked up his pack and slipped over the edge. Carefully, he made his way back down to the platform. As long as he stayed plastered to the rock wall, it would obscure him from sight. Carefully, Jared made his way back to his room.

Vanessa, Carla, and Elle eagerly awaited his arrival, all of them tense.

"What is it? Are we safe? Are you okay?"

"Is Attis out there?"

"Kitty, go check?"

All three of the girls spoke at once, their individual responses making Jared laugh despite the dire situation. As usual, Vanessa cared about the safety of everyone and specifically asked about him. Carla's first thought was about Attis, and Elle, fearless as always, thought about sending Kitty out scouting.

"Whoa, calm down and I'll explain. A city, probably the same one Scarlet and I saw before, is now floating over the place we destroyed the six drop ships."

"A whole city?" Vanessa was incredulous. Her demeanor showed one of fear, but also curiosity, having never seen a floating city before.

"Yes, a whole city that is much closer to us than I'd like. We need to make sure no one goes out there to investigate." Jared turned to Elle and Kitty. "Not even the two of you with your camouflage. We don't know what kind of scanning technology the cities have, and they might see right through your ability."

"How are we going to get out of here?" asked Carla, a note of hysteria entering her tone. She took a step toward the door, no doubt concerned for Attis.

"Don't worry about Attis, Carla. He's been around this area for quite some time and I don't think he'd draw much attention from those in the city. Now that I think about it, Kitty probably wouldn't draw much attention either, but Kitty and Attis together in the same area definitely would. There is no way two predators like that would coexist in the same area. I also don't think it's wise for anyone else to wander about. Especially not with the mutations on your bodies. One or two explorers might escape notice, but the moment they saw you weren't ordinary humans, the jig would be over."

A small frown passed Vanessa's features. He wasn't trying to sound harsh, but it was the truth. He squeezed her arm and held her close to let her know he meant nothing by it, nor did it bother him in the least.

"I can probably go out there without too much difficulty. One explorer shouldn't raise any concerns for the city. Even if they sent someone to investigate, I could just tell them I'm headed across the country."

"Jared—"

"I know, Vanessa. I won't needlessly risk myself, but it might come down to something like that so we can see how attentive the city is. If they don't notice me at all, then we might have a chance at getting out of this area undetected. Ideally, I'd stay under cover of the forest as long as possible to throw the trail off this place, and then I could head toward the open areas. I don't think I'll have any problem feigning surprise and wonder of the city and its denizens. I'll just need to make sure I mask my contempt."

"I know you want what's best for us, but let's think through some other options before you put yourself in harm's way like that. For all we know, they could abduct you and hold you hostage, or worse, they could kill you outright for no reason. It's not like there are any other humans around, at least that they know of, to witness the event. They might wipe you out just to be on the safe side."

Vanessa had a point. There really was nothing stopping the cities from taking him out immediately. For all he knew, the city itself had weapons systems that could pulverize him from way up in the sky. It was a risky bet, but if they ran out of options it might be worth the risk.

"Good point, Vanessa. I'll work with Scarlet and her brothers to see if we can find another solution to the problem."

"What about the tunnels we explored?" Elle pointed to the caverns below.

Jared thought about the direction the tunnels went. "No, I don't think that'll work. At least, not without us digging through more rock. I don't want the dragons using their fire, because last time the smoke escaped into the air. If we do that now, then they'll for sure see it and send someone to investigate. Those little probes or sensors they use will easily find the tunnel leading underground and then we're done. I'm not sure how long it would take us to excavate it by hand, but I suppose we could try."

"Scarlet help some?"

Jared turned to Elle. "We can try, but I'm not sure she'd fit. We would need to widen the initial entrance for her to get back to the dead end. The other tunnel leads directly to the lake and we can't go that way. So, if there's nothing on the other side of the wall where the water disappears, then there's no way we can escape underground. I'll tell you what, I can take the shovels down there and try clearing some of it away. We'll need to be careful we don't collapse the room on top of everyone or block the stream. We don't need it flooding down there."

Jared turned to leave but remembered he'd wanted to send Attis out to explore. "Carla, do you have a good enough understanding of Attis and how he thinks to interpret what he sees? I'm thinking we might use him as a scout to see what's going on, but I can't understand him enough to make it worthwhile. Since he won't go down to Scarlet, that leaves you."

"I—" Carla paused, her face twisting in thought. "I think so. It is difficult, and there are things that seem alien, but I think I've got enough grasp to understand him."

"Good, that might be the only viable way we have to get insight right now. I think after a time, we can have Attis fly further afield and then get Kitty out there exploring, but I don't want the two of them close to each other."

"Sounds good. Now go." Vanessa pushed Jared toward the door. "Do what you must to keep everyone safe."

Jared gave her a quick kiss, making the other girls giggle as he ducked out the door. The little moments they shared always lifted his spirits, no matter the situation. He wanted to chat with Scarlet about everything that had happened between him and Vanessa, but in light of recent events that conversation could wait. He didn't really need Scarlet to help him sort out his feelings. No, those were readily apparent to him and everyone else. What he wasn't sure how to reconcile was what his relationship meant and how they should proceed to take it to the next level.

If he wanted to honor his parents' memory, they'd need to get married first. However, he didn't know what that really meant these days. They didn't have a priest or official minister to say vows. A slip of paper or certificate binding their marriage meant exactly nothing out in the wastelands. What was the faculty of marriage, and how did it fit in his worldview? These were the thoughts Jared wanted to discuss with Scarlet. She had a much greater depth of history and knowledge to pull from than he did and might yield some insights.

Perhaps it was the cynic in him, but he'd always assumed traditional marriage was a way for people to adhere to the old ways when government made provisions and bound people together by law. He'd read stories in his parents' historical textbooks and a big oversized Bible they'd kept in their living room that talked about ancient kings and warriors who just took wives for themselves. They didn't have ceremonies, or official paperwork.

What, then, was to stop him from asking Vanessa to be his wife? He'd seen others in his old colony who'd proposed to the woman with a ring of some sort to symbolize the relationship, but again he didn't see the point. If they had mutual feelings for each other, did they really need rings?

Distracted as he was, he still held *Clear Mind* and had the wherewithal to mind his surroundings and avoid a straight line of sight to the cities. He stuck close to the walls and kept the rock and trees between him and the city at all times. There was only one time, for a split second, where he saw the cities, and that was when he sprinted from the base of the cliff to some tree cover before ducking into the tunnel.

Scarlet and several of the water folk greeted him at the entrance, demanding to know what happened and why Scarlet wouldn't let them go up. He asked them to take a step back into the cavern to avoid being exposed even a little to the open sky.

"Scarlet? Did you let anyone else know what's happening up there?"

"Only my brothers. I did not want to cause a panic."

"Okay, listen up, everyone. I've got some bad news. It looks like the cities took much more of an interest in our destroying their drop ships than I'd expected. We knew they'd send a response team, but what we didn't account for was an entire city showing up in the sky."

Jared heard gasps and shocked cries in response to his words. "There's no need to panic and freak out just yet. As far as we can tell, they don't know we're here and I intend to keep it that way. I've already set a few things in motion to learn more about them, but for now I ask that everyone remain down here."

A few people nodded their heads in agreement, needing no further encouragement to stay out of the crosshairs of those above.

"Now, I brought a bunch of shovels because I want us to start excavating the dead end down that branch of the tunnel." Jared pointed to the dark opening through which the stream flowed. "The water has to go somewhere. Whether that is straight down, or even winding back on itself I've no idea. However, the city is too close for us to try evacuating above ground. Until we learn more about their ability to detect things below, we need to exercise extreme caution.

"The other tunnel"—Jared pointed to the other side of the room—"heads right back toward the lake and the floating city. We don't want to go that way, so that tunnel is now off limits altogether. The other tunnel might lead somewhere if we can dig through. I'll need everyone's help to get this done."

Jared passed out the shovels to the group. Unfortunately, they only had a few, but it would allow them to work in shifts so they had fresh bodies on the task. He wracked his brain trying to remember if they had any pickaxes they could use for taking out the rock. A mental inventory appeared in his mind of the closet where they kept the tools and he found a few of them leaning against the back wall.

"I'll go grab more tools and anyone left up in their rooms. I want all hands on deck for this. It's going to be grueling work, but the sooner we have a viable escape from the area, the better. If you break through to the other side and I'm not here, please do not explore without me. If you have a gun, step forward and guard the entrance until I've returned."

After he'd gathered everyone, he staged them at the base of the cliff and sent them one at a time down into the tunnel, making sure they took the same route he had for minimal visibility of anything above.

Finally, everyone finished the trek and Jared followed. Passing out the pickaxes, Jared kept one for himself. Those already working had made very little progress. They'd dug a little out from under the rock blocking their way, but it only served to increase the width of the stream. If they couldn't break down the rock, or if they found nothing beyond, then digging down was also an option. The water had to go somewhere, after all.

"All right, everyone gather round." Jared waited until every last person surrounded him, Scarlet and her brothers included.

"I'll take the first crack at bringing down that rock blocking the path. While I'm working in there, I want everyone to stay out here. If the wall comes down, I'll launch myself out of the way. We'll need to haul the debris away, but thankfully we only need to get it to the entrance and Scarlet and her family can handle the rest. When I need to take a break, only two others should be in the room at a time. One with a shovel and the other with a pickaxe. Everyone understand?"

Heads nodded in agreement. Satisfied, he gripped the digging tool tighter and walked to the wall. His enhanced strength should allow him to make better progress than any of the others, but then he'd never used a tool like this to dig rocks. He'd seen others use them growing up, but he'd never had a reason to join them since he'd had a different job assignment. Shrugging, Jared took up a stance just to the side and swung it like a baseball bat.

The metal head clanged off the rock and a shower of sparks briefly lit the space. The head of the pickaxe rebounded so forcefully, he had to step back to avoid getting hit by the other side.

Okay, power swings are not a good idea.

Jared repositioned himself in front of the rock wall, but this time he tried an overhead swing. Again, the head of the pickaxe clanged off the wall, only this time, it continued straight down to the ground, making him lose his balance and topple toward the wall. He caught himself at the last minute, but he'd almost smashed his head. Embarrassed, Jared glanced back to see everyone looking at him.

"You will figure it out." From her tone, Scarlet was clearly enjoying the show.

"Thanks," Jared replied dryly. *"It's not as easy as it seems."*

It didn't look like any of the other colonists thought it was funny.

They watched with interest as he tried in vain to attack the wall. Shaking his head, Jared set himself again. He tried a cross between a baseball swing and overhead chop this time. Just before he swung down, he noticed a small section of the wall angled out and up. He twisted the axe handle at the last second to align the pick directly at the angled section.

The pickaxe crashed home, sending a resounding crack through the small room. A huge split ran from the impact point, running horizontal to the ground and extending across a four-foot section. He needed to brace his feet to get the pickaxe out of the wedge he'd created. As he worked it out, Jared used his body weight to lever the head of the tool back and forth. Another pop from the rock cracked through the room and the thin line expanded. It wasn't enough to bring it down yet, but a few more hits might do the trick.

The axe freed, Jared took up his stance once more, swinging with everything he had. It was hard to say, but it was possible *Maximum Muscle* activated for a short burst. Regardless, the axe head flew forward blindingly fast and scored a direct hit on the same spot he'd hit before. The rock split, sending an ear-piercing clap through the room.

The impact sent vibrations up and down his arms, and he lost his grip on the handle. It was probably a good thing as the section of wall fell. He dove backward as a massive segment of rock crashed to the ground where he'd stood only a moment earlier.

Already dark in the room, it was hard to see anything on account of the dust and debris in the air. However, a blast of stale, musty air indicated he'd broken through to the other side. Flipping to *Heat Sight*, Jared waited to see if any creatures moved on the other side. The noise was enough to alert anything for miles down the tunnel. No thermal signatures showed up, but a faint scratching sound started up on the other side of the now removed barrier.

"Heads up everyone, something is moving on the other side. Get back and make room for Scarlet at the entrance. I want her ready if she needs to back me up."

Jared made sure everyone stood back and took up a position in front of the tunnel, his phase pistols held at the ready. Still, nothing showed on *Heat Sight*, but the sound grew louder. Hundreds, if not thousands, of light tapping noises bounced around the chamber walls.

Shaking his head, Jared still couldn't see any warm bodies coming their way, but it sounded like they were right on top of them. He switched back to night vision, and his blood curdled.

A swarm of ebony-colored arachnids billowed out of the opening he'd made. Brilliant white hour glasses burned on their bulbous bodies. If they'd had a light source, Jared would likely find the hour glasses were actually red, indicating these were black widows the size of small dogs.

"Spiders!" Jared screamed.

His scream might have been a few octaves too high, but he didn't care, and it warned everyone else what was coming. He hated spiders more than any other creature or insect on the planet. Only centipedes and millipedes came in a close second next to these things. Seeing a horde of them surging at him like this was paralyzing.

"Jared, snap out of it."

Scarlet's words were like a splash of cold water on his face, and he shook off his paralysis, pumping phase rounds into the throng of black, bulbous bodies. It looked like there might have been other types of spiders too, but he couldn't take his eyes off the glowing hour glasses. If doom had a symbol, Jared imagined it looked similar to the design on their bodies.

His phase rounds created swathes of scorched limbs and bodies through the mass, but it barely made a dent. There were too many.

Squeezing the triggers as fast as he could, the rays of death destroyed everything coming at him. It was all he could do to take out those in the front and keep them from gaining ground. It was only a matter of time before they'd get past the phase rounds and continue forward. Jared realized he was wasting precious rounds and stepped back from opening.

"Scarlet?"

She stepped forward and drew in a lungful of air.

"Hold up," Jared said, holding up his hand. "Let's wait until they get closer. It would be nice if you can take out the whole group all at once. If they escape back into the tunnel, it means we'll just need to take them out later. I do not want to face these things in their own lair."

Jared's face was white as a sheet, and his hands shook as he watched hundreds of the spiders racing forward. It took every last ounce of his willpower to keep from sending more phase energy down the tunnel. When it seemed like the spiders would make it past the opening, Scarlet let loose a roar so great, everyone had to shield their ears.

Bright violet flames ripped through the air and into the tunnel filled with spiders. Jared heard sizzling flesh, but thankfully, it wasn't the same sickening pops he'd heard with the lizards and rats. As he watched, the spiders shriveled up and died, going belly up on the ground.

Scarlet's flames scorched everything in the tunnel for a full minute before she stepped back, her sides heaving from the exertion. To be on the safe side, Jared asked her to make room for one of her brothers in case they needed a second round of dragon fire.

The smell of the roasting spiders wasn't actually that bad, but it sent wafts of smoke curling upward. He hoped it wasn't enough to escape above the cavern into the open air, but there was nothing they could do about it. He'd worry about that later if it caused an issue. For now, he wanted to make sure they'd destroyed all the spiders and the only way to do that was to go through the mass of dead bodies to the other side.

Just before he walked through, a smile tugged at the corner of his mouth.

"Kitty? Can you go see if the spiders are dead?"

The big cat padded up to him and looked at him through narrowed eyes.

"Hey, you have camouflage. Just activate before going through, and they won't see you right?"

"It will not work on these spiders. They can see in multiple spectrums at once and sense vibrations."

"Oh…I didn't—"

"I will still investigate." She lifted her head and stalked forward, clearly flaunting her bravado for all to see.

Jared shook his head and laughed. He didn't care in the least if it made him seem like a coward. He hated spiders. There was nothing else to discuss on the matter. If Kitty could make sure they were all dead, then so be it.

Once Kitty disappeared beyond the entrance, Jared switched to telepathy.

"Let me know if you need help."

"I will be fine."

His ability to use telepathy at a distance with anyone really helped. He couldn't do it with Attis yet because the bird still had a primitive mind and needed a lot of enhancements. Kitty had had nearly a decade to develop the capability to speak with Elle. So, while it wasn't as strong as one of the water folk's telepathy, it was enough for Jared to hear her from short distances.

"Jared, you must see this."

12 ARACHNOPHOBIA

"**C**oming."

Well, he'd get there, eventually. He paused at the start of the charred bodies, dreading walking through the sea of curled up arachnids. Resigned to his fate, Jared sucked in a breath and walked into the room. The shriveled bodies crunched underfoot, causing ash to billow around his footfalls. The only saving grace was the complete absence of smell. For whatever reason, the spiders didn't have an odor. If they did, it was so faint it didn't bother him. The cave itself already smelled musty with the water running through it. Even now, the clouds of ash drifted into the water and disappeared downstream. It was a good thing this massacre happened downstream so they still had ready access to fresh drinking water. At least he hoped it was fresh with the rats upstream, but they didn't have time to investigate that anymore.

The fragments of the spiders might not be deadly to consume, but there's no way he'd even wash his clothes in it if he knew there were spider parts all over the place. He'd almost made it to the newly opened passage when a lone, spindly-legged terror dropped from the ceiling on a strand of web as thick as twine directly in front of Jared. He screeched a high-pitched cry and jerked backward. The spider might as well have been dead, as half its body was burned away, but it didn't matter to Jared. His irrational fear of spiders got the better of him and his uncontrolled reaction sent him careening backward to land in a pile of the fried critters.

The ensuing cloud of ash enveloped Jared as he involuntarily sucked in lungsful of the spider remnants. Hacking, Jared launched himself to his feet and doubled over, heaving as his insides performed somersaults. He vomited anything he'd eaten in the last day, and still the ash clung to the inside of his mouth and nose. He couldn't get it out no matter how many times he tried.

Frantic, Jared retreated to the main cavern and plunged his head into the stream, sucking in a mouthful of (hopefully) fresh water. Greedily, Jared drank his fill before standing back up. Vanessa was right by his side and looked like she wanted to comfort him, but kept her distance. Jared looked down at himself and realized that spider parts and ash covered him from head to toe. The only clean portion of his body was his head he'd just dunked under. With no decorum, he dropped the rest of his gear and weapons on the side of the stream and plunged his whole body in, clothes and all. He'd rather have sopping wet clothes than be covered in the nasty bits and pieces.

Satisfied he'd rid his body of as much ichor as possible, Jared reattached his gear and weapons and strode back into the room. The spider that'd given him the near heart-attack was still hanging in place, its remaining limbs opening and closing in death throes. Pulling his phase pistol, Jared squeezed off a round. He watched in satisfaction as the spider disintegrated entirely, leavening nothing but the strand of web hanging from the ceiling.

Jared reached up to touch the strand, curious about its strength and stickiness, but even his curiosity couldn't overcome his fear, and he sidestepped the webbing. Finally, in the clear, Jared ducked through the opening where Kitty waited, only to draw up short, his jaw dropping in shock.

Not a single wall was visible through the dense layers of webs covering the area. The only cleared portion was around the entrance where Scarlet's flames greedily consumed the webs.

"Did you see any more spiders?"

"No."

The single clipped response didn't do much to assuage his fears, so Jared clarified. "How far did you go?"

"Not far."

Annoyed, Jared knew this line of questioning wouldn't work. He looked at Kitty in frustration and swore he saw a smug expression on the cat's face. Narrowing his eyes, he glared at the overgrown pile of fur.

"Kitty."

"I went to the center of this room and discovered nothing. No more spiders, at least."

"Thank you," Jared managed through clenched teeth. Now everyone knew his aversion to the arachnoid family and would no doubt lord it over him for a while. He didn't care. Spiders were nasty things, and whoever created them had a terrible sense of humor.

"I really wish we had a torch right about now. Actually…"

Jared ran back to the other room and asked around until he found a couple extra flashlights. They weren't that strong, but with his night vision they didn't need to be. A little extra light in the room would do wonders to enhance the ambient light and thus his night vision. He set one flashlight near the entrance and walked the other out to the center of the space.

He paused there for a long moment, straining his eyes and ears for any movement at all. If there were other spiders in the area, they

RICHARD HUMMEL

weren't moving. After the ruckus they'd made earlier, it should've
awakened them by now. Still, caution was the way to go here. While
he didn't think any of the spiders could kill him given his nanite
defenses, if he somehow got covered in spiders, he might just have a
heart attack and die anyway.

Satisfied there was nothing about to leap out to get him, he
walked back to the entrance and started along the wall to his right. It
was near impossible to figure out how big the cavern was with all the
webs, so he went back and grabbed the pickaxe to see if he could tear
them down.

Slowly, the wall came into view, and a sight that would haunt
Jared for the rest of his life revealed itself. Row after row of bodies
hung suspended along the perimeter of the wall. There was no
rhyme nor reason to the macabre display of creature and humanoid
bodies decorating the walls. He saw all kinds of rodents, reptiles,
mammals, and human corpses splayed out. Every single body
was just a husk, all the blood drained, their eyes and any soft parts
of their flesh gone. Their flesh was pale gray from the blood loss. It
reminded Jared of mummies. He'd never seen one in person, but
his textbooks showed ancient Egyptian mummies drained of
blood before being wrapped in linen bandages and placed in a
sarcophagus. This entire chamber was one giant tomb.

It wasn't even as though they were all old. Many of the
bodies were still wet as if drained recently. Pools of blood, both
fresh and dried, covered the entire floor, extending out several
feet from the walls. The bodies had large cavities carved out of
their torsos and piles of spider eggs lay inside.

Jared's skin tingled, his heart fluttering with anxiety. Nothing
could have prepared him for this sight. It was worse, so much
worse than the rats' lair where he'd nearly died. Not even the
maggots ripping into his flesh had sickened his as much. His mind
wandered to the humans decorating the walls in the cave.

202

It was impossible to say where they'd come from, but a part of him idly wondered if they'd lived in the rooms above. However, he quickly dismissed that idea since they'd found no evidence someone lived there before. At least, not in recent past. Jared peered into the darkness beyond and wondered if there were more tunnels down the path and that's where these people had come from.

The closer Jared scrutinized the bodies, the more horrific the scene became. From the patterns of the webs around the body, it indicated the cadavers weren't always inanimate on the wall. And if they'd been alive when strung up, it meant they'd had to watch the scene around them as they slowly bled out, feeding the hordes of spiders. Then, they'd watched as the spiders lay clusters of eggs inside those who had died.

An uncontrollable shudder wracked his body, and Jared had to leave the room. He couldn't stomach it. Utterly repulsed by the display, he lost control of his mental and emotional barriers, prompting Scarlet to reach out.

"Jared? What is it?"

He didn't answer. Instead, he stumbled through the room, back to the opening and into the tunnel. The lone strand of web hanging from the ceiling slapped him in the face and stuck to his hair, but he was in such a daze, he didn't so much as flinch. Back in the main cavern once again, Jared sat near the tunnel leading up, needing the small shaft of sunlight to shine against his skin. The tiny amount of heat from the sun's rays did little to lighten his mood, but it helped comfort him against the horrors inside. He sat in place for a long time, unmoving. Scarlet was nearby, providing support as best she could. Vanessa came and sat next to him to offer comfort.

Finally, after nearly an hour the kaleidoscope of images stopped spinning in his mind, and he worked to push them behind barriers. He knew he'd have to see them again, but prepared now, he'd shield off a part of his mind to guard against them. He would need a massive pep talk and lots of psyching up to enter that room again. And he would enter it again. They needed a way out of this cavern that wasn't over land. If it meant going through that room and finding more underground tunnels that led away, then he'd suck it up and do it, but it would take a while for him to recover from the experience.

"**Jared, what did you see inside?**"

Looking up at Scarlet, he pressed his lips into a line. "I promise you, no one will want to see what is inside that room. It's worse than anything I could ever imagine. Worse than anything you have ever seen. Yes, I know you spent a decade under the water." Jared turned to encompass the water folk crowding around, and reached over to grab Vanessa's hand. "I'm certain this is worse. I—" Jared collected himself before proceeding. "I'll clear some of it out and burn the *things* inside, so you don't have to see what's in there. You don't want to know what I saw, and hopefully you'll never find out, but I'll never forget as long as I live."

Vanessa clinched his hand tighter. "You don't have to do it, Jared. We can—"

Jared held up his hand. "No, it has to be me. If there are more of those spiders, they can kill any of you pretty quickly. I think they'd have a hard time doing any permanent damage to me, unless I run into any larger than the ones we saw. My skin is tough, and I have a layer of nanites around my body that will protect me. It scares me to death thinking there could be another horde of those things in there and that I might have to face them again, but it is safer for everyone if I'm the one to do it. I need to get torches and things to use for burning webs and—" Jared caught himself from saying bodies at the last second. "I think a couple will work just fine. Does anyone have something I can use? If the opening was wide enough for Scarlet, I'd ask her to take care of it, but it's going to take a lot more excavation before any of the dragons fit through."

Casey hooked a thumb over his shoulder and responded. "There are old rags in my room. Maybe you can use those and a shovel to fashion a makeshift torch?"

"That'll work for now. Where are they? The rags?"

"In one of the guest room closets on the floor. You should see it easily enough. I've been using them for bandages and saving the actual medical supplies for emergencies."

"Okay, everyone wait here, I'll be right back."

Jared sprinted up the tunnel, darted from tree to tree and then up the cliff face before reaching Casey's room. He found the rags right where Casey said they'd be. He grabbed a handful and then went up to the kitchen and found a couple match boxes.

Just in case he needed them, Jared also stopped in the armory and grabbed a phase rifle with a couple spare battery packs for all his weapons. He really hoped he wouldn't need them, but it was better to err on the side of caution. He made it back to the tunnel and went directly to the entrance of the cobweb filled room before he lost his nerve.

Jared wrapped a stick with the rags, winding it as tightly as possible so it didn't fall off after a small portion burned away. Once finished, he entered the tomb and lit the makeshift torch. He wasn't sure how to eliminate all the webs, only that he must do it.

Moving to the left wall where he'd found the row of empty blood bags, Jared touched the burning torch to the webbing.

He was totally unprepared for what happened next. The web didn't catch fire as he'd thought. It ignited, like a flash grenade. The web literally existed one moment and didn't the next, leaving bright spots in Jared's vision and a small puff of smoke. It evaporated before his eyes.

Jared moved to the opposite wall. Staying as far back from the web as he could, he extended the torch and touched the web. Just like the other side, the web flashed and disappeared. A wave of bright fire washed over the entire wall, carrying it around the entire circumference of the cavern. Where the fire revealed more bodies, the flames attached to the desiccated husks and burned the dried flesh until nothing remained but bone and ash. The large clusters of eggs sizzled and popped with tiny flashes of light.

All it'd taken was a tiny flame to destroy the entire lair. The bodies, save for the bones, burned up completely, leaving nothing but scorch marks. Watching the light show, Jared found several more spiders in the room, but the flame quickly caught them and ended their existence. He hadn't needed to do anything but stand at the entrance and watch the absolute destruction.

The wall of light reached the opposite end of the tunnel and forked. It continued around the perimeter of the room he stood in, but also into another connected room. A second later, the light forked yet again. Finally, it rounded the bend and headed back toward the spot Jared stopped clearing the wall. He realized it wouldn't finish the job in this room because of the areas he'd cleared, but it didn't matter since all he needed to do was walk up to them and touch the burning rags to a single strand of the web or body hanging on the wall.

That's exactly what he did as soon as the light show ended. In only a few minutes, he cleared the whole room, leaving only the blackened bones, ash, and reddish, orange bloodstains behind. Now that the webs no longer hid the walls from view, he got a good idea of the size of this room and found it as large as the one everyone else waited in. He also noticed piles of what looked like junk in sporadic nooks and crevices within the room.

He didn't think any of it would be useful after the fire had raged through the room, but it was worth a check at least.

Jared retrieved the flashlight closet to him and pointed it at the ceiling. He'd cleared the walls, but parts of the ceiling still had webs and he had no desire to have spiders drop on his head. Wadding up more rags, Jared retreated to the edge of the room and lit one, the flames licking around his fingers before he threw it at the ceiling. Another bright flash illuminated the room as the entire ceiling lit up. From the brief flashes of light, he was glad he'd chosen to remove the webs there.

Giant sacks burst open and the flames hungrily devoured thousands of tiny spiders that'd been near hatching. None of them stood a chance. Even the ones that dropped to the floor died in an instant from the flames coving their bodies. More spiders revealed themselves and quickly succumbed to the flames, landing below with their bellies up and legs shriveled in death. These spiders were nearly twice the size of the ones they'd faced in the other room, and he suspected they were the females keeping watch over their babies about to hatch.

Just to be on the safe side, Jared pumped phase rounds into all the large spiders that fell from the ceiling. He didn't want to chance them jumping to their feet and attacking him. Nearly two dozen of these large creatures tumbled from the ceiling. All that remained after Jared finished were a few crunchy legs that disintegrated after the flames stopped.

Still exercising caution, Jared used the flashlight to examine the ceiling as he made his way across the room. There were many holes in the ceiling where the spiders and egg sacks had been and there could be something else hiding up there. Satisfied with his work, but on edge, Jared moved to the first tunnel that branched on his left.

It wasn't the tunnel through which the stream flowed. That was on the right side and likely the one that extended farther and deeper into the earth. He'd tackle that one later and would backtrack to pick up Kitty and Elle before he did.

The left tunnel proved to be much the same as the room he'd just cleared, only a quarter the size. The room and ceiling were clear of webs and there were no holes for stowaways. The only thing left in the room was a large mound of *junk* in the room's center. He didn't know what else to call the pile of things, since the assortment was random and contained everything from articles of clothing to cooking utensils.

Between the piles in the other room and this one, they had a lot of sorting to do. He'd rely on the rest of the water folk to sort through the items, as he had more pressing concerns. They needed a way out of their predicament, so he needed to keep exploring no matter what lay in his path. Jared returned to the other room and looked around at all the bones littering the sides of the walls. It wasn't nearly as bad as it had been, but he still didn't want everyone seeing the bones where they'd fallen. It was obvious from the blood spatters on the walls and large circles of orange and red on the floor what had befallen the owners of the bones.

Jared retrieved a shovel from the passageway connecting both chambers and used it to move all of the bones into a pile in one of the empty alcoves. It would still cause people to shudder, but at least they'd have a harder time figuring out what had actually happened in the room. He'd done all he could to make this easier to stomach and returned to speak with the agitated crowd.

"I finished clearing out the room and another that branches off to the left. I'd like half of you to come with me and sort through some piles of items the spiders collected. Look for anything useful like changes of clothing, any items we can use for a prolonged journey, and weapons. I'll retrieve some of our things from the rooms up above, but we won't be able to take everything with us. It's too risky to have many people moving around up there. Everything we've gathered so far is replaceable. If the city ever moves on, Scarlet and I can come back for anything we leave behind, like the solar panels. While everyone else is sorting through the piles, Elle, myself, and Kitty will follow the stream down the other tunnel. It forks off the next room. I haven't been through it yet, but I don't want to keep going without backup. Kitty's senses are much more attuned to this environment and she can take lead to warn us of anything approaching."

"I want to go."

"Vanessa—"

"If my sister is going into danger, then I'm coming with. I've learned how to shoot well enough and can help cover your back."

Jared knew he wouldn't dissuade her from coming. "All right. Just make sure you stay behind us and keep your weapon at the ready. In fact, I want you to take the phase rifle." Jared slid the weapon off his shoulder and handed it over.

She grabbed the rifle and turned it over in her hands.

He was about to ask her if she'd practiced with it, but stopped himself as he watched her check over the functions and battery charge. She definitely knew how to handle the rifle.

"Everyone ready? I don't care who comes, but only half of you should be in there at a time. Take turns if needed. Anything useful you find, bring it back here and organize your findings." Jared looked around to see everyone nodding their heads. "Okay, let's move."

Kitty took point. Jared followed up with Elle and Vanessa on his heels. Everyone else piled in single file behind them, crunching their way through the dead spiders littering the short tunnel to the other cavern. Disgusted looks marred their faces, but to everyone's credit, they trudged onward.

Once in the other room, everyone looked at the scorched walls and discolored floors. If they had seen what was there before, they would be wearing looks of abject terror and disgust. He'd need to live with the mental images for the rest of his life, but at least he'd spared everyone else. Kitty probably didn't even care about what she'd seen.

"There are two piles in here and one in the other room over there." Jared shone the flashlight into the two alcoves and the adjacent room. "I've thoroughly inspected both rooms and the ceilings and there are no surprises left. Be careful when you go through the piles in case any of the smaller spiders burrowed beneath. If there are, be ready to kill them so no one gets bitten. I don't know if these things are poisonous. My gut says they are, but no need to risk anything."

Those who accompanied him dispersed into three groups to check out the piles. Jared and his crew of three proceeded into the right-hand tunnel. Like the room that branched to the left, this one was clear of webs as well. The initial flame he'd provided was all it took for everything to burn away. This room wasn't one large cavern, but rather a very large tunnel like those he and Scarlet had used beneath the earth when they'd gone to find her family. It was a natural tunnel and easily wide enough to accommodate the dragons. The number of stalactites hanging from the ceiling could be an issue, but it would be easy for the dragons to break them off as they walked.

The width of the stream increased the farther they walked. At its widest point, it was a solid twenty feet across, but still it continued onward. There were no creatures in the immediate area, but Jared toggled his *Heat Vision* just in case. The moment he switched his sight, the world exploded into a dizzying array of colors and shades.

He stumbled, nearly losing his footing and plunging into the stream.

Vanessa reached out a hand to steady him. "Jared? Are you okay?"

"I—" He didn't know the answer to that question. "I don't know. Give me a moment, please."

Jared kneeled and closed his eyes, trying to clear the confusion in his head and the weird vision. When he opened them, he thought he'd lost his mind. The scene around him wasn't the same as when he'd entered the tunnel. His surroundings were as visible down here as if he was standing in full daylight. He could see every spectrum of light at once. *Night Vision* showed him stark contrast between shadow and darker shadow. *Heat Vision* allowed him to see the faint difference in color from the cooler surfaces and the colder water. Somehow, he could see… more.

He didn't know how to describe it other than his vision was bigger.

"Scarlet? I think I got a new ability, unless you can explain how all of my different vision enhancements are active at the same time? I know I've used Magnified Vision and Heat Vision together, but I'm literally using them all right now and it's allowing me to see in the tunnels like its day time down here."

"Your description sounds much like a spider's ability to see. Can you also sense sound?"

"Sense sound? What do you mean?"

"If you received spider senses, then you may feel sounds or vibrations."

"I…no. Nothing like that. How is this ability already active if I got it from the spiders? I didn't sleep, and I felt nothing change."

"Perhaps it is because you already had the physical changes to support the new ability."

"It's really difficult to describe what I'm seeing. I can see with Night Vision and Heat Vision at the same time, but both of those are amplified to the point they merge together to create a perfect view of everything around me. Magnified Vision also seems changed. I don't have to zoom in or out, I

can just…see farther. I can see more? Does that make any sense at all?"

"Some spiders have very wide lenses, which may account for your periphery expanding. When we have time, it will be good to explore the physical changes to see how it works. I am intrigued by this new development."

"Don't spiders usually have poor eyesight? I mean, I know they can distinguish light and dark better than many other animals, but they can't see far. How is it that my vision drastically increased?"

"I can only surmise it is your *Magnified Vision* combined with the others that enables you to preserve your excellent eyesight."

"It's very disorienting. Don't get me wrong, I'm not complaining, it's just a huge change. I don't even need light down here anymore."

"Just do not get careless, Jared."

"I know, I know, I'll still proceed with as much caution, only now I'm not as afraid.

"Jared, is everything okay?" Vanessa kneeled beside him. "You've been quiet for a long time."

"I'm okay. I was just chatting with Scarlet. It looks like I've got a new ability, though I don't know how it works quite yet, or how it manifested without resting for a time. Somehow my eyesight now combines all of my different visions into one. It's allowing me to see with absolute clarity down here as if walking out in the sun."

"You think this is from the spiders?"

"I'm certain it is, but how it happened already is what I don't know."

"If the spiders can do that, perhaps Elle and Carla should try to absorb nanites before we go farther?"

"I hadn't thought of that yet. The change was just so sudden. It's a great idea though. Elle, can you run back and find Carla and Pete? See if you can absorb the nanites in that first tunnel. I'm guessing it happened when I fell back into the pile of burned corpses."

"We have to touch them?"

"Unfortunately, that's the only way to absorb the nanites, unless you want to inhale them like I did, but I really don't recommend that. It was a horrible experience. If you can get away with just touching them, though, it's absolutely worth it. This new vision is amazing."

Jared placed his hand down to get back to his feet, and his world turned upside down once again. Only this time, the senses he experienced were more of an awareness than a new sight. He felt a mass of vibrations through his hand that cascaded into his mind. He knew the exact positions of Vanessa, Elle, and Kitty as they shifted from foot to foot right next to him. The stream burbled its way through the tunnel beside him. Even the distant footfalls of those in the other room vibrated up through his arm. Somewhere ahead of him, the patter of small feet roamed around.

He couldn't say how he knew all this, only that the information fed directly into his mind. It was like a new sense coming online for the first time. It wasn't like the usual sense of touch in which he could feel an external sensation like wind or another person. This extended his ability to sense around him. Jared closed his eyes, digesting everything. Activating *Clear Mind* and *Hyper-Cognition*, he used the momentary pause in time to ferret out everything the vibrations told him. In just a few seconds, he made sense of it all, and understood what Scarlet had meant when she'd asked if he felt anything.

Deactivating the increased thought speed, he kept his mental focus engaged. There were so many new sensations he dedicated all his processing power to understand them.

Vanessa jerked into action to help him, but he held up a hand to stop her.

"I'm fine. Another side-effect of the spiders' nanites. I can sense vibrations and understand their source from a long distance away." Without opening his eyes, Jared showed them. "Vanessa, you're standing two paces to my right and shifting back on your left foot. Elle, you are five paces behind me and petting Kitty on the side. Kitty, I can't really sense much of anything from you, but just a minute ago your claw scraped against the floor."

"I go get them." Elle's voice cracked, an edge of excitement creeping into her tone.

Jared smiled. "We'll wait for you here. Also, ask Carla if she wants to come. I don't think she will since Attis is already so far from her, but ask anyway. You two likely won't get the ability to see and feel like this right away. At least, I don't think so. It's possible, but I think the only reason my changes took place so quickly was that the physical changes required to make it happen were already present in my body. For you, there are many changes that need to happen with your eyes. I'm not even sure if you'll get the same clarity as me because I've got a few other enhancements you don't. Still, I'm curious to see what will happen."

"I be right back."

Kitty mewled and Jared walked over to lay a reassuring hand on his side. "Don't worry, Kitty, Elle will be safe. I can sense everyone in the other room moving around and everything in between. I found nothing that should concern us. There are a few creatures ahead on our path, but the vibrations were too faint for me to get an idea of what they are. I don't even know how my mind processed the vibrations, but somehow I knew."

"It is interesting. It may be better than my sight."

"We'll test it out, but let's wait until we are in a safer environment. I wouldn't doubt if you have the ability too after you rest. You walked right through the dead spiders and absorbed some of the nanites as well."

Jared closed his eyes, examining the newly acquired ability and calling out to Scarlet. *"You were right. I got spider senses. I can feel vibrations when I place my hand on the ground. It paints a picture in my head of things around me. It's not completely clear, but it's enough to extend my awareness outward."*

"That is intriguing. I wonder if it works the same for spiders. Though, I do not know if that is possible since you do not have hair on your hands for the vibrations to pass through."

"I don't know. Maybe it's just that my brain can interpret the sensations I've felt all along?"

"We must explore this new ability when we are out of danger."

"We will! I want to explore everything right now, but obviously we need to find safe passage first. Maybe there's even more I can do now that hasn't revealed itself yet."

Elle arrived with Carla. Both had bits of spiders and ash covering their clothes, but they didn't seem nearly as bothered by it as him. For a moment, he felt embarrassed at his reaction, but only a moment. Then he realized his irrational fear of spiders was perfectly acceptable.

"I wish I had a companion." Vanessa looked dejected and left out.

"Malsour?"

"I don't know yet. We had a nice chat after you left, but we've only just gotten to know one another."

"I understand," Jared reassured her and squeezed her shoulder. "Take as long as you need. This is a lifetime decision, and you need to be certain it's the right move. Obviously, I didn't have that option, but I don't regret my decision in the least. Honestly, I think anyone who bonds with a dragon will enjoy the relationship. Though I've not met any disgruntled dragons yet, if someone rushed and made an unfavorable bond, it could be a very long lifetime."

Jared started down the tunnel, reaching out to Scarlet.

"Can you please tell Pete to bring some of the spider remains out after

he's finished? It would be good for you and Kirgor to gain these abilities too."

"I have already directed him to do so."

"Thanks. I think the experience with the spiders and the new ability took over my mind, and I wasn't thinking clearly."

Scarlet didn't reply but sent a wave of encouragement to him through the bond. It helped Jared's mood, and he resumed walking up the tunnel with Vanessa by his side.

13 ON THE RUN

The tunnel grew as they continued. It was difficult to say for certain, but Jared thought it sloped ever so slightly downward. It wasn't significant, and he didn't think there'd be any issue with temperatures. While they walked, the occasional creature scurried out of the way, but nothing dared approach them. Jared wondered if it was Kitty's presence that kept them at bay. None of the creatures posed a threat to them, so he left them alone.

The stream eventually cleared up and the evidence of the spider massacre in the other room disappeared with the current. There was no way Jared would drink it, though.

"Carla? Elle? It looks like the stream is clear of spider bits now if you want to clean up?"

Elle looked at him funny and then down at herself before frowning. Carla went to the water's edge and kneeled down to scrub at her exposed flesh.

"I see nothing in the water, but just because I can't see it doesn't mean there's nothing there. Be careful, please. If they are cold-blooded, or can hide their body heat, I wouldn't see them until they broke the surface—"

Jared realized that wasn't exactly true anymore. With his new ability he could sense vibrations. He kneeled next to the water and placed a hand on the ground. A minute later, he stood back up and announced the water in the immediate area clear of any creatures.

"I've got to say, these new abilities are awesome! I really hope you all get the same enhancements. It's really something else to see a picture of the surrounding area without using my eyes." Carla and Elle both looked excited at the prospect and quickly finished cleaning themselves.

An hour into their journey, Jared called a halt to figure out how far they'd traveled. It was possible they were already far enough from the city that they could find a way to the surface from here.

Jared activated *Clear Mind* so he could keep an eye on his surroundings while he worked out where they were in relation to the surface. Pulling up a mental map of the topography above, Jared layered the tunnel and caverns onto the image. The first chamber the dragons had discovered was almost directly under the cliff where they'd made their homes. The tunnel he'd explored with Kitty and found a few rats ran east back toward the ruined city at the tip of the lake. The city floated almost exactly due north of their position. Going east wouldn't help since it would lead out of the forest and into the open terrain by the water. West was their only option.

Next, Jared calculated the distance they'd traveled, along with any deviations they'd made to the north and south. It looked like the underground stream followed the same contours as the one above ground, except the one on the surface had dried out long ago. Jared supposed it hadn't dried out, it had simply moved underground. They'd traveled about six miles in the hour they'd hiked. It was a testament to how much Vanessa and Carla had regained their strength—a few months earlier, it would have taken them several hours to walk that far.

Jared thought they were almost far enough to risk going to the surface. Once surfaced, they'd continue southwest until the city was well and truly out of range. The cities—or, at least, this one—could move overland as evidenced above, but for whatever reason they preferred to stay over the water. If Jared could get everyone far enough inland, they might not have to worry about the cities.

"I think we need to keep going. We're almost at a good point to exit to the surface, but it's still too close for my comfort. It will be easy for all of us to enter these tunnels, but the dragons won't fit until they get past the other passages. I fear when they make the hole, it will send smoke into the sky and attract unwanted attention. I want everyone else to be as far from the old place as possible before they attempt it. The dragons can run fast enough to get away if they don't need to worry about us. We'll explore for another hour and then head back. After we're certain this passage is safe, we'll go back and pack things up to make the trip."

"We should wait until tomorrow to make the journey."

Jared agreed with Vanessa. "Today has been trying enough, and it'll take several trips up to our rooms for supplies and weapons. That may take me the rest of the night."

"We help."

Jared opened his mouth to reject the offer but stopped himself. Elle and Kitty were probably better suited to making the trips than he was.

"Thanks, Elle. I'll come up with a list of things for you and Kitty to get. It will make the work go faster but I agree with Vanessa. We should wait until tomorrow. Let everyone get a good night's sleep, if they can with that thing floating in the sky, and we'll set out as soon as everyone wakes."

Another hour of walking revealed more of the same. They should be on the other side of the forest and far enough to avoid detection from the cities. There was no obvious exit above, but they could have Scarlet burn a hole to the surface if needed.

The two hours back proved unexciting. They remained silent, their senses alert for anything that might've crept in behind them. Aside from the few small rodents and insects as before, nothing showed itself. The spiders' chamber looked much the same, minus the junk scattered everywhere. None of the water folk were in the room, and Jared guessed they'd finished with the task.

Sure enough, they'd split the items into neat piles by type in the main chamber. They sorted all the clothing, belts, and packs into one pile. A small number of ancient weapons went into another, and any useful utensils sat in the third. The clothing looked like rags, but beggars couldn't be choosers, and they were definitely beggars in that regard. Thankfully, many of the water folk had salvaged some of their old clothes from homes back at their colony before everything went down with the cities.

The weapons were mostly useless. The guns all bore rust, and there was no way Jared would trust a single one with a live round. The knives and machetes they kept, but discarded the rest of the useless weapons. Most of the camping gear was good, and packed neatly into bags. Whomever it belonged to had likely been traveling when they'd ended up as blood bags for the spiders.

"Okay, I think this is a good haul. We weren't expecting anything, so to find something worth saving is a definite plus. I'll take Elle and Kitty above and gather stuff from our rooms. My priority will be boosters, weapons, and medical supplies. Please get with Vanessa and Carla and make a list of other supplies you absolutely must have. We won't have the cart this time so anything that can stay behind, should stay. If we're able to come back later, we can grab more, but assume we'll never return."

Groans echoed around the chamber, but Jared shrugged them off. Everyone's lives were much more important than goods they could scavenge again. The main thing he hated losing were the solar panels. They could probably find more, and Pete might understand them enough now to fashion his own, but it was still a loss that would bite. If only he and Kirgor had bonded before the cities had arrived, they might've been able to understand them sufficiently to replicate them. Though, Pete might already have that knowledge in his head and Kirgor could help him put the pieces together.

Everyone closed around Vanessa and made their demands. Jared was halfway up the tunnel before he heard her call out for everyone to shut up. He smirked, knowing Vanessa would get them in order quickly. She had a lot of compassion and cared a lot for her people, but she could lay the hammer down if needed.

"Elle, I'm going for the boosters first. I'd like you to come with and get as many of the medical supplies as possible. There should be bags in there you can use to hang on Kitty to help carry them. Once we've got the medical supplies secured below, we'll hit the armory. It'll probably take us a couple trips. After we've secured all of those, we'll head up to the dining hall and get as much of the dried and treated meat as possible. Finally, we'll take requests from the others, but we shouldn't make those a priority."

Just as he'd suspected, it took many trips to get the essentials lugged down. Between having to dart around avoiding sight from the city, and carrying the heavy equipment, it was slow going. When they'd finished with the essentials and food, Vanessa had a list for them. By list, it was just all the water folk lined up in an orderly fashion with requests for him.

Vanessa arranged it so everyone stood in order by room from top to bottom.

Jared appreciated the organization and heard everyone's requests. A few he dismissed immediately. They didn't need to bring extra shoes or bottled water. Sure, they'd be nice to have, but shoes were bulky, and everyone needed to carry only their essentials and keep their packs light. Though it hadn't been thoroughly vetted, they also had a fresh supply of ready drinking water, and carrying any extra was a burden they didn't need. Even if there were impurities, the nanites in their bodies would purge any bacteria. Instead, each person brought an empty water sack they could fill if the stream ended.

He limited everyone to two changes of clothes, small bars of soap, and a smattering of smaller toiletries. Everyone had their own packs in their rooms, so it was easy enough to keep everything sorted for each of them. They took another hour to gather all the belongings.

Once finished, Jared passed out all the weapons and ammo. He also added a lot of the extra ammo and batteries to a large sack which he would sling around Scarlet's neck. The extra weight would encumber the group too much. Everything sorted and ready to go, Jared lay down just to the side of the tunnel leading up. He wanted to be the first line of defense should anything try to breach the chamber. They'd been careful when moving around on the surface, but the city could've seen something and sent someone, or something, to investigate.

The night passed slowly, and waiting for trouble that never came kept Jared's sleep restless. He spent most of the night in meditation and exercised his mental abilities. It allowed him to rest but remain alert. If he grew tired during the day, he'd set his nanites to *Regeneration* to get rid of his fatigue. It wasn't a solution to help a tired mind, but it was enough for his body. He probably could've used the time to explore his new abilities, but he didn't want to distract himself too much in their current situation and opted to wait until they were safely away.

The moment the first rays of light lit up the tunnel, Jared issued a wake-up call to get everyone up and moving. He followed suit and quickly had everything strapped to his body.

"Carla," Jared called her over. "Can you please instruct Attis to fly west? If you can, try to have him fly to the end of the dried river above. That's where we'll meet him. It'll take us a while to get there, but it's best if he waits it out over there instead of us having to backtrack and find him later."

A frightened look entered her eyes as she no doubt thought about Attis out there on his own with the city in such proximity.

"O-okay, I—"

"Carla, it will be okay. Attis can take care of himself. He's lived on his own for years before this and he's only grown smarter since you bonded."

"I know, I just—" An involuntary shudder wracked her body.

Overhearing the conversation, Vanessa came over and wrapped Carla in a hug. "It'll be fine, Carla. Attis is a big boy. He'll make it. Have faith in him."

Carla melted into Vanessa's arms, needing that momentary physical comfort. Vanessa's words gave Carla the encouragement she needed.

"I need to touch Attis to give him instructions. I don't think our telepathy is good enough to explain what to do."

Jared eyed the tunnel warily. "Okay, but stay behind me and when we get close, see if you can call Attis down. Ideally, I'd like him to meet us at the top of this tunnel, so we don't have to expose ourselves at all. I know he won't enter it completely, but do your best to get him close."

They reached the top and crouched in place as Carla called out to Attis. It didn't take long before the giant griffon landed a few paces away. Careful to ensure they stayed concealed, Jared craned his head around the lip to see where the city was and realized the cliff mostly shielded them from this position.

"You're good, Carla. Show him where to meet us."

A few moments later, she nodded her head. Attis took to the air while they rejoined everyone below.

"Scarlet." Jared laid a hand on her head, pushing his love and affection along their connection. He looked into her burning, molten eyes. "I need you to wait at least three hours before you come after us." He paused, collecting his thoughts. "I don't want you to, but I need you to wait. When you clear the tunnel, it might generate enough smoke to draw attention and you all need to move fast without us in the way."

"I understand."

"We won't be able to communicate at that distance."

"Jared, we will make it. Down here, there is nothing the cities can do to harm us. If they sent people or robots to kill us, they would not stand a chance."

"We've no idea what they are capable of. We already underestimated one of their people and he almost—"

"To get down here, they must take the tunnel. We will not risk a confrontation and will take them out before they ever get close enough to use a weapon."

"All right. I know you can handle it, but I'm still worried. You can't just fly out of here if you get in trouble."

"We will get away from here and move far from any city's influence. Then we will have our freedom."

"It's a two hour hike to the place we stopped yesterday if we hurry. If you wait at least three, that will give us enough time to get there in the event we encounter any trouble. If I can find a way topside for everyone before you get there, I'll take it."

Touching as they were, he didn't need to search hard to get a lock on Scarlet's feelings. She put on a good front, but fear bubbled beneath the surface, and she understood the danger. Jared's heart clenched. There was nothing he could do differently that would keep her safer. This plan would work. It had to work.

"If there's anything you can do to delay the cities finding us, please do so."

"We will collapse tunnels as we go. Now get going." Scarlet nudged Jared away with her head.

Jared slung the extra bag of weapons and batteries over Scarlet's back, making sure to secure it firmly so it didn't impede her running. After he'd finished, he turned back to the waiting group.

"Everyone ready?" A chorus of voices affirmed their readiness, and Jared led them into the tunnel. "Kitty and Elle, please take point. Oh, wait…Elle, Carla, have you checked to see if you got the new ability?"

Several people around them looked on curiously, wondering what he was talking about. Not wanting to spend the time to explain, Jared ignored the few questions directed his way.

"I not try yet." Elle shook her head.

"Same, I haven't tried," echoed Carla.

"Okay, please give it a shot before we get moving. It may take time to get used to it, but it'll be invaluable on this trip."

"How use it?"

Jared looked at Elle, trying to figure out the best way to instruct them. Rather than wax eloquent, he kept it basic.

"When I got my other visions, I only had to think about an ability to let me see farther or see the heat spectrum and it activated. To turn it off, just think about turning it off."

"Whoa." Carla stumbled back a step.

"Wow! I see everything!" Elle danced around happily. "Kitty, I see like you!"

Jared chuckled at her childish delight. Though already a teenager, she often acted many years younger. She'd had to grow up much too fast, and he found it enjoyable to watch her act like this.

"Take a few minutes to get used to seeing like this. It's disorienting at first. Once you're confident in the ability, I want you to place your hand on the ground and try to understand the impressions you're getting from vibrations."

Fifteen minutes later they were ready to move. Both of the girls darted their eyes around like they were seeing the world for the first time. Jared supposed that was truer for Carla since she'd had terrible eyesight before. Elle hadn't experienced the same debilitating condition, but even so she usually relied on Kitty to navigate through dark places. Jared would need to check with Carla later to see if the new ability helped her see farther, or just see more.

One of the water folk shined their flashlight at them, and Jared did a double-take. Their eyes flashed a bright green when the light passed over them.

Another side-effect of the changes?

It looked creepy cool. Creepy like something possessed them, but cool because they were like spotlights in the dark. Obviously, Jared couldn't see his own eyes, but no doubt his mirrored theirs. Whatever spider netted him the ability to see like this and transform his eyes was handy. Maybe once he'd sat with Scarlet long enough, she could help him root around in his memories for something he'd learned in school. He'd tuned out any mention of spiders in his education and without spending time to drill into his memories, he couldn't recall much about them.

"Elle? Carla? Are you both ready?"

"I'm ready. It's incredible. I know exactly how many of us there are. I can even feel the dragons in the other room, the dripping of water on the ground, and the way the water moves across the bottom of the stream. It's beautiful."

"I see and feel too." Elle nodded, confirming Carla's description.

"All right, let's move. Formation remains the same. Elle, you take point with Kitty. Carla, you and I will take the rear. Keep your new vision ability active at all times. I'll stop occasionally to feel the ground and see if there's anything we can't see."

Jared turned to the rest of the group and raised his voice. "Everyone else, please stay together. If you need to rest, you can drop back with me and let me know. Otherwise, I expect everyone to keep up with Elle. Elle, please set a decent pace. We need to at least reach the spot we stopped at yesterday in two hours, which means we've got to move. Let's go."

The hike was entirely uneventful. Boring, even. Jared had already seen everything there was to see the first time. The occasional stops to check any vibrations from other creatures revealed much the same. There were a few more small creatures that seemed curious about their party, but nothing that could cause them harm. Jared suspected the spiders had scared away or killed anything worth killing long ago. It was impossible to tell how far they'd ranged from their den.

A little over two hours later, they arrived at the same location as the day before. Jared guessed they had about forty minutes before Scarlet and her brothers cleared the tunnel.

"Vanessa, I want you to wait here with Carla and the others. Elle, Kitty, and I will head farther down to see if we can find a way out. We'll head that way for another twenty minutes and then double back. If you see anything, or something comes at you, scream out with your thoughts. I should be able to hear you as long as we don't go too far."

"Okay, be safe."

"We will." Jared gave her a quick peck on the cheek, which brought a slight blush to her face. "We'll be back. Rest and be ready to move quickly."

Jared set out down the tunnel, taking point while Kitty took the rear.

The walk revealed no further signs of life or an exit to the surface. They were already beyond the edge of the forest. The entire journey was at a slight decline, and Jared believed they were a good distance beneath the surface.

"Let's head back. It doesn't look like there's anything down here. We may as well just have Scarlet and the others drill a hole to the surface from the last stopping point."

They were nearly back to the group when Jared heard a distant roar echoing down the tunnel. It sounded very far away, and Jared guessed it was the dragons making their way toward them. The sound cut off, but a moment later a cacophony of enraged snarls sounded down the tunnel.

"Something's wrong." Jared's heart thudded in his chest. The dragons were in trouble. Scarlet needed him. "Get on Kitty's back. We've got to move!"

Jared tore off down the tunnel, quickly overtaking the group he'd left. They were all standing, looking back the way they'd come. The growling and roars grew louder followed by massive crashes that sent vibrations up his legs. The intense nature of them allowed a picture to form in his mind of the dragons rampaging down the tunnel while the ceiling collapsed.

"No!"

Jared increased his speed, literally flying over the ground, but the next sound brought him to a halt. An explosion followed by a massive shifting of the earth that sent a wave of nausea through him.

Oh no.

The image that came to his mind petrified him.

"Run," Jared whispered. Then louder, he shouted, "Run!"

He sprinted back the other way, yelling at everyone to get moving.

"Kitty, get in front. Don't stop, just keep running. I don't care if there's something in the way, just keep going, we'll take it out along the way."

The crashing grew louder and louder. The ground bucked beneath him as the dragons came at them like an avalanche. Jared herded everyone forward as fast as they could move. It wasn't even half as fast as he wanted them to go, but there was nothing he could do about it.

Soon the sound echoed so loudly Jared thought they'd get trampled at any moment, but when he glanced over his shoulder, he still couldn't see Scarlet. However, a distant point of light announced the dragons' arrival as they used flames to take out the various stalactites hanging from the ceiling.

"Jared, they're coming," Scarlet finally reached out.

"I know, I saw."

"How did you—"

"My new senses. Everyone needs to move faster, but I don't think I can push them any harder."

"I think—" Scarlet paused, the feelings across their bond one of contemplation. **"I think it will be okay. We are far enough below the surface that their phase rounds can no longer penetrate."**

Jared sighed in relief. The images he'd gotten from the vibrations showed massive impacts from above, punching right through the rock and earth into the tunnel below and sending tons of rock and debris down around the dragons.

"Did everyone make it?"

"Yes, but Ballog took a phase cannon round to his back. He will heal, but his wings need time before he can fly. Wherever we are going, I hope this tunnel continues for a while or we may be in trouble when they find a way down here."

"Kitty is out front. I told her not to stop for anything."

"We will take point, but please have everyone stand to the side as we pass. Keep everyone moving and we will make sure the path is clear."

"Everyone listen up!" Jared shouted. "Scarlet and her brothers are about to come running past us. Take cover along the wall and do your best to stay out of the way."

"Kitty! Move to the side of the tunnel. Scarlet and her brothers are about to run past."

The stampeding dragons rocketed down the tunnel so fast they were a blur. In only a few moments they whipped past everyone with a wave of heat that burned Jared's exposed skin. Even an injured Ballog moved so fast it was difficult to track him.

Everyone watched in awe as the dragons were literally there one second and gone the next. The only evidence of their passing, the fallen rock formations and displaced water from the stream. Looking in the direction they traveled, Jared saw brief flashes of light down the tunnel as they cleared any obstacles in their path.

A few moments later, Kitty rejoined them, and they set out after the dragons. The sounds of the explosions from the drop ships diminished slightly, but he could tell the occasional round still peppered the area as they searched for the tunnel and whatever was inside. He doubted they knew it was dragons, but there's no doubt in his mind they knew whatever was down here was likely part of the threat posed to the city.

"Carla, make sure you're trying to reach out to Attis constantly. He'll be waiting for us around here, but we must keep going down the tunnel. Let him know to keep heading west. If he can't hear you, we'll double back for him after we're certain it's safe to do so."

"Okay." Carla sounded distraught, and Jared didn't blame her.

It was clear she was barely holding her emotions in check, and Jared applauded her composure. Given the severity of their threat, she had every right to be an emotional wreck at the thought of losing her companion. It hadn't taken Jared long at all to establish a close, unbreakable bond with Scarlet. Something about the bond drew them closer extremely fast. He'd never had time to reflect on it, but he and Scarlet had fallen into a close relationship almost immediately after their bond. Jared wondered if it had to do with the fact she'd lost her mother so suddenly, but it was impossible to say for sure.

Jared shook his head to clear it. He'd have time to dig into his thoughts at another time. For now, they needed to keep moving. The cities could send robots and probes into the tunnel, and they needed to be far from here when that happened. Somehow they'd followed Jared's path in New York City, so it stood to reason they could also follow them down here. At least in parts where the tunnel hadn't collapsed.

Before they made their escape back up to the surface, he'd ask Scarlet to further collapse the tunnel to prevent anyone from following.

Collecting everyone from where they'd watched the dragons pass, Jared ushered everyone onward. Still, they moved much too slowly, but he'd have to make the best of it. There were no sounds coming from up the tunnel, and the few times he stopped to feel the ground proved nothing followed them, or if they had, they were far behind.

"Carla, were you able to reach Attis?"

"Yes, but I don't know if he understands. I told him to go that way, but…" Carla pointed west and shrugged.

"It's okay. No matter what happens, we'll make sure we find him."

"Thanks."

They hiked for hours, the passage occasionally marked by charred bodies of indistinguishable creatures. True to her word, Scarlet cleared the path. They'd walked for five hours when Jared called everyone to a halt. If the cities were coming, they didn't seem in a hurry, and everyone could use a little rest.

"I'll run ahead for a little ways and see if Scarlet stopped yet. I don't know how far underground we are, but I need to make sure we aren't going too far, or the heat will get unbearable. Everyone else, please wait here."

They plopped to the ground, exhausted. Jared had set a grueling pace for many miles. The upside was the terrain moved downhill. If they'd had to go the other way, there's no way they'd have made it more than a few hours at that pace.

"Elle, Carla, Kitty, please take up positions around the group and keep your senses open for any threats. Everyone else, keep your weapons accessible and ready to use if the time comes. I'll be back in a little while."

With that, Jared sprinted down the tunnel. He would run for a half hour. If he didn't see Scarlet by then, he'd double back and pick up the group to resume their march. Close to the turnaround point he'd set for him, Jared found Ballog waiting around the bend at an intersection. The cavern he sat in was huge and branched in four different directions.

"Ballog! Is everything okay?"

"Yes," Ballog's voice thundered in Jared's head.

Jared winced at the volume and closed his eyes.

"My apologies."

"It's okay. It hurts, but it's not unbearable as it used to be for me."

"I offered to remain behind to show you the way and to cover our tracks. Scarlet mentioned that the people tracking us have a way to follow our path long after we've passed through."

Jared smiled. He should've known Scarlet would think of everything.

"Yes, they use electronic probes that can detect where we've been many days later."

"I will collapse all of these tunnels before we move on. Scarlet went this way."

Ballog raised a clawed hand and pointed.

"All right, I'll run back and collect everyone. It will take us an hour or more to get back here."

"I will remain here and rest."

"Are you sure you're okay? The phase round that penetrated—"

"I will be fine," Ballog cut him off. **"It will heal, given time. It is just slowing me down right now. Offering to stay and wait for you made the most sense."**

"Thanks, Ballog. I'll be back. Take no chances. If you need to leave ahead of us, do it. We can find another way to collapse the tunnel ourselves."

Ballog dipped his head in acknowledgement and Jared set off at a sprint toward the group and found half of them sleeping. He felt bad waking them after the harrowing flight they'd just endured, but the threat wasn't over.

"Get up, please. We've got to move. There's a cavern about another hour's hike away. Ballog is waiting for us. He'll help collapse the tunnels to keep the machines from tracking us. I know you're tired and we'll rest soon, but right now we must go."

Jared's assessment proved accurate as they stumbled into the intersection where Ballog waited an hour later.

"Listen up, everyone. We need to fool the people tracking us. They've a way to follow our tracks, so let's do our best to confuse them." Jared looked around the cavern at the four tunnels splitting off from the main cavern. "It'll take work, but let's move as a group down each of these tunnels. Then, one person at a time will break off and go down the correct tunnel there." He pointed down the tunnel noted by Ballog.

"Just make sure you stick to the same paths that the whole group treads. We need to make this as confusing as possible and make sure the cities spends a lot of time trying to figure out our real path. Ballog, I'll need you to do the same thing."

In the same formation they'd used so far, Kitty and Elle led them through each of the tunnels. They walked a short distance before turning around. They did this to each of the tunnels twice while Vanessa randomly tagged someone to go back to the correct tunnel and wait a short distance away. Ballog followed along in their wake, further confusing their passage.

Satisfied they'd done all they could, Jared instructed the rest of the group to go down the right tunnel and keep walking. He dropped back to speak with Ballog.

"Let's wait until they've gone a short distance before you collapse the tunnels. I don't want the ceiling collapsing too close to them. The same goes for you. Please take no chances. If we end up having to dig you out, we may not make it in time before someone from the city catches up to us."

"I do not take risks."

"Good, let's get started. I'll wait for you over at the mouth of the other tunnel. If you can make it look like you collapsed all these tunnels from the inside that would be great. I'm not sure how you'll do it, but it would further confuse our pursuers."

Ballog tromped over to the first tunnel and walked inside. He made a series of deep cuts in the wall, then blew flame into the gashes to melt away the rock. A crack resounded through the room, and Ballog quickly left the tunnel. A few more quick slashes from his claws and a spiderweb of cracks appeared. Backing up a few paces—which, for a dragon, was more like halfway across the room—he waited for the ceiling to collapse under its own weight.

It took a few minutes, but finally the fissures in the rock spread enough that a giant crack opened horizontal to the ground and the ceiling smashed into the floor hard enough to make Jared stumble from the impact. Ballog repeated the process three more times. On the last one, he reversed the process, making the cuts on the outside first and then repeated inside the tunnel.

Finished, they found the group a short while later. Thankfully, they hadn't stopped after taking the branching tunnel. This one traveled directly south, and it was the same one Jared would've chosen. It might be the logical choice for the cities to inspect first, but at least they'd done all they could to confuse and disorient their pursuers.

"Let's walk another couple of miles before stopping for the night."

No one responded, but they trudged along as fast as they could.

Finally, Jared called a halt and people slumped over, completely exhausted. It'd been nearly ten hours, and it was already late evening if his internal clock was accurate. They needed rest, and Jared used the opportunity to distribute a ration of dried meat to everyone present to help recover their energy levels faster.

"We'll stop for six hours, but then we've got to keep moving."

Everyone set up what little bedding they had and curled up to sleep. They bunched together, using each other to stay warm.

"Ballog, can you talk to Scarlet from here?"

"I can."

"How much farther are they? Is she okay? Are there other creatures to worry about?"

Ballog chuckled, the sound like that of boulders rubbing together. **"There were minor creatures along the way, but nothing she could not handle. They are nearly a day's journey from you at your previous pace. They stopped in a large cavern that should accommodate everyone until she finds a way to the surface."**

"Please let Scarlet know we'll get there as quickly as we can."

His tasks finished, Jared found a place next to Vanessa to lie down and fell asleep almost instantly.

14 HARROWING JOURNEY

The next morning, Jared woke refreshed. Though he'd only slept five hours, the nanites allowed him to recover and feel energized to tackle the next leg of their journey. Unfortunately, not everyone else felt that way. More than half of the water folk struggled to wake from their slumber. It was a slow process as their brains and then their bodies kicked into gear. Groans and exhalations sounded throughout the room. Jared always found that the best cure for sore muscles was to exercise them.

Grinning mischievously, Jared rounded everyone up. Several he roused from a deep slumber. For some reason, he thoroughly enjoyed jostling everyone awake, which was unlike him. He had no idea what had come over him, but decided to ride the high while it lasted.

An eternity later, at least in Jared's mind, everyone was ready, and they set out. Ballog took up the rear. Jared roamed up front with Kitty and Elle. It was much better to be up front and it allowed him to set the pace. It was probably more intense than anyone would have liked, but everyone pushed themselves and kept pace. He didn't need to remind everyone that the city's minions could show up at any time. They only needed to look behind them to see Ballog limping along to understand they couldn't allow that to happen. They walked through the morning, spurred on by the urgent need to put distance between them and the city. Around noon, Jared found a place where everyone could sit on some boulders comfortably and Marie passed out rations for everyone.

It wasn't much, but it would help everyone keep their strength up instead of just relying on the nanites to nourish their bodies. The radiation likely wasn't strong enough in the tunnels to sustain them at such a rapid pace, so everyone ate something to keep them energized.

Jared allowed a thirty-minute break before he waved the group into motion again. Several people threw irritated glances his way, but no one spoke out against the pace he'd set. Difficult as it was, everyone knew the severity of their situation.

They walked all day until Ballog informed Jared that he could reach out to Scarlet now.

"Scarlet?"

"Jared!" Scarlet's voice sounded relieved and weary.

"We're almost there. How does the area look up there? Have you found a way to the surface yet?"

"No, we will probably need to create our own exit. I believe we should wait a day before doing so. This tunnel took us very far from the floating city, but because the city floats so high, they may have a way to see this distance and no doubt they will look somewhere along the route we traversed. My hope is they explore south first. We went nearly twenty-five miles from that intersecting cavern where Ballog waited for you."

"Wow, was it really that far? No wonder people gave me evil looks. They've recovered a lot since the lake, but still have much further to go to

rebuild all their lost strength. Frankly, I'm surprised we made the trip so fast."

"How is Ballog?"

"As far as I can tell, he is doing great, though he's not very talkative."

Scarlet ignored his comment and continued. "I hope he heals quickly. That phase round punched right through his scales into his back, just behind his right wing. These rounds were so much more powerful than the phase pistols and rifles."

"It's probably one of the phase cannons we stripped off the ships. Who knows how much more powerful they are, but if a single round could do so much damage after passing through tons of debris, that doesn't bode well for us."

"I believe it was a direct hit. They sent a volley of rounds into the ground. The first few disintegrated the earth, and the last punched through. I agree though, a single round could cripple one of my brothers until they can use nanites to harden their skin and scales."

"Did this experience change any of your brothers' minds?"

"It may yet, but it is too early to tell. I will say this senseless act of violence at every turn from the city has renewed our hatred for some of humanity."

"You aren't alone there. I think all of us feel the same way. Unfortunately, we can't do anything about it in our current state. We also don't have enough people and companions to mount an assault and may end up looking outside our small colony for more allies. Only I've no idea where to find them."

Jared's mind briefly strayed to thoughts of Loch and Iliana. If they were still a part of the Daggers, he'd never consider working with them, but if they'd learned from their ways and gone elsewhere, then maybe they'd run into each other again someday and they could help.

"We must get everyone bonded and strengthened as soon as possible. This recent attack makes it even more obvious. Perhaps if everyone were stronger, we wouldn't need to run."

"I don't know. In either case, I think we'd run until we know what the cities are capable of throwing at us. However, I agree about getting everyone bonded and strengthened as soon as possible. In fact, once we stop for the night, we should see if anyone is ready."

"Agreed. This place we stopped—I think you will enjoy it."

"Even if I do, it's not like we can stay this close."

"Perhaps, though once you see it, you may change your mind."

"We're almost there."

Picking up his pace, he heard a few groans behind him and slowed back down.

What was it that has Scarlet so intrigued? Maybe some place like the homes we made in the cliff?

"Everything okay?"

Startled, he turned to see Vanessa looking at him quizzically.

"You sighed?"

"Oh, you heard that." Jared looked away, slightly embarrassed by his callous thoughts. "Yeah, sorry. I was just talking with Scarlet. She said the place up ahead is cool. I thought about rushing ahead to check it out, but I don't want to leave everyone."

"If you want—"

"No, no, it's okay. A few extra minutes won't kill me. There's no danger ahead, so there's no reason for me to do it. It's just impatience on my part. I know everyone is still not as strong as they will be, and our pace is slower than I'd like."

"Look on the bright side; you get to spend more time with me." She sauntered up to his side and leaned into him.

His impatience vanished. He wrapped an arm around her and pulled her close, enjoying their closeness. Little moments like this sent butterflies flitting through his stomach. Every time their fingers and lips brushed each other, little tingles of pleasure spread out from the contact. There wasn't much to look forward to in this world, but Vanessa was a bright shining star to him. She and Scarlet expanded his world and kept him from sinking back into despair. If something ever happened to them, Jared didn't know if he'd be able to handle it. Losing his parents had stolen a part of him that he'd never recover. If the same happened to his new family, there might not be anything left of him. He shuddered with the thoughts and forced himself to abandon them.

Arm in arm, they walked the remaining distance until a massive cavern opened before them. Massive was truly an understatement. This place was gigantic, and he was woefully unprepared for the sight before him.

"What is this place…" Jared's voice trailed off in awe.

"It's incredible. How far down are we?" Vanessa craned her head to look over the edge of the platform they stood on.

Jared looked up at the ceiling where tiny points of light shone into the enormous cavern below. It was difficult to assess from where he stood, but if he had to guess they were something like half a mile below the surface. The shafts of light from above gave a soft illumination to the room and allowed the whole group to see the spectacular sight, or as far as their vision allowed them to see.

Everyone fanned out around Jared and Vanessa, staring in amazement. The room descended as far as he could see in the dim light. Even his spider abilities didn't let him pierce through the darkness and see the bottom. Large, tiered platforms ringed the circumference of the room. There didn't seem to be any obvious way down to each concentric platform, but they were easily wide enough to accommodate a dozen people side by side.

The stream they'd followed, widened at the mouth of the cave and spilled over the ledge, only to crash into the platform below and split into two different streams. Those streams cascaded over the ledge and split once again. Before the water disappeared from sight, he counted half a dozen waterfalls descending below. The light from above shimmered off the surface, creating a tranquil feeling. The sound of the rushing water combined with the light show hypnotized him.

Scarlet dropped in front of him, startling those around him. They'd been so entranced they hadn't heard her flapping above.

Jared smiled, happy to see her even if it had only been a day since they'd watched the dragons rocket past them in the tunnel. He reached up a hand to caress her side.

"You're right. This place is awesome. How far down does it go?"

"Several miles. Though, I am the only of my family that can reach the bottom. It becomes too narrow for my brothers."

"What's down there?"

"A lake, filled with creatures of all shapes and sizes. I could not discern the bottom so it may be quite deep."

"Did you get the spider senses? Sorry, random thought, but maybe that would help. Does it lead anywhere else?" Jared gestured to the lake below.

"Correct, but I have not had time to rest yet, and the changes didn't happen right away for me like they did for you. This is only a theory, but I think the fall you took into the spider remains is part of the reason you didn't need to rest. You likely absorbed more of their nanites than anyone else and as such didn't need rest to assimilate them. As for the lake, it does, but I cannot go beyond as the tunnels are much too small."

"What about the creatures in the water? Can they climb up here?"

"No, there is an overhang at the bottom. There is no way

anything could climb up unless it can cling to the ceiling. I think we should be safe."

"Let's not forget the lizards and giant mantis things. If you recall, those things could cling to the ceiling."

"That is true, but based on the life forms in the water below, it does not look like there are many predators in the area."

"Or, maybe the predators are in the water."

"It is possible, though I saw nothing large enough to concern us as long as my brothers are here."

"All right, we'll be able to rest here a while, but I don't think this is our long-term solution. I want to keep moving south. We're only forty or fifty miles from the floating city. It's still much too close for my comfort."

Scarlet dipped her head in acknowledgment. Turning, she leaped off the side of the cavern and flew around the room. He brothers would have a hard time flying in the enclosed space, but it was plenty big for her. He watched her soar through the air, the shafts of light winking in and out of existence as she passed. Jared cocked his head in thought before pushing a thought to her.

"How thick is the rock above? Would it take a lot for you to punch a hole in it? Maybe that's our escape?"

"It is not thick. I am certain one of my brothers could punch a hole through without using their flames."

"The only problem is getting everyone up there. I mean, you could carry everyone yourself, but that's a lot of back and forth, and then there's Kitty."

"We could make it work, but my concern is how long it may take us and leave everyone exposed. Come to think of it, I do not believe Ballog could make the short flight on his own. Malsour and Kanundran may be able to help him through, but it would be challenging."

"All right, let's keep it as an option and we'll see if we can come up with some other solutions. If you have any other ideas, please let me know."

"We will think on it."

The conversation made Jared realize he hadn't thought to check in on Carla and Attis in a while. He found her near the back of the group looking glum.

"Carla? How are you holding up? Have you been in contact with Attis?"

"I was, but…" She looked toward the ceiling. "I can't hear him anymore."

"We're far below the surface covered by tons and tons of rock and earth. There's no reason to fret that something bad happened. Does he know to come this way? The last time I told you to check in on him, I said to send him straight west."

"He followed our path. Instead of flying ahead, he flew in circles around our position, and I told him to go south at the intersection."

"Oh, no." Jared's stomach dropped out from under him. "Can you reach him now?"

"No, I lost contact with him a few miles ago. What's wrong? You're scaring me."

"If he followed us, then the city—"

"But you said they wouldn't pay him any mind."

"Carla, it's not your fault. I should've been clearer. If he'd hung out back near our home like he's always done, it'd be harmless, but to follow us on a path like that is erratic behavior and liable to be noticed."

"I'm so sorry—"

"Carla." Jared faced her, mustering as much sincerity as he could. "I mean that. It isn't your fault. Not even a little, okay? We'll figure this out. Now, I've got to talk with Scarlet. Please just get some rest and be ready to move." Jared walked back to the ledge. *"Scarlet,*

I need you!"

Scarlet thumped down next to him and he hopped on her back. Before she jumped into the air, Jared turned back to those still awake.

"Everyone, please keep quiet and stay together. I'll be right back. Vanessa, please make sure everyone is ready to go soon. I'll explain in a moment, but I want to check something with Scarlet first."

"What is it?"

"Let's fly up to the top and I'll explain." Jared relayed the information, and a spike of alarm carried through their connection. "Yeah, I know. Our escape isn't over. I want you to take me up to the ceiling. If there are drop ships flying around up there, we might be able to hear them."

Scarlet flew him up to the ceiling. The holes were nothing more than small shafts through which the light passed. It was hard to gauge the thickness, but Jared guessed it was a few feet of rock and earth between them and the open sky.

"You think Malsour can really break through this?"

"Yes. The area is fairly wide, and with so many holes, its integrity is not sound."

"Good, you might need to make a break for—"

Jared's thoughts halted as he heard the familiar whine of drop ships nearby.

"So much for confusing them with the collapsed tunnels."

"Are you certain they know we are here? Perhaps they simply followed the bird to be diligent in their searches?"

Jared pondered the question. *If they'd thought Attis was just a common creature, why not blow him out of the sky and wash their hands of it? Did they want to capture him and that's why they followed him? Or, the more pressing question, did they assume he was part of the group fleeing underground?*

"Honestly, I don't know. There are several reasons they could have followed him, but can we risk staying here? What if they have a way to scan beneath the surface? It'll only be a matter of time before they find us."

"I see the logic in it."

Jared's brain whirred with options, every one of them worse than the one before. Finally, he settled on the best scenario he could think of, but it required Scarlet's brothers to be able to fly.

"If Malsour can break through the ceiling swiftly, then you can fly out and take out the one or two drop ships flying around the area. Then, you can head south. Go straight south for at least a hundred miles, stopping for nothing. I'll take everyone else and we'll continue walking the tunnels below."

"No."

Scarlet's tone left no room for argument.

"Care to elaborate?"

"We should not split up. You do not know what lurks further down, or if you will find a way back to the surface. No, I cannot agree to that."

"Then what do you suggest?"

"We take out the drop ships as you suggested, but we use these cavern and tunnels as shelter."

"What's keeping them from bombing us out?"

"We are nimbler in the air than the drop ships. The moment we hear one coming, we take to the skies and bring it down."

"That's not really giving me the warm fuzzies. You're just going to hope they don't bring an armada, or the city itself, here to take us out? If we stay here and keep destroying the drop ships, then the city will probably move again."

"They cannot have an endless supply of ships. If they did, why did they move an entire city into the area?"

"The city might have its own weapons systems. Maybe it doesn't even need the ships to take us out?"

Scarlet conceded the point but stood by her decision to take out the drop ships as they came.

"I don't like it, Scarlet. Not even a little. One shot from one of those phase cannons tore right through Ballog. If a dozen of them came at us at once, it could be the end of you."

"Again, I do not believe they have so many to waste."

"What if—" Jared paused as an idea formed in his mind. "What if we captured two of them and then used them to escape?"

"Remember the override on that last one?"

Jared growled in frustration. "I forgot. If only we'd had more time and Pete could've studied the pieces we confiscated."

"Also, do not forget the self-destruct tactic the cities used on that military complex. It stands to reason they have something similar in these ships."

"Okay, so capturing a ship is out until we know more about them. Splitting up is out. I don't like us waiting for them to send more ships and taking them out as they come. So, where does that leave us?"

"We could backtrack up the tunnel and take a different branch. We can make sure Attis does not give away our position again. There is a risk with any option, but at least with backtracking, we stand a chance of evading them with no confrontation."

"Then that's what we'll do. We're not ready to take on a city in a direct head-to-head battle. Besides, until Ballog recovers enough to fly, it's too risky for you to attempt to fly out of here. If we got into a protracted battle, we'd need everyone at the top of their game."

"Fair point. We will head back. As we did before, my brothers and I will lead the way, clear the tunnel, and choose another at random. Ballog will remain behind to guide you."

"When you get to the intersection, do you want to send someone back up toward our home and make sure we aren't going to get unexpected company?"

"I will send someone to scope it out. We will also explore the other three tunnels before choosing the best route."

"Good idea. Let's head back down and let everyone know."

After Jared told everyone the plan, there was a collective groan as everyone realized they'd have another day or two of marching back toward the city and certain danger. They understood it was the only viable option after Jared shared his and Scarlet's thoughts. Several suggested fighting was a better alternative, but Jared quickly dashed those voices by reminding them of Ballog. To Jared's surprise, he was the only one who thought splitting up was an option.

He'd thought it was something to consider, but everyone unanimously agreed with Scarlet that they should remain together, even if that meant heading back toward possible danger.

"All right, it's settled then. We still have half a day remaining so we might as well get a move on."

Another round of groans and dissenting voices made him reconsider.

"I know you're all tired, but the longer we delay, the more likely it is our enemies will find us. They may already have a ground force in the tunnels headed our way."

Vanessa laid a hand on his shoulder and whispered in his ear. "Just give them a few hours to rest. We can walk through the night if needed. It's not like there's a difference between day and night down here, anyway."

She made a solid point, and Jared conceded.

"We'll rest for three hours and then we move."

Jared took his own advice and sat down to rest. He couldn't sleep knowing there were ships overhead and there could be people walking down the tunnels toward them, but he'd use the time to meditate and recover some energy.

The moment he sat down, Scarlet suggested she and her brothers should move out.

"Please be careful, Scarlet. As much as I hate to say this, it's probably a good idea if you take point. If you run into any ground troops from the city, you're best suited to handle the phase rounds. I fear they'd burn right through everyone else's skin and scales."

"I planned to do just that. We can move fast enough that the robots or city dwellers would not get many rounds off before we were upon them."

"I wouldn't be so sure. You didn't have to fight that guy during the last battle. He moved with freakish speed and accuracy. If all of them are capable of such a feat, then it would terrify me to run across a group. The robots we can handle as they aren't nearly as fast even if they are deadly accurate."

"We will be careful, I promise."

"I'll see you soon."

One after the other, the dragons disappeared back the way they'd come, their thundering footfalls quickly receding into the distance. Jared's heart fluttered in his chest. He hated Scarlet being in danger, especially when there was nothing he could do to help.

Lost in thought, he hadn't seen Vanessa approach until she sat beside him, leaning into him and putting her head on his shoulder. Her presence helped to quell his fear for Scarlet, but it did nothing to stop the drumming of his heart. In fact, it did just the opposite. Jared didn't like feeling excited with Vanessa at his side while Scarlet ran headlong into danger, but he could do nothing to alter his emotions.

They didn't speak, nor did they need to. Vanessa could tell something bothered him, and she provided physical support. Meanwhile, Jared worked through his conflicting emotions. This unexpected invasion caused him so much anxiety and set back his plans. They had half a dozen people and dragons that wanted to bond, but they'd not had a moment's respite to get it done. For a minute, he thought about getting it done now, but it was too unpredictable, and he didn't know how long the bond would take. They couldn't risk a dozen people and dragons being incapacitated with enemies hot on their heels.

They needed to wait until they got to a safe place. Safe wasn't the best way to describe it. It was more like a less perilous place. The world was a dangerous place no matter where they went. If it wasn't the twisted creatures that lurked around every corner, it was mercenary bands that decided they'd steal whatever someone else had, or it was the cities being the cruel overlords they were.

Though months had passed since their encounter with the Daggers, Jared still felt the sting of the encounter. He'd wanted—no, *craved*—human interaction so much he'd overlooked the possibility they could be bad. His upbringing hadn't prepared him for the real nature of the world.

His mood turned black as he thought of the atrocities and experiences he'd been through. Expelling the negative emotions with a breath, Jared centered himself and meditated. All the recent thoughts and experiences he pushed back into the recesses of his mind and shut the door. Slowly, his mind cleared as he stood in the middle of what he labeled the byway of his mind. A few random jumbles of thought floated by, but with a quick mental shove, they disappeared until his mind was empty. No thoughts, no emotions, only quiet tranquility.

Jared sat like that for the rest of the three hours he'd allotted. The moment those three hours expired, he jolted his mind back into action and nudged Vanessa, who'd fallen asleep on his shoulder.

Jared announced it was time for everyone to get moving. No one complained or made a sound. Everyone knew the risks, and they'd resigned themselves to the fact it would take a while to get to a safe place.

Like a silent procession, they filed out of the room where Kitty took point without instructions. Once again, they set off back the way they'd come, hoping to find an escape from the clutches of the city.

15 THIRTEEN STRONG

The way back proved boring and laborious. Though no one spoke out loud, Jared caught snippets of telepathy periodically. The longer they walked, the more concerned he grew. There were a number of people questioning his and Scarlet's choices. A few even had thoughts of whether Vanessa was best suited to lead them with her obvious attachment to him.

Jared didn't understand their thought process. Everyone knew it was the most viable option, and they didn't have to like it, but to question Vanessa after all they'd been through troubled him.

"Vanessa, don't speak out loud, but there's something we need to discuss."

She grabbed his hand and smiled over at him. *"What is it?"*

"I've been listening to people's thoughts, and I don't like what I'm hearing. Some are questioning your ability to lead. They think you're just going along with everything I say because of our relationship."

"How can they think that after everything we..." Her thoughts ended abruptly. Though she tried to keep her face impassive, Jared saw a slight crease at the corner of her eyes.

"It could be George's influence still. I can partly understand. If it weren't for me and Scarlet, the city wouldn't be forcing us on this journey."

"Jared, don't." She squeezed his hand. "You can't think like that. If it weren't for the both of you, none of us would be here. It might just be nerves and lack of sleep."

"Maybe, but I wanted to let you know in case you need to spend some time reassuring them. We can't have another situation like George. We won't have another issue like him." Jared's voice took on a menacing undertone, making it clear what he'd do to anyone who tried betraying them like George.

"I'll handle it." She squeezed his hand once more and dropped back to speak with her people.

Jared had thought he'd been accepted as part of the group, but if they so easily dismissed him, maybe he was mistaken. No matter. He'd sworn to protect them no matter what, and he'd keep that promise.

The trip back took a solid portion of the day before they reached the collapsed tunnel. There was now a smooth hole bored through into the antechamber. Motioning for everyone to wait, Jared walked into the cavern to scope out the area. He found identical holes bored through the other passages, and Ballog guarding the tunnel home. All around the ground, parts of robots and sensor pieces lay scattered about.

"Ballog, what happened here?"

"We found a contingent of metal men, and Scarlet destroyed them. They shot her a few times, but they did not penetrate her scales."

Jared breathed out in relief. He'd hoped there wouldn't be any enemies, but at least it was just the robots and not another human.

"It was over in an instant. You cannot see it now, but many of the machines melted immediately when they came to investigate

the fire burning through the rubble. The timing worked out nearly perfectly, and she caught a group in her flame blast."

"Thank you. This might actually work to our advantage. I wanted to get the parts we stashed away for Pete and Kirgor, but now we can just collect some of these."

Jared walked back to the tunnel and beckoned everyone forward. Then, he scavenged parts until he had a complete robot. It didn't matter which limbs belonged to which robot as there were all identical. At least, he hoped that were the case.

"Pete. Look what I've got for you!"

The man had barely restrained glee in his eyes as he looked at the destroyed robot.

"C-c-can we keep it?"

Jared furrowed his brow. "That depends. Can you ensure the city can't track it?"

"I don't know."

Jared reasoned through the scenario. If they had no power, then maybe the cities couldn't track them. They were also far underground. However, they'd already had one instance of the cities locating them because of an innocent mistake. If they somehow had a reserve power cell, or a device powered independently, they couldn't risk bringing it along.

"Is there anything you can do to make sure there's no signal coming from it?"

"I can t-try."

"Good, you've got an hour and then we keep moving, with or without the robot." Jared turned to the rest of those gathered around him. "Everyone hear that? We've got one hour to rest and then we keep moving. Ballog, if you see or hear anything coming from the tunnel please let us know. Elle, Carla, please keep using your abilities to watch for any danger."

There were no objections, so Jared went around picking up the rest of the robot parts and put them into a pile. If Pete disabled any trackers or determined they had none, then they'd bring the rest of the parts with them.

Maybe they wouldn't need to infiltrate the city on their own after all. They could commandeer a ship using an imposter robot and then have it pilot them up to the city. They wouldn't even need to figure out how to disable anything on the ship that way. The only thing Jared wasn't certain of was if all of the robots had the ability to fly the ships and knew how to approach the city.

Jared's mind fractured into dozens of threads at all the ways they could use the robot if Pete succeeded. For a moment Jared thought carrying all the parts might slow them down too much, but then realized Ballog could easily carry everything if they fashioned a sling for him.

With that in mind, Jared took out his only two shirts and tied off the sleeves. He asked around until he had half a dozen shirts no one expected to get back. He used three more to create impromptu bags, then tore the rest into strands which he used to make slings. Testing their strength, he confirmed they'd hold against the weight of the robot. It was crude, but it'd have to do for now. In hindsight, he should've waited until Pete gave him the all clear before tearing up so many clothes.

He shrugged and sat next to the pile of parts. He watched Pete work on the robot, poking and prodding in its brain. The thing's faceplate had come off mere moments after Pete had set his bag down and extracted a few tools. Leave it to the technical genius to bring his bag of tools as essential instead of clothes or other personal needs.

Pete ended up not needing the entire hour and proudly proclaimed that the bodies were safe for transport.

"There's no electricity c-coming off any part of the brain. All the extremities are simple p-pistons and gears. Wires run through the hollow portions of their arms and legs to attach to the gears that move their extremities. Aside from those wires, there is n-nothing in them. The chest c-cavity has a variety of different c-components, some of which I'm still trying to figure out, b-but none of the wires I tested leading from it to the b-brain had any voltage output."

"Is it possible there's something hidden in a place you cannot get to?"

"Maybe, b-but it's hard to say. If there was, it's so small I doubt it would p-penetrate through this rock." Pete pointed to the surrounding cavern.

"All right, I've heard enough. Let's get these parts stuffed into the slings I made. Ballog, are you okay caring these? I can put them around the spikes on your back if so."

"I will carry them."

"Thanks!"

In no time at all, they'd stuffed the parts into the shirts and Jared clambered onto Ballog's back to loop them around the spikes. He wasn't sure how long it would last, but it if it got them to their destination that was all he cared about.

"Kitty and Elle, please walk near Ballog and make sure none of this stuff falls out. I don't want to leave a trail. I'll take point again. I know everyone's tired, but please try to push yourself. If you can't go any farther, let me know and we'll take a quick break."

The next few hours proved torturous for some. More complaints accompanied them down the tunnel, but the entire time Vanessa moved among the group chatting with everyone and doing her best to improve morale. Surprisingly he heard none of the doubt from just a few hours earlier. Vanessa really knew her people and probably knew who the culprits were. Maybe she'd spoken to them already and reassured them.

This new tunnel proved no different from the one they'd traversed yesterday. Thankfully, no one in their group was claustrophobic, and they were all accustomed to dark places. If anyone had a right to feel confined it was Jared, but he'd never been one to get scared from enclosed spaces.

Before he'd bonded with Scarlet and gained all his abilities, he'd nearly lost his nerve descending into the New York City subway, but it wasn't fear of enclosed spaces. It was the unknown and potential for predators. He'd only had his unenhanced self, mediocre night vision, and his father's Colt. Now, he could see as if it were day, had two massively powerful phase pistols, a phase rifle on his back, and a dragon at the rear of their group. In addition to all the enhancements he also had increased defenses in the form of skin hardening *Natural Armor*. If he couldn't feel somewhat safe given the circumstances, then he never would.

They hiked for hours, pushing themselves beyond their physical limits. Jared almost called a stop multiple times but decided to wait until at least one person could go no further. When the complaints and angry thoughts started up again, it was almost enough to stop, but only a few moments later Marie sank to her knees. It was good enough for one day's travel. Hopefully, it would be a while before more robots risked the tunnels. They didn't need to sleep or rest, but Jared imagined they weren't easy to manufacture, and the cities had already lost a lot.

Just to be safe, he and Ballog took up a spot in the group's rear while Carla and Elle took the front. If anything tried to follow them, they'd be ready.

Jared announced a six hour rest and took turns with Ballog keeping watch before he got the group moving again. Everyone had a little extra pep in their step, and they made good time following Scarlet. Occasionally, the tunnel branched into smaller ones, some too small for even a human to traverse. Jared kept a wary eye on these for any lurking creatures. A few times, they saw scorch marks around the entrances. Jared assumed it was evidence of Scarlet and the others destroying and warning off predators hiding in the shadows.

The gradual descent they'd made since leaving home eventually leveled out and branched yet again. One branch led north, the stream following along its path. The other led south. There was a symbol etched into the ground in front of the left tunnel. It was the symbol he'd followed in New York that had changed his life forever. Scarlet must've seen the tag during one of their mind meld sessions. It was a nice gesture, and Jared appreciated Scarlet taking the time.

Jared pressed ahead and finally caught up to Scarlet and her brothers. They'd reached a dead end with no room to even turn around. For the past thirty or forty minutes, they'd traveled uphill. It was impossible for him to know how close to the surface they were. If it was too far, the heat would suffocate them when Scarlet made a path through the earth and rock.

"Scarlet! It's good to see you." Jared squeezed his way past her brothers and joined her at the front. He didn't want everyone to hear the conversation he was about to have. "Do you know how far we are beneath the earth?"

"I guess between fifteen and twenty feet. You see the roots there? We are close enough that it should not take long to burn through."

"How long exactly? Once you start breathing fire, it's going to suck the oxygen out of the air and superheat this small area."

Scarlet didn't respond for a time as she thought it through.

"I cannot say. However, I can have my brothers block the passage with their bodies. It will not last long but should sufficiently shield everyone from the heat."

"Okay, let me get everyone together and back up a way.

Hopefully the oxygen loss might not impact everyone as much. I'll shoot a thought over when we're ready. Oh, if there's any drop ships when you get out, please take them out and move south as fast as possible. We can't backtrack these tunnels anymore. I don't think everyone can handle it and already they question our choices."

Jared made his way back to Vanessa and let her know what was about to happen. Together, they herded everyone back a few hundred yards.

"We are ready."

"Prepare yourself." Scarlet's voice thundered in everyone's head.

"Cover your face with something!" Jared yelled.

As the words left his mouth, Scarlet unleashed her fire on the rock, sending a wave of heat and roiling smoke over everything. The heat was extremely intense even from so far back, and several people cried out in surprise. It wasn't enough to harm anyone, but it was uncomfortable. The smoke was the worst of it, invading people's eyes, nose, and mouths, even covered as they were.

It didn't last long before Scarlet called him over. After the smoke cleared, some of it escaping above the surface, Jared found a small hole, big enough for him to approach. However, the rock was so hot it glowed, and he didn't think his protections were good enough to protect him. Instead, he and Scarlet bent their ears to listen for any signs a drop ship was near.

After determining the coast clear, Scarlet, followed by Malsour, prepared to charge from the tunnel.

"Scarlet—" Jared laid a hand on her side and whispered, "If there are any drop ships out there…"

"I know what must be done. We will take it out and head directly south."

"I'll find you, though it may take several days. If you're able to fly back and guide us, please do so. We can find a place to settle later. I want to head farther southwest first."

"We will clear the way of any dangerous predators."

"Thank you. Obviously, you know to steer clear of humans and colonies, but maybe keep an eye out for more explorers? I've never been this far south, so I have no idea if there are more people around. If there's more people like the Daggers, we definitely don't want to alert them to your presence."

"We will avoid them. There is no reason for us to facilitate a conflict with anyone. Not until my brothers grow stronger. We must find a way to get back to the lake of nanites. That is our most rapid path to strength."

"We'll figure out a way."

"We can send Attis. If we find him again."

"We will find him. Even if I have to hike back solo."

"Jared—"

Holding up a hand, he cut her off. "I know, I know. We'll talk about it when we're safe. Let's get this done. I want to be as far from here as possible as soon as possible."

Jared made sure everyone stood back while the dragons lined up single file, ready to punch through into the open air. Scarlet would go first, followed by Malsour and Ballog heading up the rear. Ballog still couldn't fly with his injury, so they'd need to traverse the ground, but Scarlet would fly cover for them. Before Jared joined Vanessa at the head of the group, he retrieved the makeshift satchels from Ballog. They planned to travel very fast, and the shoddy slings wouldn't survive the trek.

"Go!"

Scarlet needed no further prodding as she burst from the ground. The crashing rocks reached his ears as she launched herself through the partial opening. Malsour widened the hole further as he rocketed into the open air. One by one, the dragons disappeared from view. Once he was certain the tunnel would hold, Jared led the group in their wake, pausing at the threshold only to determine the coast was still clear.

"Let's move."

Everyone rushed for the exit, enjoying the fading sunlight on their skin. It was nearing dusk, and they wouldn't have too much time left to travel on foot before visibility became an issue. They occasionally came across a few obvious scenes of carnage. Scarlet, true to her word, had had her brothers eliminate any possible threats in their wake. Pools of blood and the limbs of a random assortment of creatures were the only evidence leftover.

They hustled for another two hours before it became impossible for the water folk to see. It was no use to stumble around in the dark. They'd rest for the night and set out at first light with everyone refreshed. He chose a small tree band to make camp. It didn't afford much protection, but it was better than sleeping in the open.

Jared, Elle, and Kitty were the only ones who didn't sleep. They patrolled the perimeter of the camp. They'd gotten a few hours the night before and didn't need much rest.

The night passed slowly. Jared expected to see a drop ship at any moment and didn't allow himself to relax. His heightened awareness proved unnecessary. Maybe they really had made their escape. It was too early for him to celebrate, but hope wormed its way into his heart.

The moment sunlight peeked over the horizon, Jared woke everyone. Sleep addled and groggy, they began their trek south.

The journey took them three days to reach the spot where Scarlet and her brothers had stopped. It was the same story every day. March from sunup to sundown with only a short break around midday to recuperate. Scarlet came back to check on them twice during the journey and corrected their trajectory both times. They'd needed to skirt around smaller colonies, but largely, the area was a barren wasteland. A couple wild dogs and a few rats that migrated to the area after the dragons passed by provided the only interruptions. It was simple work, and Jared let those with less experience handle clearing them out. Then he had Carla and Pete absorb any nanites from them. They needed them more than he and Elle.

The entire time they traveled, Jared forced himself to remain vigilant. By the end of the third day he finally let himself believe they'd escaped the wrath of the city, at least for a time.

When everyone caught sight of Scarlet and the dragons, they cheered. Jared let them have the moment. He didn't want to stay more than a couple days before they continued. If he told them that right now, they'd flay him alive.

The place Scarlet chose was in the middle of nowhere. A single cluster of buildings stood vacant in the center of barren fields. Enclosing the large area was forest as far as he could see. There was one two-lane road bisecting the plot. It was drab, lifeless, and isolated, exactly what they needed.

Before Jared let anyone rest, he cleared the buildings and made sure it wasn't home to any creatures. Like its surroundings, it was absent anything of note.

"Okay, it's safe to go in. Make yourself comfortable. We'll hole up here for a while."

Relieved, everyone dashed for the building to stake their claim and get off their feet. Jared shrugged, it was plenty big enough for everyone, and he didn't really care where he slept. When he only slept a few hours a night, all he needed was a place big enough to stretch out, and he was good.

Finally, the tension left Jared's shoulders. They'd made it safely away, and now they could take their time. He walked over to Scarlet and sat with his back to her.

"Are you and your brothers going to dig into—"

Scarlet nudged his side, making him look up at her. She jutted out her chin in the direction of the open field.

Her brothers lay in deep depressions all across the field. He hadn't seen them on first glance, but their backs were nearly flush with the ground.

"Sorry, I should stop assuming you aren't already aware of these things."

"Do not be sorry for double-checking all is secure and safe. You have many people under your charge and every right to be concerned."

Jared smiled and leaned against her side. They sat in silence for a time while Jared spun some ideas through his head. A part of him wanted to dive into his feelings for Vanessa, but it seemed like such a trivial thing to discuss when they had more pressing matters.

"So, I've been thinking about our lack of strength problem. I'm wondering if there's any reason for us to find companions other than dragons?"

"We do not know—"

"Hold on a sec. I know we don't know where they are exactly, and that's the first puzzle we have to solve, but think about it. What did Carla bonding with Attis gain us?"

"Believe me, I have. Currently, he is a liability and nearly spelled our doom. Not entirely his fault because he does not have the understanding to comprehend."

"Exactly, plus think about how long it'll take Carla and him to improve sufficiently to really add to our capabilities. I mean, it's cool and all, but..."

"I share your hesitation, but if we—" Scarlet paused to collect her thoughts.

He experienced a strange sensation as she rapidly processed a bunch of thoughts at once. He didn't know if it was their physical connection or if they'd grown more attuned to each other, but he caught snippets of her thoughts and emotions. She rummaged through her mind, looking at trajectories, locations, and distances from her mother's perspective. It was extremely confusing for him. Not only did he not understand all of the viewpoints from Alestrialia, he also didn't understand the calculations Scarlet made in rapid succession.

"It could work."

Jared couldn't help but smirk in satisfaction. "Like I said, I spent a while thinking about this. I understand that we'll need to convince them to join the fight, but I think if you consult with their matriarch, you'll be able to share your experiences and get them on board. We've got forty-four people here. Well, forty-three, since Pete's already bonded."

"There are approximately fifty-three dragons remaining, besides myself and my brothers."

"See that leaves quite a bit of wiggle room in the event others of your kind didn't survive the millennia. Razael—"

Scarlet cut him off with a snort, unhappy with that line of thinking. However, Jared would be remiss if he didn't consider the possibility that other dragons had died along the way.

"I know it's a hard topic but think about it. If we randomly stumbled on Razael, isn't it possible?"

"I suppose…" Scarlet's tone expressed her grudging acceptance of his rationale.

"I truly hope that Razael was the only one, but we must consider all angles here. If we do this, we'll need to split up. I don't think you should go yourself. Nor do I think any of the water folk should go even if they bond between now and then."

"My three eldest brothers."

"That is what I was thinking, provided they've regained their ability to fly. They will travel thousands of miles, not to mention having to find a way beneath the earth to awaken those that yet slumber. I honestly don't even know how they will reach the water dragons. Can they just, I don't know, fly over and shout for them?"

"Honestly, I do not know. It may be futile, but I can see this will provide us the highest chance of success against the cities. If the dragons united into one front, nothing could stand in our way."

An edge of defiance crept into her thoughts, and Jared watched the idea take hold. The more she thought about the idea, the more determined she became. The only thing left to do was get her brothers on the bandwagon, but Jared hardly thought that would take any convincing at all.

"Brothers, come."

Scarlet waited until they'd all assembled around her.

Though he'd been around them for some time now, the massive creatures arrayed before Scarlet was still unbelievable. It was straight out of a fantasy story he'd read as a kid. Seeing it with his own eyes was surreal.

"Jared and I discussed a plan you should hear. We—"

"We must find our kin," Ashazad interrupted, nodding his head in agreement. **"We heard your thoughts, sister. You think so loudly, you may as well shout to us."**

Chagrined, Scarlet lowered her head.

Embarrassment flooded into Jared, and his cheeks grew warm. Scarlet's emotions bleeding through him so strongly surprised him. The more time they spent together, the more attuned they became with each other's thoughts and emotions.

Jared smiled and patted her side. *"It's okay, Scarlet. You haven't needed to shield your thoughts from anyone since you were born. I wouldn't let it get to you."*

Scarlet lifted her head and stared at each of her brothers. **"What is your verdict?"**

A chorus of agreement exploded through his head, instantly giving him a headache. He wasn't the only one to experience the psionic pressure as several cried out from the nearby buildings, and people stumbled from the door holding their heads.

"Um, maybe a little less on the vocal projection next time?"

"Apologies." Malsour sounded abashed. **"I must remember to soften my thoughts."**

Scarlet spent a few more moments discussing the plan with her brothers, but Jared was left out of the conversation.

Seeing things well in hand, Jared went into the buildings and made sure everyone was okay after the mental pressure exerted by Malsour.

"Vanessa." Jared beckoned her over. "We'll stay here for a couple days to let everyone recover. If people are ready, I'd like them to bond while we're here too. Have you thought more about the bond with Malsour? As far as I can tell, there's no one else he's considered."

"If he's willing, then yes." Vanessa's voice cracked, and she looked apprehensive.

"There's no reason to get scared. It will hurt, but the benefit is well worth the experience. You'll know and understand things about yourself and the dragons that words alone cannot convey."

"I will do it as soon as he is ready."

"How about now?"

Vanessa blanched, but nodded her head.

"Can you please round everyone up who wants to bond? If someone doesn't want to, we'll respect their wishes. The same is true for the dragons, though I believe they may have changed their minds after seeing the threats we face."

"I'll round everyone up."

"Oh, after we leave here, we're going southwest until I'm confident we're far enough away from the city. Once we've settled someplace new, I've got plans to make us as strong as possible, but it will take time and luck for everything to fall into place. I'll explain later. For now, let's get this bond going so that everyone becomes familiar with their companion before we set out."

Vanessa left to collect those who wished to bond while Jared fetched eleven boosters, hoping all of Scarlet's brothers joined them. If they didn't, a mature dragon was already immeasurably stronger than most—if not any—other creature on the planet, so they still had a formidable team. On the other hand, the phase cannons had torn right through Ballog's scales. If they didn't enhance themselves like Scarlet, there was no way they'd survive a volley from an armada of the ships. Especially if they faced pilots that predicted their every move like the soldier he'd fought on the ground.

Once Vanessa rounded everyone up, they went outside to find the dragons hunkered down in their makeshift burrows.

Jared raised his voice.

"It's time!" He paused for dramatic effect, but it only yielded an awkward pause. He cleared his throat and continued. "If you've made arrangements with one of Scarlet's brothers, please go stand by his side." Immediately ten people walked over. Maria and Casey chose Ashazad and Kynderri. Vanessa lingered by his side, and Jared nudged her.

Slowly, she placed one foot in front of the other and approached Malsour. Timidly, she reached up a hand to his head and closed her eyes. Jared caught a small snippet of telepathy from Vanessa, and then it blended in with all the other conversations occurring around him.

Scarlet flared her nostrils and huffed in amusement next to him as she watched human and dragon match up for the bonding. When she didn't share her thoughts, Jared questioned her.

"Scarlet?"

"I should have known. Ashazad has always had a fascination with the human body, and Kynderri is… a glutton.

It felt like a vise closed in around his mind before Scarlet uttered that last part.

"Did you lock down your mind before you said that?"

"I did."

Jared laughed, a full, uncontrollable belly laugh. It hurt so good as tears streamed down his face. It wasn't even that funny, but for whatever reason he found it hysterical in the moment and couldn't control himself.

"What would your brother do if he heard you say that?"

"I—" Embarrassment flooded through him, her emotions bleeding into the bond once again.

"Twice in one day you get embarrassed. If I didn't know better, I'd think you're just a child…" Jared let the thought hang in the air, erupting into another fit of laughter.

Everyone around them looked at Jared and Scarlet with slight frowns on their faces. All but Kynderri that is. If looks could kill, Scarlet should have been feeling concerned.

"I don't think it matters that you shut your thoughts down. Body language speaks louder than words, you know. I'm fairly certain Kynderri knows all about this little chat. Though, perhaps because we kept it private, he won't scorn you too bad?"

"I should not think so of my brother."

"If the shoe fits…"

"The shoe? Fits? What—"

"It's a human expression, don't bother. It's not worth the time to explain." Jared calmed himself and apologized to the crowd. "Scarlet

and I had an enlightening conversation, and for whatever reason I found it hilarious."

Jared tried hard not to peek at Kynderri from the corner of his eye. The massive dragon could eat him in a single bite, and he eyed Jared with barely restrained hostility.

Treading carefully, Jared continued his explanation. "I am sorry for my outburst. It was uncalled for." He said it as much for the water folk as he did to appease Kynderri. "Let's continue, please."

One by one, the other water folk took up a position next to each of the dragons they'd spent time with. Eleven people and eleven dragons.

Awesome! thought Jared. This was exactly what he'd hoped for. Vanessa and Malsour still faced each other. He didn't know if it was a normal conversation or if Malsour was engaging in a mind meld. In either case, Jared had no doubt they'd find kindred spirits in each other, even if it took them a bit longer to decide to bond than the others.

Jared handed each of the water folk a booster and instructed them to sit down.

"You all bore witness and felt the pain when you said the vows to Scarlet. I believe this pain is worse, but this time you'll have your bond mate to assist with the pain. Carla, did you experience pain during your bonding?"

"I did."

"Pete, what about you?" Jared turned to the man.

"Y-yes, it was p-painful."

"More than the vows?"

Pete nodded his head vigorously.

"As you can see, it was painful for everyone so far. I want to prepare you as much as possible for this. As I told Vanessa just a few minutes ago, the pain will be worth the price. Of that, I have no doubt."

The moment he'd said Vanessa's name, she turned around to face him, a huge smile on her face. Jared glanced up to Malsour, who nodded his head once.

Jared mirrored Vanessa's smile and walked over to hand her the final booster. He gestured to a place near Malsour's side and indicated Vanessa should sit. Then he returned to the center of the gathered humans and dragons and turned in a slow circle, addressing Scarlet's brothers.

"Please do what you can to ease their pain. Scarlet helped with mine, knocking me unconscious before it became unbearable. I know you can isolate the pain in your own bodies, but please prepare yourselves to assist your new companions as well."

Jared had no further instructions for those undertaking the process. With nothing else standing in the way, Jared motioned for everyone to proceed. He readied himself to assist in any way he could.

Screams erupted from their throats as they pressed the plungers home. Several dragons roared, echoing the pain their human allies experienced. For those slower to inject the nanites, it made them pause, the color draining from their faces, but as Jared watched, those frightened expressions transformed into resolve. Less than a minute later, all eleven of the water folk initiated the process. All eleven screamed in agony.

Jared's heart broke as he watched Vanessa wriggling against Malsour's side. Her body, rigid and taut against the pain, looked frail. He wished there was something he could do to help, but he knew anything he did was a pointless gesture that wouldn't do anything to alleviate the pain.

The pain level appeared different for everyone. The only pair that didn't experience as much pain, was Ashazad and Casey. Besides the initial shout from Casey and grunt from Ashazad, neither of them spoke or moved. Casey didn't succumb to unconsciousness for many minutes. He sat there with wide eyes, seeing something only he could see. Jared suspected it was the encoded message left by Igor, but he could've read it over three times by now so maybe it was something else.

Jared suspected it was Casey and Ashazad's understanding of the human body that enabled them to endure or redirect the pain. Thankfully, the others' screams only lasted for a moment before they lapsed into unconsciousness. Even the dragons eventually closed their eyes and lay on the ground. All but Ballog, who seethed and growled in obvious discomfort. His sides heaved and steam curled around his nostrils.

"Scarlet? What's wrong?"

"I do not know."

She bounded over to his side and bent her head to his. A moment later, he too fell into unconsciousness. Scarlet guided his head to the ground so as not to crush Jax sitting below him.

Jackson, Jared had become accustomed to calling him Jax on account of others adopting the nickname he'd given the man. Jax usually kept to himself, so Jared barely knew him. Other than their initial meeting and a few random exchanges, they hadn't spoken more than a few sentences to each other. Jared promised himself he'd remedy that. If Ballog saw something in him worthy of the bond, then Jared needed to get to know him better. He needed to get to know everyone better. This journey would help him accomplish that.

"He could not block the pain. He was not entirely truthful with us about the severity of his injury. It is much worse than we thought, and the continued exertion these past couple days made it worse."

"Will he be okay?"

"In time, yes. Bonding will enable him to regenerate faster. It is wise we stopped here to do this before continuing onward."

"We'll take all the time he needs to recover fully. We need everyone at full strength. If the city somehow catches wind of our direction…" Jared let the thought trail off. He didn't need to spell it out for her. They couldn't let that happen.

"Thank you. It will take time before everyone comes around. We should establish a watch throughout the day and night until everyone successfully completes the bond."

"Yes, that sounds like a good idea to me." He looked around for Carla and Elle, waving them over. "We must keep a watch while they're out here. If you need to sleep before tonight, please do so. I'll keep an eye on them for now."

The girls walked off to get some rest and Jared sat next to Scarlet, gazing at the scene before him. It was surreal. After today, they'd have thirteen dragon-bonded members of their small colony, one griffon, and a giant feline. They were a burgeoning force and they'd grow in strength to become even deadlier.

"Incredible."

"Yes, yes, it is." Jared nodded at Scarlet, agreeing with her completely.

16 ADMINISTERING THE CURE

Most of the bonds had completed by the following morning, but Ashazad and Ballog were still motionless, as were Casey and Jax. Several times Scarlet checked on her brothers and found there were no complications. The most surprising news was when Scarlet told Jared Ashazad and Casey had figured out how to enter a shared thought space already, and immediately explored their bodies and nanites after the bond completed.

Neither of them wanted to end their connection for fear they wouldn't be able to reestablish the synchronicity created by the initial bond. Jared had no intention of interrupting that connection. Anything they could do to increase their skills and abilities faster was a welcome boon to their mission.

Shortly after they'd woken, Jared asked Scarlet to scout the area. Specifically, he wanted her to check back the way they'd come to ensure nothing followed them.

"Please take Kitty with you. If you so much as catch a hint of a drop ship, Kitty can investigate further. I'm still not entirely convinced we shook our tail. If everyone didn't need the rest, I'd pick up and leave as soon as the bonds completed. Unfortunately, I think we'd have a riot on our hands if we moved now, given it looks like we stayed ahead of our pursuers."

"We are three, nearly four days' walk from the city. We lost sight of it in the sky a couple days ago."

"You're probably right, but after what we watched them do with those probes, I don't want to take the chance. If we had to move quickly, do you think you could wake Ballog and Ashazad?"

"Yes, but at what cost? I do not know how it would impact the bond. That should be a last resort."

Throughout the rest of the day, Scarlet and Kitty kept up a regular cadence to their scouting. At least once per hour, they swept the area in a wide arc, ensuring they'd have no unwelcome guests.

The longer they stayed here, the more the tension he'd felt before returned. By the end of the day, he continually cast furtive looks back the way they'd come. Scarlet had just returned from scouting, but it did nothing to allay his fears.

Finally, toward the end of their second night there, Ashazad and Casey came around. Ballog and Jax remained catatonic, and Jared worried for them, but Scarlet assured him there was nothing wrong.

"Welcome back to the land of the living." Jared patted Casey on the back. "I trust your bond was…enlightening?"

Casey looked up at him and Jared flinched back in surprise. Casey's eyes had changed. They looked like a dragon's or cat's with vertical pupils. The gaze he directed at Jared bored into him and made him uncomfortable.

"Casey?"

"Jared, this—" Casey's voice halted, and he cocked his head to the side.

Casey's pupils morphed from the slitted cat-like eyes, shrinking to their normal size to reveal crystal clear blue irises. They looked like gems set against his pale skin. Just when Jared thought it couldn't get weirder, they morphed again, shimmering through a kaleidoscope of colors.

"What's happening?"

"I can see, Jared."

"Yeah, I got that."

"No, I mean I can really see *everything*. I see the modifications to your eyes, the dense field of nanites surrounding your body, the thickness of your skin, and I can even tell where the nanites suffuse your muscles to provide bursts of increased performance. Jared, this…"

Casey waved his arms around to encompass himself and Ashazad. He gawked at everything in an entirely new light.

"Your eyes? Is that how you can see?"

"Yes. No."

Jared scratched his head in bewilderment. He knew how confusing all of this could be, but Casey wasn't making any sense.

"My eyes are just my eyes, but I can manipulate them at will to see what I desire. I understand them. I know how they work. The information Ashazad shared with me allows me to understand every cell in my body."

"So, when you look at me, what is it exactly that you see?"

"I think it is the nanites that make up your body. Because they infuse every cell, it enables me to understand them and their functions."

"And you get all that from a single glance?"

"Well, I need to instruct the nanites to modify my vision to see them. I'm sorry, this is all so difficult to explain. Maybe Ashazad can clarify."

Jared looked at Ashazad with a newfound respect and had to take another step back in shock. He'd changed. Morphed, right before his eyes. A bony plate seat had already formed on his back. The spikes and claws extended ever so slowly, pushing into the sky above and dirt beneath.

"How?"

"*Body Manipulation.*" Ashazad turned to Jared. "**Rather than assigning nanites to specific categories, Casey and I determined that we will assign everything into** *Body Manipulation* **so the nanites remain free.**"

Ashazad emphasized the last word, uncertain if it was the proper way to describe the way the nanites used to remodel, regenerate, and increase *Natural Armor*.

Casey Nanites Available – 100%

Body

    Physical Augmentation

        Body Manipulation – 100%

"So… you're telling me I could've kept them all in the one category and changed my body on the fly?"

"It—" Ashazad paused, seemingly uncertain how to proceed.

"I think what he's trying to say is no, but yes. Like I said before, it is something we understand because of our knowledge of the human body. Before Ashazad, I wouldn't have known how to do this, as I'd never studied at the molecular level, but he opened my mind. It seems trivial now to adjust individual cells rapidly to perform various functions."

"So, you can do everything I can now?"

"No. And yes."

Jared sighed. "All right, this is super confusing. I think we need to do a mind meld to understand this better. It's just not clicking for me. Scarlet? What about you?"

"I understand some, but I, too, am at a loss. Though we did explore the possibility of using the nanites to permanently change your physical and mental attributes."

Casey's frown eased. "Ah, I see where the confusion lies. I…we, are not permanently changing anything. As you can see, Ashazad is making some permanent enhancements to his body. The rest remain free nanites, but we can rapidly construct and deconstruct cells."

"Brother, did you at least assign some into *Skin* and *Scale Hardening*?"

"A portion of them, yes. Though, I do not know why you use percentages for the interface you created. Why not use the actual number of nanites?"

"To you and me the numbers are negligible, but to the mind of a human?"

"Wait, what numbers are you talking about? You actually know how many nanites you have?"

"We do." Scarlet and Ashazad intoned at the same time.

"And?"

"Jared," Scarlet said, a hint of concern in her voice. "The numbers are less important than the general allocation of nanites. Each cell in a human body is made up of forty-six chromosomes. Each of those is formed by two DNA strands. There are roughly thirty-seven trillion cells. If you recall what we already discovered, the nanites automatically replicate to match the number of DNA strands—"

"Alright I get it." Jared held up a hand. "I see your point."

"Now, the nanites you're able to assign do not factor in that number, but it is still a large number. The percentages that Scarlet chose encompass the surplus beyond the DNA infused nanites."

Scarlet turned back to her brother. "May I see your assignment to understand your development path?"

Ashazad bowed his head to Scarlet and they remained like that for several minutes, giving Jared time to digest everything that Ashazad revealed. At the same time, Scarlet shared Ashazad's choices with him.

Ashazad Nanites Available – 100%

Body

Physical Augmentation
Body Manipulation – 85%
Physical Defense
Skin Hardening – 5%
Scale Hardening – 10%

When the dragons finished conversing, Jared said, "I want to see it. To understand it better. Everything from the abilities you have to the number of nanites. Ashazad, would you be open to a mind meld? And can you facilitate Casey into the meld?"

"I have not tried to renew the connection, but Casey's mind needs rest."

"Okay, let's try this once you wake up. I'm extremely intrigued by the possibilities here. Also, do you mind spending time with Scarlet to work on our technovirus problem? We still haven't isolated it sufficiently to implement a cure, or at least contain the virus so it stops killing us for good."

"It is curable."

"Wait, what? How—" Jared snapped his mouth shut and held up a hand. "Don't worry about it now. Let's wait for the mind meld so you don't have to break things down to a layman's terms."

"Very well."

Jared could barely contain his excitement. It was closer to jubilation, and it made the events of the past few days seem worthwhile. Not only had Ashazad and Casey stumbled upon a way to grow drastically stronger in a short time, they also had a cure for the technovirus plaguing mankind.

Jared didn't want to wait to dive into the specifics, but if Ashazad said Casey needed rest, he'd abide that wisdom. Jared turned on his heel and walked away. He needed a place to mediate. There were so many avenues they could take with this knowledge. For a fleeting moment, he thought about a way to make every human in the world aware of the lies told by the cities, followed by the fact there was a cure. However, that meant he'd need to reveal the bonding process. He couldn't trust that secret with humanity. It was quite possible there were others in the world already bonded. Elle and Kitty were evidence enough, but to reveal the secret to the world would cause more chaos. He wanted to bring about the exact opposite.

They'd figure out how to get the news out to everyone without causing mayhem, but now was not the time. Instead, they would use the new information to improve their small band of *Protectors* and take the fight above. Once they'd made headway in their fight against the cities, then they'd inform the rest of humanity. Hopefully, it would allow mankind to once again expand and re-populate the earth. Maybe they'd even turn earth's ecosystem back to the natural order.

He found a quiet room to think, but it was difficult for him to enter a state of meditation. His thoughts ran amok with all the possibilities. A cure for the life-ending technovirus was possible. Jared focused his attention on the nanites assigned to *Body Manipulation.* The first thing he did was eliminate their instructions for *Natural Armor* and *Regeneration*. He could change that later, but for now he wanted to see if rapid changes like Casey's were possible.

Holding up a hand, Jared sent his awareness inside, finding the nanites responsible for manipulation and guiding them to the tip of his finger. Picturing what he wanted, Jared willed the nanites to elongate his fingernail into a claw. The nanites reacted slowly, altering their coding into the shape he wanted, but nothing further happened. It was as though they needed other criteria before it kicked off.

Sleep, thought Jared.

That's how all the other enhancements worked. He programmed them, and they changed his physical self while sleeping. Pushing and prodding the large portion of nanites allocated to his current task did not enhance his understanding. It only frustrated him as he hit a wall.

Casey said it was at a cellular level.

Relaxing his thoughts, Jared activated *Hyper-Cognition* and *Clear Mind*. His awareness intensified, but through a force of will, he maintained his state of tranquility with little to no thoughts passing through his mind. Deliberately, Jared opened threads of thought, focused on microscopic portions of his genetic makeup. He followed the DNA strands, and the replicated nanite strands to understand them.

Losing himself in the work, Jared centered his thoughts on a single cell. Casey said this was how he manipulated them so rapidly. After many long moments of study, Jared couldn't figure it out.

Maybe I need to go deeper.

Singling out a single strand of DNA and its components, Jared sought to understand its makeup. Again, he failed to see and understand how to trigger rapid changes.

He went farther.

From his DNA, he drilled down into the molecules, bending his mind to understand them. Further yet, he tried to see the atoms that made up everything. Immediately, a sharp pounding at his temple halted his progress. It was too much for him to process.

Closing down many of the threads, he held only two of them open at once. One thread linked to the nanites contained in a single cell and the other on the cell itself.

Is it possible to manipulate just one?

A single nanite latched on to the cell and replicated it. He didn't know what it had created, only that he'd manipulated the singular cell. Next, he tried to understand what the cell was part of. At the risk of another headache, Jared opened another line of thought and stepped back several layers to focus on the part of his body he hoped to modify.

Slowly, he gathered the nanites to the top of his finger, located the cells responsible for growing his fingernail, and forced them to replicate.

The tip of his finger itched. Attuned as he was to his body, Jared didn't need to open his eyes to know he'd made it grow. It was barely a millimeter, but it had grown.

Satisfied with his own research and abilities, Jared left his trance and stood. The time he'd spent exploring his body seemed like only a few minutes, but from the lack of light coming in the window, it'd taken him much longer than that. A brief edge of panic entered his mind, but quickly receded. If there was any cause for alarm, Scarlet would've alerted him. They needed to get moving soon. This constant edge of panic grated on his nerves. He wanted to get to a safe place for himself, Scarlet, and his new family.

Curious if Casey and Ashazad were awake, Jared left the building to find them. Casey sat with his back to the dragon talking animatedly. From the snippets of conversation, it sounded like they were discussing how dragons reproduce.

"It's an interesting way to ensure the dragon's legacy, but it is also very sad." Jared furrowed his brow and joined the pair's conversation. "I watched Alestrialia and Scarlet's last moments together. I know her mother lives on inside her, but the sense of loss from Scarlet when her mother dissolved into the ether was heartrending."

"It should be a joyous occasion, but Scarlet went through it with no family around. It is fortunate you happened along to help her. Knowing what we do about the world and the predators that lurk among the shadows, it is possible Scarlet would have died before growing strong enough to defend herself."

"I still feel bad for whisking her away from your mother, but I see your point and am very grateful I was there for her. She's remarkable, as are all of you. Speaking of…" Jared motioned for Scarlet to join them. "Are you ready to try this mind meld? Casey, this will be a first for the both of us. While I've done this with Scarlet, I've yet to do it with any of her brothers or another human so I have no idea what to expect."

"Please sit. This will be a challenge for the both of you. It is one thing to experience the mind of a single dragon when we filter our thoughts for you, but two dragons and our thoughts mostly unfiltered may prove taxing."

"Casey, have you ever meditated? This might be easier if you can get into a state of calm before our worlds explode with information."

"Yes, I meditate, though it doesn't always work." He blushed slightly, chagrined.

"Try it again. Only this time, focus on the nanites and the thoughts running through your head. You'll get a grasp on how they function. When I found the byway, it was entirely by accident, but I think I can help guide you there."

"Byway?"

"For me, it is like standing in an infinitely long hallway, with innumerable doors on all sides. When I want to quiet my mind, I push all of my thoughts behind the doors and shut them. It leaves me in quiet solitude, a complete absence of thought. I can open them slowly or blast them all down. I've found that the only way to experience multiple thoughts simultaneously, like the dragons, is if I obliterate the room. However, I had to reach that state of utmost calm before I could do so. Once I'd practiced this enough and become proficient, I gained an ability called *Clear Mind*. It allows me to reach a state similar to what the dragons experience all the time, though not nearly with the same level of intensity."

Casey hesitated, glancing at Ashazad. "That sounds difficult."

"I won't lie, it was difficult at first. But I think you've got a major leg up on me, knowing your body so intimately. You've already shared a thought space with Ashazad, so you also know how it feels. I don't think you'll have too much trouble. At least try before we dive in. It will make things easier and you won't tire as quickly."

"I'll give it a shot."

Jared started his own exercises to calm himself. It happened almost instantly for him as he'd only just ended his earlier meditation. He could have activated his abilities, but waited and worked with Casey to achieve the desired state rather than take the shortcut.

"I've got it!" Casey shouted.

It was almost enough to drive Jared from his own tranquil state, but he managed shrug off the outburst. Calmly, Jared asked Scarlet and Ashazad to begin.

He felt a gentle nudge at his back as Scarlet placed her head against his back. A blinding flash and a world of possibilities exploded into his mind.

Casey cried out and doubled over, grabbing his head in pain.

"I warned you." Jared's voice slurred as he fought to main control of his meditative state. "Compose yourself and enter the meld again. I want you plugged in when Ashazad starts. If there are concepts beyond my understanding, you might be able to explain it for me."

Casey's breathing slowed, and he regained control. The next moment, Jared felt another mind enter the meld, and he understood Casey. His first reaction was to clamp down his thoughts, since it was a massive invasion of privacy, but he let the feeling go. He had nothing to hide from anyone.

A stray thought entered his mind and almost faded into obscurity, but something about it triggered his interest. Immediately Scarlet and Ashazad agreed. He'd randomly thought about getting their entire group into a mind meld. Maybe not all at once, but a little at a time. It was highly invasive, but they would know each other so much better. That knowledge might prove an invaluable resource in the coming days.

"It is worth asking for permission. It will allow you to choose the most effective positions for everyone. It is also how we dragons know each other so thoroughly."

Jared agreed with Scarlet and promised he'd consider it for later.

Finally, Casey made it past his initial surprise and entered the stream of thoughts swirling like a vortex between their minds. Scarlet's mind was complex and seemed endless to Jared, but comparing it to Ashazad was hard. They were so different. Scarlet's thoughts were much easier to understand. It could have resulted from how young she was comparatively, but Jared couldn't say for certain.

In contrast, Ashazad's mind was something ancient, deep and enveloping. Thoughts flitted rapidly through his mind and made little sense. Other ideas came from bygone eras and made even less sense. Disjointed ideas and thoughts confused him.

As if reading his thoughts, Ashazad commented.

"I am learning your ways. Remember, we have not walked the

earth in thousands of years. While much of the language concepts remain, many things ceased to be, or new things became a reality. It will take time to adapt to this modern era."

"I think I understand. Can we begin?" Jared chose to stick with telepathic communication while they were in the meld. It took less effort, and his words weren't slurred.

"Watch. Learn."

The next few hours were nothing short of miraculous. Ashazad led them on a journey through the human body beyond anything he'd ever imagined. The rapid-fire nature of their shared thought space meant the information was exchanged at light speed. If he tried to teach Jared all of this using normal speech, it would take weeks if not months to get through the material, and there would be no telling if he'd understand it even after all the effort.

During the instruction, Jared activated *Clear Mind* to better understand the numerous concepts and ideas presented.

Casey showcased his ability to take the free nanites and rapidly cycle through various abilities with his eyes. Other physical modifications were harder and couldn't happen instantaneously, but for his senses, they could change quickly. Sight, smell, hearing, and touch were all things Casey showed how to change in an instant. He even replicated Jared's new spider senses to a degree. Based on what Jared observed, the abilities he'd gained from the various creatures were better, but only because Casey didn't understand their genetic makeup well enough to replicate it.

All he'd need to do is spend time with Jared and he could study the nanites responsible for adding additional cones and membrane to his eyes and he'd be able to replicate it easy enough. The physical stuff was much harder for Casey, but to Ashazad, it simply extended his other abilities. Neither of them needed to wait until sleeping for changes to take effect because they didn't use "locked" nanites, or the ones he'd used to set into specific categories created by Igor.

Once Jared understood that the changes to him were more permanent, while those that Casey and Ashazad had were often temorary, it didn't feel like he'd wasted any on his choices. It was great to have options and be able to rapidly cycles through them, but Jared was glad he wouldn't have to understand his body at the same level, nor did he have to concentrate to alter one of his abilities.

That delay and extreme concentration to make it happen could prove fatal in a confrontation and he had no desire to limit his reaction time. In contrast, he saw the value for someone like Casey who was their only medic. He could use this new ability to help diagnose and treat those he worked on. He'd become much more efficient in his tasks.

"Ashazad, Scarlet and I talked about permanently changing my body so I don't have to use abilities all the time. I think it's possible, but I'd be curious to see what you think about it."

"Yes, it is possible. In time, I think you could do it. However, I suggest you continue to increase your mental abilities before attempting such a feat. This is especially true if you want to replicate *your Mind* abilities by creating new neural pathways."

"My Clear Mind ability is the one I really want to replicate. I'd love to always maintain it without the use of the nanites. I know if I assign enough nanites into it, it can become a passive ability, but if something happened to the nanites and I lost the ability to use them after becoming dependent, it would be really bad."

"The human mind, and a dragon mind, are the most complex organisms on the face of the planet. It would be much easier for you to alter your musculature, so you always used *Maximum Muscle*. Your brain is not something you should change until you are certain you understand everything completely and thoroughly."

"I didn't plan on doing it soon. It was just a conversation I had with Scarlet a while ago. It would be useful, and I fully understand the complexity. I wouldn't try something I couldn't be a hundred percent certain I'd succeed at. A wrong move or slip up could render me incapacitated."

"Exactly. Tread carefully. Learn everything you can about it, and then I will help you myself when the time is right."

"Thanks, Ashazad. I understand how you both break down and rebuild the cells in your body to create new abilities. I don't know if it's something I can do rapidly, or if I even want to, since I've already got many abilities."

"There is still much you can learn about the process of tearing down and rebuilding cells."

"I couldn't agree more, but the reality is I probably won't use it all that much in the short term," Jared explained. *"We have time to discuss it and learn more later. The technovirus, however, is something that affects us here and now. It's also something we might use as bait to lure more people to our side in the coming conflict."*

"Please attend." Ashazad spent the next hour going into detail about the technovirus and why it corrupted someone to the point of death. The nanites replicated themselves until there was a one-to-one ratio with every strand of DNA. They fused to each strand, and over time it would kill that DNA strand. However, the body needed the DNA strands intact as they were integral to that person's genetic makeup. As the strands died and the nanite took over, the host would become sick.

It often meant their death, but as Jared knew from Igor, many hosts went mad, mutating into wild beasts. It's why the cities kept such a close eye on the survivor settlements. They watched for anyone that showed signs of the corruption and then abducted them, like they had his mother. The cure for the nanites wasn't so much a medicinal cure but changing the nanites so they received instructions to regenerate the DNA strands rather than taking over.

"How would that work? Once assigned or replicated, they are static and don't change."

"Yes, and no."

"Seriously? Both of you?"

Casey chuckled at Jared's questioning. *"When you ask such a complex question, there are multiple sides to the answer."*

"Sorry, please continue."

"You cannot alter the nanites' main programming. However, you may introduce small code changes. In fact, this is how Razael controlled the water folk. Not only did he use his own version of the coding to encapsulate the nanites, he also adapted them to bend to his will. This gave him complete control."

The last few words came out sharply. Ashazad held great disgust for what Razael had become and what he had done to these humans.

Understanding Jared's thoughts, Ashazad corrected him. **"I do not blame Razael, but rather those that did it to him. If he had had his mind intact, there is no way he would have done anything like it."**

Jared didn't want to dwell on the topic and immediately moved his thoughts on to more constructive ideas. *"All right, so how do we introduce these code changes?"*

"It is a simple matter. I can guide you as I have done with Casey. Because the nanites only respond to a human, you must make the changes, but I can guide you on what to do."

"If only I can do it, then how did Razael—"

"He manipulated them and influenced their minds."

Jared shuddered. He couldn't imagine something digging around his mind, pushing thoughts and whispers of coercion into them.

Jared pushed through the revulsion rippling through him. *"Please show me how."*

The next few hours Jared spent reprogramming his nanites so they'd no longer corrupt his body. By the time they finished, he couldn't keep his eyes open. His body was fine, but his mind screamed in protest and he knew he needed to sleep and recover some of his wits.

"I'm still a little confused about how others can make these changes. Sure, I can do it because I'm bonded and understand the nanites and can control them, but if someone doesn't have the bond, they remain dormant, right?"

"I see I did not explain sufficiently. These nanites, the ones you changed, are the same ones that replicate throughout your body upon initial injection of the nanites. You do not have to bond to add the programming I guided you through. Anyone may do that. The problem arises in that most of humankind are unaware of the individual nanites in their bodies. It is why none of these people enslaved by my brother had any idea what was happening until it was too late."

"How would we distribute a cure? It's not possible, right? You'd have to—"

"Yes. I, or one of my kin, would need to manipulate their minds into making the change."

"Ashazad, I—"

"I understand and do not intend to force my will upon anyone. This would be, in effect, the same thing my brother did to an entire colony of people, and we will not stand for it."

"There's got to be another way. What about some kind of electronic signal to alter them?"

"You would have to find a way for that signal to come from the host's own mind. I honestly do not know if that is possible. Kirgor

might have a better idea on that. Perhaps the work he and Pete are looking at will yield insight into that possibility."

"So much for using the cure as a way to lure more to our cause," Jared lamented.

"If we find the professor, or his equipment, perhaps we can effectuate a global cure. At present, I know of no other way to do it."

"Thank you, Ashazad. Truly. It's just disappointing. I'd hoped we'd cure everyone."

"Do not fear. Look how far you have come in such a short time. With this new technology, anything is possible."

"I appreciate the encouragement. You're right, there's no reason for me to act like this. It doesn't help anyone. Actually, do you mind showing your brothers how to do this so they can help the others? Also, we'll let the larger group know you can do this for them, but that you'd need to take over their mind for a short time. I'm not sure if everyone will agree to it given their…experiences."

"I will share the knowledge and gladly assist those willing," Ashazad promised.

Jared nearly disengaged from the meld, but something tickled the back of his mind. *"You know, something still doesn't add up for me. I thought Professor Igor said the nanites remain dormant until after the bonding?"*

"That is not exactly true. The moment the nanites enter a host's body, they replicate, eating the radiation poisoning, and sustaining the body. They are susceptible to this micro command you just gave them, but the host cannot control them directly until after bonding."

"See, that's what doesn't make sense. How did I get Night Vision and the ability to survive extreme temperatures if I couldn't control them?"

"That is easy enough to explain. The external stimuli

influenced the nanites. Repeated exposure to circumstances that required the nanites to constantly heal or sustain your body in certain ways resulted in their alteration."

"Then why didn't everyone here gain Night Vision during their time in the water?"

"As I said previously, Razael encapsulated their nanites, forcibly preventing any external stimuli or commands."

"Interesting. I wonder if Igor even knew of this possibility. If he did, why didn't he fix it himself?"

"We may never know."

Jared thought he'd feel liberated after getting a cure for the nanites plaguing his body, but he only felt indifferent. It could have been the fact they had enough boosters to last them a long time, or that Scarlet was able to temporarily block the corruption before Ashazad came along.

The whole experience put him in a melancholy mood. He rounded everyone up on auto-pilot, explained they could have the virus removed, and then retreated to the side away from everyone else to watch the proceedings. He wasn't exactly sure everyone would want to have it done right away, but even the more hesitant got in line to have their bodies rid of the technovirus. Ridding their bodies of the virus wasn't exactly right, either. Repairing was a more apt description. They needed to repair the nanite coding to facilitate the cure.

The first thing Ashazad did was mind meld with his brothers, showing them how to cure their companions. All but Ballog learned how to help their companions. Ballog was still unconscious, but Scarlet insisted he was fine so Jared shrugged it off. They'd wait for him to wake.

The curing process went long into the night. Each person became easier for Ashazad, but he still had to work through the thirty people not bonded and it took a while to get it done. He'd set a watch through the night, but it was probably unnecessary since Scarlet had tasked Kynderri with patrolling while she was in the mind meld. Kitty also kept up her roving patrol on the ground. They were as safe as they could be, but Jared planned to move out early the next day. Already, they'd stayed much longer than he wanted and he couldn't risk delaying anymore.

The next morning brought with it a new day and everyone walked around with broad smiles on their faces. Apparently, the curing of their bodies proved a joyous occasion for them. It made Jared wonder all the more why he was so indifferent about it, but it didn't really matter. There was a cure. It wasn't ideal for the rest of the world, but at least those who joined their cause would benefit.

Shortly after the sun crested the horizon, Ballog and Jax finally woke. It'd been a little over three days since they started the bond. The dragon explained that the wound on his body had pushed him beyond his limits and it was everything he could do just to help Jax through the pain and changes. On the bright side, the wound where the phase round penetrated was almost healed.

Eager to get going, Jared gathered everyone together to talk through their next moves.

17 DRAGON HUNTING

For the next hour they talked about all of their plans, including moving farther from the city. Several people called out destinations. They had a few people suggest straight south, heading toward Florida and the Carolinas, but Jared overruled them and reminded everyone about the Daggers and what they'd almost done to him.

They couldn't do anything more to him or Scarlet, but the same wasn't true for everyone else in the group. A single stray bullet was all it would take to end someone's life. Jared didn't want to risk it.

A few more names entered the list, but only one received a near unanimous vote after he'd homed in on it.

"Is there anyone who has a good reason we shouldn't go to Colorado?" Jared spread his arms to encompass the group.

"It's too far?" a voice from the back chimed in.

"I'd argue that's exactly why it's a good option. Here's perspective for you. Scarlet can fly from our old colony to New York City in less than an hour. That's over two hundred miles. I don't know exactly how far Colorado is, but it can't be over two thousand miles. That means we can fly back here in half a day. It's not that far when you put it into perspective. Even if she didn't fly at full speed, we could easily make the journey back in a day. I'm counting on that, because once we're ready we will go back to absorb the remaining nanites in the lake."

There was no further questioning. Traveling so fast was a foreign concept to everyone. Vanessa had had a short flight on Scarlet, and Carla flew on Attis, but distance was a relative thing to most. They wouldn't truly appreciate it until they rode atop their own dragon over a long distance. They could probably get the same experience in a drop ship, but until Pete figured out a way to intercept signals, they wouldn't venture down that road.

"Okay, we know where we're going, but now I'd like to address the other matter we talked about." Jared looked at the dragons, specifically Scarlet. "I think it's time we split up."

Cries of astonishment and dissent rose from the humans present, but the dragons remained silent. They knew what needed to happen and relished the opportunity to see their extended family again.

"Hold up everyone, and let me finish explaining. Not all the dragons will go. Originally, I'd thought of sending the three oldest, but I think they should go in pairs."

"Jared, that's not—"

Jared looked back at Scarlet and switched to telepathy to explain himself. *"I know it's probably unnecessary, but I think it prudent that each of your brothers has another to cover his back. We cannot lose anyone else. I won't lose anyone else."*

Scarlet weighed his words, eventually accepting his plan.

"Do you think sending the eldest is the best way to go, or would it matter?"

"Yes, it will show the others we are serious and lend credibility. Though, I do not think it will take much convincing."

Turning back to the rest of the people, Jared resumed his explanation. "For those of you concerned with this, let me explain. Scarlet's brothers will find the remaining dragons. The earth, air, and water dragons. We need every advantage we can get, and this is a surefire way to make sure we're strong enough to take on the cities."

Many of those recently bonded looked at their new companions in fear. It wasn't his first choice to separate them so soon, but it would be a waste of time for everyone to walk to Colorado when Scarlet's brothers might find their family and be back before the water folk reached their destination. This was the most economical use of the time they'd spend traveling.

The only pair that didn't balk or look scared was Vanessa and Malsour. They hadn't even flinched at the idea. Both knew the stakes, and they both had incredible poise. Seeing her stand tall and proud next to Malsour made Jared smile. She was an incredible woman, and he still had a hard time believing she loved him. A paranoid part of him wondered if it was just the complete lack of options for a partner, but he dismissed the thoughts lest they poison his view of her.

He believed she loved him for him, not because there were no other options. A part of him had a wriggling doubt, and he hated himself for it. If she'd been around back in his home colony, and expressed an interest like this, he wouldn't think twice about it, but out here, after what he'd done for them, was a different story. Only time would tell if their feelings for each other were real or misplaced.

Jared realized he'd let his voice trail off and now stood staring awkwardly at Vanessa while everyone shifted from foot to foot casting glances between them. He felt a flush creeping up his neck and cleared this throat.

"Grab your things and be ready to move in half an hour."

Jared watched all the newly bonded members of their group conversing with their dragon companions. He hadn't said who was going yet other than at least the three oldest.

Malsour, Ashazad, and Kynderri looked ready to go, and Vanessa, Casey, and Marie made their way into the building they'd slept in to retrieve their belongings. The dragons must have already told their human counterparts about the journey.

Pete and Kirgor went back to examining the robots they had splayed out before them. Jared let him know they needed to pack up and move out soon, but Pete assured him they'd be ready and that they'd keep working until the moment they left.

"Scarlet, who will accompany your brothers?"

"I will leave it up to them."

"I think Kirgor and Ballog should remain behind, if you don't mind. We need Pete and Kirgor to crack the technology from the cities and Ballog needs to heal. I thought about asking Ashazad to stay behind since he can cure the technovirus, but now that the rest of your brothers know how, it's not critical."

"I do not believe Ashazad would stay behind even if you asked."

"All right, let's go ask them."

Jared walked closer to her three eldest siblings. "Brothers—" Jared choked on the next words as a wave of warmth washed over him from Scarlet. Instinctively, he reached up to place a hand on her side as he continued. "We must decide who will leave in search of your kin."

"Agreed, little brother." Malsour returned his greeting in kind.

The wave of emotion from Scarlet passed through their bond once again, only this time Jared's own emotions mirrored hers. Though he'd only used the word *brothers* to address them all at once instead of being impersonal with dragons, they'd accepted him into the family.

"I will go to the water dragons with Kanundran. Ashazad will

seek our kin of the air with Myndris, and Kynderri, and Braddra will seek our earthen kin."

As Malsour called forth the names, his brothers stepped forward, preparing to leave.

Kanundran's companion Dawn gave her new family one last look, sadness briefly crossing her features, before she went to collect her belongings.

Looking at all those who'd bonded, Jared realized he needed to spend more time getting to know them. He knew all their names, but he didn't really know anything about them. Who was Dawn, and why had Kanundran bonded with her?

Braddra's companion David was another mystery. Jared knew nothing about him, aside from the fact he cured all the animal hides they'd collected.

Myndris and Sean looked at each other. A quick exchange of words and Sean stepped back, leaving to retrieve his gear. Sean was another person Jared had spent little time with. The guy was tall, looked athletic, and of all the water folk had put the most amount of time into pushing his body to regain its strength.

Vanessa knew her people extremely well, but he hadn't thought to ask her about their personal lives. He chided his lack of leadership skills and promised himself he'd resolve it soon. He could ask Vanessa, but that felt like a copout. No, he needed to put in the effort himself and work with all of those in their group. They'd go into battle eventually and without knowing their strengths and weaknesses, he couldn't properly deploy them in a fight. His goal during their trek to Colorado was to get a better understanding of everyone in the group. They'd have three weeks with almost nothing else to do. It was the perfect opportunity to get to know everyone.

Scarlet's six brothers spent a short moment saying goodbye and launched themselves into the air, headed in three different directions.

"Scarlet, I don't think we have to tell them this, but they know to stay away from cities and human settlements, right?"

"Yes. I asked them to avoid any confrontation with them, but that they should continue to take down prey along the way to absorb more and more nanites."

"Can you show me where they are going?" asked Jared.

His hand still on her side, his vision swam, and Jared sat down next to her to keep from falling over. The view showed a lush earth from a high vantage point. Looking down, Jared realized they were somewhere over North America. He saw the Atlantic off to the east, the Gulf of Mexico south, and land as far as he could see to the north and west.

The view zipped by until they came to the southernmost point in North America before following the land across a narrow strip into South America. Finally, the passing landscape paused somewhere near the southern tip of the continent. Then, the scene before him shifted again, and he was once again viewing the same exodus of the earth dragons from Alestrialia's vision.

"Oh, man. I hadn't even considered that they might be on a different continent. They can't fly, so if they'd been in Europe or Asia, there's no way they'd be able to get there. I can't believe I didn't think this through."

"I saw no need to bring it up because they can get here over land. They need to cross a dense jungle, but it should pose no problem for them. Besides, they are masters of the earth and could just as soon burrow beneath any ocean."

"Do you think they'd be a liability in a battle? If they can't fly, they'd be sitting ducks for the drop ships."

"Initially, you are right. Eventually, the battle will spread to the earth, and they will be invaluable. Also, the thick hide and bone

covering the top of their body is nearly impenetrable. It may even be impervious to phase rounds."

Jared recalled the vision Alestrialia had once shown him of the earth dragons and their slow plod into the mountain that swallowed them up. They'd looked ferocious and Scarlet's explanation made sense looking at them.

"I hope your brothers can find everyone."

"Knowing how stubborn they can be, I doubt they will return until they accomplish their mission."

"Let's hope that stubbornness doesn't land them in trouble. What about your air and water kin?"

The scenes changed again, showing the ocean in all its glory: an ocean untouched by the war. That gave Jared pause. What if South America didn't look like that anymore and Kynderri couldn't find the earth dragons? He mentioned as much to Scarlet, but she didn't seem overly concerned. The dragons were far beneath the surface, and anything that transpired above wouldn't affect them.

After the view of the ocean, the scene changed one last time, rocketing over the ocean until it came to rest on a brilliant white visage. It showed a continent that looked entirely made of ice.

"Our air kin will be the most challenging to find. It should come as no surprise, but extreme cold will slow Ashazad and Myndris down."

"They'll make it though, right?"

"Yes, but it will not be a pleasant experience."

"Well, we've got a few weeks ahead of us, anyway."

Scarlet disengaged the memories and Jared stood back up. He had to blink a few times to get his bearing and regain his equilibrium. Once he'd steadied himself, he went to round everyone up.

Having the dragons accompanying them helped their speed greatly, since they could carry a lot of the equipment. Initially, they bristled at being nothing more than pack mules, but Scarlet squashed the indignation quickly. She only needed to remind them of the single phase round penetrating Ballog's scales to refresh the need for urgency and speed.

Kirgor and Scarlet could also carry one or two people at any given time. Jared wasn't sure when Kirgor made the changes, but it was clear he and Pete steadily increased their understanding of the nanites and the robots.

Both Pete and Casey had advantages over the rest of the water folk. The nanites being technological and biological hybrids allowed both to understand them much easier and faster than anyone else. It was a good thing too since both held vital roles to their success. Casey being their only medic was literally their lifeline for anyone injured in a fight. If Pete could figure out the technology and how the robots communicated with the cities, they had a real chance of capturing a drop ship to use as a boarding party.

"Hey, Scarlet, I was just thinking about the work Pete and Kirgor are doing, and I might have a viable way to infiltrate the cities. So as far as I know, there are at least two floating cities. There may be more around this continent, but I've only heard of two. One on the east coast and another on the west. I'm fairly certain the one in the east is now sitting over Cayuga Lake by the old colony." Jared hooked a thumb over his shoulder in the direction they'd come from. "What we don't know, and need to find out, is if the two cities have the same drop ships."

"I see..." Scarlet said, swiftly making the connection. "**It could work.**"

"We'll use them against each other, and they'll be none the wiser. Obviously, the ships would need to be the same, and we'd need to be certain they don't communicate with each other differently."

"**Which means we will need to capture a ship from both.**

Preferably intact so as not to damage any possible communications mechanisms. It is a risky endeavor, but I see the value. If we pulled it off, we could capture as many ships as we need from one city to ferry the whole group to the other."

"I don't think we'd want everyone up there. I mean, we have dragons that can fly and potentially more in a few weeks. No, I'm thinking about a smaller strike force that can get in and disable any defenses the cities might have. Myself, Elle, and Pete for starters. With Elle's camouflage and Pete's technical genius we should be able to figure it out and hopefully stay under the radar. I also have the uniforms we took from the various drop ships that should help us avoid immediate detection."

"That is a dangerous proposal."

"It is, but what are the alternatives? We attack from the air only to find out they have a massive fleet of drop ships, or well-fortified defenses that pick us off before we ever get close enough?"

"I am not keen on this plan, but I see the wisdom in a stealthy approach. If you succeed and disable any defenses, then we will have unfettered access to the cities."

"This is all hypothetical, anyway. I'm just trying to find alternate paths to take the fight above."

Jared walked in silence for several hours, thinking through the various ideas. Scarlet had said nothing further and no doubt she also thought through possibilities. The walk throughout the first day proved enjoyable. Everyone still rode the high from having their bonding and having the technovirus cured.

People were genuinely happy for those that'd found a companion in Scarlet's brothers, and hoped they would also find a companion when Malsour and the others returned. In the meantime, they enjoyed the wide-open world, walking through the wastelands with more protection and a sense of safety than they had in their entire lives. Nothing dared attack them with seven dragons and a giant cat patrolling the area.

Shortly after the first day, Johan sidled up to him, hesitant to speak. Jared gave him some time to articulate the thoughts churning through his mind. He'd had a couple days bonded with Midri now and no doubt wanted to discuss something they'd talked about.

"Jared, Midri and I...we have been talking, and I think we should attempt to find supplies along the way to Colorado."

"What kind of supplies? We're already scavenging along the way for clothes and other needs. What more do you want?"

"Well, I want to get some raw materials to make explosives."

"Explosives? What are we going to do with those while we're walking?"

"It wouldn't be actual explosives, just the raw materials. Most of them are completely benign until synthesized. Midri is something of an expert in alchemy. He says there are plenty of explosives we can make, and the materials are relatively easy to find. We've got the grenades you got from the armory, but they don't pack a lot of punch compared to what we've got to deal with, you know?"

"Agreed, they wouldn't make much of a dent. Even if you threw one into the cargo hold of a drop ship, I don't think it'd be enough to take one down."

"Have a look." Johan handed him a crumpled scrap of paper with a list of components on it.

Jared scanned the list, immediately recognizing some components from the explosives manual he'd read. "So, this alchemy, it's basically like chemistry?"

He didn't see the rarer components like barium nitrate, but there were entries for sulfur, calcium, barium, magnesium, and a few others he didn't recognize. There were entries for dynamite and other already made explosives, but the chances they'd stumble on any of that stuff was improbable. The armory he'd found was already a miracle and the fact that the explosives hadn't degraded to the point of uselessness or instability was a second miracle.

"Basically, yeah. They didn't call it that before Midri went underground."

The natural components on the list were something they could look into. He didn't know the first thing about finding them, but if Midri had an idea, then it wouldn't hurt to look along the way.

"So, this alchemy is for building bombs, right?"

Johan hesitated, his brow furrowing in thought. "Not entirely, but that's certainly a part of it. He knows how to make various combustible compositions and potions."

Jared mirrored Johan's furrowed brow. "What exactly is a potion? I've heard the term before, but I don't really understand it."

Johan shrugged. "Midri said it's like medicine or an elixir."

Smirking, Jared asked what an elixir was and received nearly the same response. Jared resolved to speak with Midri about it himself. It was clear Johan was out of his depth here, but Jared had to admit the idea of creating explosives and *potions* appealed to him.

"Don't you think that's kind of dangerous?"

"Yes, but that's the second part of what I wanted to talk with you about." Johan looked nervous and hesitated before continuing. "I know you want us all to work on our *Mind* enhancements, and I will, but I also want to enhance my reflexes and endurance so I can handle these materials without blowing myself up." Johan blushed crimson and looked away from Jared. He cleared his throat and continued. "There's this one combination that produces PETN." Johan pointed to a cluster of ingredients with the label. "It's more powerful than TNT, but less stable and requires precision to make. The ingredients are easy to gather or synthesize. If we get enough, we can fly it above the city and drop it down on top. Boom!" Johan smashed his fist into his hand, imitating the explosion.

"Can we transport all the ingredients safely? I don't want to carry volatile explosives for weeks."

"Yes, we need to dissolve the ingredients together and do a few other processes to create the crystals. Even then, it requires a strong shock to detonate. Not as strong as TNT, but it won't spontaneously explode."

"Okay, get with Midri and figure out where we'll find some of this stuff. Do you have any idea what kind of medicines he can help create?"

"Not really. He rattled off a few things, but I have no idea."

"Maybe grab Casey and have him talk with Midri. He might understand some of them. Also, do you need any equipment for this stuff?"

"Well, it would be easier for sure, but we'll figure it out."

"All right, sounds like a plan. Thanks, Johan! If Midri comes up with any other ideas, please let me know. As for your enhancement paths, that is completely up to you. I made a suggestion, but I won't dictate anything to you. If you think it'll help you do this and provide greater benefit to our cause, then you have my support. Do you want me to help guide you through it?"

"Yes, please. I tried, but I'm not sure how to do it."

Jared explained the process and coached him through the selections.

Johan Nanites Available – 100%

Body

> Physical Augmentation
>> *Body Manipulation – 20%*
> Physical Enhancement

Reflex – 40%
Endurance – 20%

Mind

Brain Augmentation
Intelligence Enhancement – 20%

"You sure you want to split your assignments like that? I meant what I said. If you want to push more into reflexes and endurance, I have no issues with it."

"No, I think this is good. You're right that we need to increase our intelligence. Many of these things Midri talked about, I couldn't understand."

"Okay, once you've confirmed the selections in your mind, it'll allocate them, and you'll go through upgrades when you sleep. When Midri is ready, you'll do the same thing, only think about his status screen to pull it up."

"Thanks for the help!"

After Johan dropped back with the others, Jared glanced over at Scarlet in wonder.

"Your brothers are…" Jared didn't know what to say. The diversity of their knowledge and talents amazed him. When they'd first settled at the cliffs, he'd considered finding another colony to get equipment and training for various professions, but it turned out they didn't need to after all.

"Not to sound callous, but all the water folk are babies in many respects. Only two or three of them were adults by human standards when Razael imprisoned them. Most were teenagers and some adolescents. My brothers are thousands of years old and have seen many, many human generations come and go. You saw how they used to live with some humans side by side. Many of those humans were incredible and smart, but sadly there were not

enough to fend off the hordes that came to claim their lives."

"The more I hear about your brothers and your history, the more I want to know. I wish we knew why and how you came to be. Mankind has many theories of our origination such as a divine creator or evolution from a microorganism. Personally, I can't see how something so complex as a human evolved from nothing. You told me you had a creator even if you don't know who. You're just as complex as a human, if not more, so it stands to reason that we also had a creator. The more I learn about my own body and my mind, the more I'm convinced someone created us."

"I wish we knew. It is something our water kin may know more about. I told you before, they are immensely wise and have thought about our purpose and inception often. Still, I do not believe they know the answers to your questions either. There is an instinctual part of us that knows we had a definite point in time where we came to be."

"If there were answers to these questions, you'd probably have found them already after so many millennia."

"The answer may not exist on this planet." Scarlet looked into the sky.

"You think you're not from the earth?"

"We are definitely of the earth. As stated, there is a point in time we came to be on this planet. That was our inception. This we know. What we do not know is how it happened. Did our creator also create humans?"

"Do you think there is life beyond the earth?"

"Why would you think otherwise? You believe yourself created, yes?"

"Well, yes—"

"Then your creator, are they of this world? Someone or something that could create all this would relegate themselves to a

singular planet? You have seen the stars and planets in the heavens. Surely, there is more out there."

Could there be? Jared wondered. *Are we merely one among many species in the universe?* "You know, there were rumors that the people in the cities figured out a way to venture into space indefinitely."

"That would be incredible to experience. Our air kin can fly much farther into the upper atmosphere than the rest of us. They can easily withstand the extreme cold and minimal oxygen levels. However, to venture out into space is another matter entirely."

"Someday we'll find out the truth to that rumor. After discovering dragons exist and seeing the insane creatures roaming about, it wouldn't surprise me in the least. My expectations of the world and what is real no longer mean anything."

With thoughts of the stars and what might exist beyond their tiny world, Jared walked in silence the rest of the day. Occasionally, one of the water folk joined him to ask questions. Vanessa hadn't joined him for a while, and he determined to spend more time with her soon.

Later that night, he took the time to walk everyone else through their status screens, enhancement paths, and the benefit of each.

Carla, Casey, and Pete backed him up, explaining that the extra understanding was invaluable and would help them make more informed decisions. It would also allow them to communicate better with the dragons.

Scarlet interrupted his explanation partway through to let him know she planned to meld with her brothers and show how they could best help their companions as well.

Jared thanked her and dove back into his instruction without missing a beat. "Johan brought up a good point yesterday. I won't change my stance that *Mind* is the way to go at the start, but there are other things you can work on in the meantime. For instance, eventually we will want to engage with other people and settlements. Please don't take this the wrong way, but your current appearance may exacerbate any encounter we have."

Jared held up a hand to forestall any arguments and continued. "I know it's not your fault and I have no issues with it." Jared looked at Vanessa while he said it and smiled. "That said, other humans may not accept you as you are—not at first. I don't know how many nanites you'd need to put into *Body Manipulation* for you to change your forms back, but please consider it.

"Another good point Johan brought to my attention is how he can best support the group. He's got projects where it makes sense for him to enhance some physical attributes. Midri knows how to create powerful explosives we can use in our upcoming fight. However, the substances are volatile when mixed, and Johan increased his reflexes and endurance to make sure he has a steady hand while mixing the components. These are both valid reasons to assign nanites to other areas. I only ask that you consider all angles, and if you are unsure, please talk it through with myself and Vanessa."

There was no dissent from the group, and Jared suggested they rest up and be ready to head out early the next day.

"Jared?"

"Hey, Vanessa, what's up?"

"Thank you for teaching everyone and for always helping everyone. Also, thank you for your acceptance of our...appearance." She smiled up at him and gave him a quick peck on the lips. Her touch made his skin tingle and warmed his cheeks.

"You're welcome. I meant every word. I'll admit, at first it was a little disconcerting, but now I rarely notice any of the mutations. The only time I do is when I'm talking about it like this."

"I want to assign some to *Body Manipulation* tonight. A quarter of those available. The rest I'll put into *Mind*. Out of all my people, I should be the one to focus on reverting my features back. If we make any deals or negotiations with the colonies, I need to be there. We don't need everyone to revert right away. They can do it in time, and the two of us, plus Elle, can interface with those in other colonies."

"Good idea. I think at a minimum, people should think about assigning a small amount into *Regeneration* to repair their eyesight. Many still have trouble seeing very far." Jared paused, glancing around him for Carla. "You know, I didn't even think about it, but I wonder how Carla is doing. After she got those spider abilities, her eyesight changed a lot."

"She can see better, but she still can't see at a distance. The vision allows her to see the vibrations, in the dark, and a couple other perks, but it didn't sharpen her vision."

Jared felt the shame heat his cheeks. He should've checked in on her, and said as much to Vanessa.

"Yes, you should have." Vanessa smiled coyly and tapped him on the nose. "You'll get there, Jared. I know you're still learning how to be a good leader, and everyone here recognizes you didn't choose this. You remember those thoughts you heard questioning our choices and ability to lead? I found out who it was and had a chat with them. It was born out of frustration and fear. I firmly believe that everyone here is with us, but it won't be without bumps along the way."

"Thank you." Jared drew her into a hug and held her tight, enjoying her warmth and closeness. "There's so much more I need to learn from you about all of this."

"I think you're doing an amazing job." Her coy smile appeared again, and Jared lowered his lips to hers, giving her a polite kiss so as not to make those around them feel awkward.

"Okay, so we're agreed, then? Everyone should add a small amount into *Body Manipulation*."

"Agreed."

Jared raised his voice once again. "One more note before I'll shut up and let you rest. Vanessa and I both agree that you should all assign some into *Body Manipulation*. The first thing you should do after is push them all into *Regeneration* to repair your eyesight. Once back to normal, you'll want to re-assign them to *Remodeling* to revert your appearance back. *Regeneration* won't help you there because your body believes the mutations normal. Scarlet can work with you and her brothers to help you along your path because it will require intense focus and knowledge of your anatomy to get it done. Thanks for listening, everyone."

Most of the group stayed by the fire pit they created and lit with a tiny blast of fire from Scarlet. Jared lay with his back to Scarlet, and Vanessa snuggled against his side. This moment was perfect, and he never wanted it to end. Before he nodded off to sleep, Jared nudged Vanessa.

"Do you…I—" Jared's voice squeaked. He cleared his throat and tried again. "If you'd like, perhaps we can walk together tomorrow?" He dropped his head to stare at the ground, suddenly unsure of himself.

"I thought you'd never ask. I'd love to." Vanessa pressed into his side and laid her head on his shoulder.

The smile she gave him made his heart beat so fast he feared she'd feel it through his chest. Jared returned the smile and wrapped his arm around her. He was in his own little world with Vanessa and nothing else mattered.

Jared's spirits were in the clouds as they set out the following day. He hardly remembered their surroundings because he spent the whole time talking with Vanessa and learning about her childhood.

It wasn't until dusk when Scarlet called out to him that he snapped out of it.

"Where are you?" She'd taken to the skies some time ago to scout the area and Jared didn't see her.

"I am a few miles southwest of you. There is a colony along the road we travel."

"Is it a small colony? Are there any roads that go around?"

"It is larger than the one by the lake, and there are roads that curve around. I can guide you."

Jared strained his eyes, looking for Scarlet against the sky, but he couldn't see her, which meant this little colony shouldn't be able to either. However, the massive dragons that accompanied them would be a problem.

"Is it going to be a problem for your brothers? They don't exactly have a low profile."

"I think the trees on the west side should provide sufficient cover, but it might be prudent to send Kitty to investigate."

"All right, I'll have her go check it out."

Jared contemplated walking into the village to assess the situation himself but decided against it. Eventually, he'd visit colonies, but now was not the time. They weren't far enough from the floating city just yet, and he didn't want to endanger others, nor did he want anyone to know they were around.

Kitty came back and reported that they should pass unnoticed, provided the dragons lowered their heads to stay concealed by the trees.

It took a couple hours to detour around the city, and Jared hoped there weren't any people gallivanting around outside the colony.

The rest of the day was uneventful, and true to her word, Vanessa remained by his side the entire time. They enjoyed chatting and talking about their lives and the lives of those around them. The insight Vanessa provided about her people let him understand all their quirks and personalities. It turned out that Pete was basically a hermit and rarely, if ever, spoke or talked to anyone.

Since taking on the responsibility of technologist and bonding with Kirgor, Pete's demeanor had flipped on its head. He still had trouble communicating, and his stutter often proved frustrating to both parties, but he'd made considerable improvements in the last few weeks.

The longer they talked and the more Jared learned, the more he found himself amazed at how far everyone had come in such a short time. It excited him to think about the force they'd become. Not just to fight the cities, but after they won the war, they'd have a solid group of people to set things right in the world. It was a small group, but they had to start somewhere. They had a budding colony and most of the professions they needed to see it flourish.

It will flourish, Jared promised himself. *No matter what it takes, we will persevere.*

18 WELCOME TO COLORADO

The next week passed quickly; already they'd been on the road for nine days, and the constant walking sapped everyone's strength. Jared decided they'd find a place to hole up and recover.

He'd send Kitty out to gather food. A few hearty meals and rest for two days should lift everyone's spirits. They had under two weeks to go if they didn't run into any issues along the way.

The last couple days, Jared had found himself walking hand in hand with Vanessa. Even when he talked to the others in the group, they walked together and joined in asking questions and making small talk. They presented a unified front, and it was obvious they'd grown closer.

Before it got too dark, Jared asked Scarlet to find a place for them to hole up for a couple days. If she could find someplace like the field they'd used the first few days after their flight from the city, that would serve nicely.

"I will find a resting place."

"Thanks."

It didn't take long before Scarlet let him know she'd found a small abandoned town. All the buildings were empty, many gutted by fires long ago. There were several gulches nearby that the dragons could use to keep a low profile. Once they'd arrived, Jared addressed everyone before they spread out to explore.

"We'll hole up here for a day or two and let everyone get their strength back. I need a couple folks to help me chop firewood. Daryl? Can you and Kitty head out hunting? I'd like us to have some fresh food to replenish everyone's energy."

"Aye." Daryl nodded at Kitty before dropping his gear and stalking off with only his phase rifle.

Jared gathered the volunteers for chopping firewood. They hadn't brought axes with them, but a few had hatchets. Collecting the weapons, Jared led them off the road and a short distance into the trees. It wasn't the most efficient tool for hacking into hardened, desiccated trees, but it worked well enough for the time being.

Everyone else not occupied filtered through the buildings, laying claim to an area. Jared didn't clear the buildings because his spider senses let him reconstruct the images in his mind, confirming they were vacant. Aside from a few smaller rodents, there was nothing overtly dangerous for the group. If something showed up, everyone had weapons and could fend for themselves, not to mention they had half a dozen dragons surrounding them.

It was nice that he didn't have to shoulder the burden solo anymore. They'd become much more independent, and it would only improve as they all became stronger. Several times throughout the last week when they'd stopped for breaks, Jared and Johan coached people on the use of the phase weapons. Eventually, they'd managed to get everyone in the group passingly familiar to the point they weren't afraid to carry a weapon and use it if needed. Several of them had yet to test their mettle in a fight, but Jared was much more confident in them now than when they'd first set out from the lakeside town to their home in the cliffs.

For the next two days, they lounged around the area, feasting on whatever Daryl and Kitty found. They'd had a variety of meals, including wild dogs, deer, and a smattering of rabbits and birds. Several of those that had bonded approached him, letting him know they were ready to assign their nanites. Only Johan and Casey had done so since the bonding ceremony.

When he'd asked about it before, they'd made excuses or told him they hadn't decided yet and wanted more time to think about it. Jared agreed to help everyone that night and told them he'd stay on watch to make sure everyone was okay. He also asked everyone who planned to make the changes to move into one building so he could keep an eye on them.

There was no need to set a patrol since the dragons spread out in every direction. Nothing would come for them during the night. If they did, Jared felt sorry for whatever hapless creature wandered into the area.

He sat next to Vanessa and held her hand as she fell asleep. She'd opted to dump most of her nanites into *Mind* attributes, aside from the one-fourth she'd dedicated to *Body Manipulation* as they'd talked about before.

Vanessa Nanites Available – 100%

Body

Physical Augmentation
Body Manipulation – 25%

Mind

Brain Augmentation
Intelligence Enhancement – 75%

She hoped a quarter of the nanites was enough to start changing her body back. Based on the rapid improvements he'd seen in Carla and Pete, he suspected it would be enough, but they had no frame of reference to say for sure. Without Malsour around to help guide her, Jared wasn't certain she'd be able to effect all the changes, anyway. Scarlet promised to help, but they couldn't meld the same way until Vanessa's intelligence improved enough for her to start down the path to *Clear Mind* and increase her *Telepathy* ability.

Images of Cayuga Lake sprang into his mind as he watched everyone sleep. There was so much potential for fast growth there, yet there was nothing they could do. The city floated directly above it, and a treasure trove of nanites lay below. Somehow, they needed to get back there and absorb them. If they hijacked the drop ships, there was potential he could take the bonded humans with him in the night and quickly absorb some. His only concern was the light show that was sure to follow.

The lake extended many miles though, so it was possible they could circle around to the opposite tip where he and Scarlet had hidden the robot parts, but even then, the light would be visible, especially from the sky. All the plans were hypothetical anyway, since Pete needed to figure out a way to hijack whatever signals the ships used.

These thoughts kept Jared's mind occupied throughout the night. Occasionally those going through changes stirred, but most of them lay quietly.

It was quite an interesting contrast from Johan's changes the other day. When he'd gone through all his physical enhancements, it'd had some interesting side-effects. He'd thrashed about in his sleep and Jared had ended up moving him away from the others for fear he'd accidentally hurt them.

That thrashing had lasted through the entire night, and when Jared asked Johan about it the next day, he'd said he didn't think it was something he normally did.

Jared had discussed it with Scarlet, and they'd come to the conclusion that the reflex changes had made his muscles spasm uncontrollably. It was similar to tapping the knee and the leg jerking forward. Only, with the nanites, it'd been a lot more intense.

Seeing things well in hand and the night nearly over, Jared went to find Scarlet.

"You awake?"

"I am."

"Are you good to scout the area one more time? I was thinking today might be a good time to get flying lessons in. All of your brothers now have seats formed, Ballog finished healing, and we have a couple days of down time."

"Yes, that sounds good. My brothers grow restless. The chance to stretch their wings is exactly what they need."

Plans made, Jared walked back inside, waiting patiently until everyone woke from the changes. It was midday before the first people roused. One of them was Vanessa as she staggered out of the building. Jared ran up to her and steadied her.

"There's so much." Vanessa shook her head, staggering against Jared and muttering incoherently. She squeezed her eyes shut and squinted as she tried in vain to crack an eye open.

"It will take time to adjust. Please sit down," Jared said and guided her over to a stump by the smoldering fire pit.

"There's so much."

Jared knew exactly what she meant. When he'd enhanced his mind, it was a massive influx of mental capacity; it had taken him a while to come to grips with it all. Jared waited patiently for her to adjust. Finally, she opened her eyes and stole Jared's breath.

Her eyes were no longer a milky white but shone a brilliant green. Jared had to pick his jaw off the floor as he stared into her mesmerizing eyes. There had been something exotic about her before and this change only amplified the look. Not only did they captivate him, they reflected the edge of fierceness Jared had grown to love over the past months.

"Your eyes."

A frown furrowed her brow. "What happened to them?"

"They—" Jared cleared his throat, his voice coming out hoarse. "They're beautiful."

Jared realized her disorientation wasn't the influx of mental information like it was for him, though that could be part of it, but rather her eyesight being restored.

"Vanessa." Jared cupped her cheek in his hand and grinned like a fool. "Look around."

Vanessa blinked rapidly and looked away from Jared. "I can s—" Her voice cracked, tears streaming down her cheeks.

Still grinning, Jared reached up to wipe the tears away. He stood and held out a hand for her. She took it and they walked through their small encampment. Jared wanted to work with her on all the changes, but after seeing her reaction to the world around her, there was something he wanted to do first.

They stopped in front of Scarlet, and Jared gestured for her to climb on top.

"Scarlet, can you take Vanessa for a quick flight? She had her sight restored, and I'd like her to see the world from a new perspective."

"Absolutely. Hang on tight."

The grin never left his face as he watched Scarlet soar through the sky. Vanessa whooped and hollered in Jared's mind, her thoughts streaming a thousand miles a minute as she absorbed everything around her. The moment they landed, Vanessa shimmied off Scarlet's back and ran to Jared, throwing her arms around him tightly.

"Thank you so much! I don't know how we'll ever repay you for everything you've done for us. That was amazing."

Jared started to ask if she wanted to go through all of her changes right then, but more people stumbled from the room, and Jared broke away to help them adapt. As with Vanessa, everyone had their sight restored. The milky white eyes he'd gotten used to were gone, replaced by blue, green, and brown. Unlike Vanessa, he didn't immediately take them to the dragons for a joy ride since he and Scarlet already planned on that later in the day.

Once he'd helped everyone adjust and determined they were okay, he rejoined Vanessa, and they spent the next few hours going through everything that had changed and what she should focus on. It was likely he'd need to do this again with the others, but the one-on-one time with Vanessa didn't bother him in the least. In fact, he preferred giving her a private run down of everything she had to look forward to. When he was with the group, he'd keep things succinct and revert to teacher mode.

It wasn't like that with Vanessa, and it let him tune out the world to focus on just her. She picked up on the instructions quickly and practiced meditation to explore the nanites in her body. Jared left her to it and found the other group exactly where he'd left them.

"Hey, everyone. I'm sure you noticed it, but your sight should be whole again!" As Jared looked around the small group, he saw all of them had crystal clear eyes and many shimmered from unshed tears. "I can't imagine what it must be like to see the world clearly after so long. I don't want to keep you from the experience, so I'll make this brief."

Jared quickly explained how they could learn to meditate and left them to figure out much of the rest on their own for now. Their dragon companions would be the best help, but since some of Scarlet's brothers were away finding the other dragons Jared promised he'd coach them after they learned to meditate.

So far no one showed signs of adverse effects or had trouble coping with the changes. That hadn't been the case with Johan. After he'd changed, Jared had approached the man and placed a hand on his shoulder.

It was like the touch had shocked him, and he'd rebounded like a cat, landing several feet away in a crouch. Even now, Jared smiled as he remembered the reaction. When Johan moved, he glided across the ground.

After Jared explained everything to Johan and suggested he go work with Midri to understand everything more clearly, Johan had sprung to his feet, accidentally launching himself five feet off the ground.

Jared had watched, amazed at the transformation. Every movement showed calculation and precision. For a moment, he'd regretted not adding more nanites into his physical enhancements, but the thought was fleeting. He'd come a long way from the scrawny explorer of just a few months ago. Aside from his facial features, he hardly recognized that person anymore. He stood inches taller, his muscles had tripled in size, and the wisdom behind his eyes was leaps and bounds ahead of the old him.

Jared gave everyone several hours to explore their bodies and practice meditation before he gathered them all into one place.

"I know you're all excited to keep exploring your bodies, but I also wanted you to get a taste of flying today."

Cheers went up around the group. Only Carla and Vanessa had flown besides him. There'd been a couple asks over the past week, but all the dragons were still working on making a place for their companions to sit. It hadn't been as easy for them to create the seats as it was for Scarlet since they needed to rearrange several spikes on their backs and then build the seat. Her brothers also didn't have as many nanites, and the changes were slow.

"Obviously, we must take turns, but those who just finished the enhancement process will go first. I want you to experience the world with your restored eyesight before the sun sets."

Jared had to help almost everyone up on the dragons as it was too high for many of them. Johan was the only one that didn't need help. He scrambled up Midri's back like a spider, easily making his way to the seat fashioned for him.

"Hang on tight!"

The words acted like a launch command as all the dragons leaped into the air. Jared stood with Scarlet, and they laughed together as everyone had the same reaction as Vanessa.

There were a few outbursts interspersed, but to everyone's credit they mostly screamed in their minds, cognizant of the fact they needed to keep a low profile. Scarlet's brothers had a little fun themselves, performing aerial maneuvers that pinned their riders into place and took their breath away. The first group came back, and everyone but Joe groaned in disappointment.

Joe slid to the ground on shaky legs, bending over at the waist and vomiting his dinner. Joe was the oldest of all the water folk and also one of the most reserved. Based on the man's temperament, it didn't surprise Jared at all. He helped him stand back up and checked to make sure he was okay.

Wheezing and on shaky legs, Joe rasped, "Heights. Don't like heights."

"It's okay, man. I'm sure you'll get used to it."

The look of abject terror Joe flashed at him almost made Jared lose his composure. He tried in vain to hide a smile and turned around after patting the man on the back. He rushed away to avoid shaming the man. Some people just didn't like heights. Jared didn't understand it personally, but he'd try to respect Joe's wishes.

Joe wasn't the only one who displayed an aversion to flying afterward, but he was the only one to throw up. A couple more people took time to recover and voiced they wouldn't try flying again until their eyesight was whole. Not being able to see the ground or very far around them scared them, and they had no wish to do it again as they were.

Several hours later, everyone sat around the campfire, talking animatedly about their experiences. Those that had their eyesight back spoke feverishly, describing the scene to those who couldn't see for themselves.

Jared watched carefully and noticed people forcing smiles, but he saw the pain behind their eyes. They too wanted to experience this new world, but they had many weeks, perhaps months before they'd get there.

"Vanessa?" Jared grabbed her hand and pushed his thoughts over. *"I think we may want to spend time with those not bonded and encourage them. I know it seems like everyone is happy, but…"*

"See? We'll make a leader out of you, yet. I picked up on their mood too, and I'm making a list of those I can see. You do the same, and we'll compare lists later."

Turning back to the rest of the water folk, Jared reminded them he wanted to move out the following day and that they should try to get a good night's sleep. It would be a while before they stopped for longer than a night again.

The next day brought with it hope and eagerness to get moving. They quickly broke camp and arranged themselves into a column two people wide.

"Let's move out—"

"Jared!"

Pete and Kirgor bounded up to them, scaring the pants off

everyone in the group. Pete shrieked like a banshee and showed none of his usual restraint.

"We. Did. It," he panted in between large gulps of air.

"Did what?"

"We cracked the code!"

He proved his success by showcasing two robots he's cobbled together. Pressing a few buttons on a keypad, both robots came to life and stood staring at them with the glowing red orbs.

A few more taps on the device, and one robot walked ten paces away, spinning to face them. The one that walked away looked directly at the other, raised its hand, and issued a series of beeps and warbles. Immediately, the stationary robot turned around and walked into the trees on the side of the road.

"I f-figured out how to control them. I can c-capture the signal b-between them."

"Pete, Kirgor—this is amazing!"

Jared asked a lot of questions about the robots, the likelihood was of the cities taking control, and how likely it was to capture any signals sent to the cities.

"I don't want to rely on these things if the city can just issue a command and turn them against us. You know what's at risk here as well as anyone. If we can't rely on these completely, I'd just as soon not use them at all."

Pete looked somewhat offended by the words, and Kirgor snorted in agreement.

"Hey, I didn't mean you don't know what you're doing. I just have to be careful. So many times, I've been careless and not thought about the consequences of my actions. I can't afford to do that anymore; there are too many lives under my care now."

Chagrined, Pete apologized and assured him that couldn't happen since he'd hard-wired the robot and removed the ability for it to communicate freely. It now required manual responses and input from the controller he held.

Jared gestured between the two robots. "How far does the signal extend for this control?"

"The signal b-between the robots extends at least t-ten miles. Kirgor and Zavret helped with the experiment."

Jared thanked Pete for the information, motioned for everyone to start walking, and turned his thoughts inward.

He had no delusions. People would get hurt, and people would likely die. Everyone knew the risks, and Jared repeated them all the time. The idea of using the cities' technology against them thrilled him, but also sent shivers of icy fear down his back. If they used the robots to infiltrate the city or capture drop ships, and if the city somehow overrode the changes made by Pete, it could mean the death of everyone here.

The trip to Colorado took a little longer than he'd estimated. They stopped twice more to rest for a day or two, giving everyone plenty of time to recuperate. Scarlet's brothers hadn't returned yet, but it could be weeks before they made it back.

For the past two days, they'd seen imposing mountain ranges in the distance. Now, they were close enough to make out the snow-capped peaks. Jared called a halt to their progress when Scarlet let him know there were a couple large colonies at the base of that mountain range. He and Scarlet made plans to fly out after dark and scout the area. Thanks to their combined abilities to see at night, they'd have no trouble locating a place to stay. He established a watch rotation and checked all his gear before heading out with Scarlet.

"We'll be back before the sun is up, but make sure you stick to the watch rotations."

"We got it," Vanessa said and waved him goodbye.

"Ready?"

"Let's do it."

After so many weeks walking, it felt liberating to once again soar through the sky. He could've flown with Scarlet over the intervening weeks, but after that first week he'd let others take turns riding on her back. He was already familiar with it, and flying almost felt second nature to him. He wanted others to reach the same level of comfort.

Several minutes into their flight they passed over one of the large colonies Scarlet had viewed from a distance. With a simple thought, Jared activated his vision enhancements. Instantly, the world came into focus.

"Stay high enough they won't hear the beating of your wings. No need to draw too much attention to us. I doubt they'll be able to see us, but then the flames in your eyes and wings might be visible below."

"Jared, look west."

"What are those?"

Something stalked through the mountains many miles away. He couldn't make out many details from the distance, but massive bodies moved against the backdrop of the mountains. They weren't as big as Scarlet's brothers and they also ambled slowly.

"I do not know, but this appears to be a good hunting ground for my kin."

"Can you fly closer to the mountains?"

Scarlet shot forward, and Jared noticed a large wall running parallel to the mountain and the colonies. It was likely the only thing keeping those monstrous creatures from attacking the residents. Based on their size, it seemed like they could climb right over, but upon closer inspection Jared found a dozen people patrolling the top of the wall. They carried an assortment of weapons, and many large caliber weapon emplacements lined the wall.

"It looks like they're prepared for anything that might come out of the mountains. If these people are friendly to outsiders, they could make great allies."

"Or we find another group like the Daggers."

"Let's hope that isn't the case, but I won't take any chances this time. Once we've settled down, I can make a trip back here to see if they're friendly. We need to stock up on some essentials and new clothes for everyone."

"If we use this as a hunting ground, they might get suspicious if the creatures disappear."

"Maybe. I suppose it depends on how often they get attacked. We can observe them for a time to see what their reactions are, or if any of these creatures even go near the colony."

The walled city was massive, many times the size of any colony he'd ever seen. It was easily twice that of a floating city and looked well-organized. They had a variety of crops growing both inside and outside the walls. They had at least one hundred people patrolling the entire wall. They circled the largest town several times before Jared suggested they move on and find a place to live.

Roughly seventy miles farther south, there was another town, though not as large. Both towns boasted many people. The buildings were in good repair, the crops full, and those patrolling the walls armed to the teeth.

"This is impressive, Scarlet."

"There are so many people and weapons."

"It's nothing like where I grew up. Our colony was small, and you could easily walk around the whole thing several times in a day. These settlements are massive. I hope that doesn't mean they get more frequent trips from the cities. If we settle close by, we'll always be on the lookout for drop ships."

"What about Pete's research?"

"It's promising, but until we can capture more of the robots and ships, I don't want to rely on it yet. I think his research will help, but we don't want to tip our hand too soon by taking out a ship. None of the ship parts we scavenged are available to us and I'd like it if he experiments with them before we commit to a course of action. Once we're settled, we can scout for more ships. I'd imagine these cities see their fair share of drop ships so that shouldn't be difficult. It might take us a few months, but perhaps we can find a lookout position that affords us a view of the colony. We'll keep a constant watch, which will allow us to plan our actions."

"I do not think that will be difficult with these huge mountains shielding us from sight."

"We aren't in a rush to attack the cities, so I'm okay if we take our time in this phase. Plus, we've got to wait for your brothers to get back. Then we have the honeymoon phase where the water folk will court your kin for bonding. Further, they've all got to upgrade themselves. I think we should also send the weakest out to hunt these creatures in the mountains, so they grow stronger."

"We should also return for Attis soon. He has the best chance of scouting this area without raising suspicion. Look to the north."

Jared followed Scarlet's gaze and watched several massive birds fly over the mountains. It looked like they'd made their home in a perch high on the mountain's face. They looked like eagles, but of massive proportions. They were as large, if not larger, than Attis and there were quite a few.

"That looks dangerous for him."

"Observe. Attis is much faster and nimbler. It will be dangerous for those birds with him around."

Scarlet was right. The birds floated around the mountains, but they were all ponderous, and Attis could easily fly circles around them all.

"Maybe once we've settled in, you can fly back and get him. If you do it though, you've got to promise you won't get too close to the city. Go as far as you need and reach out telepathically. I know you're fast, but you can't outrun the ships and we don't need them tracking you back here."

Scarlet agreed and they let the topic rest. There was much to do yet, but first they needed to find a new home.

19 SEARCHING FOR ANOTHER HOME

They flew for several hours, exploring the mountain passes. The eagles Scarlet had observed earlier came to investigate, but after getting a good look at Scarlet, they kept their distance. It would have been super easy for Scarlet to snatch a few from the sky for dinner, but she left them alone. She and Jared had decided that having them around was good cover for anything the colonies or drop ships might observe. Especially if they stuck to flying around at night.

The night passed swiftly while they searched. It wasn't until they'd returned the following night when Jared found a couple large clusters of buildings nestled deep into a ravine. He wanted to stop and investigate, but it was nearing sunrise, so he marked it in his mind and returned the following night.

It wasn't a city, but a small cluster of buildings isolated at the base of some of the tallest mountains in the range. One building looked decrepit and falling apart, but there were two other large brick apartments mostly intact.

"I'll check out these buildings to see if they're safe for people to live in."

"I will look around the area and keep an eye out for those large creatures we observed yesterday."

Jared paused at the door and looked around. If this ended up being the place they hunkered down, it was a superb location. Everywhere he looked, mountains pierced into the sky. There was no direct view to anything beyond. The only way to get here besides over the mountains was a very windy road. The road was mostly useless, since most of the bridges had collapsed a long time ago, and the only viable way to get here was on foot. It was a perfect place to escape the clutches of the city that pursued them.

Jared walked up to the first building and whipped out his pistols. Kneeling down, he placed his bare hand on the ground and closed his eyes. Small vibrations of the building settling and a slight wind whipping through the valley created a three-dimensional replica in his mind. It wasn't perfect, but enough to confirm there was nothing large and dangerous inside.

Standing back up, Jared walked into the four-story brick building. Along the hallway, dozens of doors lined the passage. Most of them stood ajar with garbage strewn about. One by one, Jared cleared all the rooms. Every room had basic furniture and would make a great place for them to live if the integrity of the building checked out. On impulse, Jared checked the sink to see if there was any water, or water pressure.

Twisting the handle, nothing happened. Jared shrugged and left the room. If there was a septic tank and reservoir around, they might figure out how to get it working, but it wasn't the end of world. It shouldn't be too difficult to find drinkable water up in the mountains. Even if some rain was caustic, he had a hard time believing they wouldn't find fresh water springs to use.

The first two floors were entirely devoid of life. On the third floor, he killed a few normal rats. He'd almost finished the fourth floor when something jumped out at him and latched onto his arm. Jared panicked until he realized the small rat's teeth couldn't penetrate his skin. It screeched and clawed to no avail. It tore his clothes a little, which irked Jared, but at least it couldn't hurt him. If it'd been one of the large, dog-sized rats he'd encountered so many times, the teeth would likely penetrate even through his defenses.

Grabbing the rat behind its head, Jared yanked it from his arm and launched it out the door into the hallway. The rat hit the wall and slumped to the ground. Jared didn't think he'd killed it, but a closer investigation revealed he'd snapped its neck. He picked up the rat and tossed it out of a window so it wouldn't rot or attract other creatures to the building.

Jared fingered the new rips in his shirt and cast an angry glance at the window. "Stupid rats."

"Scarlet, how's it going out there?"

"I killed a few rats, but otherwise nothing in the immediate area. There are some larger creatures at a distance, but nothing we cannot handle later."

"I've got three more buildings to clear. There are a few less rats in the world, but that's it so far."

"I will expand my search radius while you clear out the buildings."

"Sounds good."

Jared cleared the next building quickly. The third building didn't look like an apartment building. It was larger, but only one story and included large open areas with lots of tables and chairs. One corridor revealed several rooms with metal grates covering them. He decided to explore them later since it didn't look like anything could get inside.

The buildings cleared, Jared moved to the last apartment. The moment he opened the door, a pungent smell punched him in the face. Jared knew immediately what waited for him in this building. It was the same smell that had assaulted his senses beneath New York City.

Rats.

"Scarlet, I think I found where all the rats are coming from."

"On my way."

Scarlet thumped down beside him, and they stared into the darkened building. All desire to clear this building evaporated. He'd rather just burn it down, but it was nighttime, and the fire would attract way too much attention from everyone and everything in the area. The best way to clear it was Jared to walk the corridor and take out anything that got in his way.

Four floors, nearly a hundred rooms, thought Jared. *That's a lot of places for rats to hide.*

"This will take me a while, Scarlet."

"Lure them out."

"Good idea."

Jared found a piece of pipe lying nearby and banged it on the side of the building.

"I've got this. You pick up any stragglers, or if it looks like they'll overwhelm me. I want to try something."

"Jared?"

"Don't worry I'm not planning to stab myself."

Scarlet snorted. She didn't say anything further, but stepped back to give him space.

Jared secured his phase pistols, dropped his pack a few yards away, and drew his knives. The overwhelming dread he'd felt last time was gone. In its place was a confidence in his abilities and a desire to test himself in battle. One on one, these rats were nothing, and he had little to fear, but if a horde of them overwhelmed him, well, thousands of claws and teeth could still take him out. His main concern was finding another rat king. If there was another, he'd bow out to Scarlet. His legs still twitched when he remembered how they'd shattered to pieces. Scarlet was more than a match for any rat, no matter the size. She could make mincemeat of the smaller ones too, but Jared needed to hone his combat skills.

It didn't take long before a chorus of chittering assaulted his ears. Jared set himself in front of the exit and prepared for the onslaught. When he saw the angry rushing horde running at him, he almost changed his mind and unsheathed his pistols. He chose not to give in to the cowardly feelings and braced himself. Still, a horde of bloodthirsty rats the size of dogs rampaging toward him made his heart hammer and his nerves shudder.

Instead of letting the rats make it out of the room to surround him right away, Jared crouched and pounced into the first wave pouring from the building. In mid-flight he activated *Clear Mind*. As if in slow motion, he knew exactly where he'd land, which rats were closest, and which he needed to dispatch first. Precision and speed were his ally as he mercilessly mowed down the rats. Fur, blood, and limbs flew in all directions, creating a vortex of death around him. Unheeding of the obvious death, the rats clawed their way forward until Jared needed to jump away to make room for his acrobatic dance of death.

These rats weren't as deadly as those in the subway, and they didn't devour their fallen comrades, but there were easily just as many.

Activating *Hyper-Cognition*, Jared paused a moment to assess his position while the seething horde surrounded him. He didn't need a reprieve, but a moment of inspiration struck him, and he wanted to try adding a new element into his fight. While in the suspended state,

Jared opened his mind to the surrounding vibrations, using the spider senses he'd gained to build a picture in his mind. He closed his eyes and used the vibrations of the surrounding creatures to build a complete rendering of everything around him.

Though he'd already eviscerated dozens, he had hundreds yet to go. The clarity he gained from the spider senses amazed him. With his mind running as fast as he was, and the clarity to see and understand everything, he looked at the scene through his new eyes as if a bystander. He could literally rotate the view, spin it around, and look from above. None of this was possible using his naked eyes since he never changed his point of view.

Rats surrounded him, vying for position to sink their sharp incisors into his exposed flesh or land their sickly yellow claws on his exposed back. If he relied on only his physical eyes, there's no way he'd survive once the rats surrounded him. He would have to admit defeat and let Scarlet take over.

Not going to happen.

Jared mapped a pattern out in his mind, showing precisely where to slash, stab, or kick out. Drawing in a long, slow breath, Jared prepared himself. This would be a test of his mettle. He planned to keep his eyes closed and fully rely on the three-dimensional images in his head. *Clear Mind* helped him process the information fed to him from the vibrations. Jared heart pulsed faster, expecting the renewed battle.

Before deactivating *Hyper-Cognition*, Jared sent a quick thought to Scarlet, letting her know his plans. She cautioned him but backed up.

"If you get into trouble, just jump out of the way and I'll finish them."

Jared's world lurched back into motion as his consciousness returned to normal speed. He missed a small step, but he used the stumble to roll into a new position. He came up in a spin, slicing the jugulars on three rats arrayed behind him. The blood pumping out of the rats' severed necks, which created more vibrations, painted a gruesome spectacle in his mind.

The rats didn't stand even a fraction of a chance. If Jared had been a whirlwind of death before, now he was a god of death and destruction. When the rats joined forces to jump at him, he vaulted into the air, landing several yards away to renew the slashing and hacking. *Maximum Muscle* activated without conscious thought as his mind applied just the right amount of exertion to use the skill without putting too much strain on his muscles.

Jared hit a rhythm in the battle, tuning out everything but the fight. The mental clarity and perfect synchronicity of his body thrilled him. The battle ended much too soon for Jared's taste. He relished the opportunity to continue the fight, and sprinted into the now empty building. Jared frantically searched room after room, hoping there were more rats to satisfy his bloodlust. By the time he reached the second floor, the adrenaline had faded, and his legs grew tired, slowing his pace.

He pushed forward, determined to ride the rest of the high until he finished clearing the area. By the time he'd searched the last room, he wanted nothing more than to lie down and sleep. The fight, while exhilarating, took a lot of energy, and he needed time to recover.

Dragging himself down the stairs, Jared collapsed on his back near Scarlet, several dozen yards from the mayhem that had ensued outside the building. Even at this distance, the blood from the rats ran in rivulets and nearly reached his position.

"Feel free to"—Jared tried catching his breath with a huge lungful of air—"take your share."

"No. This is your kill. Recover your strength and then capture the nanites. I will wait and feast on them after."

Jared groaned. "At least. Wait. Until I've gone. Elsewhere."

Scarlet wheezed out a laugh, and Jared rolled his head side to side at her shenanigans.

"You know, I'm looking forward to this area. Maybe you'll get to eat normal prey for a change."

"I do not know, I may prefer rat meat now."

Jared giggled in his delirious state. "You are something else, Scarlet, you know? Something else. Oh, how far out did you go?"

"I circled in a ten-mile radius."

"All right, works for me. Now, let's see if we can find the best way out of here." Jared rolled to his stomach and pushed up into a kneeling position. Summoning his willpower, Jared stood and made to climb on top of Scarlet's back, but she backed away.

"You are not getting on my back looking like that. Besides, you need to collect the nanites."

"Oh, come on, you talked about eating rats as a snack, and you can't deal with a little rat guts?"

"Have you looked at yourself?"

Jared looked down and his mouth opened in horror. He had rat entrails and blood coating his body. Somehow, a rat tail had gotten wedged into his belt like some kind of trophy.

"Well, I don't see many places to wash up around here." Jared waved his arms around as he started the arduous process of absorbing the nanites from all the rats he'd killed.

"There is a stream a short distance away you can use."

After Jared finished absorbing the nanites into his body, he walked in the direction Scarlet had pointed to wash up. The moment he rounded a building, he heard Scarlet crunch into the rats, raising his hackles.

The stream was a tiny thing and barely enough water to immerse himself fully. Jared hissed in pain when the water washed the filth from his skin. He hadn't noticed it while fighting and riding the adrenaline high, but he had dozens of lacerations across his body. His clothes had holes in dozens of places, and his skin bore the evidence to match. The cuts were shallow and would heal quickly, but they stung, and the fabric scraping against them hurt.

Scarlet had finished eating her fill by the time he got back, and thankfully there were no half-eaten remains. He'd half expected Scarlet to take a few nibbles from some corpses and intentionally leave them for him to see.

There were still a couple hours of darkness left, so Jared suggested they fly through the mountains instead of over. They needed to plot a course through. If they weren't able to find a good path, then the dragons could take turns flying the group to the location. It might even be easier to just do that, but Kitty wouldn't ride on a dragon, and Jared didn't want to leave her and Elle to walk through the mountains alone.

It took an hour, backtracking several times, before they found a viable option that would also avoid the colonies at the base. It would take them another few days to hike the distance, but they didn't have a timetable to keep, anyway.

Everyone was still asleep when they got back to camp, and Jared snagged a few hours rest himself. They'd have the entire day to figure out what to do and begin their trek at night. As close as they were to the settlements, Jared had no desire to go tromping across open areas and risk detection. There were enough people in the colonies and on the fully manned walls, someone would see the dragons if they traveled during the day.

Jared woke a few hours later to find the entire camp awake and milling about. He called them over and explained the situation to them. He received a few questioning glances at his clothes, but he ignored them for now. He knew he'd need to let Vanessa know what had happened, but not everyone had to know.

"We found several apartment buildings at the bottom of a ravine about eighty miles from here. It's a three or four-day hike on account of the rough terrain. I know many of you are getting stronger, but we've been walking for three weeks, and I understand that fatigue is real. We'll camp here for another day and then head out tomorrow night."

"Why are we traveling at night? That's prime time for predators, and most of us can't see in the dark."

"Thanks for bringing it up, Daryl. Scarlet and I flew over a couple large colonies at the base of the mountains. When I say large, the smaller one is four or five times the size of your old colony. The larger one is three times that size. They have massive walls between them and the mountain. On top of the walls I counted at least one-hundred men, all armed well."

"I see. Thanks."

"Don't let the news discourage you. We need to avoid them for now, but I want to contact them soon. I also want to take Vanessa and Elle with me when we go. I think they'll be more receptive to that than a lone explorer."

"You can't mean—"

"I do, Carla." Jared held up a hand to interrupt her. "If you hadn't noticed, Vanessa reverted much of her appearance back to the way it was before. We said nothing, as she wanted to make sure it worked. Vanessa?"

Vanessa stepped up next to Jared and pulled down the collar of her shirt. Pink lines replaced the gills that existed several weeks ago. Her skin had no trace of the faint bluish tint. She smiled a big, toothy grin, and several people gasped in surprise. Her teeth were back to normal, the sharp predatory smile gone. She still needed to work on her feet and hands to eliminate the last of the webbing, but as long as she wore gloves and shoes, no one would be the wiser. Jared was surprised people hadn't noticed already, but then it was a gradual change so maybe they hadn't noticed the incremental changes.

"How long?" Marie looked at Vanessa with wide-eyed wonder.

"I started just over two weeks ago. I assigned twenty-five percent of my nanites into *Body Manipulation*. Since I haven't needed *Regeneration,* I had all of them working to revert the changes back. It only works while I sleep, and it's a very slow process. When we saw what the dragons could do, manipulating their body to create seats, I thought maybe it'd be that fast for us too, but it takes much longer."

Jared picked up where she left off. "A large part of that is a dragon's intelligence. They're able to understand and manipulate the nanites to a far greater degree than any of us. I may be on the same level as all but Scarlet, Kirgor, and Ashazad. They can compartmentalize their thoughts and control the nanites to greater effect. Still, two weeks is not all that long to return to your original bodies. Part of the reason it took so long is that Vanessa needed to visualize the changes before falling asleep. She could only make one change at a time. If Malsour were here, that timeline might speed up a lot. I'm proud of Vanessa for what she managed so far."

A murmur of excitement ran through the group, and Jared studied the hopeful faces. Only Johan and Pete looked saddened by the news. Johan had assigned a quarter into *Reflexes* and the rest into *Mind*. Pete had pushed all of his into *Mind*. They each had different objectives, so Jared didn't think it was a loss, but he could see how much it meant to everyone to have their bodies changed back.

Jared quieted them down and outlined his plans for the trip through the mountains. As he'd thought, everyone opted to stay together and make the hike as a group. They had no desire to be without three of their primary lines of defense. Jared reminded them of Scarlet and her brothers, but still it wasn't enough to convince everyone to part ways. He smiled inwardly, proud of all these people for their decision to suffer through a difficult hike for Elle and Kitty.

"Thank you, everyone. Take the next couple days to rest and relax. Daryl, Kitty? Can you get us some grub?"

"On it!" Daryl jumped up from his seated position, grabbed his weapons, and walked off with Kitty.

"While they are out finding us a meal, I suggest everyone check your gear and have a ready means of defense if we need it. None of us knows this area, the creatures that live here, or how often they're visited by the cities. We must be ready for anything that heads our way. We also don't know how often these colonies get visitors or send people out to explore, and we can't afford to be complacent just because the end is in sight."

The group dispersed and Jared followed his own suggestion, setting up his bedroll. Once he finished, he found Pete to go over some ideas churning in his head.

"Hey, Pete, I wanted to run an idea by you about the robots and parts you've been working on."

"Sure."

"Is the signal always on? Are they always communicating with the cities if you let them?"

"No. They're p-programmed to p-perform a specific task and only reach out during d-designated times."

"Could you, I don't know, make the signal stay on? Or rather, can you program them to do something like that?"

"Maybe, b-but why?"

"I was curious if there's a way to trick the cities into staying away from us. Like a constant warning or message, signaling the pilots of drop ships that there's no reason to come to this area. Or, we can do the opposite and can lure one to our location to capture it."

"I guess we c-could send out a d-distress signal. I don't know about keeping a ship away."

"It was just a random thought, but figured I'd ask. If we could program them like that, we could set up a wide perimeter wherever we stop to make sure the cities can't find us."

"We will think on it." Pete's eyes had already glazed over as he leaned against Kirgor's side.

"If you think the distress signal is possible, try to work out the details, but be very careful you don't activate it. The last thing we need is a drop ship dumping on our heads when we're unprepared."

Pete acknowledged his instructions with a grunt and closed his eyes. Jared guessed the man and dragon were already hard at work figuring out the technical aspects of his ask. Their appetites for technological advancement and knowledge was insatiable.

Sometimes Jared wondered what it would've been like to live in the early twenty-first century. There were so many wonders he'd read in the books growing up. Often, it was hard to separate fact from fiction because so much of the old world seemed impossible. Cloistered as he'd been in the small community back home, they rarely saw or heard from anything beyond their borders. They hadn't seen a single soul outside the occasional drop ship until he was sixteen.

That was four years after Igor dispersed the nanites to the world. He didn't know how it was in other parts of the world. Maybe there were whole states or countries unaffected by the war. It was possible the nuclear radiation wasn't as concentrated on other continents like Australia, or smaller places like Puerto Rico, and Cuba, but there was no way for him to know. At least, there hadn't been before Scarlet. Now, he had the means to fly to other continents.

One day, after they brought the cities to heel, he and Scarlet would set out on an adventure to explore the wonders of the world.

That future was far away, but it was hope. Without hope, there was no future. No matter how unlikely an outcome it was, Jared needed to keep his dreams alive and remember why he fought.

20 RETURN OF THE DRAGONS

"**J**ared?"

Snapping out of his daydream, Jared turned to find Carla approaching.

"Hey Carla, what's up?"

"When will we get Attis?" she demanded.

"Scarlet and I were just talking about him. As soon as we get to our new destination, Scarlet will go back and find him. I've asked her to exercise caution and stay as far from the city as possible. If she can't get to Attis without exposing herself, she'll come back and get me. Then, she'll drop me as close as she can go, and I'll continue on foot the rest of the way until we get to his last known location. I don't think the cities will care if one explorer passes, but if they caught even a whiff of Scarlet, you know they'd commit as many resources to her capture and destruction as possible. She can't outrun the ships and we don't know how many there are. I'd rather be cautious and not even expose her to that risk."

"I understand." Carla sniffed and turned away.

"Carla." Jared laid a hand on her shoulder. "I promise we will find him and bring him back to you."

"Thank you," Carla said as she fought back the tears. She gave Jared a quick hug and retreated.

"She's had a rough time."

Jared hadn't seen Vanessa approach, but he leaned into her and grabbed her hand. She knew he felt a sense of deep obligation to all the people here and that it would eat at him until he made things right again. She pulled him away from his quiet contemplation and they retired to their bedrolls.

Jared and Vanessa spent the next two days laying out their plans for the new home. They wanted to get things established as fast as possible. When Jared mentioned the stream nearby and the possibility of running water in the apartments, Vanessa squealed in delight. He was quick to set expectations they may never get it working, but that the buildings were at least intact and with a little work and luck it could happen.

He almost didn't tell Vanessa about the rat infestation but changed his mind. To his surprise, she wasn't all that upset about his risky endeavor. She knew Scarlet had his back if it got out of hand.

"I'll warn you now, the scene is...gruesome. Scarlet wouldn't even let me on her back until I cleaned the blood and guts off. I—"

He'd been about to say he didn't even know what the last apartment building looked like on the inside, but he did, since he could pull up the images.

"Hold on a sec. I'm an idiot and forgot to replay the last apartment building in my mind. I ran through it so fast, I didn't pay much attention to anything."

Jared closed his eye and cast his mind back to the battle. Slowly, and then faster, he replayed the walk-through in his mind. The rooms were filthy, and there was little chance they could make it into a living space. Bottom to top, they were all the same. The only saving grace was the lack of foot-long maggots they'd encountered in the subway.

He concluded they should get rid of the building and use the materials to build up a wall around the area. It wouldn't be enough material, but they could chop down the dead trees around the area and use it to fortify defenses.

"Okay, sorry. That last building where the rats lived is worthless. The entire place reeks, there's mold on everything, and none of the furniture survived. We should just destroy it and use the materials to build a wall."

"How many rooms do the other apartments have?"

"Oh, there's plenty of space. Each apartment has around one-hundred rooms. There's also a large building that has a dining hall. In another corridor, there's a bunch of smaller rooms that have cages in front of them.

"Cages?"

"I'm not sure what they were, but there seems to be a bunch of items on display, and metal grates cover the entrance."

"It sounds like a resort."

"A resort?"

"Yeah, I remember seeing them in old magazines as a kid. It's where people would go on vacation. If I remember correctly, Colorado was a big destination for skiing."

"Sorry, I must sound dumb, but skiing?"

"I know little more than you, but it has something to do with sliding down the mountain on snow with long flat things on your feet."

"Why would you do that? I mean, it could be fun, I guess." Jared wondered if it would be any different from riding on Scarlet's back.

"I wonder if we can find any of them and ski down the mountains here."

Vanessa laughed. "Well, there has to be snow first."

"There's some on the peaks." Jared gestured to the tallest mountains partially obscured by clouds. "I wonder if it even snows anywhere but up there. We saw snow occasionally back home, but everyone said it used to be much heavier before the apocalypse. Not that they knew either. It's all just word of mouth passed on from generation to generation at this point."

"I wonder if the world will ever right itself. Think about it, if the nanites can convert radioactive waste into nutrients for our bodies, couldn't someone program them to clean and scrub the rest of the earth? Look at me." Vanessa ran a hand over her neck and slid her tongue between her teeth which were no longer pointed.

Jared shivered, watching her show off her body. She was so beautiful, and even a simple action like that sent his pulse racing. Vanessa continued speaking, but he hadn't heard what she'd said. He blinked and nodded noncommittally, pretending he'd heard her.

"I hope so," Jared said. "Who knows, maybe Pete and Kirgor will figure it out. I find it hard to believe the cities above would just sit back and screw the rest of humanity for hundreds of years if they could do that. Then again, there's nothing I've seen so far to refute their callousness."

Jared and Vanessa spent the rest of the day chatting, and he almost stayed an extra day just to spend more time with her. Unfortunately, most of the group were antsy, and Carla's mood declined rapidly. Jared spurred everyone into motion, and they packed their meager belongings to set out.

"Let's move. We need to hurry to get past the colony before dawn. When we get closer, I'll let you know and make sure that everyone keeps their voices down. Scarlet, it will be best if you and your brothers fly from above. Anyone that wants to fly, may do so."

Jared paused for a moment, thinking who should ride on Scarlet. He'd almost asked Vanessa, but he knew she'd refuse. Her people were on the ground and would suffer so that's where she would want to stay.

"Carla?"

"Yes?" she responded timidly.

"Can you ride atop Scarlet for this part? Besides Elle and I, you have the best eyesight, and I want you to keep an eye on everything around us."

"Okay."

He wished there was something he could do to set her at ease, but short of retrieving Attis, nothing he said would change things.

Vanessa caught the glance he shot her way and nodded her head. Before Jared turned back to the rest of the group, he saw Vanessa walk up to Carla and lay a hand on her back. Maybe she could provide some encouragement to keep her going.

Jared set a fast pace with Kitty and Elle bringing up the rear. To everyone's credit, they all kept up with him and they made it past the colony well before the sun came up.

"Does anyone need to stop and rest?"

Jared saw the exhaustion warring for dominance, but no one raised a hand to stop. Just before dawn, Scarlet and her brothers landed, creating a perimeter around them.

"Scarlet, did you see any of those creatures again?"

"No, all is quiet. I do not know what we observed from a distance, but they are conspicuously absent now."

"What do you think they were?"

"I can only guess, but they walked on four legs."

"I think we should set a watch on every side when we stop to rest. At least until we're certain they won't bother us. If they're anything like what we've encountered so far, they might just attack the second they catch wind of us. Though I have to wonder where they disappeared to."

It was midday before they stopped to rest, and Jared called it for the day to give everyone some time to recover. The next morning, Jared let the others set the pace. The path became so grueling for some they needed to ride atop the dragons to continue. They only managed ten miles before they needed to stop for the night. The next day proved even more difficult, but it saw them through the worst part of the trek. The following day was all downhill, and the time went much faster. Finally, the buildings came into view, and a quiet cheer echoed around the group.

Jared paused at the third apartment building, expecting to see the mass of rat carcasses littering the ground, but only blood remained, mixing with the dirt to create a thick brownish red sludge. The building itself looked like an abstract painting with arcs of arterial spray shooting as high as fifteen feet off the ground.

"Scarlet? You didn't—"

"No. There were many bodies here when we left."

"It looks like we may need to get that wall built sooner than we thought. I know it took several days to get back here, but that was a lot of bodies."

Jared addressed everyone before they delved into the buildings. "Please be careful as you explore. There are other predators in the area that carried off many rat carcasses that Scarlet and I killed. There could be creatures lurking in these buildings. It might be a good idea to have Carla or Elle check the building before you go too far."

Jared went through the disgusting rat den again but found nothing waiting for him inside. A few bodies littered the rooms at random, and Jared guessed that whatever creature had cleaned up the massacre couldn't fit inside or had their fill and moved on.

"My brothers want to hunt."

"You need not ask my permission, but if you don't mind, can you split into two groups? One group head south and the other north so you can push our boundary and cover both approaches? I doubt anything will come at us from up the mountain on the east and west, but if it does, we'll see it long before it gets here and be ready to defend ourselves."

The feast Scarlet and her brothers brought back was nothing short of impressive. They'd gorged themselves on deer, various mountain cats, moose, and the occasional bear. They found none of the larger creatures Jared and Scarlet had observed from a distance. Jared wondered if they were only active at night, or they knew the dragons had moved into the area and stayed far away. It didn't matter, they would hunt them down eventually no matter where they were.

Jared constructed a huge fire pit, dragged a bunch of chairs out of the cafeteria, and fashioned a spit for the meat. Maria gathered up all the excess and staked her claim on the kitchen behind the cafeteria. It was a mess, but it had everything she could want, including a massive walk-in refrigerator. Jared doubted the seal worked anymore, but it was as good a place as any to store any food they had and keep creatures out. If they got the electricity up and running, maybe they'd even have a place to keep that food fresh longer.

Jared walked around the area after dinner and found a metal ladder leading to the roof. It was only two stories, he could just jump to the top, but used the ladder which proved sturdy enough. Once on top of the building, Jared's eyes widened. Banks of solar panels lined the top. He hadn't seen them from below because a three-foot high wall rimmed the roof, and he hadn't seen them when they'd flown over at night because they blended with the roof itself.

Looking over the edge of the building he shouted for Pete to join him.

"There's a ladder around back."

Pete quickly scrambled up and mirrored Jared's own surprise.

"Scarlet?"

"Yes?"

"Did you know about the solar panels?"

"I did. Wanted. Surprise."

"Sorry, I can barely hear you. We'll chat about it when you get back."

Jared shook his head. If he hadn't found them so quickly, they could've gone days without looking into them if Scarlet kept it a "surprise" until then.

"Well, what do you think?"

"It will take work, b-but I think I c-can get it working."

Jared left Pete to his work and walked over to an access panel that led into the kitchen below. Dropping through the opening, Jared found himself in a dark, cramped closet. As he'd thought, it spilled out into a utility room in the back of the kitchen. A lot of the equipment was in disrepair, but if they got it cleaned up and running, it would be a huge morale booster.

Many pots, pans, utensils, and every conceivable manner of small appliance lined a row of shelves on the last remaining wall. A four-by-four-foot window looked into the cafeteria and a bulky machine with a bunch of buttons sat next to it. Jared suspected it had something to do with recording meals, but he wasn't familiar with it. In a small community like where he'd grown up, everyone received an equal share of any goods, food, and services. It was a true communal setting, and as far as he knew everyone lived like that these days. Though, the more he thought about the people he'd encountered along the way, a different story unfolded in his head.

He never figured out why the Daggers didn't use the boosters they had on them to replenish their stores. Clearly, there was something else at play. Maybe they had some contribution requirements they had to meet, or they couldn't go back. Jared didn't know what the situation was, but a part of him wished he'd gone back to get the whole story.

Jared moved over to the first apartment building and hiked up the staircase. There was no ladder on the outside of the building like there'd been with the other, shorter building. Once on the fourth floor, Jared went door to door looking for an access hatch to the roof. A few of the water folk had chosen rooms up there, so Jared knocked on the doors before barging in.

None of the rooms had an access hatch, and the only place he had yet to look was the stairwell opposite the one he'd ascended. Opening the door, Jared immediately found a shorter staircase leading up to a door. The door only opened from one side, so he used a cinder block sitting next to the door to hold it open. The moment Jared stepped on the roof, a loud groaning pop echoed across the rooftop. Jared froze. Carefully, he spread out his feet and dropped to all fours, distributing his weight more widely.

It could have just been the many years since anyone had stepped foot on top, but he didn't want to risk smashing through a rotted roof. Carefully, he inched his way along. Thankfully, the creaks didn't persist, and he chalked it up to not being used in years. The door he'd exited faced north, parallel to the ravine. He could see for many miles standing up here and it would make an excellent lookout position.

Rounding the corner to face the other side of the roof, Jared's lips curled into a smile. More solar panels lined the surface. Looking across to the other apartment buildings, Jared found every building had a full array. Some panels bore cracks, but the majority of them only held layers of dust and debris from years of neglect.

"Yes!" Jared's voice echoed off the mountain walls.

When he looked over the side of the building, Pete stared up at him from the top of the shorter building.

"There are more solar panels on top of all the apartments," shouted Jared.

Pete mouthed something, but Jared couldn't put the words together. Judging by the man's smile, he was as excited as Jared. They easily had five times the number of solar panels they'd taken from the old colony, and that amount of electricity had been plenty to sustain the group for anything they needed. If Pete got these up and running, they wouldn't even need to conserve their usage.

The fact these panels and buildings remained in such good repair made Jared wonder about the weather patterns in the area. The panels back in the old colony had been in good shape because it'd been less than a decade, and the winds and occasional acidic rain hadn't been enough to deteriorate them. However, there was no telling how long this place had remained vacant, yet everything was in good shape. The obvious conclusion was that the climate wasn't as harsh, and the rain didn't carry with it any of the abrasive chemicals he'd become accustomed to.

That could be the reason the colonies at the base of the mountain were thriving. If they didn't need to worry about acid rain, they could easily live a normal life—except for the all the mutant beasts, but they had a wall to protect them.

His mind spun as he worked out the possibilities. There was definitely still radiation in the air because he hadn't felt hungry like he did beneath the earth, but maybe it was less than usual, which could explain the massive size of the two colonies.

Maybe the mountains block the spread of radiation?

There were too many variables, and he had no data to back them up. For now, he'd take it as fate smiling on them and use it in the best way he could. His next mission was to explore the reservoir and see if there was a way to get water running again. He knew next to nothing about plumbing other than pipes go from one place to another. He'd have to rely on someone like Pete to figure out how it worked, though, it wasn't a pressing matter and Pete had many other things to occupy his time for now.

For the next week, everyone busied themselves making their new home presentable, purging everything, and attempting to clean out the third apartment. Jared finally called it quits and realized they'd never neutralize the rat infestation from the building. He asked Scarlet and her brothers to knock the building down after he removed the solar panels on top. They moved a lot of the wreckage to the perimeter of the area to burn while the panels went up on top of the cafeteria where Pete added them to the existing array.

Before they'd turned the pile of rubble into a massive bonfire, Jared asked Scarlet to fly a distance away and make sure the mountain obscured the smoke trails from the colonies. Thankfully, the mountains thoroughly blocked them from view. Jared's only concern was a drop ship passing overhead, but they also needed to get rid of the nasty rubble. All the dragons contributed to the burning and reduced the pile to ash while Jared and the others piled dirt on the embers to snuff it out. They'd waited in tense silence inside the apartments for hours before he gave the all clear.

Over the course of the past week, Jared had gone out to explore a few times and ended up finding massive lengths of steel cables running up the mountain. Vanessa explained it was how people used to get up the mountain so they could ski down. It wasn't until he found one of the bucket seats that ferried people up and down that he understood how it worked. He traced the cables down to a small building with a massive steel pole thrusting into the sky.

After he'd described his findings to Scarlet, she informed him there were many of them dotting the side of the mountains. It was then Jared got an idea for a perimeter.

"Scarlet, can you and your brothers gather up these steel poles and cables? I think we can create a wall using all the materials."

"We can gather them and help create the wall. Though, I have to wonder, do we even need a wall? Nothing we have seen in the mountains would be a challenge for us to defeat."

"What about those big creatures we saw?"

"They have not shown themselves yet, and I am increasingly confident they will not approach while we are here."

"You're probably right, but if you and your brothers leave for any reason, it would provide comfort to everyone here."

"I hardly think you are defenseless."

"Still, if we've got the materials and the time to do it?"

"Then there is no harm. We shall start tomorrow."

Another week passed as everyone spent the bulk of their time working on the wall. Scarlet fused the ends of the cables together using her dragon fire and then again to mount the cables on the steel poles. Having dragons around to do the heavy work made an arduous process simple.

About the time the walls went up, Pete finally got all the solar panels working fully. His next task lay in making sure all the wiring to the buildings and rooms worked. Pete conscripted half a dozen people to help him look for areas they needed to fix. They finished the job in a couple days.

Now all the buildings and rooms had electricity, but what they didn't have were working lights. Nearly all the bulbs burst when flipping on the electricity for the first time. There was a small stockpile of unopened bulbs in a utility closet, but it wasn't enough to install a new one into everyone's rooms. The cafeteria used a bunch of high-powered LED lights, and they had plenty of those in the utility room.

Marie took charge of the kitchen and gave it a complete overhaul. The entire room looked pristine, the cafeteria itself cleaned and organized, and the ovens were functional once again. She'd also found rubber seals to place around the walk-in refrigerator that kept a tighter seal on the door. Contrary to his initial thoughts, they couldn't use it as a refrigerator because the chemicals they needed to generate the cooling effect had expired long ago. Instead, she converted it into a storage room to prevent any rodents and bugs out of the butchered meat Daryl and Kitty brought back.

Everything looked great, but Jared couldn't help feeling they'd done all this for naught. How much time would they really spend in the place was anyone's guess. They had a war to fight, and that war could take them anywhere. Finding a place like this had an undeniable effect on everyone's morale. They couldn't commit to any action until Scarlet's brothers returned, anyway. Jared shifted his troubled mind to the here and now and went back to making the lives of everyone around him easier and safer until they were ready to move on.

Two weeks went by in a flash as they had ample work to keep them busy, but Jared grew concerned. Scarlet didn't seem overly worried, but Jared felt the angst across their bond and knew her brothers' continued absence weighed on her heavily.

"Do you think they got into trouble?"

This wasn't their first conversation on the topic and Jared already knew the answer she'd give because she always said the same thing...*be patient.* He asked more for his own sanity than to hear a different answer.

"I do not know."

Startled, Jared looked up at her. "You don't think they—"

"I honestly do not know. None of us expected it to take this long."

"They'll make it back!" They had to make it back. Their future hinged on it.

It wasn't until week seven when Kynderri returned with the earth dragons.

He felt the dragons before he ever saw them. The vibrations running up through the floor painted a clear image in his head. A throng of giant dinosaurs galloped down the mountain toward them. Dinosaurs were the first thing that popped into his head since they resembled their prehistoric brethren so much, but these were, in fact, earth dragons. The picture in his mind was clear. Every jolt of their powerful legs sent thrumming vibration up through the soles of his feet that easily projected a complete three-dimensional rendering of everything around for a ten-mile radius.

The information bleeding into his mind was too much, and *Clear Mind* activated of its own volition to compensate for the overload of information. He tried to keep the ability activated at all times, but when he slept, it wasn't a feat he could do just yet.

Vanessa and Elle saw him jump to his feet from across the room and looked at him in concern. That's when they felt the thumping of the earth. To be on the safe side, Jared blasted a mental note to everyone in the area not to freak out, and that the earth dragons had arrived at last.

Jared sprinted to greet the new arrivals. Scarlet's brothers led the charge, gliding on silent wings over the mountain, outpacing their land-restricted kin. They moved across the ground at frightening speeds. Steeling his nerves, Jared stood his ground and faced the stampeding mythical beings, praying they arrested their seemingly reckless descent down the mountain.

He almost lost the spirit to remain in place, and only Scarlet walking up to his side prevented him from running the other direction like a scared child. It really didn't look like they'd stop in time, but somehow, they arrested their momentum.

A series of things happened all at once that left Jared scratching his head. Scarlet stepped forward and roared in defiance at the newcomers, while one of the earth dragons pushed through and roared right back.

Jared cocked his head in confusion, wondering if this was some kind of dominance thing. If that were the case, he wondered if any of the other dragon kin would submit to her will because she was the newest addition to dragonkind. She had more knowledge of the current world than them, but aside from technological advancements, mankind was much the same as they were thousands of years ago.

The standoff continued for many minutes and the tension in the air was a tangible thing. The air tingled, and Jared was certain there was a psionic war waging between them. Looking behind him, Jared found the water folk who'd come out to watch on the ground holding their heads. It hadn't affected him, and he wondered if it was because he held *Clear Mind* active.

He quickly jumped between them and felt the pressure in his head explode. He dropped to his knees in pain. Both dragons snarled and snapped out of their posturing match.

"Jared! Why did you—"

He cut Scarlet off with an upraised hand pointing back to those behind her.

"Jared, I..."

"It's okay. I know you didn't mean to. My head. Feels like it got crushed in a vise."

"This is a tradition passed from one matriarch to another. You should not interfere."

The voice wasn't one he recognized, and it sounded condescending. Jared assumed it was the matriarch of the land dragons. It was female, but more guttural than Scarlet's silky-smooth voice. Thankfully, the being speaking into his mind didn't exert nearly as much mental pressure as Alestrialia had, and Jared only cringed slightly.

The fact he didn't drop to his knees again surprised the dragon as Jared watched her head cock to the side. Deciding it was a good idea to keep her unbalanced and allow Scarlet to regain her composure, Jared opted to use telepathy to reply.

"It may be a tradition and I apologize for interfering, but you hurt my people." Jared motioned behind him again at those still on the ground writhing in pain. Low growls rumbled from her throat when Jared spoke. Apparently, Scarlet's brothers hadn't told them about his or any of the others' ability to use telepathy. It seemed like an oversight on their part, unless they'd wanted to use it as further leverage to integrate the earth dragons into their budding army.

"Yes, I can use telepathy, as can every one of my people. Only, they have much further to progress before they can project their thoughts or mind meld like I can."

"You can meld? How?"

"I assume Kynderri didn't tell you everything, or he wanted to wait until you spoke with Scarlet yourself. You have much to catch up on, and I will let you acquaint yourselves, but please dial back the mental pressure for the sake of everyone here."

"We will... comply."

It was obvious she didn't care for Jared's lack of subservience, but at least they'd hold themselves in check long enough for Scarlet to brief them. The conversation over, Jared walked away from them and let Scarlet pick up where he'd left off. They'd chosen to make their conversation private, so Jared heard nothing they said. He glanced back to see Scarlet and the earth dragon matriarch, whatever her name, bow to each other and then place their heads together.

The moment Jared got back to his room, a deep, booming voice blasted into his mind.

"We have returned."

Jared turned back around but paused in the doorway. He didn't need his gear, but after the brief but rude, encounter with the earth dragons, he brought his weapons.

Jared dashed outside to see Malsour fly in from the north. The water dragons were so much more impressive in person than when he'd seen them from Alestrialia's point of view. Though it was dark outside, Jared easily made out the dark forms blotting out the stars and moon. They were massive creatures that dwarfed Scarlet and made Malsour look like a child.

How could creatures so big exist anywhere? How did mankind hunt these things?

Jared couldn't wrap his mind around how anyone would think to kill one. They floated through the air languidly as if the sky itself held them aloft. Magic was one word that came to mind. Malsour landed just outside their newly erected walls and fourteen water dragons touched down behind him. Jared hadn't counted the earth dragons, but quickly rebuilt the image in his head when they rampaged down the mountain. There were fifteen in total.

Fifteen earth dragons, fourteen water dragons, and thirteen fire dragons. Forty-two dragons in total, and they had yet to meet the air dragons. If they all joined in their fight against the cities, they'd have no problem taking down one of the floating cities. If just the water dragons attacked one, they could probably take it down themselves.

The only notable difference between all the other dragons and the water dragons was that they didn't have much defense or attack capabilities. Their size was their only advantage he could see. Their legs and tails ended in wide, membrane-like paddles rather than sharp claws.

Jared's mind raced back to Razael in his underwater cage and his heart broke for them all over again. Razael was small compared to some of these floating in the sky. Seeing them in person reignited the raging bonfire of vengeance that always simmered beneath the surface of his emotions. Water dragons didn't look the least bit violent, and everything about them exuded peace and tranquility.

Scarlet walked by him, startling him from his reverie. Instead of locking gazes with the matriarch of water dragons, she embraced her, wrapping her neck around the largest of the water dragons. There was a moment where the air felt charged, but when he looked at those around him, they didn't react the same way as the earlier introduction. Jared much preferred this welcome over the earth dragons.

Jared watched the earth dragons move to the south and land a half mile from their home. After Scarlet finished greeting them, they walked farther away and bedded down.

"They must rest. The long journey and prolonged exertion taxed them greatly. We will speak to them and introduce everyone in three days' time."

"Three days? Why so long?"

"They were asleep for millennia and tire quickly. It will take time for them to regain their strength as it did with my brothers' ability to fly. I suspect that is what took them so long to reach here and likely why my air kin have yet to arrive. If they needed to wait to regain strength and fly here, it may be awhile yet for them to arrive."

"I hadn't even thought about that. It makes me feel better knowing it could just be a delay in their ability to fly versus getting into trouble with the cities. I am a little curious how Malsour and Kynderri coordinated their arrival."

"Agreed, I did not think of it until speaking with Layonia, the

matriarch of our water kin. They swam to the coast and met our earth kin at the southern edge of this continent. Kynderri and the others took the lead because Layonia cannot move so fast across the earth. They regained their flight and caught up to them today. It is a coincidence they arrived at the same time."

"Did you mind meld with them?"

"I did, but we discussed nothing of import to our current situation. It is customary for a matriarch to acknowledge her peers and they all expected to see Alestrialia. The time we spent communing was to acknowledge my rightful place and honor my mother's life. The time will come to speak of current events."

"What of your brothers? Surely, they would have said something, right?"

"They gave only the minimum amount of information. Enough to get their consent to leave hibernation. I will check with my brothers, but it is possible they only informed them of the world's current state and the decimation of the human population. That would bring them from their slumber. It is my place to ask them to join our cause, which I will do with as much persuasion as I can. As for bonding…"

"I understand. I know your brothers had a hard time with it, but I believe in time they'll come to see the value in it."

"We must hope for that outcome. Though, as you can see, Layonia and her kin are not battle ready. A phase round would tear right through their skin, and our earth kin cannot fly."

"There might be a use for them yet. If you recall the conversation I had with Johan about creating bombs, we'll need someone to fly overhead to deliver the payloads."

"Possibly. Though they abhor violence."

Understanding what little he did of the water dragons, he saw how it would be difficult for them to take part in a battle against humankind. They did not like conflict and would prefer to remove themselves from the affairs of the world again rather than face a battle resulting in massive loss of life on both sides. After they learned of Razael, they might change their mind, but it wasn't his place to show them unless asked. He would let Scarlet handle everything where her kind were concerned. She would know how to do it properly with the least amount of pain.

With nothing left to do, Jared retired to his room. He couldn't fall back asleep and eventually went up to the roof. From up top he observed all the dragons. Earth, water, and fire, and the view sent chills up his spine. The raw, primal power these beings portrayed dumbfounded him. If he saw this group headed toward him with hostile intent, he wouldn't even think about putting up a fight. He'd just roll over and die. The only reason he could see the cities putting up a tangible fight was their army of robots and ships. They could deploy them with impunity and never need worry about dirtying their own hands. That would definitely change soon. If the cities wanted to put up a fight, everyone would need to get involved.

21 DRAGON FIGHT

The next three days proved an intense lesson in patience. Scarlet made certain everyone stayed away from the two groups until they went through a more formal greeting process. Scarlet assured him it wasn't anything to concern him or the other humans. It was simply a three-day mourning period for her mother.

Scarlet shared memories and events with the other dragons. Every so often, a long wailing growl echoed across the ravine. By the end of three days, everyone was on pins and needles. They hadn't dared venture out beyond their small enclosed space, and only Jared, Elle, and Vanessa would go to the rooftops. They'd grown used to having the fire dragons around, but with the number of different dragons now roaming the area, they were scared.

Jared didn't experience quite the same level of fear and nervousness from the dragons, but then he'd been around Scarlet for much longer, and he'd met Alestrialia. None of these dragons were as fierce and dominating as her. He tried to put himself in the shoes of the water folk, but try as he might, there was no getting around the fact he'd transformed. These great mythical beings no longer scared him. That was probably not a good thing. Any of them could snuff his life out in a single breath or stomp of their foot, but he knew they wouldn't. At least, he hoped they wouldn't.

Finally, Scarlet announced it was okay for him to greet the matriarchs. When the time came, only Vanessa, Elle, and Kitty joined him. That needed to change if he hoped to unify his people with the dragons. They couldn't start off this initiative with everyone being deathly afraid of them.

"Scarlet, did you tell them of Razael yet?"

"I did not."

Jared paused as they walked toward the earth dragons. "Uh, I think maybe you should do that before we get these introductions kicked off."

"No."

The abruptness in Scarlet's words made him flinch. "Why?"

"I want it to come from you."

"You can't be serious…" His words trailed off, thinking of the inevitable outpouring of emotions, psionic outrage, and physical reaction to the news he had to share. "Scarlet, I—"

"It must come from you, Jared. I want you to mind meld with each matriarch. When you do, show them through your eyes and your emotional feelings from the moment you met me. Leave nothing out."

"Ah, you're hoping they see me for who I am, rather than another pesky human that killed off their kin."

"Correct. It is not without risk, but this is the best chance we have persuading them to join our fight."

Jared drew in a deep breath, expelling it slowly as he thought about telling the water dragons that one of their own had died after being brutally mutilated at the hands of humans like him. He shuddered, knowing the news would be a hard pill to swallow and not knowing how they'd react.

"All right, I'll do it. Vanessa? Elle? I don't want you around while I do this. If they take the news badly, there's no telling what they might do. An errant thought by one of them could severely hurt either of you."

"What about you?" Vanessa latched on to his arms and looked into his eyes, alarm skittering across her face.

"I'll be fine." He put on a disarming smile, hoping to set Vanessa at ease, but inwardly his stomach flipped somersaults. "I'm fast enough to get out of the way of any physical outburst. Their psionic pressure hurts, but I can withstand it for a time. You cannot. Besides, if it gets too bad, I'll just jump on Scarlet and she can get me out of the way."

"I not like it." Elle placed herself in front of Jared and crossed her arms.

"Look, both of you, I get it. It's not an easy thing to do, but when has any of this—" Jared motioned around him, "—ever been easy? I'm losing track of how many times I've almost died at this point."

"That doesn't mean you should invite more opportunities for de—" Vanessa's voice hitched and a tear trickled down her cheek.

Scarlet bent her head to their level and nuzzled Jared's side. "**I will keep him safe.**"

Her words left little to doubt. It was the push Vanessa and Elle needed to step aside.

Jared cast a glance over his shoulder as he walked away. "I'll be careful, I promise!"

With a heavy heart and lead steps, Jared resolutely marched to his first encounter with the matriarch of the water dragons.

"**Normally, you would greet Gayana first, but because the news you must share pertains to our water kin, I persuaded them** to accept my slight deviation from decorum."

"Gayana is the earth dragon matriarch, I presume?"

"Yes."

"So, all this posturing, the three-day period, and order of introductions seems antiquated. After all these years, you still stand on decorum. Why?"

"It..." Scarlet paused while she thought through his question. **"I do not know. It has always been. A time of change is upon us, and with that change, perhaps our traditions will evolve. For now, this is how it must be."**

"All right let's get this over with."

"Hold nothing back. Show them your every emotion. Lay bare your innermost thoughts and turmoil. They must see you for who you are."

"That's asking a lot. You know how I feel about the events in my life."

"I do, but yet you must do as I ask. How you respond and react to the things you endured are precisely why I, and my brothers, trust you implicitly. My kin must see that side of you."

Jared's chest constricted. He didn't want to relive those memories again. Not only would he need to relive them, he'd need to do it three times because of their annoying traditions. The thought set his heart racing and his vision darkened. This was the last thing he wanted to do, but Scarlet's words carried truth. This was how he'd win them over to his side. Locking down his misgivings, Jared pushed them to the dark recesses of his mind, slammed the door, and threw away the key. It was time for him to man up and face his fears and heartache head on. He'd no longer let them rule him. No, he'd wear them proudly like a badge affixed to his chest. He had nothing to fear and no one to hide from.

This. Is. Who. I. Am.

Jared bowed his head in greeting to Layonia. "My name is Jared Cartwright."

"I am Layonia, matriarch of water dragons. Greetings, young human."

Her voice was smooth, calming. It gave him a sense of serenity. It was like a gentle lapping of a stream against its banks. With only a few words she set him at ease and quieted his mind. He could listen to her talk for days on end and never tire. Scarlet snorted next to him, understanding his surprise at hearing Layonia's voice.

"You are stuck with me, Jared."

Jared glanced to his side and saw Scarlet grinning like a fool. It brought a smile to his lips and made the last of his hesitation vanish. He reached up to touch her side, expressing his thanks. *"I appreciate the levity; I know you're trying to help this go easier on me."*

"I need not say it again, but be yourself."

"It's nice to meet you, Layonia. I'm informed that our greeting is out of the norm as it should have been Gayana first. Scarlet thought it important that we change tradition this once. The information I have for you pertains to all dragonkind, but specifically one of your own."

A deep sense of sadness and foreboding settled over him as the gigantic head of Layonia lowered to his level. His shoulder sagged under the enormous weight, and he plopped on his rear before his knees gave way. This would not be an easy task at all.

Jared looked into the icy blue eye of this great giant and found himself overcome with emotion. There was great wisdom in her gaze, but also an unfathomable depth he couldn't explain. Layonia's sorrow and pain seeped into his bones and robbed of his will to continue.

"Please, speak."

The words weren't a command. They didn't spur him into action. But he couldn't ignore them either. His body betrayed him at first. Jared summoned the last vestiges of his willpower and scrambled over to Layonia.

"I think it would be better if I showed you."

She drew back in alarm, but Scarlet was quick to assure her it was all right.

"How can such a primitive mind accomplish a meld?" The question was genuine and held no malice.

Jared held up a hand letting Scarlet know he was okay to handle the questions. "The same way your telepathy hasn't rendered me unconscious. We have a new technology called nanites that allows me to manipulate and alter my mental abilities. I will leave it up to Scarlet and her brothers to educate you fully, but mankind invented it only in the last decade and only in the last few months did we discover the ability to bond."

"Consider me intrigued."
Though the conversation changed, it didn't lessen the deep sorrow pressing in around him. Her voice oozed into every pore of his body, taxing his mind.

"Please, let me show you. I should warn you," Jared raised his voice to carry to all the water dragons, "I want to warn all of you this will not be pleasant. I promise you, I will do nothing to hurt Layonia, but I know she will not react well to this news. Please know I do not intend her harm."

Layonia dipped her head in acknowledgment and he reached a shaky hand up to lay it on her. Layonia's skin was cool and smooth, almost slimy. Jared pictured her slicing through the water as it parted to allow her passage.

Jared activated *Clear Mind*, entered a meditative stance, and recounted everything.

The emotional roller-coaster he experienced was unlike anything he'd ever been through. The highs and lows of his life paled compared to the overwhelming waves of emotions rolling off Layonia. She amplified every emotion to the point he felt his heart would burst open. It crushed him to the ground, and he lay there panting.

There was none of the righteous fury of vengeance he'd expected, only a deep sadness and sympathy for Razael. Jared now understood Scarlet's explanations about their desire for peace and acceptance. Confusion clouded Layonia's mind, making Jared feel utterly lost. Adrift in the sea of emotion.

"Scarlet, I... can't do this any... more."

"Sister."

The pressure lessened as Layonia looked to Scarlet.

"Please, sister. You are projecting your thoughts onto Jared. It is not a weight one man should carry."

The giant behemoth blanched and looked down at Jared's tiny form. The pressure dissipated and the overwhelming sadness fled. It left a hollow ache in his chest and there was no way he'd ever forget. He'd thought his reaction to seeing Razael the first time left an imprint on his soul. Now he knew, it was but a fraction of the loss experienced by his kin.

"My deepest apologies, Jared. I...We need time to process this loss. We will remove ourselves from this area while we mourn. I believe it too much for you and your people to endure."

She turned to leave but halted and looked back and Jared.

"Thank you for laying him to rest."

The finality of her words brooked no response. He and Scarlet watched Layonia leave, her family falling in behind her.

"Will they be okay, Scarlet?"

"Yes, but I do not know if it was enough to convince them to join

our fight. To bond, perhaps. To send dragon and man into harm's way? Uncertain."

"I'd be content with them bonding. It will help everyone else get stronger even if they don't fight. Honestly, with just you and your brothers, I think we can handle a lot of what a single city throws against us."

"We will want our air kin. They are nimble and...flighty."

"Flighty?"

"Whimsical? They go where they want, solve problems as they see them, but rarely rationalize their motivations. They will join us, but do not delude yourself into thinking we can corral them."

"If they're willing to fight with us, that's all that matters. If they're faster than you, then it's exactly what we need to combat the drop ships. You stayed just out of reach of their phase cannons, but your brothers are slower."

"Correct. Though, I may yet grow faster with my enhancements. It is difficult to tell. Also, Zavret is fast."

"I suppose as a hunter he must be quick."

"The biggest problem is size. Because my brothers are much bigger, the chance of being hit by a phase round increases. The air dragons are of a size equal to me right now. It is why they are so quick."

"Hopefully they get here soon."

"Hold that hope close. I fear after you share your experience they will want to take off and attack these cities."

"That would not be good. We must make sure we get Layonia and Gayana on board to help shepherd them."

"That would be for the best."

"Do we need to do this again with Gayana right now?"

"We do."

"I don't know if I can go through that again."

"It should not be as emotional with Gayana. Though, she has a violent personality and may react entirely differently."

"That's not helping, Scarlet."

"I will try to support you through our bond. I should have tried it with Layonia, but her emotions affected me too."

"All right let's get this over with."

"Please be careful with Gayana. If you feel she may react violently, put as much distance between you and her as possible. Her predisposition is one of violence as you witnessed the other day. Pay close attention to her feelings and reactions much like you did with Layonia, and you will be fine."

Jared jumped on her back and they walked the mile back through camp and to the other side where the earth dragons rested. At first Jared couldn't see them, but it turned out they'd burrowed beneath the earth with only their bony, plated backs exposed.

"Wow, good luck trying to root them out. I wonder if their backs can withstand a phase cannon round."

"I am almost certain the answer is yes. However, a sustained barrage would eventually break through."

"Which one is Gayana?"

Jared didn't know how to tell the dragons apart looking at their backs. They all had a distinctive pattern, but he'd only seen Gayana from the front and couldn't tell what her back looked like, let alone know how to separate her from the rest.

"She is closest to us. Do you see the symmetric rows of spikes running parallel to her head? She is the only of her kin with spikes like this. Everyone else has a random assortment scattered across their plated backs."

Jared thought he saw a slight color difference too, but it was almost imperceptible. The spikes, though, established a clear contrast between Gayana and the rest. He and Scarlet walked up to her and announced their presence.

"Gayana, it is time. Forgive me again for breaking tradition. I think you will agree it was the right choice in a few moments."

The matriarch of earth dragons didn't answer. She merely lifted her head to glare at them as if the change in formalities affronted her.

"Tread carefully, Jared."

"You need not tell me again."

As he'd done with Layonia, Jared reached out a tentative hand. She bared her teeth at him, her dark eyes drilling into him.

"I must touch you for the mind meld."

A slight widening of Gayana's eyes was the only response he received. It was a start.

Scarlet explained Jared's abilities and with great reluctance, Gayana lowered her head to the ground.

Jared kneeled next to her, positioning his body so he could launch himself away if needed. He didn't think sitting sounded like a good idea if she reacted physically.

Delicately, he showed Gayana his life and the events leading up to this moment. It wasn't as thorough as he'd been with Layonia, but he couldn't bring himself to relive certain parts. Layonia set him at ease, while Gayana had the opposite effect and he wanted nothing more than to leave her in peace and let Scarlet handle any further interactions.

The reaction to Razael wasn't as powerful as what he'd felt from the water dragon, but once he'd finished with Razael's story, Scarlet interrupted him.

"Jared, prepare yourself."

Jared opened his eyes to glance at her, his brow knit in confusion. Gayana's emotions weren't running rampant, and he hadn't seen her so much as flinch at the news.

"Feel the earth."

Jared opened his new senses, and pain stabbed behind his eyes. The entire ground pulsed. The ripple effect emanated from the dragon in front of him, pushing out in all directions. It rose and fell in waves, gradually drawing closer together. He quickly shut it off and snapped his eyes to Scarlet.

"Get out of here. Run! Tell everyone to get out of the apartments. Go. Now!"

Jared didn't hesitate. He sprinted for the buildings, yelling with his mind the whole way. Scarlet's sense of urgency spurred him on. He activated *Maximum Muscle* and rocketed forward, careful not to push himself too far. He made it back with great, bounding leaps, quickly passing Vanessa and Elle who waited at the entrance of the wall they'd erected.

Jared shouted over and over, hoping everyone heard him and got out of the buildings. He didn't yet know why, but he trusted Scarlet implicitly and would do whatever she wanted. As he passed the wall, he heard the steel cables scraping against the supports. A snap somewhere down the wall, announced a cable detaching from the support poles.

"Vanessa, Elle get away from the wall!"

More pops echoed around the area as the sloppy welding came undone and the cables fell to the ground. By this point he'd reached the buildings and almost sprinted inside, but caught himself at the threshold. The windows and any glass remaining rattled in their frames violently. A moment later they shattered, and he instinctively covered his face as shards of glass fell around him. His hardened skin prevented any damage, but there were still people exiting the buildings and many cried out in pain as the shards of glass cut them.

The chorus of cries pushed everyone to move faster and the last of the water folk stumbled from the building. Jared quickly counted to make sure they had everyone. Everyone accounted for, Jared corralled them into a wide open area with no buildings or steel cabling around.

"Scarlet! Is there any way to stop this?"

"I am trying."

"Can they go somewhere else?"

"I do not think they can move when entrenched like they are. Gayana generates the energy from her body, much like my mother could with psionic pressure and shields. Worse, all the earth dragons amplified her actions when she started."

"This is not a good place for this." Jared's glanced up the mountains. If their actions caused an avalanche, they'd be in serious trouble.

"Gayana!"

Scarlet's voice pounded into his mind. The rest of the water folk dropped to their knees, holding their heads. Carla and Elle experienced the worse of it when their bare hands contacted the ground. They screamed in concert, grabbing their heads and rocking back and forth. Kitty mewled and pawed at her head.

"Turn off your senses."

The effect was immediate, and they stopped rocking back and forth. Carla looked at him through tear-filled eyes and a trickle of blood streamed down her nose. Elle and Kitty didn't look much better, and they lay on the ground, their sides heaving.

A spike of alarm pierced his chest when the matriarch of earth dragons snapped out of her stupor and with it, a tremor that knocked Jared off his feet. An earsplitting crack followed. He eyed the buildings warily, hoping they'd stand firm.

Before he rose to his feet, a secondary crack echoed across the mountain range. Crinkling his brow, Jared scrutinized the mountain. At first, he saw nothing out of place, but a second glance revealed a large section of earth breaking off the mountain. It started slowly, but picked up speed, sending a ton of rock and earth cascading down the mountain, directly for their new home.

"No!" Jared surged to his feet. He ran through the group and pushed them to their feet, urging them to run. The spike of psionic pressure that pierced into his body had a much greater effect on everyone else. It was everything he could do to get them moving. He pushed them to the other side of the ravine and urged them to climb up the mountain as fast as they could.

"Scarlet! Can they do something?"

"I do not know, but I will try."

"Move faster! Go!" Jared ran back and forth, sometimes carrying people and sprinting forward. He willed them to flee faster.

"Scarlet, if you can't get them to do anything about this, just get out of there. Don't risk yourself."

Scarlet's brothers soared into the area and their companions sprinted forward, scrambling onto their backs. Each dragon carried three people, but that still left twenty-three. Elle rode atop Kitty, and they easily ate the ground, scaling up the other side of the mountain, well out of the path of the avalanche.

Jared didn't think they'd make it in time. He could, but there's no way he'd leave the rest of the water folk behind. If he had to carry them, he'd do whatever he could until the end.

The avalanche made the ground bounce precariously under their feet and many people had trouble keeping up a steady sprint, stumbling frequently. Jared bounced around like a rabbit, picking people up and giving them a shove forward. They'd sprinted only a mile by the time the massive wave of rock and earth hit the steel and cable wall they'd erected. It tore through it like tissue paper, smashing into the buildings and leveling everything in its path.

"We won't make it, Scarlet."

"You will."

In the next instant, Jared felt himself lifted in the air, borne away in Scarlet's claws. Another person in her other claw.

"Help them!"

An unknown voice thundered into his mind. A moment later a wall of pure white streaked by him as dozens of smaller dragons, rocketed over the top of the roiling debris, snatching water folk out of the way. Jared watched in horror as Damien stumbled before one of the white dragons grabbed him. He face-planted, struggling to get back on his feet, but there was no way he'd make it in time.

Right before the rampaging earth reached him, Gayana's head burst from the out-of-control landslide. She roared in defiance, bunched her muscles and jumped right on top of Damien, tucking her head and tail beneath her as the earth and debris crashed over them.

No.

Seconds later, it was over. The entire ravine looked foreign. Nothing remained. The buildings were gone.

White, hot rage burned within him. Gayana's carelessness had destroyed their home, Damien might be dead, and all their equipment and weapons were under tons of rock and earth. All their efforts and preparation gone in only a few minutes.

"Put. Me. Down." Jared seethed in a rage.

"Jared, do not be a fool."

"Put me down, Scarlet."

Scarlet opened her claws a few feet off the ground and Jared stalked over to the last place he'd seen Gayana buried. Pushing as much vehemence and anger into his thoughts as possible, Jared roared at her.

"Gayana!"

"I do not think this wise."

"Scarlet, she destroyed everything, and who knows if Damien survived. It's gone! All of it! Three times now our world's turned upside down, and this was entirely preventable."

Turning back to the spot in the earth he'd chosen to direct his rage, Jared yelled again, and again.

A slight shifting of rubble was the only warning he had before the matriarch burst from the earth, shooting straight up twenty feet before dropping to straddle the hole her exit made. Jared sprinted to the edge of the new crater and saw Damien laying directly beneath her, blood oozing from his face.

Jared didn't waste a single moment. He dropped into the hole, picked Damien up, and jumped out. He didn't care if it pushed his muscles too far, he needed to get Damien some help. As he flew from the hole, Jared called out to Casey.

"Casey! I need you here, now!"

Jared laid Damien on the ground next to Scarlet, and Ashazad landed, carrying a pale Casey. He immediately jumped off and ran over. After a long, tense moment, Casey announced that he was okay and just unconscious.

The immediate crisis averted, Jared instructed Casey to carry him away from the area. Steeling himself, his rage a barely contained hurricane, Jared whirled on Gayana.

"What was that!" Jared exploded in a rage, spittle flying and his face burning a bright red.

"I do not answer to you, human."

"You destroyed everything we've built these past few weeks. All our weapons are down there. You almost killed my people."

"Your people killed Razael."

"Wrong! We have the same enemy, but your stupidity just set us back months, if not years."

"What. Did. You. Say?"

"You heard me! Your stupidity!" Jared yelled as loud as he could, his voice echoing off the mountain.

Gayana lashed out with her tail, but Jared proved faster, vaulting over the swing, and grasping the studs lining her tail. Surprising himself, he scrambled to his feet on the still moving tail and sprinted up her back.

She twisted her neck and tried to bat him from her back, but she wasn't fast enough. Thankfully, she didn't have razor spikes like Scarlet, or it would have ended badly for him. The pointed studs on her back were hard enough to avoid.

Gayana leaped forward, intending to dislodge him from her back, but it failed again.

"Get off!"

The mental blast nearly succeeded where her physical actions failed. Pushing back with his own psionic blast, Jared yelled at her. *"Never!"*

"Jared, I think this has gone far enough. Gayana, stop this farce." The new voice was one he hadn't heard, and it made him pause until Gayana responded.

"Stay out of this, Sildrainen."

Jared could see he wouldn't get through Gayana's thick skull without drastic measures. A part of him balked at what he was about to do, but the fury wouldn't abate, and he shrugged off common sense. Whipping out his new phase pistols, Jared carefully lined up his shots and fired a flurry into the exposed section of her neck when she glanced back at him.

She roared in anguish and rage, bucking and thrashing around. She even tried rolling onto her back, but no matter what she tried, Jared was just too fast, and his *Maximum Muscle* kept him a step ahead of her every time. He saw the scorch marks on her skin and realized that the phase rounds didn't do more than mar the surface after the first volley.

After a series of particularly close calls with Gayana hot on his heels, Jared pivoted and rushed at her. Startled, she drew up short, but not before he released another round of phase energy into the same spot as before. Jared knew he'd done damage this time. The other earth dragons wailed in protest and started toward them. Scarlet and her brothers blocked the way.

Jared was about to pull the trigger for another round when Layonia's voice dropped him to his knees. Immediately, Gayana stopped moving. She knew her superior and wisely submitted as the giant water dragon dropped in front of her.

"Stop this at once. Jared, put your weapons away."

Jared didn't obey immediately, prompting Layonia to apply more pressure.

"Now!"

The weapons clattered to the ground as he grabbed his head. Excruciating pain filled his mind, and a trickle of blood leaked from his nose.

"Gayana, leave him be. He is right to be angry. We all grieve and in our own way, but you destroyed his home and put those he loves in danger."

"He is just a paltry human." The vehemence in her voice made Jared cringe.

Layonia looked at Jared curiously. "A human, sworn to protect mankind and dragonkind. Frankly, I am surprised he could harm you at all, given the vow he made. That tells me only one thing. He did not want to harm you, but you gave him no choice."

"What vow?"

Gayana didn't sound so certain of herself anymore. If only she'd let Jared finish showing her everything, she'd know what vow. In hindsight, he should have shown her the vow when he rehashed Alestrialia passing on her legacy.

Did I skip that part? Jared wondered. *Maybe she ignored it?*

"He swore to protect Scarlet on pain of death. An excruciating death. He also vowed to see dragonkind thrive once more side by side with humans. Did you not see this in his memories?"

"I…" Gayana sounded chagrined. "I did not give them any mind."

"Then this is all your fault and yours alone. You will aid Jared and his people to recover their equipment and gear, or what little of it remains."

"I—"

"This is not a request, Gayana. As the oldest and appointed overseer of our kind, my word is final. Do you understand?"

"I understand."

Finished with Gayana, Layonia turned her massive head toward Jared.

"Jared. Never confront a dragon or inflict harm on one again. Do you understand?"

"But, what if—"

"Never."

His mind exploded in another spasm of excruciating pain and more blood oozed from his nose.

"I. Understand."

"If one of our kind steps out of line again, we will deal with them. Is that understood?"

She looked between the two of them and they both nodded their heads, chastised by this ancient being.

"Jared, finish showing Gayana the events leading up to your encounter."

"You can't seriously—"

Layonia tilted her head to the side, and Jared snapped his mouth shut.

"All right, I'll finish the recounting."

Once finished, without incident this time, Layonia directed Jared to Fayle, the matriarch of air dragons.

"Fayle, I warn you now. The information is not pleasant, but I will not take kindly to brash reactions."

Dutifully, Jared sulked over to Fayle. Amidst the chaos, he hadn't gotten a good look at these new arrivals. They shone as if a light source unto themselves. He knew it was just the sun's reflection off their pristine white scales, but it almost hurt to look at them. Squinting, Jared craned his neck up to look at Fayle. She lowered her head to Jared's height, a smirk twisting the corner of her mouth into a smile.

"Consider me impressed, Jared. It is possible you could have won that sparring match. These weapons you carry. They are impressive, no? To penetrate the flesh of an earth dragon is no small feat. I must know more. How did you move so fast? What manner of man are you?"

Jared stared stupidly at this beautiful creature in front of him. Her piercing white irises roved over his body, weighing him thoroughly. Fayle's voice was a high-pitched and whimsical tone, perhaps to match her nature as an air dragon. Scarlet warned him they were often unpredictable and given to impulse. His first impression didn't disappoint, and he found himself at a loss on how to proceed. Layonia saved him from the predicament.

"Fayle, let him show you his mind and all will become clear."

Fayle had much the same reaction when she learned of his ability to mind meld, but overcame her hesitation much faster and laid her head next to him. He sat down, exhausted from his encounter with Gayana. For the next thirty minutes, he showed Fayle all there was to see. Contrary to the reactions of the other two matriarchs, she didn't react outwardly to his reveal of Razael, but Jared knew there was a slight shift in her perception of mankind. He didn't know how, but he knew she directed her ire at the humans responsible rather than him and his group. It was strange, since it didn't seem like there was a difference in her mind, but the way her thoughts shifted and jumped about made it impossible for him to get a solid read on her.

Fayle's next words shocked Jared altogether.

"We bond now?"

"I—" Jared didn't know what to say. "We—"

Scarlet saved him from having to respond himself. **"I think we should let tensions lapse before we consider more bonds."**

"Thanks, Scarlet. Her mind is…"

"I know."

The exchange amused Scarlet, and despite the recent events Jared smiled in response to the emotions traveling across their bond.

Layonia inclined her head. "I suggest we all remove ourselves from each other's company for a time and regroup. Scarlet, Fayle, Gayana, and I will spend the rest of the day and night together in conversation. Tomorrow we decide on our path."

22 NEW DENVER

No one got any sleep that night save Damien, who spent half the night unconscious. He panicked when he finally woke up, confused about how he was still alive. Jared explained what had happened and a strange look came over his face.

"I thought—" Damien collected his thoughts, "—it was just a dream. I don't know how to explain it. Someone invaded my mind after darkness enveloped me, but I thought it was just my imagination. That was Gayana?"

Jared watched Damien look around as if he wanted to see the dragon that saved his life.

"Yes, it was Gayana. She's also the one responsible for destroying our home, burying all our gear and weapons, and almost getting you killed."

"But she saved me."

Jared couldn't believe Damien's insistence on this point. Damien, the one who'd previously supported George and was quick to express doubt of Jared and Vanessa when things didn't go smoothly. Sure, he'd eventually come around, but Jared thought

Damien would hold a grudge against Gayana after what she'd done, not look around for her in reverence.

Could this day get any weirder?

Jared shook his head and pointed in the direction the earth dragons had gone. Damien tried to stand on shaky legs, but Jared pressed him back down.

"You're in no condition to be up and about. Besides, Layonia made it very clear we're to remain with our own groups for the night. She is not someone you want to cross. Trust me on that." Jared reached up and grabbed his head where he felt pulsating pain from her mental blast.

"But—"

Jared held up a hand to silence him. "I'm serious, Damien. It's not worth it tonight. Wait until tomorrow after Scarlet speaks with them. We'll know more then. But until then, please try to get what little rest you can."

"Fine," Damien spat the word.

Sighing, Jared retreated and found Vanessa. If he disobeyed Layonia's command, Jared didn't want to know what would happen. He idly wondered if she would *take care* of him. Immediately, he admonished himself for the thoughts. He knew Damien would never betray them like George, and wishing death on someone just because they didn't always agree with him wasn't the attitude a leader should have.

The night passed ever so slowly, and Jared itched for the sun to crest the mountain tops. Looking at the mound of debris covering the area where the apartments used to be, he saw a metric ton of work and time lost. He wanted to get started right away, with or without the help of Gayana and her kin.

It was several hours after dawn before Scarlet returned to him.

"They will join our cause. Though, as we surmised, Layonia

and her kin will not partake in direct battle. They will, however, ferry some of you to the cities if needed."

"Gayana?" Jared wasn't sure if she wanted to join the cause after their disagreement.

"Yes, but she has a rather odd request. She wishes to bond with Damien."

The surprises wouldn't stop coming. "Seriously? She—I—"

"It surprised us as well, given your confrontation."

"Do you think that's such a good idea? You've seen Damien can cause problems. Wouldn't this bond exacerbate that even further?"

"Likely, but it is the only way the earth dragons join our cause."

He didn't like it but had no other choice but to agree.

"Scarlet, about the fight—I didn't want to hurt her, I—"

"I know, Jared. As Layonia said, had you wanted to cause her any real harm, or worse, your vow would have destroyed you. I tried to warn you, but you would not listen to reason."

"I'm sorry, I let my rage consume me. It's just"—Jared waved his arm around him—"everything we worked toward is no more. Who knows if the weapons survived this?"

"Gayana will help." Scarlet seemed certain, even though Jared didn't know how she could.

"With Fayle and her kin, we have sixty-six dragons and forty-five humans. Jared, we have an army. What are a mere handful of weapons compared to a force such as this?"

Put into perspective, his rage-fueled idiocy seemed petty and juvenile. Ashamed, Jared admitted he'd wronged Gayana and promised to apologize.

"She knows what she did was wrong. I believe the two of you may yet get along if you but give her a chance."

"I'll try."

"Gayana will help clear the rubble and recover as much gear as possible. Though, Layonia suggested we have a bond ceremony first."

"Scarlet, the boosters!"

Alarm shot through their bond as they both whipped their head to the buried buildings.

"Gayana!"

The giant earth dragon looked over to Scarlet.

"We must carefully excavate the building that used to lie here. There is a crate filled with the boosters that enable the bonding. Without them, we cannot unlock the nanites."

Jared watched Gayana dip her head. It looked like shame, but he didn't know her well enough to understand her mannerisms.

"Gayana—"

"Jared—"

"—I'm sorry for attacking you."

"—and I apologize for destroying your home and putting your people at risk. It was not my intention."

"Thank you, Gayana. Let the past stay in the past?"

"Indeed."

Jared pushed the negative feelings from his mind and reverted to business mode. "So, I've no idea if the building is still in this location, or what survived, but we've got to try."

"This is an area where we excel. Please stand back and let us work." Gayana closed her eyes and pounded her tree-trunks-for-legs into the ground.

"Are you sure?"

Gayana opened one eye to glare at him.

"Hey, okay, okay. Moving back."

"Family, come."

Jared watched the earth dragons surround the area, creating a large circle around where the apartments sat. Once all the dragons were in place, the ground vibrated again.

"Oh no, not again."

"Peace, Jared. She is in control this time. Watch, for this is not something any other human has witnessed before."

Concerned, Jared listened to Scarlet and watched the dragons from afar, turning his mind to the vibrating sensations running up his legs. He forgot all about the avalanche as he watched the vibrations pulse and move beneath the earth. Directed beams of energy flowed into the ground, pinging off anything that wasn't of the earth. The beams of energy cut straight through rocks and dirt but bounced off parts of their broken fence and anything else that didn't belong. It reminded Jared of sonar where the wave of a frequency bounced off objects and returned a simplistic picture. The waves of energy manipulated the objects beneath the ground. If it didn't belong, the pulsating vibrations pushed and prodded the object. Slowly, the foreign objects moved upward. Not just one, but all at once. Shocked, Jared couldn't believe it.

"Scarlet, how are they doing this?"

"They are of the earth and understand its nature."

"Really, Scarlet? Cryptic much?"

"I am a fire dragon, and fire cannot harm me. My body is in communion with it. I can harness it, breathe it, thrive in it. Air dragons harness the air, aiding their speed and agility They can even manipulate it to a degree, creating a cone in front as they fly and using it as a projectile. Water dragons can do much the same with water. If attuned to an element, we can feel that element and shape it to our will."

"Why didn't we speak of this before?"

"It never came up before. You asked of my fire breathing, and

you got an answer. After you witnessed the changes to my body on our journey to find my brothers, you saw the fire coursing through my veins and behind my eyes. Was any explanation necessary?"

"Good point. Are there any other hidden talents I should know about?"

"None I can think of. Though, like my own brothers, there are those of my kind here of earth, water, and air with their own special interests in the sciences or philosophy. Once Kirgor catches up on modern technology, and Ashazad on modern medicine, we will not lack for sufficient knowledge to speed up humankind's development."

"Let's not get ahead of ourselves. We've still got a city to take over, and that's just the start. No one knows how many of these things exist. First, though, we need to get everyone bonded."

"Patience."

"Easy for you to say. You live for thousands of years."

"Your point?"

"What do you mean, my point? Humans don't live that long. I'll die in mere decades from now."

"I do not think so."

"You think these nanites can sustain us that long?"

"I do. Perhaps not indefinitely, but centuries, yes."

It seemed unfair to him. So many people in his life died around him. He'd killed others barely older than himself. What right did he have to live centuries? It never occurred to him he'd live that long, given the technovirus and no cure, but that no longer plagued them so why not? The idea appealed to him. The main question was if he'd survive long enough to live for centuries. His future was unclear, but now he knew it possible, he added it to his goals. If he could live with Vanessa for centuries, he'd be the luckiest man alive.

"A few hundred years is nothing to a dragon, but I am only

centuries old so I understand your thoughts better than you might think."

Jared said nothing. He sat watching Gayana work. As if the last day wasn't enough to wrap his head around, Scarlet dropped another world-changing idea on him like this. If anything else happened in the same day, Jared might have a heart attack from the sheer ludicrousness of everything.

Several hours passed before Jared realized that Elle and Carla had joined him. They sat with their eyes closed and expressions of wonder on their faces. Watching their heads move in tandem, Jared knew they also watched the choreographed vibrations beneath the surface.

Finally, around midday, the rubble on the surface shifted as tons of material poked through. Another hour passed before anything not of the earth lay on the surface. All the earth dragons dropped to their bellies and fell asleep immediately.

"Are they okay, Scarlet?"

"Yes, they must rest."

"Is it safe to walk on the ground?"

Scarlet showed it was by walking out, herself, to sift through the collapsed apartment building.

Jared jogged over to the water folk and asked everyone to go help find anything worth salvaging. Weapons and medical supplies were the priority, but if there was anything else they could take, they should do so.

"Jared, over here."

Running over to Scarlet, Jared saw part of the crate they'd used to store the boosters. All around the ground, the blue liquid seeped from beneath a partially collapsed wall.

Please, no.

Scarlet lifted the wall and Jared gingerly levered the mangled crate from the wreckage. Fingers shaking, Jared ripped off the lid and promptly fell back against a fallen support beam.

"Shattered." They were all shattered to pieces.

"We will find more."

Vanessa ran over to him, pausing when she saw the ruined crate. "Oh no."

She carefully reached inside, moving broken vials out of the way. She pulled her hand back and held one intact syringe. They'd had over one hundred boosters, and now they held but one.

"Give it to Damien." Jared didn't hesitate. He and Gayana already knew they wanted to bond. It was a non-decision for him.

"Are you certain?"

"I am. We've not spent enough time with the others for anyone to find a companion and Gayana made this her one request to join our cause. I don't care how much of a headache it'll give me. If it means we get the support of all the dragons, it's worth it."

"I'll do it now." Vanessa squeezed his shoulder. "We'll survive this, Jared. We'll survive and come out stronger than ever before."

She was right. They would survive. As much as it pained him to lose so much yet again, they were all alive, united with all the remaining dragons, and of one purpose to create a better world for man and dragon. It was a time to rejoice, not wallow in despair. Dragging himself to his feet, Jared forced himself to move on, taking a page out of his own book and leaving the past in the past.

To take his mind off of the loss, Jared threw himself into the work, digging through the destroyed building for equipment and weapons. After a full day searching, they salvaged half a dozen phase rifles, a dozen phase pistols, and two dozen of the handguns. He found his pack almost untouched, except for the few boosters he kept inside, which had broken like the others. Miraculously, all the phase batteries remained intact. He wondered if that was an intentional design of their manufacturer, so they didn't accidentally explode. It made sense. One of those blowing up in someone's face was a sure death sentence.

The crate of medical supplies was mostly salvageable, as were all the manuals for the various weapons. The gunpowder and other supplies they'd collected for bomb-making weren't among the rubble. Jared guessed because the bulk of the materials were natural and the dragons hadn't known to levitate them to the surface.

Johan assured him it wouldn't be an issue. With the earth dragons on their side, they could easily produce all the materials they needed from the earth, and Scarlet could refine the materials in fire. He'd mumbled something about ice and the air dragons, but his voice became faint as he turned away to find Midri.

Whatever it took, Jared would definitely see that Johan and Midri had all the help they needed. Those bombs could be the difference they needed for a surprise attack against the city. They could use the air dragons to deliver the payloads since they'd easily blend in against the sky and clouds. They only needed an overcast day and they could bombard the city into submission. The thought gave him pause as he thought about the innocent life they might take out. It's possible many in the city didn't know what transpired on the earth. He wasn't sure it was a decision he could make without violating his vow to protect the innocent, but how could they not know? He definitely wouldn't lose any sleep over it, no matter what they decided.

A stealthy infiltration appealed to him more and more, and it would allow him to assess the situation before committing many people and dragons to the fight. It was risky and, if discovered, it could be the end of a thing before it ever got started. However, he had Vanessa to take up the fight in his stead if that happened. Elle could easily get lost in the city and evade capture until help arrived, if he brought her with them. Overall, it was the least risky plan he could come up with and would risk the fewest lives. It was a worthy gamble to protect those he loved.

Pete had figured out the signal for the robot and believed he could use it to lure a ship in while also preventing it from communicating with the city. First, they needed to get more boosters, and everyone bonded. While he worked, Jared came up with a plan. It made him slightly queasy to think about it, but it was their best bet.

He'd hike with Vanessa, Elle, and Kitty to one of the nearby colonies at the base of the mountain. They'd travel to the city like normal explorers, Kitty with camouflage on, and see what kind of reception they received. If the city welcomed them, and helped them out, then they'd ask for boosters. If they refused, they'd trade one of their phase rifles for them. Jared also had credits in his pack. If everything else failed, then Elle and Kitty would go into stealth mode and steal the boosters.

Jared couldn't risk the colony finding out about the water folk and dragons and wouldn't be able to bring anyone else to the city as proof of those that traveled with him. If the colony was anything like his own back home, they likely wouldn't give any up without something in return. He only hoped a phase rifle was sufficient compensation for twenty-nine boosters. That's how many they needed after Damien and Gayana finished bonding.

That was a tall ask for most colonies, but considering how large these were, he hoped they'd have the resources on hand to help.

He outlined his plans to Scarlet and informed everyone they'd set out at first light. They planned to travel quickly, so Scarlet and Malsour would accompany them part of the way to carry him and Vanessa.

"It'll take us a couple days. Everyone else, please take the time to get to know our new allies. If possible, I'd like everyone to get acquainted and find a dragon you'd like to bond with. If there are some that don't want to bond, I'll not force it upon anyone. After you've bonded, please work with Ashazad to understand the changes to your body and how to enhance yourselves. We should be back before that happens, but if not, then you'll have something to keep you busy."

The next morning, Jared, Vanessa, and Elle mounted up and took off for the larger of the two colonies. They made it through the mountains and passes in half a day. Scarlet and Malsour promised to wait for them there, and the four continued on foot. They took half the day to reach the city as the sun set over the horizon. Those on the wall called out for them to stop when they were within a few dozen yards of the gate.

Jared looked around and didn't see Kitty. Thankfully, the feline knew how to evade detection well. Jared swept his gaze back to the wall and caught a slight movement out of the corner of his eye. Kitty scaled the side of the wall, right below the person who called for them to stop.

Jared smiled, knowing Kitty could easily decapitate the man if he intended to harm them. A few minutes later, the gate opened, and a retinue of armed guards marched up. They didn't point their weapons threateningly, so that was a good sign. Jared had wisely kept his phase pistols back in the ravine with the others, and only sported a couple long knives and his Colt. The phase rifle and spare battery were in his pack. He had no intention of revealing them if he didn't need to.

"What is your business here?"

The man's voice brooked no nonsense. He was a burly, older man with a white beard, shaved head, and skin the shade of night.

His body armor looked military grade, and he wore clean pressed fatigues.

"We're just explorers passing through. We hoped to take shelter for the night. There are some rather vicious creatures up there and we barely made it through the mountains."

The man eyed him suspiciously, not believing his story for a second.

"How did you survive in there? There's no way you made it through the mountains in a day, and we've seen what lurks in there."

"We have explored most of the western parts of the country for almost a decade and know how to become invisible to the creatures around here. We can also see in the dark. It makes it a lot easier to go unnoticed."

After a long, intense scrutiny, the man finally relaxed and held out his hand. "Sergeant First Class Johnston. This is my command post. Welcome to New Denver."

"Johnston, nice to meet you. I'm Jared Cartwright, this is my family, Vanessa and Elle. It's nice to meet someone who knows what they're doing out here. We've been across many other settlements and just walked right through their small fences and gates without so much as a sideways glance."

Jared cringed. It sounded much like his own home colony. They'd been so naïve to the world and it's a wonder they'd lasted so long. Looking around New Denver made Jared realize just how much they'd limped along. In the years he lived there and as far back as he knew, their colony had never grown. This New Denver was clear evidence it was possible to enjoy a normal life. Normal was subjective. He knew the truth now, so no matter how nice it would be just to settle down here and live out their days, he couldn't ignore the cities. They needed eradication for the world to prosper once again.

"Carlo?" Johnston turned to look at a man standing at the open gate. "I'll take our new friends into town. Stand in my post until I return."

"Roger that, Sergeant."

After they'd passed through the gate and it shut behind them, Jared found an entire platoon of soldiers drilling in the yard. They worked with bayonets, hand-to-hand combat, and even had medieval training pits set up for swordplay, spears, throwing daggers, axes, and an archery lane. Jared eyed everything in wonder.

"Impressive ain't it?" Johnston nudged him with a brilliant white smile painted on his face. "We ain't brought no one through these gates before and never had an excuse to show this off. Don't let these sorry louts fool you, though." Johnston raised his voice, ensuring it carried over the group of men practicing. "They jumped up to practice after they heard you approach the gate. We're just about to change over duty to the night rotation. They insisted it was worth staying to put on a good show."

Jared smiled back at Johnston's casual demeanor. He'd initially presented a strong, stoic front, then, he'd greeted him like long-lost friends, and now treated him like his drinking buddy. The man was clearly a people person and adept at making him feel at ease.

"This is just the rear garrison. We've got another two battalions stationed on the east gate, and one each on the north and south. We should probably have two battalions back here, but with these walls we ain't had nothing get passed them or even try in a long time."

"I've got to hand it to you, this is one impressive fortification. I've not seen anything like it in all the time we've been out here exploring. Although, we've never been this far east."

"There's another colony close by, but they aren't as big. We split this city up decades ago when it expanded into higher radiation zones. I suppose it doesn't matter now with nanites, but the split happened so long ago no one cares to merge the two up again. Maybe someday the colonies will naturally grow large enough to become one big settlement.

"I can take you to some place to rest for the night, somewhere to get grub, or if you'd like to see the mayor I can see if he's got any visiting hours?"

"You all have an elected official here?"

"Of course! We ain't barbarians. We've got schools, police, emergency responders, you name it. There's electricity from our solar and wind farms. Our vehicles are all battery operated. We ration electricity, but we get by just fine. Our farms produce livestock, fruits, and vegetables of all kinds. We even get fish from the lakes in foothills of the mountains."

"Do you still get help from the cities if you can sustain yourself here?"

"We got to get nanite injectors somehow, don't we? We could just stay in the safe zone boundaries, but even then, folks got sick with radiation poisoning. Now, we all got to take them by order of the boss man."

"I'm assuming you all produce materials for the cities then?"

"Yep, gotta give them something for the little buggers. Circle of life and all that. So, what'll it be?"

"Maybe someplace to eat, rest, and time with the mayor tomorrow?"

"Priorities. Good choice my man. Yes, I've got just the place in mind. Serves the best chicken dumplings and beef stew."

"Lead on."

Jared smiled at the thought of a fine home-cooked meal. Marie's food was good, but it paled compared to the meals his mother used to make.

Johnston led them to a plain two-story building with a wooden sign out front that announced it as "Marie's Inn & Tavern." Jared nearly burst out laughing. He caught himself at the last moment, remembering his cover story they'd been exploring for almost a decade. It could get a little awkward if he needed to explain the outburst.

This Marie proved to be quite the opposite of their own. She was a spindly old woman with a shock of white hair tied neatly behind her head. She wore a red-checkered apron around her waist and greeted them warmly. Her smile was genuine and touched her eyes, making him feel warm and welcomed. Permanent crow's feet adorned the dimples on her cheeks and the corners of her eyes, clearing showing this was a woman who enjoyed life and serving others.

Jared treated her with utmost respect and asked about room and board for the night.

"We have little to offer for the hospitality. I've got a few munitions credits, but that's about it. We've been traveling for so long, we carry only essentials and live off the land."

"Your payment ain't good here, anyway. Johnny boy, you stick around for some dumplings, you hear?"

"Ah, Ma, I wish I could, but the missus ain't gonna forgive me if I miss another meal for your kitchen."

"Now, listen here. You tell that girl if I gotta come over there and give her a what for—"

"Now, now, she didn't mean nothing by it. I miss mealtime often on account of my shift change. It ain't your cookin' she's jealous of. It's just my time."

"Well, then whatcha waitin' fer? Get ya gone from my inn, boy."

Jared watched the exchange with a broad grin on his face. Before Johnston ducked out of the room, he glanced at Jared, winked, and shut the door.

Jared's face fell as his mind ticked back to the reason for their visit here. He hated the fact they may end up stealing from these people. He really hoped the mayor obliged his request.

"All right, up ye go. Wash up. Dinner be ready in half an hour. Jerry!"

A boy no older than ten bounded into the room.

"Show our guests up to their rooms."

"Yes, ma'am." The boy snapped to attention with a formal salute. He turned on his heel, beckoning them to follow, and marched up the stairs.

Their room turned out to be an adjoining suite, complete with a full bathroom. When Vanessa and Elle found out there was running water and a boiler, they shut Jared out of the room and spent almost the entire half hour basking in the luxurious hot water. Jared didn't blame them. The moment the hot water hit his body, he wanted nothing more than to stand underneath the torrent of scalding water the rest of the night. Fate was a cruel trickster as Jerry rapped on their door not a moment later. He announced dinner was ready and Nanna didn't tolerate tardiness. He said it with such a matter-of-fact politeness, it made Jared chuckle and shut down the glorious stream of energizing liquid. Stepping out of the steamy bathroom, Jared felt like a new man.

A pair of clean linen pants and a shirt waited for him on the bed. He slipped into them, obeying Jerry as he asked to gather up their soiled clothes for washing and mending. Ready to enjoy a succulent dumpling, Jared joined the girls in the other room and his jaw hit the floor. Vanessa practically glowed. Her skin shone, and a soft pink hue decorated her cheeks. Her silky black hair reflected the light, shimmering when she ducked her head.

"You look so beautiful!"

Consumed by her radiant beauty, Jared jumped when Jerry

forcefully cleared his throat from the doorway.

"Nanna is waiting."

"Shall we?"

Vanessa took Jared's proffered arm, and Elle followed behind them, a huge smile on her face.

"I didn't overlook you either, Elle." Jared winked at her. "You look stunning! I haven't seen you smile this much since you first reunited with Vanessa. The look suits you. Both of you!"

They all knew this moment wouldn't last, but they enjoyed it for what it was, a brief respite before the storm. That night, they left any talk of the future and upcoming plans aside, choosing to live at the moment and enjoy each other's company.

As much as he didn't want to part from Vanessa that night, duty and his moral compass drove him to bed alone. Sometimes he hated his conscience. He loved Vanessa with everything he had and wanted nothing more than to be with her for the rest of their lives. Unfortunately, the nagging voice in the back of his mind railed at him to follow his parents' example.

The thought made him stop in his tracks. "Wait, surely there's a minister in this city who could—"

Jared ran to the adjoining door and asked to speak with Vanessa alone. Elle eyed him askance, but Jared assured her it wouldn't take long.

When the two of them were alone, Jared's forehead broke into a sweat and he opened and closed his mouth several times before making an approximation of sound.

"Vanessa, I—we have something between us that is so precious. Something I didn't expect to experience in this life. The love I feel for you is the same love I saw in my dad's eyes when he looked at my mother. I want nothing more than to be your husband. In this life, the next, and any other we find ourselves in."

"Jared, I—"

He placed a finger on her lips, cutting her off.

"Vanessa Carlisle, will you do me the honor of becoming my wife?"

"Yes!" Vanessa shrieked. Elle and Kitty materialized in the room, crouched and ready to face any intruders.

"Jeez, we're fine!" Jared laughed, joy filling his soul.

"Why you yell?"

"Elle, Jared asked me to marry him and I said yes!"

It was Elle's turn to shriek and jump on Vanessa with a huge bear hug. Next thing he knew, the door flew open and old Nanna barreled into the room with her shotgun primed. Luckily, Kitty had disappeared a split second before the door opened, or they'd have had a lot of explaining to do.

"What's all this racket!" grumped Nanna.

Vanessa positively beamed as she ran over and wrapped the old woman in a bear hug. "Jared just asked me to marry him!"

Nanna narrowed her eyes suspiciously. "I thought you married already?"

Vanessa's smile faltered for a moment, but she quickly recovered and explained.

"No, we've been together for a long time, but we've never been to someplace where we could formally make this happen. Surely you have a minister here, right?"

The suspicion turned into a beaming smile until she realized she still held the shotgun at them. "Sorry 'bout that. Never can be certain these days. We have a minister. My brother runs the church just down the street."

"Can we do it first thing in the morning?" Vanessa looked to Jared and Nanna hopefully.

"Nanna, do you know when we're meeting with the mayor?"

"Nonsense, that stuffy old git can wait. Yer wedding be more important. I'll make sure that old badger attends the wedding himself. You can kill two birds at once."

"Oh, thank you, thank you!" Vanessa couldn't contain her energy, bouncing from foot to foot.

Jared couldn't wipe the grin off his face. He'd never seen this side of Vanessa. Up to this point, she'd been so reserved, carrying the weight of her people on her shoulders. He'd caught glimpses of this side with the elusive and sudden kisses over the months. He never thought she'd devolve into a bouncing teenage girl like this. They'd already discussed what marriage even meant these days, but apparently it meant every bit as much to her as it did him.

"Thank you, Nanna. What time should we meet you downstairs?"

"Nonsense. Vanessa and Elle be coming with me right this instant. You ain't allowed to see your bride on yer wedding day until she be walkin' down the aisle. We still hold to tradition here in New Denver. You might be a guest, but ain't no exception under my roof."

Jared didn't enjoy letting them out of his sight, but he felt confident they would be safe with Kitty looking out for them.

"*Stay with them, Kitty.*"

The giant cat brushed his side. "**I will.**"

"All right, then, I guess I'll see you in the morning...fiancée."

Vanessa squealed again, jumped into his arms and planted a kiss on his lips.

"All right, that's enough, you two sinners. Ain't no kissy kissy till after yer married."

Grinning like a fool, Jared walked the trio to the top of the stairs and waved them goodnight.

Back in his room, Jared lay back in the bed, more content than he'd ever been in his life.

"Jared? What is happening down there?"

"Scarlet? How can you reach me this far?"

"I am flying over the city right now with Malsour. Yours and Vanessa's emotions are hard to ignore."

"Scarlet! We're getting married in the morning!"

"I do not know why you trouble yourself with something that no longer matters. You told me this is just a construct of a rule of government, right? So, why do it? When my mother walked the earth—"

"But it matters. It does. Marriage aside, we would've eventually gotten past it, but this is more to honor my parents than anything. Also, even though Vanessa didn't come out and say it, her reaction when I asked was a clear indication she wants this too."

"Human relations are...odd."

Jared smirked. She experienced the emotional surges through their bond, but she did not understand what it meant to have a relationship. Since dragons didn't mate like other creatures, she couldn't understand, and he hadn't spent the time he wanted with her to work through and explain all these feelings. He'd need to remedy that when they had a moment to spare.

Jared ignored her comment. *"This place has been nothing short of amazing, and the little old lady we're staying with has a brother who is a minister. She whisked Vanessa and Elle off to get ready for a ceremony at first light. She'll also wrangle the colony's mayor to come to the chapel, and we can have a chat about the boosters."*

"All that happened in a few hours?"

"Amazing, right?"

"I am happy for you, Jared. I don't understand it all, but after so much tragedy, you deserve happiness, and I am thrilled you get to honor your parents' memory by following in their footsteps."

"Thank you. That means a lot."

"I..." Scarlet paused and for a moment Jared didn't think she'd continue. **"I think Malsour and I will need to teach the both of you to lock down on your emotions better. It could become... awkward."**

A blush crept up Jared's neck as he realized the implications. *"Oh, I—"* Jared didn't know what to say. Embarrassment washed through him. He could endure the increased scrutiny from Scarlet, she already knew his innermost thoughts, but Malsour...

"Scarlet should we wait?"

"Think nothing of it for now. We will speak of it later. We will remove ourselves from the area to create a buffer between us." Scarlet projected as much mischief as possible along their bond, inciting a wry chuckle from Jared.

"Sorry, again." Jared winced, hoping it didn't cause too much discomfort for them. *"I promise we'll work on shielding our emotions as soon as we can. As for our timeline here, that hasn't changed, and we intend to meet you tomorrow."*

"Are you certain? We could—"

"Yes, I'm certain. As much as I'd love to take more time, we have people waiting for us. I won't put my wants and desires over theirs."

"Very well. We will be waiting. Goodnight, Jared."

23 BARGAIN STRUCK

Jared slept like a rock, getting more than his customary three to five hours. Between the reason for his visit and the events leading to the following morning, Jared didn't think he'd sleep at all. However, the incredible meal, hot shower, and comfortable bed compounded to render him unconscious. A knock on the door startled him from his sleep. Bleary-eyed, Jared opened the door to admit an equally bleary-eyed Jerry.

"You look tired. Didn't you get any sleep last night?"

"With all that yammering in the other room? Nope, not a wink."

Jared grinned at the little boy as he stumbled from the room. Poor little guy. Jared imagined the girls chittering all night, and he couldn't wait to see the fruits of their preparation. He basked in another hot shower, washing his hair for the first time in months.

As if reading his mind, Jerry announced that the barber had arrived to give him a haircut and shave. Feeling like a king, Jared leaned back as Benny expertly cut the stubble from his face. His skin tingled from a salve Benny applied after he used a straight-edged razor to remove any trace of hair from his face. He'd never grown his beard long, but he hadn't shaved it all off in years. Next to go was the hair he'd grown out for the past five years. His mom was the last one to cut any of it off but getting married to Vanessa was the perfect opportunity to chop it all off for the close-cropped look he'd once preferred.

By the time Benny finished, Jared looked like an entirely new man. No longer did he resemble the world-weary traveler wearing blood-stained rags for clothes. While Benny cut his hair, Jerry had brought in a black suit, complete with a bowtie and shiny black shoes.

"Wow, Marie thought of everything!"

Benny guffawed. "She's been waiting for Jerry to get old enough to marry off. All her kids long since up and ran off with their brides. If you hadn't come with your own lass, she'd have invited half the colony to the inn last night to find you a match. Just be glad you already had yours picked out."

"You sound like you're speaking from experience?"

"Aye, you could say that. Penny and I are happy enough, but it wasn't a love at first sight if ya catch my drift. We were young and, well, Benny and Penny. You can imagine the teasing we incurred along the way. I don't regret it, mind you, just coulda done without the public scrutiny when old Nanna announced to the world that Benny and Penny were freshly minted the night after our wedding, you know? We didn't live that down for years. Even now some folk bring it up."

Jared had to hold back a chuckle himself, forcing his face to remain passive. "I can only imagine." Jared clenched his teeth, doing his best to keep a stoic expression. "Thank you for all your help, Benny. I appreciate it. Sadly, I have no coin—"

Benny waved him off saying that Nanna took care of payment. The moment the door closed, Jared buried his head in the pillow and roared with gut-wrenching laughter. It really wasn't that funny, but he'd almost made a pun on Benny's wife's name by saying pennies, but changed it to coin at the last second.

He had no right to be this happy, but he couldn't help himself. It was a wonderful day and the events of the last few days couldn't darken his thoughts at the moment. Quickly donning the suit, Jared had no clue how the bowtie worked and opted to just leave it on the bed. Ready to head to the chapel, he found Jerry waiting for him by the door.

"It's about time."

"My apologies, young sir. Please, lead on."

Jerry led him up the street to the chapel. Jared entered to find the room filled with foreign faces. He balked at the sight, until he glimpsed Sergeant First Class Johnston at the front of the small auditorium. The Sergeant beckoned him forward and motioned for him to stand at the head of the room. An aged, white-haired minister stood behind a podium, holding what Jared assumed was a Bible. He saw the physical resemblance to New Denver's Marie down to the smile creases on his pale face.

"I'm Max." He extended a hand, and Jared shook it firmly. "You've made my sister a very happy old woman today. She's been pining to throw another wedding, but it's been years since anyone wanted to get married and well, we ain't getting any younger, ya know?"

"Hi, Max, Jared Cartwright. It's nice to meet you, and I'm happy to oblige Marie. Vanessa and I talked about this, but we wondered if it even made sense anymore. My parents would have wanted this if they were still around."

Max made to respond but stopped with his mouth open and pointed down the aisle. Elle came first, dressed in a beautiful blue summer dress that caressed the tops of her calves as she walked. She was even tinier than Jared imagined, but he'd only ever seen her wearing clothes five times her size. Even though she was in her teen years, she looked no older than twelve as she walked down the aisle with a beautiful smile splitting her face. Her chestnut hair was spun into a relaxed bun atop her head with flowers placed strategically throughout. She wore makeup and positively radiated happiness. She wore white heels, and it was clear she didn't know how to walk in them as her legs wobbled with each slow step forward. Jared heard her breathe a sigh of relief when she finally stopped near the front of the small chapel.

After Elle reached her position next to the minister, Max asked everyone to stand. The doors opened, and an angel entered the building. Jared felt his knees go weak as he looked at the most beautiful sight he'd ever beheld. The girl of his dreams sauntered down the aisle. She wore a strapless, pure white wedding dress with a glimmering sequined bodice emphasizing her hourglass figure. Her raven colored hair hung in ringlets around her face, cascading from a sparkling golden circlet. Her smile blazed like the sun. Her makeup amplified her already gorgeous face a thousand times, her skin glistening in the morning light.

Jared couldn't look away. He drank in her beauty hungrily, his heart fluttered rapidly and threatened to escape his chest. As long as he lived, he'd never forget the image of perfection in front of him. A tear trickled from Vanessa's eye, unconstrained joy bursting to break free. Jared ached to wrap her in his arms and wipe all tears from her face, but he didn't trust his legs to carry him a single step before giving out.

He seared the images in his mind, willing himself to never forget this moment. No matter what difficulties lay ahead, this picture-perfect scene would always be a simple thought away and bring a smile to his face.

The next moments passed in a blur, so enraptured was he with the beautiful woman before him. They exchanged vows with each other, fully intending their words to be the only sign of their matrimony they needed. Apparently, Nanna had had other ideas as, miraculously, a pair of wedding bands materialized out of thin air. Elle carried a simple silver band for Jared and Jerry snatched a gold band from his pocket for Vanessa.

They promised to love each other no matter what life had in store for them. If the entire world turned against them, they would always remain true to each other.

The ceremony ended when Jared swept Vanessa off her feet and kissed her passionately to the cheering of the crowd and mental congratulations from Malsour and Scarlet.

They'd done it. They were husband and wife, and nothing prevented them from being with each other any longer. For a moment he contemplated ignoring his own words and staying another night, but he knew it wasn't right and everything he'd done up to this point was to take the right path. He didn't plan on changing that now no matter how strongly he desired to do otherwise.

The ceremony over, the crowd quickly left, Johnston stopping only briefly to say congratulations before making his way over to his post at the wall. Nanna and Max sat together at the front of the chapel, tears in their eyes as they witnessed the joy of young love once more in their lifetime. Jared thanked them for everything and ensured them they'd be by the Inn shortly to change out of their formal attire and grab their gear.

"Mayor?" Jared approached the man Max pointed to and proffered his hand. "Jared Cartwright."

"Please, call me Corey. Mayor is such a stuffy title."

"All right, Corey, it's a pleasure to meet you. I want to say thank you for everything here. We never expected such a warm welcome. After what we've seen and been through, it's refreshing to find such wonderful people left in the world."

"We've chosen to carry on just as it was before the war. As far back as I can remember, we've always run the colony this way. When they elected me, I vowed to carry on the traditions, as has every mayor to run New Denver since the calamity."

"We're so grateful for everything."

"Ah, Vanessa, such a lovely bride." Corey reached for her hand and kissed it with a flourishing bow. Jared felt a prick of jealousy but kicked himself for being so petty. Everyone in this town had been nothing but polite and he had no reason to fear any malicious intent.

"So, Nanna threatened me on pain of death and told me I had to come to this wedding and speak with you." Corey raised his voice loud enough for Nanna and Max to hear, eliciting chuckles from them both.

"Do you want to chat someplace else?"

"Here is fine." The only people left in the room were the mayor, Max, Nanna, and Jared's small party. "We're all part of the senior council. There's nothing old Max and Marie don't know around here."

"All right, we'd like to request your help with some nanite injectors."

"For three of our special guests, absolutely! We're expecting a new shipment any day now."

"That's just it…we need more than that."

"I see." Corey sat down on a pew as Max and Marie joined them.

"Why do you need more?" The suspicion shown the night before returned to old Nanna's face.

"I assure you, it isn't for us. We encountered a nomad colony up in the mountains and they're liable to die without some injectors." Jared hated lying to them. It made him feel dirty, even wearing the pristine tuxedo and having just taken a shower.

"Bring them here! We've got more than enough room and if we don't, our sister colony does."

"Unfortunately, I don't think they will. They'd rather die than join another colony. Someone razed their last one to the ground."

"How many are you talking about?" Max's voice held a growing note of alarm.

"Twenty-nine to be exact."

Corey blew out a breath. "I—"

"Jared, that's an awful lot to ask of any one colony, let alone as an outsider."

He turned to look at Max. "I know, and I wouldn't be asking if I didn't think it was important. You can see we aren't your usual variety of explorer, and we only want to help everyone. As much as I don't want to give it up, I can offer you something in return. Elle, do you mind grabbing my pack from the inn?"

"Sure, be right back." Elle unfastened her heels and jogged off toward the Inn.

"We told you we'd been out exploring for almost a decade. That's not entirely true. Vanessa and Elle have been without a colony for that long, but I come from a colony in the northeastern part of the continent. I've been exploring for about two-and-a-half years. My mother passed about five years ago, and my father a couple years later. I tried to go through the motions for a year back home, but everything I did just brought back the memories, and I struck out on my own.

"I stumbled on Vanessa and her people, and they've truly been homeless for just under a decade. All of their supplies and homes destroyed three times over, and now they have almost nothing but the clothes on their back and some weapons. It's one of these weapons I want to offer you in exchange for the injectors."

"We've got weapons. Lots and lots of weapons. You came

through the west gate, so know."

"I do, but I assure you, there is no weapon like this inside these walls. If there is, then I apologize for wasting your time. Truly. This is all we can offer at the moment, but we're happy to open trade if there is anything outside your walls you need from us."

Elle re-entered the chapel and handed Jared his pack. "I urge you to keep what I'm about to show you a secret. This is not something you want escaping your walls and getting to mercenary camps."

Jared pulled the phase rifle and a full battery from his pack and set it on the pew beside Corey.

The mayor's mouth dropped open, and he fell back into his seat. Max and Marie craned their heads around the front pew to see what he'd pulled out. Similar reactions came from both.

"How?" They all asked at the same time.

"We found a downed drop ship and scuttled it before another came to clean up the wreckage."

"This is worth a fortune, and you're offering it in exchange for some injectors?"

"Yes, the lives of my new family are worth more than any weapon in the world." Jared understood the Mayor's plight, but he thought the tradeoff more than worth it considering what they'd use the injectors for.

"I'm inclined to agree, but I must bring Johnston back here before we decide. He may not look or act it, but he's in charge of all the military-trained people around here. I'd like him to verify the weapon and test it before we concede. Agreed?"

Corey directed his question at Max and Marie as much as Jared and his party. This was entirely new territory for everyone, and they wanted to ensure both parties came out winners.

"I'll fetch him." Elle didn't wait for a response as she sprinted out the door once more.

"She's quick!"

"You have no idea, Nanna. She can outrun almost anyone back home. Anyone, but Jared that is. Elle—"

"You don't have to talk about it, Vanessa." Jared placed an arm around her, rubbing her shoulder for comfort.

"It's okay. It's in the past now. Elle was on her own for nearly a decade. We got separated when she was only five, but Jared found her and reunited us."

"That poor sweet girl." Nanna covered her mouth in shock. "She spent all that time alone? Was she in a colony?"

Vanessa shook her head and Nanna's eyes widened, a tear leaking down her cheek. "It's a miracle she survived at all. You shoulda started with that story to begin with and I'd have given you all the injectors you wanted, myself."

"No, fair is fair." Jared reassured them. "I find this trade perfectly acceptable, and we'll do just fine without the phase rifle. We've got many other conventional weapons to keep us safe."

It took Elle and Johnston a few minutes longer to return. As soon as Elle walked into the chapel, Nanna all but threw herself on Elle, muttering about the poor child and how brave she was.

"*Easy, Kitty,*" Jared warned the large feline when he saw her shimmer just beyond everyone's view. The cat winked back out of view, realizing there was no danger.

"Sergeant Johnston. We got an interesting proposition to consider and we need your military expertise to be the final say. Jared is asking for twenty-nine of our injectors for—"

"Twenty-nine! Whatever for?" Johnston barked his response, immediately reaching for a pistol at his waist.

"Calm down, you. We're having a civil discussion here. We believe their story, but what they have to trade is more in your realm of responsibility. You need to examine and test if it works; preferably, someplace no one can see. If all checks out, they'll have those injectors."

"Would could be so valuable—"

Corey lifted the rifle from the bench and proffered it to the sergeant.

"Holy mother of all that's good! Where...how?"

"Stop yer splutterin'! Don't ya think we already asked these questions? Hmm?" Marie smacked her clutch against Johnston's arm.

"Right, okay, whoa. This is really a phase rifle? I've always wanted to, but..."

"No more questions, sergeant." Corey stepped into his mayor role rather efficiently, and the bubbling sergeant immediately quelled his attitude and started a thorough examination of the weapon.

"It checks out from what I can tell. I've only seen them on the drones from the drop ships and never held one, but it looks identical."

"Drones? You mean the little ball things?"

"No, those are just sensor probes. The metal humans are drones. They're remotely controlled by the cities. We've gotten a little information over the years, but unfortunately never got our hands on any phase weapons. I've only every heard of colonies getting dated pistols. If someone knew we had—"

"We will not speak of this outside this room. Understood?"

"Sir, yes, sir."

"Now, can you test this without raising suspicion?"

"This church still has a basement correct?"

"Yes, but...ah, why didn't I think of that? Okay, lead the way."

Jared made to follow, but Corey motioned for everyone but Sergeant Johnston to wait. "We can't give up all our secrets, now can we?"

He winked at the group before disappearing into a back room with Johnston and the phase rifle.

After fifteen minutes of waiting, Jared grew concerned by the long absence, but his senses indicated Kitty wasn't in the room and he surmised that she'd followed them into the basement.

Good Kitty. Jared smiled, imaging what their reaction would be if they knew a giant cat the size of a horse stalked them. He relaxed and waited patiently for them to return.

He glimpsed Kitty walking back through the open door several minutes before Johnston and Mayor Corey. Brushing his side, Kitty let him know they had an underground tunnel that led several miles under the city. They'd walked down them for a time before they reached a bend in the tunnel. Johnston set up a couple targets and squeezed off few rounds. After he confirmed it worked, he'd done a little happy dance exclaiming it was well worth the trade and that he felt a little bad for how lopsided it was.

Jared thanked Kitty and smiled to himself. If only they knew the water folk had five more plus a bunch of phase pistols. They'd fall over in shock. Johnston was ready to give them the world just to have the rifle. It was blatantly obvious when he clutched the rifle to his chest with a vise-like grip.

"I see you enjoyed your test?"

"Very, very much! I'll sleep with her on my pillow. My wife might hate ya for a while, since she's gonna share a bed with her." Johnston stroked the side of the rifle with affection.

In only a day, the man had grown on Jared, and he'd miss his open nature. Someday, he wanted to come back here. If they succeeded against the cities, perhaps it would be sooner than later. Based on his interactions with the inner council of New Denver, it was obvious they sided with the people surviving on the earth. If they knew the truth of the world, he suspected they'd join their cause.

Unfortunately, now wasn't the time to tell them. All he wanted right now was the boosters.

"Then it's settled?"

"It is. Marie, please take Jared and his beautiful new bride back to the Inn. I'll send Jerry to the hospital to get the boosters."

"Is it far? We've people waiting for us midway up the mountain. I don't want to keep them waiting too long."

"An hour tops. It's a five-mile hike, but Jerry will take the scooter. Shouldn't take him long at all."

"Up ya go. No lolly-gaggin'. We gots to get ya outta that dress."

Vanessa smiled and let Marie pull her along. They marched to the inn where Jared parted ways to head upstairs, and Vanessa disappeared into a back room on the main level. He stripped out of his clothes and folded them neatly on the bed. His travel clothes were waiting for him, washed, mended, and pressed. The service at this place was amazing, and he definitely wanted to stay there again if they ever came back.

He was just about to slip his pants on when a timid knock at the door stopped him.

"Jared?"

"You're done already? I'm still—"

Vanessa opened the door and Jared fell on his back, one leg tangled in his pants.

"Nanna says we have time before Jerry gets back and—"

Jared needed no further invitation. He jumped to his feet, slammed the door shut, and spent the most wonderful hour with his new wife. Words couldn't describe the experience. It was unlike anything he'd imagined, and as a married couple, this was now their life. To have and to hold, from this day forth. He couldn't wait to experience every second of the rest of their lives together.

24 CAPTURED

True to his word, Jerry arrived back almost one hour on the nose. The knock on the door was an unwelcome sound and if not for the amazing hour Jared would have snarled out a rebuke at the interruption.

"Your package is waiting downstairs with Nanna."

"Quite the little gentleman in the making." Jared flashed a brief note of irritation, but Vanessa quickly squashed it.

"He's such a sweet little boy, and Nanna raised him well so far."

Jared swung his feet over the side of the bed. "Shall we?"

"If we must."

Jared rolled back over, pinning her to the bed and kissed her with all the love and affection he could muster. "We're married now. We can *get away* whenever we want."

"Well, we don't exactly have a home anymore."

"That's fair, but that will change."

"How so?" Vanessa's voice sounded muffled as she moved to the adjoining room to retrieve her belongings.

"Corey said they're expecting a ship any day now. Pete is ready to intercept the signals from the ships. I think there's no reason to delay the recon mission any further, given our current homelessness."

Vanessa didn't answer and Jared knew why when he heard soft weeping coming from the other room.

He dropped his gear back to the bed and joined her, wrapping his arms around her. "We don't have to talk about it now and I know you're not a fan, but it's our best chance of success."

"I know, I…It's our wedding day. Let's talk of this tomorrow, please."

"As you wish, my love." Jared kissed her nose and finished strapping on his gear.

They found Elle waiting for them in the common room. Nanna and Max came out from the back to say their goodbyes and hand them a satchel filled with boosters. He jiggled the bag slightly, closing his eyes for a split second as the image solidified in his mind.

"Twenty-nine boosters as promised. Though, like Johnston, I think you're getting the short end of the stick here."

"It's okay, Max. Really. We have plenty of protection, and we've survived this long without the phase rifle."

"If you say so."

"You've been such a wonderful host, Marie. And Max, we can't thank you enough for your help with the ceremony. Jerry, you've been a huge help and I want to give you something for your trouble." Jared fished a credit from his pack and handed it to Jerry. His eyes lit up in glee and he raced from the room. Nanna's voice lashed at him before he'd made it two steps.

"What do you say, mister?"

"Sorry. Thank you. Be Safe. Bye." With that, the little fellow was out the door, Nanna's muttering the last thing on his mind.

Jared chuckled and turned back to see Vanessa and Elle hug

Nanna, repeating Jared's sentiments.

"If we get the chance to come back through here, we'll stop in for a stay. We'll never forget the kindness you've shown."

"It's been our pleasure, dearie! Please come visit again, lovebirds."

They turned around and left the inn, Kitty silently trailing behind. Sergeant Johnston hadn't made it back to his post yet, but Carlos saw them off and promised to keep an eye out for them if they ever returned.

Glancing over their shoulders, they found Jerry up on the wall waving to them until the guards chased him from the ramparts. At the same time, a large flock of birds the size of massive eagles flew over the town. None of the soldiers so much as flinched, but Jerry looked at them in wonder, flapping his arms as the soldiers shooed him off the wall.

The birds almost made Jared rethink their strategy of bonding all dragons. It would be really handy to have a giant bird that could fly with impunity anywhere it wanted. They couldn't even use Attis because most people likely had no idea that griffons were real. Even if they couldn't use him as a scout, Jared needed to go retrieve him soon. No matter his usefulness, he was a part of their group now and Jared didn't like the idea of leaving anyone, human or creature, behind.

A shout drew his eyes back to the wall and he saw Jerry dart around the person herding him down the steps.

Laughing joyfully, Jared grabbed Vanessa's hand, and they hiked through the afternoon until reaching the pass where Scarlet and Malsour waited.

"Scarlet?" Jared frowned. He didn't see the two of them abandoning their position without good reason.

"Let's keep going, maybe they moved back."

"Scarlet? Where are you?"

"Jared! Are you on your way back?"

"Yes, we passed the meeting place half an hour ago."

"Sorry. We needed to put some distance between us."

"Why? Oh."

"We will teach you to lock down your emotions. Until then, we would appreciate a heads up."

"Sorry, Scarlet. We didn't plan to...you know. I wasn't thinking of much else at the time."

"There is no reason to apologize. You are perfectly within your right to be with your mate. The bond complicates things, slightly."

Jared's cheeks flushed crimson as he imagined exactly what Scarlet and Malsour had felt. They didn't experience the same relationship as humans, so he wondered what equivalent feelings they'd have. Shaking his head to clear the thought, Jared apologized again and ensured Scarlet they'd warn them until they could lock down their emotions.

"We will be right there."

A few minutes later, Scarlet and her brother climbed over the ridgeline and landed before them. Everyone mounted up, and they raced through the rest of the mountain range until meeting up with the group. Everywhere Jared looked, he saw dragons intermingling with humans, many in deep conversations.

"What's the status here, Scarlet?"

"The rest of the water folk are ready to bond."

"Everyone found someone? Just like that?"

"Remember, it does not take long for a dragon to root through your human minds. Compatibility would not take long to achieve. Most of those left want air dragon companions. It makes sense, given their ability to fly and willingness to engage in our fight. Also, Damien finished bonding yesterday."

"Is it too fast? It took a few days to figure out who your brothers would bond with."

"I do not think so. The dragons scrutinized the bond and how it works with my brothers. That is precisely why they are ready so soon."

"All right then, let's get this done. There's really no reason to delay any further."

Jared called everyone over and announced he had boosters ready to hand out. Twenty of the remaining water folk would bond with air dragons, five with water dragons, and four with earth dragons. After handing out the boosters, Jared walked everyone through the process again. He also advised them to spend any available nanites immediately, pushing as much as possible into *Mind* for the humans and *Body* for the dragons. He amended his earlier instructions slightly and encouraged everyone to put a small portion into *Body Manipulation* so they could revert to their old human forms. They may end up joining another colony, but they couldn't do it without explaining the mutations. Jared wasn't ready to reveal the nanite capabilities just yet.

While Jared instructed the water folk, Scarlet formed a mind meld with all the dragons and showed them how everything worked. The moment everyone was ready, Jared motioned for them to proceed. Just like before, several people immediately passed out, some remained awake for a time, but thankfully no one screamed in obvious pain like Jax and Ballog.

Everything moved so fast, and he had learned none of the new dragons' names, save for the matriarchs. Every one of the air dragons was white as snow, and their spikes and claws glittered like diamonds. The only clear differences were the shape and sizes of the horns adorning their heads and backs. Jared tried to listen to the various conversations taking place, but there were so many whispers of telepathy and verbal conversations it was nearly impossible to absorb it all. The dragons not bonding mingled with their kin. Thousands of years was a long time to remain apart, and they had much to catch up about.

Seeing everything under control, Jared called Scarlet over.

"I'd like to go find Attis while we're waiting for this to finish up."

"I thought you wanted me to go solo?"

"I think it would be more efficient if we both went. Especially if I need to go the rest of the way on foot. We'll get as close as we dare. If we can't find Attis, I'll hike for half a day to find him. With any luck, we can be there and back in a day if you travel at top speed."

"You must find something to bind yourself to my back first. We will be flying faster than we have in the past and I do not think the seat I made is sufficient to keep you on."

"Can I put a chain or rope around your neck?"

"If it does not impede my movements, yes."

"Okay, let me see what I can dig up. Oh, actually, you remember those big machines where we found the cables? There were chains inside them. We didn't need them when we built the wall, but they might work. Let's head over there and grab some. I'll let Vanessa know what's up."

Jared quickly informed Vanessa of their plans and they set off to collect the chains. It turned out to be more than he needed, and it took a couple phase rounds to separate the chain into the proper length. That done, Scarlet blew on the chain with her fire to fuse it together.

Scarlet ducked her head, and Jared placed the length over her horns where it settled at the base of her neck, right in front of the bone seat he used.

"How's that? It's not too heavy or restricting?"

"No, it works."

"Perfect, let's head back. I want to let Carla know we're heading out to get Attis. She's been pining after him ever since we left."

Jared found Carla sitting on a rock, removed from the group and looking out at the mountain pass despondently.

"Hey, Carla."

She looked up at him, her eyes dull. Seeing Jared's broad smile, she jumped up in anticipation.

"It's time? You're leaving to get him now? Can I come? Please?"

She pleaded with him and Jared heard the hope and pain in her voice.

"Sorry, Carla, I wish you could, but we're planning to move fast, and it'll be hard enough for me to stay on Scarlet's back. I don't want to risk a second person."

"Okay." Her crestfallen face saddened him, but it was in her best interest to stay put so they could get back faster.

"We'll be back in about a day, maybe two. It depends on how long it takes to find him. If I have to journey on foot, it'll take longer."

"Please find him, Jared!"

"You have my word; we'll do everything we can."

"Thank you." She gave him a hug before returning to her seated position to brood.

He hoped it wasn't an empty promise, but everyone needed a little hope these days. If he could give that hope with a few words, for even just a couple more days, he'd do so. If Attis was no more, they'd address that when the time came.

Deep in thought, Jared walked back to Vanessa to say goodbye and make sure she had things in order. If Attis was, in fact, dead, Jared didn't know what he'd tell her. He thought it was unfair that a bonded creature could die with little side-effect on the human companion; but if the human died, the nanites would break down and turn the creature into a rabid, mindless beast. He'd spent time talking to Scarlet about this, but there was no way around it. The upside of bonding with a dragon is that they could shield their minds and then isolate the nanites to prevent it like Alestrialia had done when sharing her essence with Jared. Carla and Attis didn't have the luxury, and probably never would.

Jared wondered if Igor had programmed it so that massively overpowering creatures didn't run rampant if their companion died. He likely hadn't known dragons existed or that they could defeat the programming.

"Jared, are you okay? You seem distracted."

"Hey, Vanessa. Yeah, I'm good. I was just thinking through some things. I don't exactly want to talk about it though. It's kind of morbid, and I'd prefer to keep the thoughts to myself for now."

"If you ever need to vent, I'm here for you...husband." Vanessa gave him a deep kiss, his cheeks turning the lightest shade of pink.

A smile stretched across Jared's face. He'd never tire of hearing her say it, nor of kissing his new bride. "Thank you, wife. I gotta say, it sounds amazing. I'm the luckiest man in the world and surrounded by some amazing women. I'm not sure that Scarlet counts as a woman. Dragonnette? Is there a female form of the word dragon?"

"There is."

The voice surprised Jared, and he looked around for its source. It sounded like Layonia, but she was far away, and he didn't think she could hear so far.

"You guessed correctly. I may not hear your voice, but I can hear your thoughts when you forget to shield your mind."

"Oh, sorry about that. Then you heard..."

"I did. It is something we must explore in greater detail, but you are correct, now is not the time. To answer your question, though, the ancient form of the word dragon, or drakon, has a female derivative, drakaina. We have not gone by that name in ages,

but it was the name given at our creation."

"Do you know who, or what, created you?"

"Yes and no. As with your previous thoughts, now is not the time for such discussions. We will speak of this more another time. Go, rescue your friend's companion. Your people will remain safe with us."

"Thank you, Layonia." Jared bowed in her direction and turned back to Vanessa. "Did you catch all that?"

"I did. These dragons are remarkable. I'm constantly amazed at what they can do. Have you seen how fast the air dragons move? Or when Gayana and her kin pushed all our gear up through the earth like that? Seeing so many impossible things just makes me realize how small we really are in the grand scheme things."

"As small as we might seem, you're one of the best parts of the world." Jared grabbed her around the waist and pulled her in for another deep kiss. Reluctantly, he released her and stepped back. "Okay, we've gotta get going. I want to be back before everyone finishes bonding in case there's any difficulty. Also, if Corey and Max are right, there will be a drop ship visiting soon and this could be our chance to capture one. We'll wait until after it does its business in the colony and then ambush it."

"What if it's different from the ones in the other city?"

"We'll tackle that when the time comes. For now, this is our best bet. Can you make sure that Pete and Kirgor are ready to go? If the ship comes by while we're gone, it's up to you all to capture it."

"Jared, I don't—"

"You'll succeed, Vanessa. I know you've got it in you. Between you and Malsour, you can handle a single ship. Just make sure Pete gets on board as soon as possible and that he has all of his equipment ready to intercept any signals. We're just lucky the parts from the robots survived the avalanche. Otherwise, we'd have to collect more before attempting this."

"We'll try, but if it looks hopeless, I'll call it off."

"I wouldn't have it any other way. I've got to get going now." Jared turned to leave but turned back to Vanessa and kissed her one last time for good measure. "I love you."

"I love you, too. Please be safe."

Jared jumped on Scarlet's back and grabbed the chain around her neck. "Let's go, Scarlet."

His heart skipped into his throat as Scarlet launched into the air and rocketed forward. It was all he could do to hold on to the chain and keep from falling off.

Scarlet's estimations proved accurate, and they reached a point close to their old home in a little over nine hours. It was the middle of the night, and they heard nothing to suggest drop ships flew around. Scarlet slowed her approach to a lazy float, and they scanned the area looking for signs of Attis. The first thing they did was trace back both paths they'd taken in the underground tunnel. When neither of them turned up Attis, Jared thought the bird had returned to their old home.

"Let's fly as low as you can. The moment the city comes into view, we stop. If we can't reach Attis by then, I'll go the rest of the way on foot."

"You will have about four hours of darkness left. I suggest you spend only two hours walking in that direction before returning. I do not want to remain exposed this close to the city during daylight hours."

"That should be plenty long enough. I'll run to cover as much distance as possible."

They didn't find Attis when the looming spires of the city peeked over the horizon.

Scarlet set down amongst a cloister of bare trees and Jared hopped off, his limbs sore from the tense hours traveling at top speeds.

"Be careful."

"I won't take chances."

He maintained a fast, steady pace just short of a sprint as he made his way back along the route they'd traveled. His mental clock ticked away the seconds rapidly and before he knew it, an hour passed. Periodically, he called out to Attis. Though he didn't expect a response, the silence made him uneasy.

Jared ran up the creek bed toward their old home. When he got close, his pace slowed to a walk. He had only a few minutes remaining before he needed to turn tail and run back. A commotion coming from the cliffs where they used to live made him pause. He slunk through the trees, careful to avoid a direct line of sight. Once the cliff came into view, he found a dozen robots and several dozen sensor probes ranging over the area. A drop ship sat in the clearing next to the tunnel they'd burned into the underground cavern.

Holding his breath lest the slight sound or movement show up on a sensor somewhere, Jared reached out again.

"Attis?"

A squawk and gentle flapping of wings announced his arrival as he shot up from the hole Scarlet's brothers had made into the earth. The machines in the area glanced at the griffon, but otherwise ignored it and continued their patrol.

Why are they ignoring it?

He'd need to figure it out later, because right now they needed to get out of there. If one of the sensor probes turned in his direction that'd be the end of the line. He couldn't outrun a drop ship. This close to the city, they'd have more of them converge on him before he got to Scarlet. That wouldn't do at all. He needed to move.

"Attis, fly west. Just keep flying west and don't stop."

There was nothing else he could do here, and ever so slowly Jared backed away, careful not to turn his back on the machines in the area. When he confirmed they couldn't see or hear him, he turned around and sprinted back the way he'd come. The pause and slow retreat put him behind scheduled and he needed to make up ground.

Scarlet would see Attis approaching and call him down. Even if she missed him, they could catch up. Jared just hoped the bird understood him enough to travel directly west. When they'd fled the first time, Carla told the creature to do something similar, so he hoped that it knew what the words meant.

Making it back with only a few minutes to spare, Jared vaulted unto Scarlet's back and they rocketed through the sky.

"Attis?"

"He follows."

Jared trusted Scarlet rather than look behind him at these speeds.

"Did you check him over?"

"No, why?"

"There were a lot of robots, sensors, and even a drop ship right by him when he heard my call. They ignored him entirely when he took off."

Scarlet slowed her speed and craned her head back to find Attis. They couldn't see him, but Scarlet said he wasn't far. Sure enough, a short time later, the griffon flew into view. Scarlet waited until he drew alongside them and matched his pace. Jared looked the creature over.

It didn't take long for him to understand why the robots let him go so easily. Strapped around one of his legs, a slim black box nestled against his feathers.

Jarod's heart sank. "He's being tracked, Scarlet. I see no cameras or anything, but no doubt they can follow his location."

"We can use it to our advantage. We should lure a drop ship with Attis and leave New Denver alone."

"Agreed. We won't have to worry about the ships being different, either. We can fly ahead to get Pete and Kirgor so they have their jamming equipment ready to go. Can you give Attis enough information to fly to a place between here and Colorado?"

"Done. I chose the clearing where we had the first bonding ceremony."

"How far away is that?"

"For me? Only a few hours. I instructed Attis to land there at sunset. We should make it back with Pete in plenty of time."

"Excellent, let's head back."

Once again, Jared found himself plastered to Scarlet's neck, clinging to the makeshift bridle. Many tense hours later, they made it back to the ravine. It was nearing evening, and they'd needed to skirt around the side of the mountains to avoid flying over the colonies along the way.

Jared informed Carla and Vanessa of the plan, collected Pete and Kirgor, and set out for the rendezvous. They couldn't move as fast with Kirgor trailing Scarlet, but they'd still make it ahead of Attis to get everything into place before the ship came into view. The jamming equipment needed to be in place before the ship's occupants radioed for help.

Dropping Jared and Pete at the houses next to the empty field, Scarlet and Kirgor flew a short distance away, found a depression in the forest, and tucked themselves between the decaying branches.

"What do you need me to do, Pete?"

"Take the sensors and p-place them around the c-clearing."

"Okay, can we bury them so they don't see them right away? Will they already be transmitting when the ship gets here?"

"Yes and n-no, I will turn them on remotely with this."

Pete held a circuit board in his hand with a tiny switch fashioned on one side. It looked like a child threw a bunch of random parts together, fused a few wires by accident, and put a little lever on it thinking it might look cool.

Jared eyed the electronics skeptically. "You sure that'll work?"

"Yes."

The unwavering confidence in Pete's voice set Jared at ease, and he buried the sensor probes around the area. Finished, Jared retreated to one of the nearby buildings and rebuilt one of the fire pits they'd used on their initial pass through here. He started the fire and quickly snuffed it out. He wanted to show signs of a recent vacancy to lure the ship in for a landing.

It took Attis several more hours before he showed up in the clearing. Pete removed the tracker from the griffon's leg and tossed it into some trees next to the clearing. Jared directed the bird to fly over to Scarlet and hide. Several hours passed, and no drop ships arrived to investigate. The waiting pained him, and he wondered if the tracking device on Attis couldn't transmit far enough. Thinking they wouldn't show, Jared stood up to go outside.

Before he cracked the door, the telltale whine of a drop ship's engine announced their arrival. Based on the sounds, it was only one ship.

Perfect!

"Pete, it's here. Get ready. The moment that thing lands, if it lands, I want your jammers online. Can you send them a signal to stand down from here as well?"

"N-no. I n-need to change their p-programming. The p-probes are only for jamming."

"Okay, just stay in here until I give you the all clear. I don't want you getting in the line of fire if I need to kill anything out there. Scarlet and Kirgor can hold the ship in place until you've reprogrammed it. They're strong, but even they might not hold it in place long without damaging it and we need to make sure it's intact. Also, if the phase cannon on that thing shoots, it could get messy."

"I'll be quick. I p-practiced over and over."

"Scarlet, get ready. As soon as the ship lands, you two need to get over here and hold it in place while Pete does his thing. I'll take care of any robots and probes that come out. The jamming equipment is in place and ready to fire up."

"We are ready."

The drop ship hovered over the area, refusing to descend. Jared wondered what they waited for and goaded them. He walked through the house, pausing by the open windows long enough there was no doubt someone occupied the room. The tracking device was only a few dozen yards from the house, and it tied whoever was in the building to the griffon.

The ruse paid off as the drop ship descended into the clearing. The moment it touched down, Jared instructed Pete to activate the jamming signal.

"They won't know it's on, right?"

"N-not unless they are expecting something from the city."

"Scarlet, now!"

Jared dashed out of the building at the same time the ramp descended, and a trio of robots exited amongst a swarm of sensor probes. The robots raised their weapons, but Jared proved faster and put three rounds cleanly through their torsos. They slumped to the ground, smoking holes in their chests.

"Pete, go now!"

Scarlet and Kirgor landed on either side of the drop ship, pinning it in place as it tried to rise off the ground. The whine of its engines increased as it attempted to push into the sky. It bobbed up and down in agitation, unable to overcome the weight of the dragon.

Pete raced up the ramp behind Jared. One quick look in the interior and Jared realized the only other occupant was the robot in the pilot seat. Jared put a phase round into its head and kicked it out of the seat. Pete jumped into the vacated seat and rapidly pushed buttons. He also pulled a device from his pocket and swept over the console. Pete pushed another series of buttons and let out a sharp exhale.

"It's d-done."

The ship stopped bobbing and Jared bounded down the ramp to take out the rest of the sensor probes, but they'd all stopped, motionless.

"They n-n-need instructions. Without the robots, they have no direction."

"Should I shoot them, or can you use them?"

"Use them. We use them to scout the city."

"Huh, I didn't even think about that. Maybe we won't even need to leave the ship at all when we get up there. Can you see what they see?"

"We can now." Pete pointed to the display in front of him. Jared watched a half dozen images of himself look back as he glanced at the surrounding probes.

Jared grinned, they wouldn't need to risk anyone. Now, if only they could remotely pilot the vehicle.

"Please command the probes back on the ship, and let's head back to Colorado. Also, see if there's a way to drive the ship slow enough to prevent the whine we normally hear. I don't want to alert anyone to the ship's presence."

"Give me a few m-minutes."

Pete set to work, tapping buttons and talking with Kirgor. Satisfied with their brief pow wow, Pete announced his readiness.

"Be careful with the controls. I wasn't last time, and it didn't go so well." Jared rubbed his head, remembering the impact with the displays.

Slowly, the ship rose into the air and jerked into motion, accumulating speed. As soon as the pitch in sound changed, Pete backed off the controls to slow down.

"Scarlet? Can everyone keep up?"

"Yes."

"Do you mind flying ahead to let everyone know we're coming? I don't want to surprise anyone."

The ship bucked slightly as Scarlet shot past to announce their arrival. It took a couple hours to get back. When they did, Pete landed the ship in the ravine, lightly touching down as the ramp hissed open.

Jared walked down the ramp, and Vanessa ran into his arms. He picked her up and swung her around.

"You did it!"

"I only took out a few robots. The credit belongs to Pete and Kirgor. We took this ship with little effort and no casualties. We also jammed their communication signals, so the city is unaware of our little mission. Also, Pete thinks he can control the probes to scout the city for us. We might not even have to leave the ship at all. We'll just dock, let them refuel, and leave again. The probes will allow us to observe on the monitors."

"Can you control it from here?" Vanessa looked hopeful.

"Unfortunately, no. Pete doesn't think so. I don't know what it would take, or how long it would take to get that set up. Depending on what we find during this scouting mission, we might need to rig that up, anyway."

"When will you leave?"

"Right now."

"Jared—"

He placed a finger on Vanessa's lips, cutting off her protest. "I know, love, but we can't risk the city catching on to what we're doing. It might already be too late. Scarlet and Kirgor will follow at a distance and come to our aid if we need it."

"Please be careful, Jared."

"I'll return, Vanessa. I promise." Jared crushed her to his chest, feeling the warmth of her body. She didn't object to the move. He knew she didn't like the plan, but it was also the best option they had.

"Let's get this done, Pete."

"Scarlet, Kirgor you ready?"

"We are ready."

"Please stay with us until we get close enough to the city to see and then drop back."

"Here we go," announced Pete and hit the throttle.

There was no turning back now.

25 THE CITY

The city came into view much too soon for Jared's comfort. He spent the few hours in flight exploring the ship and meditating. His nerves were all over the place. He could only imagine what Pete felt. The man put on a brave face, but Jared knew he was a nervous wreck.

"Jared, we can see the city now. We can go a little farther on the ground, but it is up to you now."

"Thanks, Scarlet. Be ready if we need you. I don't know if it's too far for us to hear each other, but I'll keep my abilities active and hope it's enough."

"Be careful. If you think they will discover you, get out. That ship is fast. Even if more ships chase you, head for Colorado, and my family will help you take down the other ships. Kirgor and I will catch up when we can."

"See you soon." "All right, Pete, let's take it in nice and slow."

"The city is hailing us. I replied with a pre-p-programmed response we n-need to refuel."

The ship soared ever closer, the towering spires coming into focus. This was the same side Jared observed from a distance. The images of the other explorers standing on the platform flashed back into his mind. Remembering the pink cloud of their bodies exploding sent a fresh shiver down his spine. The platforms on this side of the city were mostly empty. A couple drop ships sat dormant, but otherwise there wasn't a single soul in sight and no evidence of a welcoming party to greet them.

The closer they got to the city, the more details he saw through the display. The towering structures of the city's buildings were a true work of art, twisting and arcing through the skies. Plants, trees, and flowers bloomed everywhere he looked, making this place look alien to the earth below.

Once again, he saw no people, and wondered if they didn't venture out to the edge of the city, and rather relied on all the robots to take care of the ships coming and going. If they had robots to do all this, chances are the robots maintained the city too, leaving no reason for people to hang out on the outskirts. It's not like there was much to look at below, anyway.

One platform lit up along the edge and Pete nudged the aircraft in the right direction. When they'd gotten within a hundred yards, the ship went on auto-pilot and glided onto the platform.

"I hope they aren't expecting the robots piloting this thing to leave. If they are, we'll get company pretty quickly."

"They are sending a signal. Asking if we have c-c-cargo to d-drop."

"Just let them know we're still on recon looking for the creatures and humans and we've got nothing to drop off. Just need to refuel to follow the strange bird creature."

Jared watched the digital readout on the display and the word *Affirmative* crawled across the screen. The ramp descended with a hiss as several robots shambled from a nearby building with a long hose. They hooked it to the side of the ship, and a thrumming noise echoed through the interior as the fuel pulsed into the ship. The robots didn't ascend the ramp, but a couple unassuming probes rolled out, controlled by Pete. He sent them into the building vacated by the service robots.

It was a large warehouse where row after row of drones lined the walls. None of them held weapons, and Jared assumed these were here for servicing the city and the ships. There had to be at least a hundred in the large room. The probe rolled into an adjacent warehouse where more rows of robots stood side by side. There were another fifty, only these held phase rifles. They were the same robots that had killed the two invaders months earlier.

"Can you send it further into the city? I want to see beyond the docks here."

"Let m-me t-try."

Pete found a door leading farther into the city and sent the ball through it. The moment it crossed the threshold the screen flashed and went dark. Sending the second probe to the door, they saw nothing beyond but static. Something shielded the passage.

"Can you rewind any of the footage?"

Pete pushed a few buttons, and they watched the first probe enter from the perspective of the second. It passed through an insubstantial barrier and disappeared on the other side. There were no electrical discharges, and the ball looked fine physically, but they abruptly lost the signal.

"Maybe it's a jamming signal to prevent people from spying?"

"M-maybe…" Pete's voice trailed off as he played the scene back several times. "I think you're r-right. Look here."

The place he pointed out shimmered and closed around the sphere. Pausing at just the right frame, Jared saw the corridor beyond.

"Do you think you'd be able to hijack one of these service bots and send it through? Maybe they aren't as susceptible to the jamming signal."

"Yes."

The small probe rolled back the way it'd come and waited by the entrance to the service building until the last robot reached it. Pete pressed a button, and the robot turned around and walked up the ramp to their ship.

"I sent it inside to check the c-console operations. I'll turn a jammer on when it boards."

Jared ducked behind the pilot's seat and crouched next to Pete.

"Tell me when you jam the signal and I'll subdue it."

"Now!"

Jared sprang into action, vaulting over the seat and tackling the robot to the ground. A series of beeps emanated from the robot, but thanks to Pete, it couldn't communicate with the others.

Pete ran over and pried off its faceplate, twisting a few wires and flipping a switch. The moment Pete flipped the switch, the robot stopped struggling to escape and calmly stood to its feet awaiting a command.

"Give me a minute. I n-need to hook its c-camera up to the display here."

Pete sent the service bot back into the warehouse to continue down the corridor as they'd done previously. Pete also sent the probe so they could observe what happened with the robot if they also lost communication with it.

The robot passed the doorway and ended up in a long corridor stretching to the left and right. The first probe they'd sent in was sitting next to the doorframe. When the robot kicked it back into the room, it immediately came back up on Pete's display.

"The signal output from the drone is much stronger than the

probe and must be able to work through the jamming signal." Pete looked at the screen and the corridor, unsure which way to go.

"It doesn't matter which way you go. We want to explore everything we can while we're here. I only hope us staying docked this long raises no suspicion."

The robot turned left and walked a hundred yards before hitting a dead end with a door on its right. Trying the handle, the door wouldn't budge. It was a good bet the robot could go right through the door, but that could trigger some kind of alarm and their jig would be up.

"I wish these things moved faster." Jared impatiently tapped his foot on the ground as the robot lumbered down the hallway. Two hundred yards in the other direction, the corridor turned left and opened into a massive hangar. A gigantic ship rested inside. It resembled the drop ships in shape but was easily ten times the size. Sensor probes and service bots milled around the ship at random. Standing in the room's corner observing, Jared watched the robots milling about. For all the activity, Jared didn't see them do anything. Piles of material lay to one side, untouched. Scaffolding built next to the ship was empty. Not a single robot or probe entered the huge ship.

"Wow, if we could get our hands on that..." Jared's eyes must have looked like they'd pop out of their sockets. He practically salivated at the thought of using it as a transport and attack ship for his people. Sure, they had dragons, but the ship was awesome and could probably fly faster than all the dragons. At least, he suspected it could if it was as fast as the drop ships.

"Send it into the hangar and let's see if we can get a better look at that ship."

While Pete sent the robot in farther, Jared tried to reconcile the massive hangar with what he'd seen as they approached the city.

Something wasn't right as he brought up the image of the city and what they observed from the monitors. Right where the hangar sat, there should be a large courtyard with lush grass, plants, and a few trees. The end of the hangar sat where one of the sloping spires began.

"Pete, is there any way to tell if the hangar is underground? It didn't look like the robot walked down, but maybe we can't tell on the cameras?"

"I don't know. There's n-nothing to show it did, b-but it's p-possible."

The robot left the corner of the room and walked toward the open ramp of the giant ship. Before it ascended the ramp, another robot stepped in front and issued a series of beeps. The text scrolled across the screen:

ACCESS CODE. WHAT IS YOUR DESIGNATION?

"Uh-oh. Is there a pre-programmed response to use?"

"N-no."

Jared's mind spun. A moment of inspiration struck him. Tell the truth.

"Send *Inspector*."

Pete complied and the robot in front of them paused, straightened from its position and issued a loud beep.

An announcement scrolled across their display.

RETURN TO OPERATIONS

The change that came over the place shocked Jared. No longer did the robots mill about as if performing busy work. They synchronized their movements and marched with purpose about the room. On closer inspection, Jared realized the ship needed work and there was a lot of equipment waiting to go inside.

A series of complex instructions flitted across the display, informing Pete's robot the inside needed an inspection and to load a pile of gear onto the ship.

"Will the robot do this task automatically?"

"I don't know."

"All right, let's assume it won't. Follow the instructions, and load that pile into the ship. If it's supposed to inspect the interior, it'll give us an excuse to look around."

Watching the organized activity from the robot's eyes, Jared wondered why the drones in the room couldn't perform their tasks until this new robot showed up. It seemed like an egregious flaw in the whole operation.

Pete shrugged and guided the robot up the ramp. The interior was equally impressive. Several corridors split off the loading area. The cargo hold could easily hold a full-grown dragon. The robot carried the cargo deeper into the ship and it immediately became clear that no one had set foot inside it in a while. Where the hangar itself was in perfect order and clean, the interior of the ship held a layer of dust so thick, clouds of it puffed around the footfalls of the robot.

Jared got an uneasy feeling from everything he'd seen so far. Why hadn't a human come to check on the operations here? In fact, where was the human oversight for this operation? Jared asked these rhetorical questions of himself as he tried to make sense of everything. His curiosity piqued, they watched the robot enter the core of the ship. It sported several lounge areas, a forward display, and many rooms leading to the sides and front of the ship. Setting down its cargo, Pete searched the room.

The cockpit proved larger than the entire ship they now stood in. The controls looked the same, only there were many more buttons and levers. There were also multiple stations. The pilot seat was separate from the communications array and it looked like there was an entire console dedicated to weapons systems and shields.

"Okay, send it back out to grab more cargo. We don't want to give any reason for that other robot to come check on this one."

It took forty minutes of back-and-forth trips for them to explore the rest of the ship. They found a dozen comfortable sized rooms across three stories of the ship. Along with the common area, there was a futuristic-looking cafeteria with machines that listed an array of items to eat. Every room sported a complete bathroom stocked with all the amenities one needed. On top of the ship, there were half a dozen pods. After checking one out, they found it led up to turrets mounted on top of the ship.

The engine room was probably the most impressive. The reactor, as Pete called it, could power an entire colony for a lifetime. It looked like it ran on nuclear energy, but the entire topside of the ship also acted as a solar array, harnessing energy and funneling it back into the ship.

Once completed, this thing could self-sustain for decades. Jared knew he had to have this ship.

"I wonder why we've never seen one of these before. You'd think if they wanted to catch us, they could've sent one to take us out."

"It's n-not done?"

"True, but if we randomly stumbled on something like this, wouldn't it make sense they'd have more?"

Pete shrugged and worked the robot back and forth from the ship to the pile of cargo.

"I think it's time to cut the robot loose. If we extract him from the hangar now, it'll raise alarms. Let's move back to using the sensor probes and find another way to enter the city. Also, is there any way to check for a camera or sensors around this area? If there's nothing around here, I can go out to explore."

"That is not a g-good idea. I don't want to stay b-by myself."

"What if I stay close? Also, you can just keep one of these sensor probes nearby and let me know if anything moves around. Remember, I can hear your thoughts if you project them forcefully enough."

"B-but what if that shield p-prevents you from hearing me too?"

"Good point, I didn't think about that. Okay, let's get another service bot, and you can work your magic on him."

Rolling the sensors into the first warehouse, it looked like all the robots were offline.

"I'll go get one."

"Jared, I—"

"You'll be fine, Pete. I'm just going to go grab one quickly and bring it back here."

He didn't wait for a response and dashed from the ship. Something flickered at the corner of his vision, but when he turned to look, nothing was there. Frowning, Jared picked up his pace and grabbed the first robot in the room. He slung it over his shoulder and raced back to the ship. Once on board, Jared lay the bot down and motioned for Pete to get working while he watched the view from the sensor probes to make sure nothing came after him.

"All clear."

Pete didn't seem at all thrilled, but grudgingly admitted his fear misplaced. Pete finished synching the robot's camera to the ship and sent it exploring through the rooms. Instead of entering the warehouse, they sent it to check out an adjacent dock that was empty. The platform led to yet more warehouses on the other side which proved much the same as the ones they'd just explored. One hundred service bots lined the walls, and an adjacent warehouse revealed another row of fifty drones with phase rifles.

Feeling a sense of déjà vu, Jared had Pete send the bot down the same series of tunnels that also led into another large hangar with another ship. The difference in this hangar was immediately clear. There were no active robots milling about, only a row of them stood in front of an open ramp leading into a completed ship.

Comparing this to the previous, Jared realized how much work there was yet to go on the first one. This massive behemoth of mechanical engineering was incredible. Sleek, precise, and deadly, the ship sat entombed in the hangar with nowhere to go and no one to witness its beauty.

Their enslaved robot marched into the open room and paused in front of the motionless robots. They didn't move. Just like the interior of the previous ship, the entire hangar held a solid layer of dust from many, many years.

"Let's look at the ship."

The layout was identical, but the interior much more luxurious and fully stocked with all imaginable goods and desires one could want. Fine rugs and tapestries hung from the walls and adorned the common areas and rooms. As the robot walked from room to room, lights winked in and out of existence, illuminating the space.

"Pete, what's going on here?"

"I d-don't know." Pete's voice held the same note of hysteria reflected in his own.

"Jared? What happened?"

Scarlet's voice made him jump and sent his heart racing.

"Geez, Scarlet, you scared me half to death."

"Is everything okay?"

"We're safe, but there's something wrong up here. Scarlet, there's not a single human being around, and the robots here are in a seemingly endless loop. They have massive ships, one of which is complete and sitting in a vacant hangar. Dust covers the ground as if ages passed and no one cared."

"Maybe they do not need the ships? They have not left the cities in generations."

"I hope it's that simple and I'm freaking myself out for no reason."

"There must be an explanation, but be careful."

"I will. Another thing that makes little sense is the layout of this place. These hangars should be wide open courtyards with trees and plants on them."

"Underground?"

"I thought so too, but we can't tell using the robots to scout for us."

"Please keep me apprised of the situation and let me know if you need me to come."

"I will, thanks."

Jared returned his attention to Pete, who had been muttering something about the controls. Jared didn't think it was important and shrugged it off. "Hey, Pete, just had a chat with Scarlet. She suggested that maybe the people in the cities don't need these ships and that's why they're empty."

"M-makes sense I guess, but it seems wasteful."

"I agree. I think I need to go out there myself and check it out."

"B-but, if you—"

"I'll be fine, I promise," Jared interjected. "We've seen enough of this area to know all they have are attack bots. Fifty is a lot, but they are dormant, and as long as I don't trip an alarm, I'm hoping they stay that way. Even if they activate, there are plenty of places for me to hide around here. I could even try to abscond with that huge ship in there. However, if they do wake up while I'm out there, I want you to take off and head back to Colorado. I'll find another way off the city."

Jared didn't let Pete protest anymore. He stripped off his rags, ripped open one compartment in the ship's cargo area and pulled out the uniforms he knew lay inside. Finding one his size, Jared donned the outfit, used the holster provided with it and slipped his phase pistols in the belt. Finding a sling for a phase rifle, he also slung that over his back.

Seeing himself on the monitors in the ship, he realized he looked just like the city dweller he'd fought a few weeks ago. If he'd still had his long hair and a beard that wouldn't be the case, but the cut and shave a few days earlier completed the picture.

Jared paused at the ramp and fixed a stern gaze onto Pete. "I mean it. If I don't make it back before the attack bots activate and come here, I want you to leave, and don't look back."

Pete shakily nodded his head and went back to monitoring the area through the probes and robot eyes.

"Before I go, I'll bring two more robots in here for you. I want you to gather as much intelligence as possible and two will help you branch out more."

After laying the robots in the cargo hold, Jared took off toward the hangar with the completed jumbo ship. He passed through the service room with the hundreds of robots, fully expecting them to all come online at the same time and chase after him. They didn't, and it made the next room even more tense as he passed the fifty attack bots. Again, he made it through the room without incident, Pete's sensor probe following dutifully behind him until he reached the hallway leading to the hangar.

In the large hangar, Jared followed the footprints from the robot they'd sent through into the ship. He traced its path right into the cockpit of the ship and flicked buttons. He'd seen Pete operate the drop ship and knew what most of the buttons did. Sitting in the chair for the pilot, Jared realized they'd designed it for a human rather than a robot. Aside from the ships flown by the humans from the city, most of the drop ships had much smaller, narrower seats to support the frames of the robots.

Diagnostics readouts ran across the screen in front of him and the exterior cameras flicked on. He watched his surroundings for any movement, but the robots stayed offline. One by one, he read through the lines of text and every line signaled readiness and one-hundred percent operational.

Jared couldn't believe it. How could the city let something so awesome go to waste? The layers of dust suggested this place hadn't seen use in many years.

"Scarlet! This ship is just sitting here ready to launch and no one around to stop me."

"Are you inside it?" It was Scarlet's turn to push a little hysteria through their bond.

Oops.

Jared hadn't told Scarlet his plan to explore on his own, and he hoped she didn't make a brash decision and fly up to meet him.

"Sorry, I should've told you what I was doing. There was no one around and Pete saw no surveillance to suggest someone watched us and I needed to check this out for myself."

"Are you sure that is wise?"

"No, but there's something about all this that just doesn't make sense and, call it a hunch, but I needed to see with my own eyes."

"Just be careful and do nothing stupid."

"All right, you win. I won't try to take it now, but you can bet I'm coming back for this baby. We can have Pete disable any tracking devices it might have."

Reluctantly, Jared left the cockpit and continued exploring. He reached the *galley* as noted on the plaque and found the cafeteria. The kitchen held many non-perishable food options and small packages with tasty looking meals decorating the side. There was a stack of them next to a strange box with only a single button that said *start*. Curious, Jared placed one package into the box and pressed the button. In only two minutes, a ding sounded through the room. Jared opened the box and found a full meal sitting on a disposable carton inside.

His mouth immediately watered as the smell wafted to his nose. It looked amazing and he couldn't pass up the chance to see if it was edible. His nanites would protect him from anything spoiled, anyway. Grabbing a fork from a nearby counter, Jared speared a perfectly golden potato and popped it into his mouth. It melted on his tongue. Salt and something sweet filled his mouth, pulling his lips into a smile. It reminded him of his mom's home-cooked meals, but with a mystery ingredient that amplified the butter and salt fused into the soft potato.

Before anything interrupted him, Jared wolfed down the potatoes, followed by a slab of meat he couldn't identify. It looked like beef but tasted more gamey, and he couldn't put a finger on it. A dispenser next to a sink poured out fresh water, and he greedily gulped down the luxurious liquid to cleanse his palate. Thoroughly refreshed from the quick meal, Jared left the galley and the ship altogether. He wanted to find what was beyond the hangar. At first, he couldn't find a door, but a staircase set into the far wall led up four stories. In the middle of that balcony a pair of double doors led out the other side of the hangar.

"Looks like this place is underground, Scarlet. I still don't understand how it's so far down, because I didn't feel myself descend on the way here. There's also a pair of doors on the other side of the hangar leading farther into the city."

"Are you going through?"

"I'm heading up now and will take a quick peek. I don't think I'll venture into the city on this scouting mission. We can return later with more people. If there are several more of these huge ships, maybe we commandeer them at the same time and bring the city to its knees."

"Recon mission now, attack later. That sounds like a good plan."

Jared bounded up the stairs and paused at the top to admire the ship in front of him. Standing about the same place as the cockpit, he saw the top curve of the sleek ship and all the weapons placements, and realized how powerful this thing really was. The phase cannons mounted on top were triple the size of those on the drop ships and had room for a single person or robot to man them individually. This thing could dish out a lot of firepower, which made him even more confused why they hadn't sent it after Jared and Scarlet when they took down the other drop ships.

If all the ships they'd encountered so far were part of an automated protocol, how did he explain the humans he'd encountered? There were many puzzles to unravel, but the first of which was the doors in front of him leading into the city itself. Through these doors lay the people responsible for holding the planet hostage. A part of him really hoped to glimpse actual humans, but the rational part of him wanted to stay invisible until they were ready to start the war.

Jared tested the doors and found them unlocked. Breathing deeply, he pushed open the door.

In front of him lay the most beautiful visage he'd ever seen. The grass was a deep shade of green, the blades swaying in the wind. Fields of tulips and roses dotted the courtyard and tall trees provided shade from the sweltering sun. Beyond the courtyard, the towering spires rose high and majestic, sweeping around each other to create a latticework of bridges and walkways.

Not a single piece of garbage or rubble marred the beautiful landscape, and Jared stood for long minutes admiring the peace and tranquility before him.

Even amidst the beauty, a part of his mind radiated alarm. There were no birds, animals of any kind, or insects buzzing about. He saw no people walking the gardens or children playing. In fact, it was empty. As desolate as the nuclear fried wastelands below.

What is going on here?

Jared knew he should turn around and go back to the ship, but he couldn't. Pushed forward by an unseen force Jared stepped onto the lush grass.

His foot clanged down, and his vision shifted. Shaking his head, Jared blinked the glitch away and took a second step. Again, his foot clanged down. Jared didn't know what was happening, but nothing made sense. His vision swam again, and he stopped to gather his wits.

Squeezing his eyes together, Jared centered his mind and opened his eyes. The world around him blinked in and out of existence, creating a staccato display of static and fog around him.

Did I finally crack? Am I losing my mind?

Jared took two more steps forward, his mind waging a war with him as his feet clanged against the green grass below him. The moment his second step touched down, the world around him shattered into a million pieces. No longer did he stand in a futuristic world with vibrant greenery around him. There were no spires. The gardens disappeared. As far as he could see there was nothing. He stood on a metal surface that extended to the edges of the island in every direction. Looking behind him, he realized the facility he'd emerged from molded into the contours of the island. This door was one among many lining the circumference of the floating island.

Mounted atop the doors, huge steel beams rose into the sky. They crackled with electricity, and the surrounding air shimmered. It made Jared's eyes itch watching them.

He didn't know how to process all this. His mind clamped down, forcefully shoving him from his *Clear Mind* state.

Nothing made sense.

Where was the city?

Where were all the people?

Jared stumbled back toward the door he'd exited, and his vision shuddered again as the image of perfect beauty once again interposed itself across his vision.

"Jared? What is it? Are you in trouble? Jared!"

"Scarlet, it's not real."

"What is not real? What are you talking about?"

"It's fake. The city? It's just a hologram. There's nothing here, Scarlet."

"What about the ship you found? All the robots?"

"Oh, those are real enough, but the people? There's no one here. Not a single living soul in sight. It's just a giant metal platform with doors leading to more hangars where I found the ship."

"But we saw—"

"What we saw were attack bots executing stowaways."

"What about the people you fought a few weeks ago? The human that put a hole in my side?"

"I don't know what to say, Scarlet. It's empty. There's no one here."

Jared sank to his knees. He didn't know what to do next.

What is vengeance without people to exact it on?

Who is to blame for my mother's death?

Who killed Razael and covered it up?

Are the robots in charge?

So many questions, and no answers in sight.

TO BE CONTINUED...

Thank you so much for reading Radioactive Revolution! I hope that you enjoyed the book and would love it if you left a review on Amazon!

If you'd like to keep in touch and follow progress on my next book, join my Newsletter!

Check out my website - https://hummelbooks.com

You can also keep in touch on my Facebook Group, Facebook Page, Discord server, or Twitter.

ACKNOWLEDGMENTS

I want to send out a special thanks to the author community that has been a huge help to me as a new writer. Without fail, there's always someone in my new circle of friends that has a ready answer for something I'm researching. I really appreciate everyone's support and continue to lean heavily on people like Dawn Chapman, Dave Willmarth, Steven Rowland, KT Hanna, Bonnie Price, and Nick Kuhns. You folks are awesome and will always hold a special place in my heart.

I'd also like to send a shout to my wonderful editors over at Chimera Editing, Jami Nord, and Evan. They've been a tremendous help as I learn the ropes. This time around, the editing pool expanded some and I wanted to give a special thanks to Tamara Mataya for helping me out and providing a ton of feedback during the proofing stage.

Last, but certainly not least, thank you to all of my readers and fans. You're support and comments have been a huge encouragement to me and keep me chugging even with life throws curveballs.

Looking for more Gamelit & LitRPG? Want to follow other authors and engage with readers?

Join the Gamelit Society's <u>Facebook Group</u> and <u>Discord server</u>

Join <u>LitRPG Books</u> for recommendations and reader engagement

Curious about Russian LitRPG (frontrunners to the genre)? Follow <u>MagicDome Books</u>

To learn more about LitRPG, talk to authors including myself, and just have an awesome time, please join the LitRPG Group.

BOOK RECOMMENDATIONS

Did you enjoy Radioactive Revolution? Looking for more Gamelit/LitRPG to sate your appetite?
Check out these other LitRPG's that take place in Dystopian or Post-apocalyptic worlds including Adam Online, from Magic Dome Books (I love Russian LitRPG!):

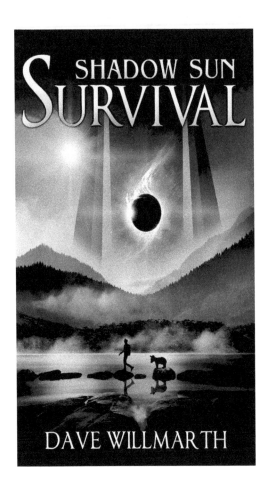

<u>Available on Amazon</u>

How would you survive the apocalypse?
After the earth is drastically altered and the human race is targeted for culling, Allistor and a few desperate survivors struggle to do just that.

Can they work together to stay alive?
Or will human nature doom them all?

<u>Available on Amazon</u>

Digit 36589900 lives among the masses of other nameless and Forgotten humans under the thumb of the Government and Bankers.

After one abusive push too many, Digit 36589900 finds himself exiled to a frozen prison moon. Vowing to make a change, the wheels of war are put in motion.

With limited supplies, no shelter and constant threat of attack, a small band of newly christened humans fight to survive, even as repercussions spiral further than anyone could have imagined.

The only hope is constant evolution, but they aren't the only ones...

Available on Amazon

Leonarm, an Adam Online ex-champion who hasn't played the game for ten years, logs back in - this time on an assignment from the secret services. He needs to get to some of the game's closed locations and seek out the entities called Mentors who are rumored to have solved the problem of digitizing the human mind - which would allow human beings to live forever.

Still, completing quests and finding his way around the unfamiliar game mechanics is the least of Leonarm's problems. He soon discovers he's being hunted down by a clan of mercenaries. He has no idea who hired them - but whoever it is, this person doesn't want their fellow human beings to live forever.

CPSIA information can be obtained
at www.ICGtesting.com
Printed in the USA
FFHW020820090519
52359284-57736FF